ALSO BY CAROLINE PRESTON

Jackie by Josie

LUCY CROCKER 2.0

A NOVEL

>>

CAROLINE PRESTON

SCRIBNER
NEW YORK LONDON TORONTO SYDNEY SINGAPORE

SCRIBNER
1230 Avenue of the Americas
New York, NY 10020

Designed by Colin Joh

Set in Sabon

Manufactured in the United States of America

1 3 5 7 9 10 8 6 4 2

Library of Congress Cataloging-in-Publication Data

Lucy Crocker 2.0: a novel/Caroline Preston.
p. cm.
1. Computer games—Programming—Fiction. 2. Mothers and sons—Fiction. 3. Women librarians—Fiction. 4. Married women—Fiction. I. Title.

PS3566.R397 L83 2000
813'.54—dc21 99–088095

ISBN 0-684–85449–X

To my sons Matthew, Luke, and William, who taught me everything I know about computer games.

ACKNOWLEDGMENTS

My thanks to Yaddo, Ragdale, and the Massachusetts Cultural Council for their support. My deepest gratitude to Jane Rosenman, Pat Eisemann, and Henry Dunow for their enthusiasm and guidance, and to Chris, my first and best reader.

CONTENTS

LEVEL I: The Clockwork Castle
11

LEVEL II: The Never-ending Forest
99

LEVEL III: The Lumberjack's Lair
219

LEVEL IV: Return to Mink Cottage
309

LEVEL I

The Clockwork Castle

CHAPTER 1

>>

Gossip Net

Maiden's Quest priestess, Lucy Crocker, was nowhere to be seen at the latest P.C. gamer convention at the Monterey Hyatt. Her husband, Ed Crocker, prez of Crocker Software, was there handing out Maiden's Quest II T-shirts and mugs. Where's Lucy? we asked. Back at home putting the finishing touches on Maiden's Quest II, said Ed. And when will the sequel to the world's most popular fantasy game be released? By Christmas, saith Ed Crocker. Every good little MQ I fanatic better write Saint Nick right now to make sure a pentagon-shaped package is waiting under the Christmas tree. Ed says anyone who can't wait until then can visit the Maiden's Quest II web page at www.Crocker.com.

CHAPTER 2

>>

Lucy woke at 10:10. It was not the first time she'd woken up that morning, of course—the alarm had gone off at 8:30. That's the time Ed set it for so she wouldn't sleep until noon. The alarm made a bleat of surprise like a robot having one of its limbs torn off. The clock looked like a robot, too, with space-age metal and red-lit numerals. Ed bought it to give her a clearer sense of time passing, at least that's what he said when he chucked out her old beige Baby Ben. Every time it went off she pounded at it blindly until it stopped, with any luck, forever.

Their bedroom faced east, and in the morning big cheerful bars of sunlight streamed in through the bay window, across the shiny orange floors, and onto the bumpy hills of the bed quilt. When Lucy was up and about, all this brightness was reassuring, but now it only highlighted the puffy blue veins snaking down the backs of her hands. She shut her eyes again and tried to remember the dream she'd been having, the surreal kind you have when you've fallen back to sleep instead of getting up and off to work.

She had been dreaming about her father's fishing locker in the back hallway of the cabin at Little Lost Lake. Her hand had turned a corroded hasp and tugged until the tongue and groove door gave way with a shudder. Inside was a jumble of fishing gear—green rubber waders, a fishing net, a straw creel hanging off hooks. When she lifted the lid of a tin tackle box, a hinged tray unfolded like a tiny staircase of fishing flies—yellow fuzzy ones, red ones with long tails, tiny ones with barbs no bigger than a pinpoint.

Little Lost Lake, now where had that come from all of a sudden? Lucy was usually pretty successful at suppressing the memories of her father's cabin, but sometimes they managed to seep out from her unconscious. That was probably the price she paid for sleeping late—stirring up the murky past.

She jumped out of bed, considered for a moment taking a long, purging shower, and decided she wasn't up to it without coffee—there was probably some left over from Ed's breakfast. She straightened the rumples out of her Lanz nightgown, pulled on some kneesocks, and skated toward the stairs. Ed had insisted that they refinish the wide, warped floorboards of their two-hundred-year-old house with four coats of bowling alley varnish. At first Lucy objected until she discovered that she could take a running start out her bedroom door and slide the length of the hallway to the top of the stairs. Every morning she leaned back, shut her eyes, and felt the wind in her face, imagining that she was back on the pond in Libertyville, Illinois, laced into her old black figure skates, in the pre-global-warming days when it was still cold enough to have natural ice all winter long. But this morning her running start was a little weak, and she stopped short outside of Benjy and Phil's bedroom, where these days she did not feel particularly welcome. The door was open for a change.

"Boys?" she said timidly, even though she knew perfectly well they'd left for school two hours ago. Emboldened by the silence, she stepped inside. Their room was as gloomy and dank as an underground grotto. She snapped up a shade and shuddered at the squalor of two unmade beds, two heaps of yesterday's clothes on the floor where they'd been dropped. The only furniture in the room besides the beds were two hulking computer workstations, side by side, with printers, scanners, and a speakerphone. She walked over and inspected a fresh stack of invoices for Benjy/Phil Computer Consultations (BPCC) waiting to be mailed. Four years ago the twins had been relatively normal fourth graders—a little nerdy and unathletic, but normal. The space occupied by computer terminals had once held baskets of Legos, a chest of wooden blocks, and a Playmobil castle. Sure, they enjoyed the occasional kid's computer game that taught multiplication with purple elephants, but they weren't fanatics. Then one day, egged on by their father, they had run an ad in the local newspaper, the *Crowley Crier.*

COMPUTER CONSULTANTS
Need help understanding the latest software?
We will install your hardware and provide on-site training.
References on request. We are in fourth grade.
Call Benjy and Phil, 555-9402

Every adult who read the ad thought simultaneously, Oh, how cute, and, That's just what I need to understand computers—a nine year old. By the end of the first week, they had fourteen jobs lined up. By the end of the month, there was an article about them in the *Boston Globe* and they were interviewed by Natalie Jacobson on Channel 5. The Legos and Playmobil were dumped in the attic, the tree house Lucy had had built at ruinous expense was left to rot. The first year Benjy/Phil Computer Consultations had a net of $1,280. At the end of their second year, they restructured BPCC, with Phil specializing in computer services and Benjy handling the financial end—billing and attracting new accounts. By sixth grade, they had hired two high school students with driver's licenses so they didn't have to be driven to appointments with clients by their mom anymore. Last year BPCC, thanks to their new worldwide Web site, billed $17,560—not bad for a business run part-time by seventh graders.

Lucy spun slowly around, wondering as she did on a daily basis what had happened to those little boys who loved dressing up in pirate costumes and listening to her read *The Hobbit*. There weren't even any real books in their bookcase anymore, just a few tattered computer manuals and Dungeons & Dragons player guides. The twins now spent their days in a darkened room surfing the Internet.

Benjy recently complained that they were required to read books printed on paper at school. "I mean, like, linear reading?" he whined at dinner to his father. He didn't even bother complaining to Lucy. As a former children's librarian, she could hardly be expected to understand the irrelevance of books.

Guiltily, Lucy bent over and straightened up the bookshelf, then made the beds and scooped the dirty laundry off the floor. The boys had forbidden her to clean up their room since the time she had turned off both of their computers and erased God knows what. She stood at the door and inspected for signs of trespass. No, they probably wouldn't even notice made beds and the absence of dirty clothes; the twins were oblivious to everything in the tangible world.

She dumped the laundry off in the boys' unused clothes hamper and strolled downstairs to the kitchen, left in a shambles by Ed, Phil, and Benjy in their mad dash out the door at 7:30 A.M.—milk jug on the counter, open jar of mayonnaise, a bowl of messily mushed-up tuna salad, a bread loaf unwrapped and strewn, half-eaten bowls of cereal and half-drunk glasses of juice left on the breakfast table. Lucy liked to imagine the helter-skelter breakfast scene she'd slept through. At first, Ed would be in his high speed mode—shaking out bowls of Frosted Flakes (Ed and the boys would only eat sweetened cereal), throwing together sandwiches, yelling at the boys to pack their homework and put on their shoes. And then, suddenly, there would be a distraction—the boys would check their e-mail on the kitchen computer for BPCC, or Ed would check his for Crocker Software—and things would digress.

"Ah, crap. That moron at Palmero Travel reads in the newspaper that there's a tiny bug in one billionth of the Pentium chips, so now he wants us to get all seven of his computers fixed," Benjy would say.

"So we're thinking of having a focus group of fifteen-year-old boys at the next gamer convention to test the new game," Ed would answer. The three would settle back, pour out more cereal, and by the time someone checked the clock, the school bus would have rolled by half an hour ago and the twins would have to be driven to school, missing fifteen minutes of first period —again.

She sat down with a cup of reheated coffee, pushed the cereal bowls to one side, picked up yesterday's *Boston Globe,* and flipped to the crossword puzzle. This was one of her procrastinating habits that Ed disapproved of, rather unfairly, Lucy thought. It was her lifelong addiction to crossword puzzles (she had been the Midwest Under-12 champ for two years) that had made her so good at designing computer games, after all. She breezed through the clues: fortune-teller—seer; coral island—atoll; fruitbearing cactus—saguaro; Agamemnon's daughter—Electra.

Next she inspected the list of Saturday's flea markets and reached for the phone to call Rosemary at the children's desk of the Newton Public Library. "What about Newburyport? Says there are going to be two hundred dealers with everything from Chippendale to Barbie dolls." Every Saturday since they'd been in library school at Simmons in 1982, she and Rosemary had gone to flea markets. Eventually, they started specializing—Rosemary in Dick and Jane-era children's books, Lucy in tin lunch boxes and salt and pepper shakers.

"I was thinking of Portsmouth. We haven't been to New Hampshire in a blue moon," said Rosemary with a mouthful of something doughy.

"Okay, let's try Portsmouth."

"Unless you have to work Saturday."

"Why would I have to work?"

"Ed says you've got this killer deadline," she said in a stern voice. When had Ed started complaining about her work habits to Rosemary?

"It's not for a couple of weeks. No rush. In fact, I'm just having breakfast."

"At ten-forty-five? Lucy, I'm starting to get worried about you. . . ."

"See you Saturday," she said, hanging up. Okay, Ed, you win. She walked back upstairs, paused at her bedroom door, and once again considered taking a shower and getting dressed, checked her watch—now 10:52!—and slunk down the hall to her studio.

Lucy's studio had formerly been an old sun porch sagging off the rear end of the house. Four years ago, when they bought the house, the building inspector had predicted that if they let one of their children so much as step out on it, it would surely come crashing down in a heap of timber and glass. Ed had hired a burly team with a dump truck to tear it off the minute they took possession, but then Lucy had gingerly inched out onto the sloping floor. Three walls of windows looked out over a rolling back field dotted with spilling milkweed, a gnarled pasture fence edged by a winding brook, a distant hillside turned crimson and orange with autumn leaves. She banged up a window and poked her head out just as a beefy guy was plugging in his Sawz All. "Stop," she yelled, holding up her arm like a traffic cop. "It stays." And so it had gotten completely rehabilitated, along with the other fourteen rooms of the Trask homestead (the picturesque name used by the threadbare old lady who sold it to them), into something unfunky, unsqueaky, unsloping, smelling of oil paint and varnish.

Lucy settled gloomily at her worktable and examined her latest watercolor sketch for Maiden's Quest II—Princess Arabella entering the Minotaur's maze. She called it her latest sketch, but in truth she had started it two weeks ago, and should have produced at least four more sketches by now. Instead she had been adding lavish details to this one—Arabella's dress was now covered with cryptic symbols. The dress was a new plot element she had dreamed up a few days ago. Arabella finds the dress in a lead chest at the entrance to the Minotaur's maze. Unknown to Arabella, it belonged to an evil sorceress and had some kind of magical powers, yet to be determined. Being invincible from the Minotaur was one possibility, but a little boring. Maybe the ability to make any man fall helplessly in love with her, but Arabella was so beautiful that men always fell in love with her anyway.

So, Lucy considered, how about the ability to *never become lost*? Maybe it could glow or something, like a fluorescent green, when she's going in the right direction, guiding her on like a beacon. But if she always knows where she's going, that kind of defeats the purpose of the game.One thing Lucy did know was that the evil sorceress was going to get really pissed when she discovered that Arabella had walked off with her dress. Arabella always got embroiled in some kind of showdown with another jealous female superhero. When Maiden's Quest I hit the top of the software bestseller list, a feminist writer had proclaimed, "Here for the first time we find women who are problem solvers, warriors, healers, not just the usual big-breasted victims." But as far as Lucy was concerned, Arabella's relationships with women were pure seventh-grade catfight.

Lucy studied the runes on Arabella's dress, then jotted them down on a piece of scratch paper, wondering what she could make of them. She'd used up her stash of word games on MQI—acrostics, scrambled words, transposed letters. What else was there? Maybe the Nazi Enigma code. Her father, the one who had taught her all those word games in the first place, had been enthralled with the World War II codebreakers. His stutter and myopia made him 4-F during the war, but she had always wondered why he didn't get some kind of job as a codebreaker. She had even asked him once, but since he could never give long thoughtful answers to questions like that, he only shrugged and said, "Im-pa-pa-pa-sible." *Check Nazi codes* she wrote under the runes.

Every time she dreamed up some new angle for the game, she seemed to slip further behind, although Lucy didn't like to consider exactly how far behind. She opened the portfolio with the other sketches and spread them in order across her worktable—Arabella outwitting the Cyclops, Arabella holding up the magic mirror to protect herself from Medusa's head, Arabella in the underworld, being tempted by Pluto to eat the pomegranate seeds. Nothing but a senseless hodgepodge of Greek myths.

I don't know what Arabella is searching for, Lucy sometimes wailed when Ed complained about her delays. Truth, justice, self-knowledge, what? We're talking about a computer game for a bunch of teenagers and immature adults, said Ed. It doesn't have to be Tolstoy, Lucy. Ed was probably right. Why couldn't she just make herself draw a bunch of scenes, throw in a few of those tried-and-true devices used in every computer fantasy game—the secret diary with the missing page, the treasure map, the hidden staircase, the underground passageway?

Lucy stared down at her maze. All right, she was plodding along as instructed, one foot in front of the other. She plucked the finest sable brush from the water can and added a string of saliva dripping from the Minotaur's fang. The watercolor was finished; even she couldn't dream up another procrastinating stroke.

Lucy jumped to her feet and started along her regular pacing route. First, she stood at the bank of windows on the southwest corner of her studio and surveyed the grounds. The vegetable garden was rototilled into a rectangle of black composted earth and planted in neat rows, with the first emerald green shoots of lettuce and radishes poking through.

Usually, Lucy spent hours of each workday during the summer puttering around her vegetable garden, but this year Ed had hired a landscaping service to take over. Don't even set foot in that garden, he warned. I'm going to check for footprints every night. They'd also mulched the perennial bed and weeded along the stone walls. There wasn't so much as a fallen twig for her to pick up.

Next she wandered over to her desk, but that had been denuded of distractions, as well. Usually there was a five-inch stack of bills, but Ed had recently turned over the bill paying to the Crocker Software accountants. She'd even been deprived of her fan mail (incomprehensible tomes from teenage MQI addicts), but that was because it mostly came via e-mail, which she could never quite get the hang of; she was always accidentally erasing messages or firing off responses to the wrong e-mail address. Now Ed's assistant, Marla, handled her e-mail. The only correspondence she was trusted with these days was what Ed derisively called "snail mail," two pieces of which sat in her in basket. The first was a letter from her brother, Larry, about the cabin at Little Lost Lake. So here was the source of her dream—how boring. She unfolded Larry's letter and reread it. It was one of his typical missives, printed on his *Lamb and Levin, Arch.* stationery in a minuscule eight-point type that Larry undoubtedly found artistic and she found infuriating.

Dear Lulu,
Enclosed are my latest expenses for the renovations of the Little Lost Lake cabin. I'm sure these seem awfully high, but labor is *très cher* in the old north woods, and I'm insisting on the very best materials. I'm assuming you and Ed have no plans to visit this summer. If you do, let me know, and I'll arrange to have the cabin opened up.
Hugs and kisses to everyone, especially those boys!

Larry

replace front porch screens	$1,500
paint window sash & deck	$1,900
new gas refrigerator	$ 950

repair roof on boathouse	$1,500
annual consulting fee	$2,000
	$7,850

On the bottom of the letter, Ed had scrawled in his boyish round hand: *Can't you get your baby brother to do something a little less cher? Seriously, Lucy, let's sell him our share in this dump, okay?*

When her father died fifteen years ago, he'd left the cabin in northern Wisconsin to Lucy and Larry. But since she couldn't bring herself to either deal with it or sell it, she'd turned the maintenance over to Larry, which had proved a bit costly. As a struggling architect with fancy tastes and few actual jobs, Larry considered Ed and Lucy to be his well-heeled clients who didn't mind footing the bill for a fishing shack worthy of *Architectural Digest.* Oh, well, Lucy thought as she wrote out a check for Larry's latest indulgences, since when can you buy off a guilty conscience cheaply?

The other item in her in basket was a brochure from Camp Kinahwee, the wilderness survival camp where she had gone every summer when she was a teenager. She'd sent away for the brochure with the pathetic hope that she could interest Benjy and Phil. Lately, she'd been squabbling with the boys over their summer plans. They had schemes for expanding BPCC's client base over the summer into western Massachusetts and Rhode Island, but she had gotten fed up with their pasty faces and slack upper arms and decided they should spend the summer outdoors, doing something "normal." By "normal" she meant what thirteen year olds did back in her day. But when she'd shown them the Camp Kinahwee brochure a few days before, they'd been unimpressed. With a barely suppressed smirk, Benjy read out loud, "At Camp Kinahwee, we believe in teaching campers to find their own inner strengths. By the end of a summer at

Camp Kinahwee, campers will discover that they can easily portage a canoe over a mile-long trail, or paddle solo across a five-mile lake."

Phil, who was always more sensitive about people's feelings than Benjy, switched to a soothing tone. "Look, Mom, we don't have anything against your old canoe camp. I'm sure you had a great time there, but let's be practical. Benjy and I can't even swim. We'd probably drown the first day, and then you'd have spent all that money for nothing."

It was true, the twins didn't know how to swim, at least not real strokes that could propel them anywhere. Like Ed, they felt it was only necessary to master a rudimentary dog paddle. Just enough so that during their annual two-week vacation at the Cape, they could wade out to their armpits and jump up and down with the waves. Lucy would swim laps in the ocean, a mile each day, while their three heads, in baseball caps and shades, bobbed like buoys.

"Face it," Benjy had said, his braces flashing, "summer camp is for kids."

"What do you think you are?"

"As Nicholas Negroponte says, in cyberspace, there is no chronological age," he said pushing down his glasses in a sagelike manner.

Lucy studied the girl on the front of the brochure—she had thick brown braids, and carried a backpack the size of a refrigerator. She reminded Lucy of herself at that age, standing at the crest of the hill above the thousand lakes of Wisconsin, her biceps well defined and gleaming from six weeks of portaging canoes, a cocky smile on her face that announced, With the strength of my back and the power of my mind, I can do anything. She didn't know yet that she had no control over the fateful turns of her life—that she'd end up in suburban Boston, not the wilderness, that she'd be a computer game designer, not an artist, that she would marry an oddball violin-playing math genius who would turn into Steve Jobs, Jr., that her sons would transmogrify from whimsical little boys into screenagers, that her dream for a baby girl would end in a bloody wash of miscarriages.

Now Lucy reached the final destination of her pacing, the chintz-covered couch next to her desk. She stretched out, pulled an afghan over her, and fell asleep, dreaming of Benjy and Phil paddling a canoe, swiftly and effortlessly, without splash or wobble, like Iroquois, across the Lake of the Woods, up the Saint Lawrence, on and on to Hudson's Bay.

The phone rang. She startled awake, checked her watch—12:45!—and grabbed it on the fifth ring.

"Lucy, it's Marla. Ed wanted me to check and see if you'd left yet."

"Left?"

"For the meeting. Everyone's here. We're all waiting."

The big summit meeting for Maiden's Quest II, the one that had been planned for weeks, with the programmer, animator, musician, the publicity director, the new financial officer, and Ed. The one where she was going to present her final drawings and storyboards. How could she possibly, possibly have forgotten? She glanced frantically over at the jumble of drawings on her worktable, down at her flannel nightgown and kneesocks. "I'm just leaving," she said in the crisp imperious tone she once used to silence noisy children at the library, and hung up before Marla could answer.

CHAPTER 3

>>

Ed's spirits sank when he saw Lucy come bustling through the double glass doors of Crocker's new corporate conference room (oval table fashioned from a garishly striped rain-forest tree, lighting so recessed that every human seemed to radiate an aura), forty-five minutes late, harried, panting. Shit, she could have at least *tried* to dress appropriately, considered their corporate image for once in her life. She was, after all, the Crocker Software figurehead, and here she was in some droopy flowered skirt that hung down to her ankles, rubber-soled Bass sandals, a scallop-edged pink T-shirt, and weepy black hair pulled back with a plastic hair band. She'd dabbed on a bit of lipstick, a lame attempt at vanity that somehow made it worse. That old crummy black portfolio left over from her college watercolor class was under one arm, and a piece of oaktag covered with pastel Post-it notes under the other. She looked like a cross between Joni Mitchell and a Wellesley-Grads-for-Literacy volunteer.

Russell Mott, Crocker's brand-new CFO with a freshly minted Wharton MBA and a South Park necktie, peered up from his laptop, pushed up his shirtsleeves (the only shirt in the room that actually had buttons or cuffs), and poised his fingertips to start tapping. The formal presentation had, in fact, been his idea (a "dry run" he'd called it) for making the pitch to various venture capitalists (VCs he called them) for the three million to tide Crocker over till Christmas. Ed had been able to prevent Mott from going face-to-face with Lucy just yet—he didn't want the boy to get discouraged, after all.

"So, you must be the famous Lucy Crocker," Mott said in a daunted way, as if the magnitude of packaging Lucy Crocker for VCs was slowly dawning on him.

"I guess," she said, plunking down the portfolio and oaktag on the table as the assembled Maiden's Quest II team swiveled back and forth uneasily in the black ergonomic conference chairs. Jason, one of the programmers, loosened the already floppy laces of his bulbous skateboarder shoes splayed over his chair arm, while Ingrid, the director of publicity, peeled the label off a bottle of kiwi-flavored iced tea.

Usually these meetings started with Lucy arranging her drawings in order down the length of the conference table as everyone paraded around. The first time she had presented sketches for Maiden's Quest I, when she had come shuffling in with that same beat-up portfolio and meekly tossed out the drawings one by one, Ed could still viscerally recall his astonishment, his joy. There, laid out in front of him, was the salvation of Crocker Software, and the unexpected agent of that salvation was . . . his wife.

When he'd asked her to try and design a computer fantasy game, it had never occurred to him that she might actually produce something that was any good. He'd only proposed it as therapy after the second miscarriage, when for no apparent reason the fetus's heart had stopped beating after four months. After the D & C, Lucy had spent days in bed with the shades drawn even though the OB said there was nothing physically the matter with her. When the doctor suggested that maybe a project or hobby would help ease her sorrow, Ed had come up with the charade that he desperately needed her help to develop some kind of fantasy game for the Crocker Software Christmas catalog.

It had seemed like a plausible idea. She had been the Midwest Under-12 Crossword Puzzle champ, after all. She'd majored in art and could paint tiny imaginary landscapes filled with gnarled trees and jagged lavender mountains. He had pleaded—the sales of Crocker's military strategy games had plateaued (which was true), if they didn't come up with a new product soon, Crocker was toast (also true). And lo and behold, out of that disheveled, inscrutable mind of hers had sprung Maiden's Quest—a fantastical tale of knights, trolls, soothsayers, spellbooks written in code, all weaving through the catacombs of castles, the winding alleyways of marketplaces. The first time Ed had seen those drawings, he knew MQI would go platinum, which it did three months after it hit the shelves, and he remembered why he had fallen in love with Lucy Lamb in the first place.

But today was clearly not going to be like that heady moment four years ago, no siree. Lucy now sat with her hands folded neatly on top of the poster and portfolio, its black laces still tied tight, like a substitute teacher waiting for the class to come to order. Well, if she wasn't going to get on with it, Ed better do something fast to salvage this fucked-up situation. He got up and ambled slowly over to Lucy, as if this was all part of their well-scripted "dry run." Of course, Ingrid could have coached her through a practice session last week. He could have brought it up over dinner last night. That way, she would have at least *remembered* the meeting, for crying out loud. But Ingrid had convinced him that to nag Lucy day after day, the way he'd been doing, was reinforcing what Ingrid called (she had studied child psychology at Skidmore) her "learned helplessness." "Just send her an e-mail about the meeting, like all the other members of the staff, period." Actually, it had been a relief not to be on Lucy's case for a change. Because whenever he did bring up MQII, asked her how things were going, and she answered in that vague I'm-an-artist-and-can't-be-pinned-down-to-details way, honestly, he felt like putting his hands around that slender neck and throttling her.

"I would like to welcome our new CFO Russell Mott to a historic moment at Crocker Software—a presentation of the drawings and storyboard for Maiden's Quest II. We here at Crocker Software have worked long and hard to create the most exciting, most ingenious, most entertaining computer fantasy game, not only in the United States, but in the entire world. Maiden's Quest I is sold on six of the seven continents, in thirty-six countries, and is translated into nine languages."

He glanced covertly down the table at Ingrid, who had appropriated the seat at the opposite end, second in command to Lucy. She was bobbing her head up and down, up and down, in a satisfied way. Her spiky hair, the eyebrow ring, the skimpy clothes that showed off her slutty lace bras (today's was the color of grape Kool-Aid)—all Ingrid's punk fashions (who au naturel would be a very pretty girl) that usually bothered Ed seemed quite lovely today, maybe in contrast to dull, drab Lucy.

Ed was losing his train of thought and forced himself to peel his eyes off Ingrid and turn back to Russell Mott, who was alertly tapping notes into his laptop, and then to Lucy. She still wasn't moving, hadn't untied the portfolio, so Ed decided he'd better keep going. "I would first like to introduce the creative genius of Maiden's Quest." He stopped. Nope, better not describe Lucy as a genius, even if what she'd done with Maiden's Quest was goddamn brilliant, because she certainly didn't look like any genius right now, and Mott might start to think that no one else at Crocker knew what they were doing, either. "What I really mean to say is that Lucy is only one, a very important one, but only one of many creative people who have worked collaboratively to create Maiden's Quest." This introduction did not seem to be having the desired effect of reassuring everyone that Maiden's Quest, and ergo Crocker Software, was in safe, collective hands. Ralph, the head programmer, Ingrid, and most importantly, Russell Mott, looked a little baffled.

"And so without further ado, I give you Lucy Crocker." As he said this, he put an avuncular arm around Lucy's shoulders and gave them a little squeeze. Suddenly, he had a sharp memory of the first time he had put his arm around Lucy Lamb's narrow shoulders. He had been an impoverished graduate student living in a dilapidated wooden tenement in Cambridgeport, and she was a lovely standoffish girl with a curtain of dark hair who lived across the hall with her creepy forest ranger boyfriend. For months he had wistfully watched her long hiking boot-shod legs sprint up the stairs, the black hair swinging. Then one day as he was coming home from orchestra rehearsal, he heard the sounds of weeping coming from behind her closed door. He stood for a couple of minutes listening for the boyfriend's voice offering tenderness or further wounds, but he heard nothing except wails, which were escalating. Finally, he knocked timidly, then again a little louder until the beautiful tear-stained girl, dressed in a turtleneck, kneesocks, and lavender bikini underpants with a black butterfly embroidered on the corner, opened the door. Are you okay? he asked. A couple hours later, after she had poured out the tragic tale of her boyfriend ditching her, after Ed had tried to cheer her up with mugs of tea and cartons of takeout kung po chicken, after she had started crying again, Ed had put a bashful arm around her to offer comfort—and his undying adoration. The dark hair and heaving shoulders had turned limp, melting into him with gratitude.

But now Lucy stiffened at his touch, then ducked slightly to one side and shifted her weight, in the process leaving his arm extended awkwardly into midair. He let it slowly drop and shoved his hand nonchalantly into a pocket, as if this were all part of the script.

She stepped forward to the table, smiled in that disarming way of hers, flipped a piece of hair back over one shoulder, and stared down at them like a preacher sermonizing to his lowly flock from a lectern. "In Maiden's Quest II, Princess Arabella is once again on a quest of profound consequences. This is not your basic sadistic computer game where some psycho Mortal Kombat guy aims an assault weapon at helpless civilians and then splatters body parts in every direction. No. MQII is very, very different. Morally superior. Literary. Socially conscious."

Uh oh. It was always dangerous when Lucy began to spout off about computer games. Anyone over the age of four knew that Mortal Kombat was a video game, not a computer game, but the pathetic thing was that Lucy probably didn't realize there was a difference.

Russell Mott had stopped typing, seemed half-mesmerized, half-repelled by Lucy, and Ed could imagine what he was thinking—was this lady expecting him to find a VC willing to sink three million bucks into a morally superior, literary, socially conscious computer game? What kid—even a precocious, oboe-playing, AP calculus kid—with sixty bucks in his pocket would buy that when for the same price he could get Quake IV with all the latest rocket launchers and plasma rifles and high-resolution gore?

Just as Ed was considering how to put some spin control on Lucy, Jason the programmer jumped to his feet, bless his neon nylon soccer-shirted, blond dreadlocked heart. "I mean, you don't have to convince us, Lucy. We know the deep thinking gist behind MQII. But you've got to show us the storyboard, because we've got to start programming this mother, or we . . . are . . . fucked." Jason was a mere twenty, had just dropped out of Rochester Polytech after three semesters, and had widely spaced, buggy eyes that made him seem as if he was seeing the planet Earth for the very first time that day. He spoke in such a slow, awe-filled way that *fucked* came out as innocently as *holy smokes.*

"Right," said Lucy, abashed as if she was just now coming to her senses. She held the floppy oaktag with one hand and pointed at the curling Post-it notes one by one with a Bic pen. "Okay, here's the storyboard. It's still kind of a first draft, but each Post-it note is a different scene. Um, you start here, at level one which is pink Post-its, then move on to mint green, yellow, and blue." The poster was about as polished as a third-grade book report, a bad third-grade book report. Not like the storyboard for MQI, which Lucy had calligraphed like an illuminated manuscript on a parchment scroll.

Russell Mott was the only one who even tried to make sense of the scribbled jumble, squinting through his oval wireframes down the conference table, but even he finally gave up and sank back in his chair. "I think investors might find your storyboard a bit, um, abstruse. How about showing us the drawings instead."

Abstruse, Ed thought. That was the kind of word they taught you to say in b-school instead of *shitty.*

"It would be, like, helpful," Jason chimed in.

Lucy opened her portfolio just a crack and slid out a single watercolor drawing, which she held up for the assembled throng. "Okay," she said, in a truculent, have-it-your-way tone. "Here's the first scene of level one, Arabella at her island in the Aegean when she hears from the winged sprites that her beloved has been captured by the king of the underworld and the only way she can free him is by completing three impossible tasks."

Everyone rose up out of their seats and clustered around for a closer look, and Ed had to stand on tiptoe and sort of wedge himself between Mott and Jason to get a peek. Amazingly, even though they lived in the same house, and that goddamn studio of hers which they'd had renovated to the tune of thirty thousand bucks was just down the hall from their bedroom, Ed hadn't seen any of Lucy's drawings for MQII yet. He'd asked a couple of times, but she'd acted almost offended as if he was asking to read her diary.

He gazed at the drawing with a leaping heart—the first glimpse of his baby, MQII. He always forgot what an exquisite painter Lucy was, and this was one of her best efforts, as complex as a Dürer woodcut. There was Arabella, in a sexy one-shouldered toga, standing on the balcony of a fantastical Greek palace with columns and pediments, and pawing stone Minotaur gateposts. Ralph the head programmer, Dave the composer, Alissa the animator all let out a few appreciative *wows* and *cools*. "It looks," said Jason, again wonderstruck, as if he had never seen a painting before, and probably never had, "like those neat scenes they paint on the side of vans."

Lucy carefully slid the drawing back in her portfolio, sat down in her chair, and folded her hands in front of her as if the presentation was all done.

"Do we get to see any more?" Ingrid said in the aggrieved tone she used when she complained about Lucy to Ed. She had slipped her compact, personal-trainer-trained body behind him and casually pressed a taut calf muscle against his out-of-shape flaccid one.

"Sure," said Lucy, opening the portfolio just a crack and pulling another drawing out, this one of Arabella at the helm of her boat heading off in search of the king of the underworld, slate gray waves leaping up over her head like menacing claws. The reaction was more muted this time, a few subverbal grunts and then silence.

Ingrid jumped in again. "Look, Lucy, it's hard for Russell and the rest of us to get an idea of the whole story if you just show us the drawings one at a time. Can't you just lay them out all at once." It was not a request. Ed usually approved of Ingrid's take-charge attitude, but now it made him squirmy, and he stepped back to disengage his calf from hers.

"Thanks, Ingrid. I was hoping someone would say that," Russell Mott added officiously.

Lucy sat back down, straightened her silly hair band, glared at Ingrid as if she was going to tell her where she could stick that eyebrow ring. But then, out of nowhere, the resolve seemed to dribble away, her narrow shoulders in the shell pink T-shirt sunk. "All right," she said in the same flat, dejected voice she had used after the miscarriages. "Why not." She opened the portfolio, lifted out a tiny stack of drawings, and set them oh-so-carefully down in perfect alignment with the edge of the table, as if she were hanging a museum show.

There were only thirteen of them, eleven more in addition to Arabella on the castle balcony and on her boat. They were more elaborate and accomplished than the ones for MQI, beautiful in fact, covered with tiny artful brushstrokes, but . . . there were only thirteen of them for Christ's sake.

Jason seemed to be slowly arriving at the same conclusion, tallying up the pictures on his fingers. "Wait a second, let me see if I get this. There are six levels, with about seven different scenes in each level, so that's like forty-two scenes. What we've got here is only thirteen drawings, so. . . ." He trailed off and then gave one of his gee-whiz-it's-so-neat-to-be-alive smiles and shrugged, as if there was surely some obvious explanation that he was missing.

"The rest of the drawings aren't quite finished yet," said Lucy sullenly, her eyes lowered.

"Could you possibly define 'not quite'?" said Ingrid, who had resumed her place at the head of the table. As she said this, she set her palms flat on the table and leaned menacingly toward poor Lucy; Ingrid's well-defined arm muscles flexed impressively, her large breasts in that purple bra pushed together and out against gravity into a formidable prow of cleavage.

"I mean that I have rough pencil sketches of the other characters and scenes, but they aren't ready to show yet," Lucy said, sounding more tentative by the second.

"And how long do you think it will take to get them 'ready'?"

"A few weeks," said Lucy as if it were an open question.

"We don't have a few weeks, Lucy. MQII is supposed to be in production right now. We are already months behind. Even if we had a complete set of drawings *today,* the whole team would have to work around the clock to catch up. And, obviously, Russell can't woo any investors without a product to show." Ingrid punctuated the sentence with a loud, petulant sigh as Ralph, Jason, and the rest of the Crocker drones nodded in vigorous agreement.

Of course, Ingrid was overstepping herself, Ed reminded himself—taking over this meeting, chewing out Lucy, getting the rest of the disloyal, spineless staff to join along. But Lucy had really screwed up this time and somebody had to say so. And he couldn't very well do it himself, could he?

Ed slumped down in his chair as he watched this catfight unfold, feeling humiliated and helpless, the way he used to on the basketball court in eighth grade, nearly naked (or so it seemed to him) in his skimpy uniform, with his pale, skinny arms and legs on display for everyone to see, and his ridiculous size-ten basketball sneakers, bought a size too big by his mother who said he would grow into them though he never did. The fresh rubber edges would somehow catch against each other and send him sprawling to the floor at midcourt. And his hands, which were always so adept when playing the violin, held the basketball as if it were a splintery lump of wood, the orange bumps on the ball actually abrading his fingertips.

Lucy jumped up and placed her palms facedown on the table, a mirror image to Ingrid. Unfortunately, she didn't cut quite such a persuasive image. Unlike Ingrid, with those breasts that swung forward like weighted pendulums, the only thing that happened when Lucy bent over is that the scalloped neck of her T-shirt gapped, her tiny pearl dangle earrings jittered, and her hair band got crooked again. But at least she was taller than Ingrid by a good five inches and height always created an advantage. And she was truly prettier than Ingrid, Ed thought, with those big blue eyes, if she would only dress better and whack seven straggly inches off that hair. Ingrid did have a certain base, animal appeal that Lucy could never achieve, but did that matter in the long run?

"Okay, Ingrid, what do you want me to say? That I haven't done fifty drawings, that I've only done thirteen? That I haven't even figured out the basic story for MQII? That every day I sleep late, I sit for hour after hour staring at my drawing board and nothing comes, that I take two weeks to do a drawing that should only take two days? That I'm single-handedly destroying this company and your aspiring careers as software tycoons? Okay, I admit it. I'm nothing but a fraud." Lucy's voice was loud and hysterical, like those witnesses at the end of Perry Mason who finally crack in the witness box and are led off screaming, "*Yes,* I did it! And you know what? I'm *glad* I did it."

Russell Mott had a pained expression on his face, as if he'd been caught between a couple bickering about their sex life on a city bus. He closed his laptop, closed his folder of Crocker Software financial data, and wistfully eyed the doorway. Undoubtedly, he was thinking of all those other software companies he could have signed aboard with rather than the leaky, mutinous vessel of Crocker Software.

"So you're actually telling us that this is all you've done in the last eighteen months. That all those rosy progress reports from Ed were nothing but a sham," said Ingrid, now directing her wrath toward Ed, as if he had been deliberately misleading her in all those private chats they'd been having over the last few months, when he whispered in her ear that it would be okay, that Lucy was coming along, that Crocker would make its Christmas deadline. He had promised her, as she rubbed her hands over his shoulders and neck, kneading out all those knots of tension.

"It's not Ed's fault. It's my fault. I didn't actually lie. I just let him believe that I was further along than I was," said Lucy quietly, no longer sounding testy, only resigned. Ed felt a pang of shame; Lucy had always defended him. To her boozer suburbanite mom, Corky, who thought Ed was a math geek loser and couldn't understand why Lucy, if she was determined to marry a bore, couldn't at least marry a lawyer. And to his dad, Harry, the high school math teacher, who was baffled that anyone would design computer games for kids when they could contemplate the sublime beauty of numbers. Sitting in the folding aluminum chair on the poured concrete patio behind his parents' house in Marshfield, politely sipping one of those sickly sweet strawberry daiquiris his father whipped up in the blender as a special treat, she'd give him a little playful nudge with her foot and say, "Oh, come on, Harry. Ed isn't just designing kung fu arcade games for a bunch of juvenile delinquents. He's on the ramparts of a revolution and he'll make us millionaires to boot." Sweet, really, how Lucy could defend the merits of technology, at least to someone as clueless as his father, when she herself was a Luddite to the very core.

Back in those early days, when Crocker Software consisted of a single Tandy computer and himself in the rear bedroom of their two-family in Arlington, she never doubted him, didn't mind supporting them on her librarian's salary. The time he showed her his first game, Fighter Pilot Alert, with its crude jets lurching across the sky, the bullets plodding toward their target when you pounded the alt keys, the explosions that sounded like stereo static when they hit their target. She squinted at the screen, saying vaguely, "Oh, that's really clever, I guess" as he explained all the programming wizardry. But afterward she had wrapped her arms around his shoulders while he sat in front of his monitor, murmured what a genius he was while kissing the rim of his ear, her hair smelling of Herbal Essence shampoo, a scent he used to like, and he had felt validated.

And now here he was sitting by impotently as Ingrid the director of publicity, and . . . why didn't he just admit it . . . his tantric masseuse, trashed his wife in front of everyone. Okay, time for the president and founder of Crocker Software to take charge. He stood up, placed *his* palms flat on the conference table, and thrust his body forward in what he hoped was a muscular and authoritative way. He probably didn't cut a very persuasive figure, either. Although he had a hard time believing it, Ed knew he was considered to be quite handsome, in a boyish, Kurt Cobain kind of way. His high school yearbook had nicknamed him "the thinking girl's heartthrob." *Wired* magazine had named him one of its twenty sexiest men, not that the other nineteen with their sagging bellies and Buddy Holly glasses were such stiff competition. These days he dressed in the standard software company garb—some freebie T-shirt from a P. C. gamer magazine, baggy pants cinched up with a belt that was woven from shredded tires, and (his one indulgence) six-hundred-dollar Armani leather shoes. He also sported the ubiquitous software CEO's ponytail, a thick blond one now slightly streaked with gray.

"I think what we're seeing here is the natural growth cycle of a technology company. As president and founder of Crocker, I take full responsibility for not recognizing the weakness in the organizational hierarchy of our product development sooner," he said, glancing warily toward Russell Mott, who wasn't looking reassured by any b-school mumbo jumbo.

"Lucy, as we all know, was the creative genius behind MQI. She did everything—the story, the puzzles and clues, the fantastic illustrations. The job of the rest of the team was to transform her text and artwork into a computer game. The creative and technology components were completely separate." As he said this, he held his hands up on either side like a scale that was balancing huge but equal weights. This was going quite well, he thought.

"Our big mistake was to try to duplicate the process this time. With its additional levels and graphics, MQII was simply too big for one person to design all by herself. We all owe her our thanks for trying so hard to solve this impossible 'quest.' " At this very small joke, Ed paused, hoping there might be at least a couple of smiles or something to lighten the dreary mood, but all he saw was Ingrid's eyes roll up in disgust under a swath of black eyeliner.

"So Lucy, you are *off . . . the . . . hook*. From now on, MQII is a completely collaborative effort. Starting today, Jason, Alissa, and Ralph will program and animate the game directly, no pencil and paper stage anymore. Ingrid, Russell, and I will evolve the marketing and financing strategy. Lucy's role will be one of consultant. She'll be available for brainstorming whenever the team needs her. And so I would like to adjourn this meeting. The new MQII team will convene in one hour so we can revise our production schedule."

Nicely done, Ed thought. The problem of Lucy was gracefully handled, made it look like she had actually been promoted; that was the beauty of the term *consultant*. And now there was a ghost of a chance that they might get back on schedule, if they hired a few extra programmers, and be able to ship by Christmas.

Well, Ingrid certainly look pleased, tossing her spiky head back and giving Ed a coquettish sideways nod of approval as she gathered up her papers. She headed toward the door, calling over to Jason, Alissa, and Ralph, "Come on, guys. Let's grab some lunch before the meeting." Russell Mott grabbed his laptop and scurried to catch up with Ingrid, whom he seemed to find more compelling than Ed, leaving Lucy and Ed all alone at the empty conference table.

Lucy collected her drawings, placed them in a neat stack in the center of the portfolio, and then tied the three laces. Ed was having a hard time reading her mood. He thought she would be thrilled that her days as Maiden's Quest creator were over. Hadn't she been complaining in that irritating, passive-aggressive way of hers for the last three years about the burdens of unwanted fame and responsibility. Ed busied himself gathering up the empty Pellagrino bottles, Snickers wrapper (Jason's), bags of organic potato chips. Why was everyone at Crocker such an inconsiderate slob? He would send a memo reminding the staff to clean up after themselves—again. Lucy was done with her tying and now just sat there, all alone, looking vacantly at the other end of the table where only minutes ago Ingrid, his publicity director/masseuse, had her drawn and quartered.

"Come on, let's grab a bite to eat before the meeting," he coaxed. They could go down the street to that Thai place she liked, have big platters of Pad Thai washed down with two bottles of beer apiece, and cheer up.

"I'm not going to the meeting," she said, but remained motionless as if she were planning to stay put while the meeting took place down the hall in Ed's office.

He sat down in the swivel chair next to hers. This was the closest he'd been to her all day; he could see that dusting of tiny freckles that always appeared on her arms with the first blast of summer sun. "Why not?" he said quietly.

"Because you just fired me, remember?"

"I didn't fire you. You're going to be a consultant. Weren't you listening?"

She blew out a cynical snort. "Oh, come on Ed. *Consultant* is a polite term people use for getting canned. My uncle was a consultant for the last twenty-five years of his life. It meant he sat around all day watching game shows and drinking screwdrivers."

Ed felt his old exasperation return with a vengeance. "I don't get it. For months and months you've been like Princess Arabella caught in the cave of despair. Now you're finally free. You can sleep late, spend all day gardening or going to flea markets with Rosemary and I won't gripe. I thought you'd be happy."

"I thought I'd be happy, too, but I'm not. Weird as it seems, I guess I think of Maiden's Quest as my baby." She flinched slightly at the word *baby* as if she realized that this is what it had come to—a computer game had taken the place of a real baby.

"But we still need your ideas. It's still your baby," he said, regretting his word choice.

She turned around to face him, then suddenly pulled her hair band off, tossed it on the table, and raked one side of her hair back with her fingers. It stayed in place for a moment and then a wave cascaded down over one eye, like those big-hair models. The effect was surprisingly sultry, and Ed felt startled as he sometimes was at his wife's babe potential. Not that he wanted to be married to a babe, but was being slightly provocative, exuding a whiff of sexual chemistry, such a bad thing? And it certainly would have made her a more plausible figurehead for a hip, cutting-edge software company. But she probably wasn't the figurehead of Crocker anymore, was she? he mused. So who was—Ed with his ponytail and Italian shoes?

"I don't think Ingrid is going to be really eager to hear my ideas," she said.

"Ingrid isn't the boss," said Ed.

"Could have fooled me."

Ed dropped his eyes, shamefaced, hoping his cheeks weren't turning any incriminating colors—when he was embarrassed, he tended to blush. It was true that things had evolved with Ingrid—accidentally, inadvertently, at least by him—into what might be described as an inappropriate relationship. He probably hadn't reflected deeply enough about the possible consequences—on his marriage, on company morale. But when Ingrid had him stretched out on the couch in his office and was kneading ginseng oil into his shoulder blades it was difficult to reflect too deeply about anything.

Ingrid's uppity behavior at the meeting had nothing to do with the fact that she was occasionally helping the boss relax his overtensed muscles. In her defense, she was only doing her job as publicity director. She was the one who was catching all the flack from the software chains and the computer press about the MQII delays. No wonder she was pissed off at Lucy's antics. Let's face it, Lucy had led everyone at Crocker—including Ed—down the primrose path, with her vague assurances that she was right on schedule. But it was hard for Ed to feel too indignant as she sat plaintively in front of him, her dark hair now drooping all over her face, making her look unkempt and unemployed.

Lucy didn't seem to be waiting for a reply. In fact, she seemed to have forgotten all about his betrayal at letting Ingrid publicly lambaste her and had turned her attention to the dozens of thick black cables snaking across the ceiling of the conference room. After the first flush of Maiden's Quest

I's success, they had moved Crocker out of their two-family in Arlington and into this old candy factory in Somerville. The trendy Cambridge architect who had designed the renovation had insisted on running the miles of souped-up electric cable for the computers on the outside of the walls. "It's a visual statement of Crocker's gestalt," he had said. The building had smelled of wintergreen and chocolate until the day the electric wire went in and blotted everything out with the fumes of plastic and solvents.

"I miss the old place on Spruce Street," she said softly. By the time they had finally moved, Crocker had taken over most of their two-family, with terminals and telephones jammed into closets and pantries. Ed, Lucy, and the boys had been relegated to three bedrooms on the third floor, and the boys had used Crocker's ragtag office space as their playroom. Once Phil jammed three Lego space men into Ed's disk drive and crashed out the whole system for a week.

"Yeah, I do, too," said Ed. Back then, running a software company had seemed carefree and fun. It was like being back in college, eating greasy takeout food, staying up all night with his one or two part-time employees, bouncing zany ideas off one another, laughing.

Sure there were cash flow problems, but no one seemed to mind too much if their paycheck was a few dollars shy, or sometimes missing altogether. They were a team, they had a common cause, and the not-entirely-unrealistic dream that Crocker might make all of them rich. Which it had.

Back then Lucy fit right into the corporate culture, not that you could call the early Crocker corporate. The programmers had found her endearing—the way she asked befuddled questions about technology, put mason jars of cut flowers on their desks, and answered the telephone: "Hi, it's Lucy—I mean, Crocker Software." Of course, his early programmers had all been misfits themselves—Laszlo and Vlad and Victor. Overweight, unwashed, smokers, mostly mute unless they were discussing their latest programming feats or their comic book collections, keeping the same working hours as bats or moles. When Crocker expanded to the point where it required regular hours and minimum standards of social graces and hygiene from its staff, they disappeared. Ed occasionally ran into Vlad or Victor in Harvard Square, coming out of a comic book store with an unfiltered Camel dangling from his lips, and was always relieved to hear if either one was working at some month-old start-up somewhere. But as for Laszlo, the genius Hungarian who had stormed out in a huff when Marla got on his case for leaving an open sardine tin on his desk for a week, he seemed to have vanished off the face of the earth.

The new Crocker staff was about as intolerant of Lucy as it had been of Victor, Vlad, and Laszlo. It did not find her techno-stupidity lovable, tended to think that maybe she was feebleminded in other ways, too. Ed once overheard a programmer explaining to her in patronizing tones how to operate the water cooler. Ingrid and the others didn't understand that all Lucy's oddball interests in medieval literature and board games and flea markets were what made Maiden's Quest so quirky and original in the first place.

Ed sighed sadly for those good old days on Spruce Street, for his own losses. Running a software company sure wasn't fun or zany anymore. He spent his time reviewing employee benefit packages, writing up policies for maternity leave and sexual harassment. If there was so much as fifty cents missing from their paychecks, they'd probably drag him out to the parking lot and drive over him with one of those sports utility vehicles they all seemed to be able to afford.

Lucy stood up stiffly, tucked her portfolio under one arm, slipped the hair band back on—now her hair really looked like Morticia's—and headed toward the door. "So long, Ed," she said with finality, as if she never planned to lay eyes on Crocker Software or him again.

"Are you going home?" he asked.

"Of course. Where else would I go?"

"All right, then. I'll see you at dinner. Don't take this so hard. Why don't you go on a vacation for a few days. You deserve a little R and R."

She stopped and turned back toward him, actually smiling. "There's a thought. We could go hiking with the boys in the White Mountains, do the huts. Remember when we did it the year before the twins were born, how much fun it was? Maybe I could get reservations for this weekend."

Ed did not remember doing the huts with Lucy as fun. By the end of the first day, he was limping in agony behind Lucy, who bounded ahead on those long legs, with a canvas rucksack she'd used at that stupid canoe camp she was always hearkening back to, Camp Kimona, or whatever it was called. She'd be waiting for him on the top of every peak, and when he finally arrived huffing and puffing, dragging his blistered feet, wishing that a Sherpa was there to administer oxygen, she'd want him to partake in the beauty of nature. He was supposed to listen raptly as she identified all the peaks, the landmarks in distant states, the rock formations and flora. "I can't go on vacation right now. We have to get MQII back on track, and I'm doing a P.C. gamer convention in New York all next week." With Ingrid.

"Forget it. I don't know why I even suggested it." Lucy turned and marched off, down an interminable corridor of beige cubicles where the programmers and graphic artists dwelled, surrounded by leaning towers of hard drives, monitors, and extension cables. Ed took after her at a trot, but her long strides easily outpaced his, just as they had on Mount Lafayette. By the time he caught up to her in the parking lot, she was sliding into the driver's seat of her beat-up Taurus station wagon. (Another one of Lucy's perverse possessions. Ed had been trying to persuade her to buy something a little snazzier, maybe one those SUVs that everyone else at Crocker had, but she had stubbornly insisted she needed the Taurus to haul those barn loads of junk she and Rosemary picked up at flea markets.)

Ed held the top of the car door so she couldn't slam it and leaned down. She'd already slipped her sunglasses on so he couldn't see her expression, but her mouth had a pinched look as if she was holding back tears. "Why don't you go with just the boys? They've never been to the White Mountains."

"Oh, come on, Ed." She pushed down her glasses so she could glare at him. " You know they refuse to be away from their e-mail for more than twenty-four hours. Just like their dad." She fairly spat out the words, and Ed was truly offended. Lucy was always complaining about Benjy and Phil, about their lack of exercise and hobbies, but he practically busted with pride over their accomplishments. Teaching themselves C++ computer language at the age of eleven, designing those Web sites, expanding the client base of Benjy/Phil Computer Consultations until they had accounts receivable for $17,000. They knew more than half the programmers at Crocker. When he heard other parents bragging about their kids who were in youth orchestras or on all-star teams, he never felt diminished. He knew that Benjy and Phil would achieve fame and gain someday that would far surpass any French horn player or soccer goalie. And he was grateful that they felt at home in the world, were appreciated for their skills (at least by everyone except their mother), would never have to stand naked and mocked in basketball jerseys.

"Well, why don't you go a few weeks early to the Wheeler bungalow colony. The boys and I will join you in August."

"Right, Ed. Go on a whale watch. Play miniature golf. Have the clam roll platter at Sylvester's lobster shack. Sounds like a blast."

Well, actually, it did sound like a blast, at least to him. He loved the simple pleasures of their annual two-week August vacation at the Wheeler bungalow colony in South Dennis with Rosemary and Alfred and their two bratty kids. An afternoon of bobbing the waves side by side with Alfred at Cold Storage beach, followed by a game of horseshoes in the sandpit behind their bungalow with the shamrock shutters, double-dip pistachio cones with jimmies from Ruby's ice-cream palace, then hitting the video arcade with Benjy and Phil for their daily Duke Nukem face-off. But it's so unadventurous, Lucy would say, as they loaded up the Taurus every August with the cooler and low-slung beach chairs. So . . . ordinary. What was the matter with ordinary, Ed always wondered.

Before he could make another unadventurous suggestion, Lucy slammed the door, started the engine, and backed up so fast Ed had to leap back out of the way. As she made the righthand turn out of the Crocker parking lot, tires squealing, Ed heard a whap of something hitting the pavement, and saw the portfolio of MQII drawings lying in the center of the drive, waiting to be flattened by the next Federal Express truck that pulled in. Lucy was always putting her purse or packages on the roof of the car while she unlocked the door, and then forgetting about them as she drove off. Her purse had been retrieved by honest citizens from some remarkable places—the center of Storrow Drive, the parking lot of Disney World. He walked over and picked it up; luckily, Lucy had tied those laces so tightly that the pictures were still snugly inside. The only damage was a smashed corner, and a dusting of gray grime. Shaking his head almost fondly, he straightened out the dent as best he could, wiped the cover clean against his cargo pants, and walked back inside.

He found the staff all crammed into his office, eating Chinese food out of white cartons stained with grease. Why was it that every time the staff was eating something messy—pizza or meatball subs—they had to do it in his office? He scowled as a jet of hoisin sauce squirted out of the end of Jason's moo shu pancake onto the all-wool citron-colored berber that had cost eighty bucks a yard. Ingrid had settled comfortably into his chair, but at least she had spread a plastic bag tidily under her carton of Szechuan spicy green beans (she was a vegan), which was a mere three inches away from the elliptical, ergonomic edges of his brand-new behemoth P.C. Ed sat down cross-legged on the floor and set Lucy's portfolio protectively next to him, out of splattering range from Jason. He didn't mind, though, when Ingrid or another staff member sat in his chair during a meeting. He prided himself that Crocker was still nonhierarchical, that they still saw him—at least occasionally—as one of the team.

"Ed, you're finally here," said Ingrid, lowering her chopsticks and giving him that saucy smile she'd bestowed on him earlier. His heart sped up as he thought ahead to the massage they'd arranged for later in the afternoon. His sciatica had been kicking up and she had invited him back to her apartment so she could stretch him out on her massage table and try out some pressure points recommended by her acupuncturist. But Lucy was expecting him home for dinner, and tonight, a mere six hours after he had demoted her, was not the night to be skipping out to explore the frontiers of sacred tantric massage. He scowled again.

"We've been reviewing the revised timetable and flow chart, and it looks like we're back on track," said Mott, who had made himself right at home in the center of Ed's custom-made maroon leather arm chair and was in the midst of taking tidy bites out of the fleshy rump of a dumpling.

"Great," said Ed. Maybe they would make the Christmas ship date and Crocker's sorry ass would be saved after all. "Listen, guys. Lucy is sorry she couldn't make it. But she left me these for you to work from." He patted the portfolio by his side. The staff as one lowered their eyes toward their take-out food cartons, the latest issue of *Wired,* anywhere but his face or one anothers'.

"What?" he asked.

"Before you came in, Russell was suggesting that maybe our whole concept for MQII was too . . . ah . . . rigid. " Ingrid was picking her way through this speech very cautiously, as if she were dealing with some cantankerous elderly person who might any minute fly off the handle. "All along, you'd seen

MQII as basically a clone of MQI, with the same type of storyline and graphics." Ed noticed that Ingrid had somehow exchanged "we" for "you." The screwups with MQII were now all his fault, his and Lucy's. "So now that Lucy is out of the picture—" She stopped, and corrected herself. "Now that Lucy's serving in a new capacity as consultant, we thought maybe it was time to rethink MQII from the ground up. But of course," she said, leaning forward toward him, revealing a few tantalizing peeks of her gumball-grape bra, "you have the last word. You're the boss." Was it his imagination, or was there a distinct note of sarcasm as she said this?

Ed stood up, feeling defensive for Lucy. No one had even asked where she was. How dare these little twerps dismiss her so easily? Who did they think had made Crocker Software what it was? Since a palace coup seemed in the offing from his new CFO, he might as well prepare himself to receive the blow. "Always happy to hear any ideas you have on how we can improve our product, Russell," Ed said in what he hoped was an affable way.

Mott dropped his dumpling back in the container, carefully wiped his fingers one by one on a fistful of tiny napkins, then pulled out a thick packet of pie charts. "According to the latest market survey. In addition, over eighty percent of all gamers prefer a male to a female protagonist."

"Go on," said Ed.

"So we've decided that Princess Arabella as a heroine seems dated," said Marla. Now even his personal assistant had turned against him. "When people think princess, they think Di, you know?"

"So, who would seem more heroic?" said Ed, with the distinct impression he wasn't going to like the answer.

"We still want a female heroine, of course, but maybe a less overtly female one," said Ingrid. "No long hair. No fancy gowns. Modern dress, short hair, androgynous. Someone that both male and female gamers can relate to."

Ed didn't know about the others, but he was much more

interested in relating to a sexy, brainy princess than some androgynous creature with a crew cut and breasts. "So would you still call this new heroine Arabella?"

"We were thinking of something that would *remind* everyone of Arabella, but *not* be Arabella. So what about, simply 'A'," Ingrid said, punctuating the sentence with a flourish of her chopsticks.

"I was also pointing out gamer preference for an interactive game-playing experience. So instead of getting from one level to the next by solving puzzles, which is essentially passive, players in Maiden's Quest II would progress by doing something more, um, proactive," Russell said holding up a chartreuse bar chart.

"Such as . . . ?" said Ed, not able to surpress the sarcastic edge creeping into his voice. This was getting boring. Why couldn't they tell him all the bad news at once and be done with it?

"Arabella's gotta pack some heat," Jason said, taking aim with his forefinger at Ed's forehead. "*Phip, phip, phip.*"

"Oh, I get it. Guns instead of thinking. How proactive," said Ed with a bitter smile. Too bad Lucy wasn't here to witness this great moment in their corporate history. Until an hour ago, Crocker had prided itself on its commitment to nonviolent games.

"Not traditional guns, of course. Just little laser weapons for self-protection. No shooting at humans allowed. You'd only get points for hitting non-humans—droids, trolls, aliens, the like. No blood or gut-splattering. Very tame, *Star Wars* kind of stuff," Ingrid explained.

"Okay, let me see if I've got this straight. You want an androgynous woman named 'A' with a buzz cut and a tiny laser gun who blows away cyborgs, right?" Ed asked glumly. Maybe he was getting too old to design computer games. Maybe kids like Mott and Jason were going to take over Crocker and turn him into a consultant, too.

Heads and chopsticks nodded around the room.

"I need to think this over. We'll discuss this more tomorrow." The others stood up and started meandering toward the door. "And would you all *please* take your litter with you."

"Oh," said Jason with surprise, as if he had never heard this notion of cleaning up after himself before. "Right. Cool."

Ed sank down in his desk chair, which Ingrid and her Szechuan green beans had vacated, and dropped his head down on his folded arms the way he had been forced to spend naptime in second grade. They had to keep their heads down on their desks with their eyes closed, while their teacher played Mexican folk music on a giant record player. If you were caught squirming or poking anyone, you got your name written down on the blackboard. A sly goody-goody girl named Daria Cotrell kept poking him, but for a reason he was never able to fathom, he was the one who got his name written on the blackboard.

God, what a fucked-up day—starting with firing his own wife, and ending with listening to MBA-speak about how Maiden's Quest II should be played with a gun scope. His head throbbed as if it had suddenly sprouted a golf ballsize brain tumor, his neck muscles felt as if a giant had been strumming them like a banjo.

He heard the door of his office click closed, soft footsteps gliding over the nubby carpet. "You look like you're in pain," Ingrid murmured softly.

"I am," he said without raising his head. He felt her sinewy body press into his back, her strong fingers push his ponytail to one side, and start to pummel and stretch out the taut ropes of his neck.

"Ooh, you're so tight. How does that feel?" she cooed.

"Mmm, hmm, mmm, hmm," Ed said, as if he was gagging on something round and slippery. He had noticed that he was unable to conduct intelligent conversation when he was getting one of Ingrid's massages, probably because he got so relaxed that he tended to drool.

Suddenly, the magic fingers retreated and his neck clenched up again, worse than ever. "You're too stiff," she said. "You'll have to wait until I can stretch you out flat and work on your whole body."

"I can't come," Ed said mournfully, his words still sounding wet and garbled. "I have to go home for dinner. Lucy's pretty upset about what happened at the meeting, and frankly, I don't blame her." He felt like the headline on a romance magazine story—"His Head Said No, While His Body Screamed Yes!"

"I got some new massage oil with kale and liverwort I was going to try out."

Even though kale and liverwort did not sound particularly appetizing, Ed's mouth started watering again. "Maybe I could drop by. Just for a few minutes."

CHAPTER 4

>>

Phil was hunkered down with Benjy in front of a computer terminal, trying to download a neat new shareware game called Revenge of the Ninja, when he heard his mother knocking on the door. He could always tell it was his mother, because she rapped so softly—like a bunny's paw—and then waited for one of them to let her in. His dad never knocked, just came busting in the door like a kid, so hard that the knob ricocheted off the wall. His mother had hollered at Phil about the round dent in the plaster, and he said he'd try not to do it again, even though it was all his dad's fault.

"Come in," Benjy yelled, but there was no more activity on the other side of the closed door. Finally, Phil got up, walked across the room, opened it, and there, as predicted, stood his mom.

She didn't look so good. Her hair was a big tangled mess, like she hadn't brushed it, which was ironic because she was always on Phil's case to brush his hair, which in the morning tended to stand up straight in the air like porcupine quills. He didn't see the point in brushing his hair, when he usually jammed on a baseball cap and wore it all day, but she insisted anyway. And her clothes were all rumpled and crooked like she had been sleeping in them, which was a possibility. He'd noticed that she liked to take a lot of naps on that couch in her studio, when she was supposed to be working on her drawings for MQII.

"Hi, Mom. Come on in," he said. She always acted like she

wasn't welcome in their room, so he made it a point to invite her.

"Are you sure? I don't want to bother you if you're doing something important," she said tentatively.

He sat back down next to Benjy, who was now clicking his tongue with disgust at the sluggishness of Revenge of the Ninja, and wondered if there was anything that he did in his life that could be considered truly important. Doing his French homework, installing Windows 98 on some lawyer's computer? That didn't seem too important to him.

His mother trailed after him and now stood hovering behind his shoulder, which made him nervous. Usually she wandered in after they came home from school, asked if they had any homework or were hungry, and then wandered out again without really listening to the answers. Now, she put a hand on Phil's shoulder and rubbed it, and then ran her fingers through the back of his bristly hair. He dropped his head limply to one side like a spaniel getting its ears scratched; he loved it when she touched him like that, not that he would admit it, especially with Benjy sitting right there.

"What are you guys doing?" she asked.

"Just checking out this new computer game," Benjy said, without raising his eyes from the screen.

Phil knew that she disapproved of them spending time playing computer games. All of their friends thought it was incredibly cool that their mom designed computer games, especially a really famous one like Maiden's Quest. Little did they know that their mom was just like any of the other moms—anticomputer games, anti-Nintendo, anti-Sony PlayStation, anti-R-rated movies. Actually, Phil was glad that the kids at school had this illusion that his parents were cool—it seemed to be his only claim to coolness—and he wasn't in a big hurry to set anyone straight.

"What's it called?"

"Revenge of the Ninjas," said Benjy, sounding suspicious

that this conversation was working its way around to him getting yelled at for something.

She bent down so her face was level with the screen. "You mean those little guys in black kicking those other little guys in black are ninjas?"

"Uh huh."

"But I thought ninjas were big green guys with shells."

"That's Teenage Mutant Ninja Turtles. This is different."

"Oh." She straightened up. "Shouldn't you boys be doing your homework?"

Benjy slid a sideways glance over at Phil and rolled his eyes behind his wire-rim glasses—so much for her interest in the latest shareware game. "We don't have any homework because this is the last week of school."

"That's right. I knew that," she said uncertainly, crossing her arms and staring out the bay window with a vague look. "Have you boys decided what you're going to do this summer?"

Benjy and Phil exchanged nervous looks. Was she going to make another pitch about the pleasures and thrills of paddling across Wisconsin? "We've got it all planned out, Mom. BPCC is going to expand its client base into western Mass. and the Cape. We've hired some temporary summer help—a couple of sixth graders," said Benjy in a grown-up way that Phil admired. Benjy was really good at sounding like he knew what he was talking about even when he didn't. Whenever they had to make a presentation to a prospective client, Benjy did all the talking, while Phil handed out the company brochures and work samples.

Benjy tended to take charge anyway because he was the oldest, by eleven and a half minutes. Even if he didn't look like the oldest, at least these days. In the last year, Phil had grown a bunch, while Benjy had stayed exactly the same size, so Phil kind of towered over him. Nevertheless, people who didn't know them still asked if they were identical twins, which seemed like an unbelievably dumb question. Phil's stock answer was, "What do you think?" Benjy, who never missed an opportunity to throw around a big word, would say, "We're dizygotes."

"So you're going to work on your little company all summer?" she said. "That's nice."

Phil truly started to worry when his mother behaved like this. How could she not know it was the last week of school? And why did she think it was nice all of a sudden that they were spending the summer working on BPCC, when she'd been lecturing them for the last two months about spending more time outside and going away to canoe camp. Although it wasn't unusual for her to get weird notions in her head—like the time she decided she wanted to buy this house from some strange old lady and move them all out to Crowley—and no one, not even Dad, could change her mind. But today she seemed much worse, like she'd snapped or something.

Everyone teased Phil that he worried too much, and maybe he did. His grandmother—his mom's mom, who insisted they call her by her first name, Corky—nicknamed him the little professor, which really pissed him off. He certainly worried more than Benjy, who didn't seem to care whether or not he was popular, or got good grades (even though he always did), or had the right clothes, or whether BPCC might accidentally erase some big company's data files and they'd get sued.

Phil spun around in his chair and studied her standing in a big puddle of afternoon sunshine, which made her look really exhausted, like she was coming down with the flu. And she looked older, too, with lines like parentheses on either side of her mouth. Not that she still didn't look really pretty—Phil thought his mother was prettier than all the other moms he knew, but once when he told this to Benjy, he just snorted and said incredulously, "Mom? I guess I never really thought about it." Maybe he thought she was attractive because he looked like her—tall with dark hair and blue eyes—while Benjy was small and blond like Dad.

He got up and walked over to her. Now that he'd shot up

all of a sudden, the top of his head was about the same height as her eyebrow. He wasn't exactly a grown-up (even though now he was taller than some shrimpy grown-ups like Mrs. Rogers), but he felt like he wasn't a kid anymore, either. He just stood there, next to her, until she stopped staring out the window at the vegetable garden and noticed him.

"What?" she said.

"Why don't you come sit down, so we can have a little talk." He grabbed hold of her elbow with one hand and her shoulder with the other and kept tugging until she started to come along, like a stubborn dog on a leash. Then she smiled a little bit, the first time he had seen her smile since she had come in, as if she was pleased that someone was paying attention to her for a change. He steered her over toward his chair and yanked on her elbow until she finally sat down.

Benjy was staring over at him, as if he were the one who was acting weird. Everyone always assumed that just because someone was your twin you could read his mind, and he could read yours, and you had all the same opinions and tastes. It was true that Benjy was his best friend, but that was probably because they hung out together all the time. Phil sometimes wondered what their relationship would be if Benjy weren't his twin, if he were just another kid at school instead; he wasn't sure if they would even be friends.

Phil sat down cross-legged on the floor, next to his mother's feet, in those old sandals she wore when she was gardening (although dad had forbidden her to do any gardening, because she was so behind on her MQII drawings). "So," he said, "How was your day?" As he said this, he felt like a complete moron, like he was pretending to be a grown-up. This was the way his grandmother talked to him—so Phil, how is school going? —which always made him squirm.

"My day sucked," said his mother.

Benjy and Phil were never allowed to say something sucked, unless of course it was something that really did suck, like an octopus. They were also not allowed to say *pissed off, butt* or *butthead, God, asshole, shit,* or the f-word. These rules, made by his mother, were technically hypocritical, because his father said all of these words all of the time, but Phil didn't mind. It somehow seemed the proper order of things—that his mother would not swear, that his father would because he was head of a software company with college-age employees who swore a lot, that he and Benjy would also swear, but secretly between themselves, when they were sure no grown-up could hear them. Therefore when his mother said *suck,* Phil didn't know whether he should even ask why.

Benjy had finally gotten fed up with the lousy graphics of Revenge of the Ninjas and switched his laserlike scrutiny onto their mother. He leaned back in his swivel chair and pushed his glasses down, so he could study her more closely with his nearsighted eyes.

Phil wished Benjy wouldn't do that because it made him look like a nerd. One of the many things Phil worried about was whether kids at school thought Benjy was a nerd. And if your twin was a nerd, then everyone would assume you were one, too. He'd been trying to get Benjy to dress better—in Nine Inch Nails T-shirts and cargo pants and skateboarder sneakers for example—but Benjy couldn't be bothered and just wore his same old Crocker Software T-shirts and Reeboks day after day. Benjy's hair looked funny, too, kind of grew in clumps, because he always let the barber cut it any way he wanted to. And also, Phil thought it was time for Benjy to stop using that babyish nickname and shorten his name to plain old Ben.

"Wasn't the big MQII meeting today?" asked Benjy.

"Ye-e-es," she said, giving the word at least three syllables.

"So, how'd it go?"

"Well, let's see. First, I forgot all about the meeting. Marla had to call and remind me and I got there forty-five minutes late. And then I had to admit to this whole room full of people, including the new financial officer that your dad brought in, that I had only done thirteen drawings."

Benjy frowned. "Wait a second. I thought there were six levels with seven scenes each, so you should have had something like fifty drawings."

"Right. I really fucked up." She said *fucked* so matter-of-factly it seemed as if she had forgotten she was talking to a couple of thirteen year olds and was supposed to be setting a good example.

Now it was Benjy's turn to look alarmed. "Mom, I don't think you should talk like that."

"You're right. I'm sorry." She looked over at them sheepishly. "I really goofed up."

"So what happened? Did Dad get mad?"

Phil wished Benjy would stop asking all these questions. He, for one, didn't want to know what happened next or if Dad got mad. He was starting to feel queasy, like when his French teacher Madame Miller announced at the beginning of class that she was going to give them a surprise vocabulary quiz.

"Mostly, Ingrid got mad. She chewed me out for screwing everything up."

"Which one's Ingrid?" Benjy asked.

Sometimes Benjy was so out to lunch, Phil just couldn't believe it. How could he not know which one Ingrid was? She was the one with the big boobs, like Jenny McCarthy on TV.

"She's the one with the eyebrow ring," said Phil helpfully.

"Oh, yeah. I guess I remember. So then what happened?"

"Well, after Ingrid was finished, then your dad fired me." She leaned back in her chair and stared at them defiantly, first at Benjy, then at him. Phil thought her eyes looked feverish and wild, like those raccoons on warning posters about rabies. Could she have possibly been exposed to rabies? he wondered. It was theoretically possible—there were bats in the attic, raccoons regularly knocked over their trash cans.

Benjy, for once in his know-it-all life, seemed to be at a loss for words. "What do you mean he fired you?" His voice sounded tiny and scared.

"I'm not working at Crocker Software anymore."

"That's not possible," said Benjy, with a hollow bravery, like a third grader standing up to an eighth grader who had swiped his lunch money. "You started the company with Dad. Who's going to design MQII if he fires you?"

"Ingrid and Ralph and Alissa. They don't need me anymore." Her voice was flat and dejected, as if no else in the world needed her anymore, either, including Benjy and Phil and Dad. Phil felt the urge to crawl into her lap, wrap his arms around her, and kiss her—the way he had done when he was about three. He remembered kissing her again and again, loud wet smacks, saying between each one "I love you" and her saying back, "I love you, too," like it was a game. But of course he couldn't fit in her lap anymore and would probably break or tear something if he tried. With Benjy here, he felt too self-conscious even to hug her, so he clasped his arms around his long legs and sighed sympathetically.

"So what are you going to do now?" Benjy seemed to have recovered from his momentary alarm. His mother's joblessness was now an intellectual problem to be solved.

"I don't know," she said, standing up, tucking in her T-shirt, and brushing down her skirt, not that much could be done to straighten out those clothes. "I might go back to being a children's librarian. Maybe they can use me at the Crowley Library."

It was all too strange. First his mother wasn't going to design Maiden's Quest games at Crocker anymore. Now she was going to work at the children's room in the town library—gluing up posters of Winnie the Pooh reading to Piglet, doing story hour for little kids, stamping out books, and yelling at him and his friend to quit making so much noise. Phil was pretty sure this would affect his status of having a cool mom.

But he had to admit she looked a little less depressed as she said this, so maybe it wouldn't be so bad. It wasn't as if she liked designing computer games very much. She was always saying how stupid they were, and how he and Benjy spent too much time staring at computer monitors with their thumbs on a joystick when they should be outside doing something, although he wasn't exactly sure what she expected him to do—ride a bicycle, go bird watching, play baseball? But the irony (this was Phil's new favorite word ever since he had written a paper about irony in *Huck Finn* and gotten an A) was she was so good at dreaming up cool computer games, kind of brilliant really. Benjy thought Maiden's Quest was boring, but for Phil, playing the game was like exploring the inside of his mother's mind—with all the bizarre rooms and landscapes and those complicated word puzzles.

"I thought I'd make something special for dinner. What do you boys want?" she said.

"Fajitas with guacamole and lots of sour cream," said Benjy.

"And steak," Phil added hopefully. Usually they didn't eat too much red meat because his mother worried about growth hormones or something.

"Fajitas coming up. I'll see if I can find a nice thick sirloin at the Ayer meat market," she said almost cheerfully and glided out of the room.

Benjy waited until the door closed and then turned to Phil. "So what do you think?" he asked.

"About what?" said Phil, even though he knew perfectly well about what.

"About Dad firing Mom. Do you think this means they're going to get divorced?" Benjy said this in a perfectly normal way, like you might say, What's the math homework, as if their parents getting divorced wasn't a big deal, was something that happened every day. Phil just didn't get Benjy sometimes, when he acted like he was a computer brain with no feelings.

"Of course not," said Phil. "Mom and Dad really love each other. They never fight."

This wasn't quite true, because Dad had been awfully fed up with her lately, and kept making sarcastic comments about her sleeping late and procrastinating. But then she would just ignore him instead of getting mad and saying something sarcastic back, so technically you could say they never fought. "And they have a lot in common. Crocker Software, for example." Well, this was hardly true anymore. Phil tried to think of something else. "This house." Another lame suggestion. His dad despised their house, with all its leaky windows and buckling floors and thought Crowley was a dump, which it basically was. He'd wanted to buy a modern house with huge windows in a fancy suburb like Lincoln. The only reason they'd moved here was because Mom had a shit fit and insisted.

"Us," he added. Now that was true. Sometimes Phil tried to figure out which one of his parents loved him more and decided it was about equal, although they showed it in really different ways. Dad thought everything Phil and Benjy did was cool and interesting, especially whenever they got a new client or redesigned the BPCC Web page. Mom mostly worried about them, whether they were eating right or doing their homework or taking showers when they needed to, or wearing clothes that weren't too disgusting or were cleaning up their room. And gave them hugs and back rubs, when they would let her. No, his parents were like iron and carbon. Separately, they were rusty and fairly useless, together they were pretty efficient, like the stainless-steel scissors on his Swiss Army knife.

"Mom and Dad will never get divorced," he announced a little too loudly. He remembered saying this once before, when Lila Shea told him in fourth grade her parents were getting divorced. He knew Mr. and Mrs. Shea a little bit, because they lived around the corner on Foxglove and sometimes he and Benjy went over there to watch movies on their wide-screen TV. Phil was so upset when Lila told him that he thought he might actually start to cry, right there in the middle of social studies. But she didn't seem upset at all, said that she was actually kind of glad because her parents hated each other's guts—those were her exact words. And then he had said, "My parents will never get divorced," but that time he had meant it.

Of course, now he never talked to Lila Shea anymore or went over to her house to watch television, not since he had decided that she was by far the prettiest girl in seventh grade (a conclusion that a lot of the other guys seemed to have come to, except Benjy, of course, who still thought girls were gross). Back in fourth grade, he once made her laugh so much that cranberry juice dribbled out her nose, but now when he actually worked up the nerve to say anything to her, she gave him one of those superior "boys are so stupid and immature" looks.

"What difference would it make if they did?" asked Benjy.

"Maybe we should call Dad at work," Phil said, even though he had no idea what he'd say after he got his father on the line. Dad's voice would sound the way it usually did when he was rushing around a million miles an hour at Crocker—impatient, buzzed on too much coffee. He would say, "What's up, Phil?" and then what would Phil say back? "Why did you fire Mom?" or "Mom's acting really strangely and you need to come home."

"You know he hates to be bugged at work," said Benjy, turning back to Return of the Ninjas.

When Phil went downstairs for dinner, he was relieved to see his mother had mostly recovered from whatever she'd been suffering from earlier. She'd taken a shower and changed her clothes for starters, into blue jeans and a tight, long-sleeved red T-shirt, and her hair was wet but combed, hanging like a long rope down her back. She'd also changed her shoes, into these clunky black sandals with shiny square heels that Dad had brought her back from Palo Alto last month. Even though they made a clomping noise when she walked, Phil thought that seemed like a good sign, divorce-wise.

He liked her better in regular clothes than when she tried to dress up. She tended to go for these filmy, long skirts with kind of abstract designs in blues and purples that came with a little shirt in a matching color, and then pulled her hair back with a big barrette and wore long dangly earrings. Phil never found the overall effect that impressive. This was ironic, because her clothes were really expensive. Once he'd looked at one of the tags on these outfits and it cost about three hundred dollars, because it was handpainted and made of silk and an original work of art. Could have fooled him. It basically reminded him of the way lady folk singers dressed on the covers of Dad's old LPs—Joan Baez and Mary of Peter, Paul, and Mary. Actually, he thought his mother should consider dressing a little more like Ingrid, although he couldn't exactly put a name to her style of dress—short and black mostly, in stretchy elastic-type material. He wasn't entirely sure that this would be appropriate for an older, mother-age woman, but he suspected she might look pretty sharp. It wasn't like she was fat or anything.

She had made an effort to set the table nicely, which Phil also thought was a good sign—with a red tablecloth and napkins and matching Mexican pottery bowls for the sour cream and shredded cheese and guacamole, a platter of sliced sirloin with rich pink centers, swimming in a bath of their own red juices. She'd cooked up the steak on that fancy built-in grill, and there was tons of smoke pouring into the kitchen like a steak house, even though the hood above the stove was going full blast. Phil took a deep whiff of the greasy, decadent smell of charred meat and decided his mother quitting (which sounded better than being fired from) the computer biz might not be such a bad idea after all.

This was the first time she'd cooked a decent meal in months. Ever since she had started pushing hard on the big MQII deadline (although in retrospect, it seemed like she'd probably spent more time napping in her studio than drawing), it had been organic frozen entrees from Bread and Circus health food store night after night—lasagna, teriyaki chicken, finnan haddie, enchilada platters. At first, it had seemed kind of exciting, better than real homecooked food, but after a while Phil thought that it all started to taste alike—salty and mushy—even though it didn't make sense that lasagna could taste like fish.

She sat down and elegantly served up their plates for them—a tortilla with a tidy pile of steak and toppings, followed by a dusting of cilantro. This was also a pleasant switch—usually they just helped themselves from the pans on the stove.

"So," she said, pouring herself a Corona into a frosted mug, no less (Corky had once sent them four mugs, which were supposed to live permanently in the freezer, and, as far as Phil knew, this was the first time they had ever been used). "I want to hear everything you boys are doing. I feel like we haven't talked in a long time."

Benjy looked over at Phil as if to say, Is she out to lunch or what? Had she forgotten that she'd talked to them this afternoon? "So what do you want to know?" asked Benjy, warily.

"How's BPCC going? Got any new clients or anything?"

"Well, yes, in fact," said Benjy, pushing down those stupid glasses again. Phil wondered how he could tell him he looked like a dork without hurting his feelings. "We just signed on a group of lawyers in Fitchburg specializing in personal injuries. They've asked us to create a Web page for each of their services—medical malpractice, car accidents, workmen's compensation. So, using Java . . ."

Blah, blah, blah. Benjy could go on for hours about Java or C++ to anyone who was dumb enough to ask. He was always cornering kids in the hall at school and when they started making faces like they were going to start screaming with boredom, he didn't even notice. Although Mom actually looked interested, or at least pretended to be.

"Java allows you to create better Web sites than other programming languages, right?" she said.

That was the mysterious thing about his mother. Just when you thought she was dumber than dumb, hadn't been paying attention at all, out she came with something like this. Next she turned her scrutiny on Phil.

"So, how'd your French final go?"

Madame Miller and French had been completely torturing him all year. He studied and studied lists of irregular verbs and those diagrams in his textbook, like the one of the kitchen with the contents of the cabinets and refrigerator labeled in French, but when there was a quiz he always got something really pathetic, like a seventy-one. And then when he said something in class perfectly correctly, she made him keep repeating it over and over. "Non, non, non. Comme ça, Phil," she'd say, pronouncing his name like *feel*. He was pretty sure he'd messed up on his French final, but couldn't quite bring himself to admit it, at least not in front of Benjy. "Okay, I guess."

"How about you, Benj?"

He gave a thumbs-up. "Aced it."

"Good going, guys. I was always really lousy at French, until I went to live with a French family near Rouen the summer after my junior year," she said. Lousy at French, had lived with a family in France for a summer? How come she'd never told him this before, when he'd been so miserable night after night doing his homework that sometimes he hid in the bathroom and cried. He'd thought he was the only one who was ever stupid at anything. Now that he thought about it, he probably hadn't really told her how much he hated French, just expected her to guess somehow.

"Maybe we should go to France this summer, now that I have time on my hands all of a sudden. Stay in Paris for a week, then rent a car and drive around in chateau country. We could even go on a bike tour." As she said this, her face sprang to life, and Phil could imagine them zooming along windy roads in some tiny French car with a sunroof, stopping at a cafe with red umbrellas to eat escargots in that town on a big hill that got buried by water every day. What a cool vacation, even though he couldn't imagine speaking French to a real

French person. Madame Miller seemed to have a hard enough time understanding him, and she was from New York City.

"Sorry, Mom. But we couldn't possibly take the time off from BPCC. We're swamped with jobs until the end of the summer. It's going to be hard enough for us to get away to the Cape for a few days," Benjy pronounced, as if that was that, end of discussion.

Phil wanted to say, Oh come on, Benj, let's screw BPCC and go to France. Why not actually take a different vacation than two weeks at the Wheeler bungalow colony, year after year. But Benjy was kind of right. They *were* swamped with work, and Benjy made all their clients sign contracts and pay fifty percent in advance, so they could hardly take off for a month. "Maybe we could go for a week in the end of August," said Phil miserably.

"You can't go to Europe for a week. It doesn't work that way." She sounded really ticked off.

"Where's Dad, anyway? I thought he was coming home for dinner," said Benjy, as if the notion of tramping around France for a month in metros and Citroëns and motorbikes meant nothing.

"He called on his car phone and said he was tied up in Cambridge traffic. He should be home any minute," she said, but he didn't drive in until Phil and Benjy had almost finished the dishes. Phil had offered to do the dishes to try and make up for turning down the vacation to France, and it had actually been kind of fun. He and Benjy were probably spoiled; they never helped with the dishes or laundry or other chores, but he would have if his mother had asked. Anyway, she had sat there and had another beer and talked to them, while they covered all the little dishes with Saran Wrap and scraped the plates and put them in the dishwasher. She had put on a CD by a famous black singer named Billie Holiday, who had had a very sad life until she finally died when she was pretty young of drug abuse, and Phil thought you could tell that just by listening to the way she sang.

When his dad came in, Phil was relieved that he seemed all relaxed and happy, too. He wasn't quite sure what he had been expecting—maybe that Dad would still be pissed off at her, or Mom would still be pissed off at him, and that they would have a big fight and yell at each other, not that Phil had ever seen them do that before. Mom warmed up a plate of fajitas for Dad in the microwave and poured out a Corona in another frosted mug. Dad sat down and shook out his red napkin. "Well, this is pleasant. We haven't had a real family dinner in a long time."

"Yeah," said Mom, pouring out her third Corona. "Too bad you were so late."

"Cambridge traffic is getting worse and worse. And I'd be home earlier if we lived closer," he added pointedly. Another one of Dad's complaints about Crowley was that it was so far away from Cambridge. I drive for an hour every day, and then where am I? he'd say. The middle of nowhere. But then, as if he didn't think this was getting off to a very good start for a family dinner, he looked her over, up and down, and said, "You look really nice, Lu. A lot better than you did this afternoon. I like those shoes on you."

She pushed her chair back, so she could poke out one black, platformed foot and give it the once-over. "Yeah, I like them, too, even though they're the kind of thing Ingrid would wear."

"Well, actually, Ingrid picked them out for you when we were at that software convention in Palo Alto."

"Oh, really?" she said, frowning down at her frosted mug. "How thoughtful of her," she added, not sounding particularly grateful.

Benjy and Phil sat down with bowls of Ben & Jerry's Rain Forest Crunch ice cream, their particular favorite at the moment, which she had remembered to pick up at the grocery store. Normally they disappeared up to their room with their dessert, but it seemed like they should stick around because this was supposed to be a family dinner.

Benjy, who was sitting next to his father, sniffed loudly. "What's that disgusting smell?" he asked. He leaned closer toward his father and sniffed again. "You smell like skunk cabbage," he said. Benjy was so out to lunch he didn't know it was bad manners to tell a person, even your father, that he smelled disgusting. Especially when you were having family dinner, and all trying to get along and say polite things. Although now that he mentioned it, Phil noticed that something did smell like skunk cabbage.

"I've had a hard day," said his father, looking embarrassed.

"Oh, yeah, that's right," said Benjy, doing that thing with the glasses again. "You fired Mom, didn't you?" This was Benjy's idea of pleasant dinner table conversation—what a jerk.

His dad's face turned dark; crossing over from the usual bent out of shape to seriously angry. "Is that what you told them, Lucy? That I fired you? That's a nice thing to tell our children." Phil had never heard him refer to him and Benjy before as *our children* and it felt ominous, like when the school principal said *pupils* or *youngsters* instead of *kids* it meant she was going to blow her stack about something. Usually his parents said *the boys,* or *the twins,* or *the guys.*

His mom stared straight back and Phil thought she looked more than just the usual bent out of shape, too. Goddamn Benjy, anyway. "They asked me how the meeting went, and I told them the truth. That I had only done thirteen out of fifty drawings and everyone got fed up with me for holding up Maiden's Quest II, and you fired me. How would you describe what happened?"

His dad turned away from her, toward Benjy and Phil, and he furrowed his eyebrows, as if he were putting a lot of careful thought into what he was saying, like Judge Judy. "What your mother says is basically correct. There was a big meeting today, and some of the staff were disappointed that more progress hadn't been made on MQII. It was decided that it was too much responsibility for a single person to do all the drawings and game design. So from now on, a team of Crocker Software staff will develop MQII and your mother's going to be a consultant, which means that she'll give advice when anyone needs it."

He was talking to them like they were five-year-olds or complete idiots or something. Here he was explaining the word *consultant* when the name of their company was Benjy/Phil Computer Consultations—duh! And he was also using the passive voice, which was something that Phil's language arts teacher, Mrs. Chadwick, had explained was completely bad English, because you could tell what was done, but you couldn't tell who had done it. Her example was "the ice-cream cone was eaten," which did sound pretty ridiculous. So his mom had been made a consultant, but Phil couldn't tell which person, or even if any person, had done it. His dad made it sound like she had done it to herself.

"So you mean that the staff is going to use all of Mom's drawings and ideas, and then just turn it into a game," said Benjy.

"Ah, well, sort of," said Dad, lowering his eyes from their faces and back to his mostly empty plate of fajitas. He speared a lone piece of steak with his fork, pushed it through a glob of guacamole and sour cream, and chewed on it thoughtfully for a while. "They'll probably want to make a few changes. The graphics might look a little more modern than MQI."

Mom, who had been looking bored through most of Dad's explanation, suddenly seemed to be paying attention. "More modern, huh? That was quick. I wonder whose idea that was," she said, staring down at her shoes again.

Dad shrugged, as if this whole conversation was starting to get boring, which it basically was.

"Mom can't be much of a consultant anyway, because she

says she's going to go work at the Crowley Library," Benjy observed, like she wasn't even in the room.

For some reason, this made Dad grin over at Mom, as if this was the best news he'd heard in a long time. "Really? That's a great idea, Lucy." Now, this didn't make any sense at all, because Dad usually said that being a librarian was stupid because libraries were going to be replaced by the Internet in ten years and besides, she could make about a hundred times more money designing computer games.

"Glad you approve, Ed," said Mom in a really unfriendly way. The other thing that was strange about this conversation was the fact that they were using each other's first names, as if they had just met.

Mom cleared away Dad's plate and frosted mug (which wasn't frosted anymore, only drippy on the outside), and he stood up and stretched, tipping his head back so his ponytail swung around. Phil was kind of embarrassed by his dad's ponytail. They were the only ones at school whose father had a ponytail, although everyone seemed to think it was perfectly normal because he ran a software company, and lots of CEOs of software companies had ponytails. But personally Phil thought that his dad's looked dumb, maybe because it was so thick that it looked like a girl's, and that he should just cut it off and have a normal haircut. "Well, guess I better go take a shower," Dad said, and left the room before Benjy could make any more comments about how bad he smelled.

Benjy followed along, too, because it was getting pretty late—9:15—and they usually were in their room by now, even if they didn't go to bed for another hour. But Phil thought he better hang around for a while and make sure that his mother was okay or that nothing else bad happened. Not that anything bad had happened so far, but Phil was still feeling unsettled, even though dinner had ended on a cheerful note. He sat at the table, stirring the melted soup at the bottom of his ice-cream bowl, watching how the little chunks of toffee and nuts floated around like icebergs, or polar bears. "You going up to bed soon?" he asked.

"I'm going to do the dishes," she said, although as far as he could tell, the dishes were all done except for putting his father's plate in the dishwasher. She turned off the overhead light so the kitchen was dim, like a fancy restaurant, put the Billie Holiday CD on, and then started spraying the fronts of the white wood cabinets with a bottle of cleaner and wiping them really hard with a rag. This was the kind of work she usually saved for their cleaning lady, Karen. As she wiped, she started singing along with the CD to "Stormy Monday" in a low, mournful way that sounded more like Billie Holiday than Phil would have thought possible.

CHAPTER 5

>>

For three days, with the brackish taste of humiliation still in her mouth, Lucy played the meeting over and over again in her mind, like an anxiety dream. Herself tiny and meek as a third grader who had forgotten her homework, waiting in terror to be exposed and publicly shamed. Ingrid—who oddly enough resembled Lucy's third-grade teacher, pretty Miss Swenson, gone punk—lunging down the table toward her, the blonde hair gelled into ice picks, the purple spaghetti straps falling off the muscle-bound shoulders. Ingrid's lovely face—or at least would be lovely if she didn't wear all that ghoulish eye makeup and pale lipstick—twisted into a sneer, as she said, "So when *will* you have the rest of the drawings ready?" The other Crocker kids, as Lucy tended to think of them, contemptuous as they checked out her thirteen measly sketches.

Then there was the worst part of the dream; then there was Ed. Slumped down as if he had no more authority than a junior programmer, looking about as old as one, too, with his unlined face and lithe boy's body; the only evidence of his thirty-eight years were a few strands of gray creeping into his blond ponytail. It was his eyes that Lucy felt so betrayed by, those moony eyes that had once stared at her with ardor as she stood in the doorway of her Cambridgeport apartment, dressed only in a stretched-out turtleneck and underpants with tears streaming down her face. At the meeting, those same eyes had been averted while Lucy was toyed with and then slowly torn to pieces by Ingrid, like a toddler in the jaws of a rottweiler.

But each wave of indignation against Ed was quickly followed by one of remorse. He had every right to be disgusted with her. For months she'd lied to him about the drawings, she'd forgotten about the meeting even though she'd been reminded at least half a dozen times. Then she'd tried to bluff her way through like some slacker teenager who hadn't studied for the midterm, as if they might not catch on that there were thirty drawings missing.

I've failed him, she thought—as a business partner, as a wife, as mother to our children. Back in the old days on Spruce Street, she'd agonized over his every setback with Crocker Software—the computer that shorted out and melted three months of work, the investor who had sneered at Fighter Pilot Alert. Now she ignored Ed as he thrashed around in their bed at night, tormented with worry over how Crocker would meet the next payroll, the next ship date. She never laid on a comforting hand or said, "What can I do to help?" The boys were turning feral—microwaving their own frozen gourmet entrees most nights, dressing in any tattered, outgrown garment they found in their drawers.

And what was Lucy doing, as she ignored every duty and responsibility? Wandering, dozing, procrastinating. Still mourning over the last miscarriage almost a year ago, the cause of this one as mysterious as the others. I'm useless, she muttered over and over to herself. Plain useless.

By the time Ed was packing to leave for the P.C. gamer's convention, Lucy was ready to forgive him and be forgiven. She sat cross-legged on their four-poster bed and watched him haul out the hip wardrobe he used for his public appearances—a bomber jacket of creamy mocha suede, pants of cocoa linen, custom-made Egyptian cotton shirts in russet tones. Ed looked quite dashing when he was dressed in one of these cuddly, earth tone getups, and she always had an impulse to stroke him, like her old brown hamster, Misty.

He was humming to himself as he packed his fancy pair of leather shoes (each in its own yellow flannel pouch) and then a stack of press kits with the Maiden's Quest logo (Arabella with her leonine hair flowing) embossed on the cover.

"You seem pretty chipper," said Lucy.

He stopped and studied her. "You do, too. I'm glad you don't seem so mad at me anymore." He cautiously rested a hand on her knee, then ran an index finger down her bare calf, along the top of her foot. They hadn't touched each other for days, had slept spine to spine, with two feet of cold sheet between them.

"I'm glad you're not so mad at me." She shivered slightly under his smooth touch. When they first met, his fingertips had thick calluses from the violin. Now his violin sat under this very bed, collecting dust.

She was relieved that Ed wasn't going off completely empty-handed; the Crocker kids had managed to put together some kind of press kit for the convention complete with a demo CD Rom. She reached across the bed, flipped open one of the glossy folders, and pulled out a cover letter. "Meet 'A,' a super heroine for the digital age," she read and then paused to scrutinize an 8 by 10-inch glossy of a platinum blonde, shorn creature with missile-shaped breasts and bionic muscles, clad in molten silver and ass-kicker black boots. An ammo belt was slung around her snake hips, a gun dangling phallically. "Kind of a departure, isn't it?" Lucy said mildly. She waited to feel slighted, but instead was oddly elated. Now Maiden's Quest II was truly somebody else's job, the somebody who dreamed up super-heroine "A."

"Sure is," said Ed, plopping down next to her with a long sigh, and giving "A" a bemused once over. "According to Russell Mott's latest marketing survey, gamers want biceps and bullets. Princesses are passé, but the old Arabella still turns me on. Guess I'm getting passé myself." He leaned over and nuzzled his slightly bristly cheek against her bare upper arm, then slid his arms around her waist and leaned until they both toppled over backward on the bed, right on top of a pile of his freshly laundered shirts.

"I like passé guys," she said, hooking her thumbs through his belt loops and nuzzling him back, behind one ear. He smelled like sandalwood soap from the Body Shop, which he bought by the dozen in small wooden crates lashed together with hemp. Years ago when they first made love on the swaybacked Castro convertible in his overheated Cambridgeport apartment, he had smelled like peppermint castile soap—his whole body, even his hair. She'd been relieved he'd smelled sweet; she'd feared the worst—the majority of MIT students she'd encountered seemed to reek of overheated coffee, cigarettes, and too many all-nighters in the same clothes. Later she learned that Ed always smelled soapy and fresh—even those few times he'd exercised enough to work up a sweat. Everything about him was smooth to the touch, as well—his well-laundered T-shirts, his silky hair, the lanolin-soft skin of his back and neck.

As he slipped off her tank top and slid one of those uncalloused hands down along her spine to the top of her shorts, she considered briefly if one of the boys would barge in. Most certainly not, she decided, even though it was only 10:30 on the first night of summer vacation and they were still awake. She could picture them at that moment, propped against either arm of the big overstuffed couch in the "library" with a bag of nacho chips resting between their entangled bare feet, bathed in the moonglow of their brand-new projection television with surround sound (an impulse buy of Ed's). They had reached a stage where their parents' room was off-limits—probably out of the terror of witnessing the kind of repulsive scene that was currently unfolding. Lucy leaned her head back, closed her eyes, and pressed Ed's head gently against her chest, imagining for a moment that it was as mountainous and taut as "A's."

> > >

The next morning, Rosemary called to announce she was taking Lucy out to lunch at Buddy's rib house, their favorite eatery back in library school days. "I always take my friends out to lunch when they get divorced or fired."

"Who told you I was fired?"

"Well, first Benjy told me, 'Dad just fired Mom' when I called last Thursday, so I sort of called up Ed at work to get the story, his side of the story, of course."

"Yeah? So what's his side?"

"He was very diplomatic. He said that coming up with the creative concept for the sequel was too multitasked—I think that was the term he used—for one person, so that you had decided to serve as consultant. In other words, he fired your lazy ass. What's your side of the story?" Rosemary had a way of stating the truth that was hard to deny.

"That, I guess. But I think you're really just looking for an excuse to eat ribs." Rosemary, who had formerly been called zaftig, had in recent years tippytoed over the line to letting-herself-go. Her husband, Alfred, had taken to inflicting strange diets on the family, the latest consisting of miso soup and barley shakes.

"That, too."

Over pulled pork sandwiches and dirty rice, Rosemary interrogated Lucy about her career plans. "So, now what?"

"Well, I've been checking out the job listings in the ALA newsletter. They need a part-time children's librarian in Lancaster specializing in after-school programs. I figure Maiden's Quest is kind of an after-school program, so I can bill myself as an expert."

Rosemary lowered her yam fritter so she could wrinkle her nose with disdain. "Take it from one who knows. We're talking glorified janitor and baby-sitter. The most exciting part of my job is putting cellophane covers on books. Pays great, too—like minimum wage. Any other bright ideas?"

Lucy was getting the distinct impression that Rosemary

had already figured out what her next job move should be, but they had to go through this charade first. "How about starting an antique store in the barn and then we could sell off all the junk we've bought."

"A store in Crowley specializing in tin lunch boxes and salt and pepper shakers? Now we're talking subminimum wage."

"Maybe I won't get a job. The boys are growing up so fast. Phil has a pimple on his nose, and their feet are huge, like extraterrestrial growths. All of a sudden they smell bad—their shirts, their socks. Whew!"

"If I remember correctly, when you get pimples and smell bad, you don't want to spend a lot of time hanging around with your mom," Rosemary said, reaching over with a slightly jiggly arm to spear some of Lucy's red pepper slaw. She had taken to wearing nonconstricting clothing—baggy jumpers and Chinese canvas slippers. If Lucy had Rosemary-style bluntness, she would confiscate her utensils and deliver a lecture about the dangers of overeating. But fortunately, Rosemary seemed to think honesty was a one-way proposition.

"Okay, I give up," Lucy said, handing the remains of her lunch across the table. "Any suggestions?"

"Look, Lucy. You are talented—really talented. If I could design some neat fantasy game and make a few million bucks, do you think I'd be sitting on my big butt behind the children's desk at the Newton Library?"

"But I just got fired, remember?"

"Okay. So do something that uses your talent for fantasy stories and illustrations, like a children's book. You could do a whole series, by the best-selling author of Maiden's Quest." Rosemary's plump index finger airwrote the jacket blurb in front of Lucy's nose.

Best-selling author, that had a nice ring. "I'll think about it."

"The point is, Lucy, you've got to figure out something to

do with yourself. All this sleeping late, moping around stuff has got to stop. You're driving us crazy—me, Ed, your kids. Why are you so miserable, anyway?"

Miserable—not a word she would have used to describe herself. Distracted, at loose ends, maybe blue, but not anything so melodramatic as miserable. But if Rosemary, the truth-teller in her life, said she was miserable then she must be. "I don't know," she said with a shrug. "I look at my life and I don't like what I see."

"From where I'm sitting, your life looks pretty good."

"I guess after four miscarriages I'm finally accepting that I'm not going to have any more kids, and that makes me really sad. And I keep wondering how I ended up where I am. Me, designing computer games when I basically disapprove of technology—how did that happen? We moved to Crowley so the kids could be outside building forts all day, and now Benjy and Phil refuse to step out of their pitch black bedroom. I always thought I'd end up married to a river rafter in Montana, you know?"

Rosemary stopped her feasting and studied Lucy with a furrowed brow of concern. "Not being the type of person who wants to be married to a river rafter, no, I don't know. As I recall, you had a chance to live happily ever after with your forest ranger, but you said no."

Which was true, sort of. Her old boyfriend, Sam the forest ranger, had tagged along after her to Boston, but after three months of being cooped up in her tiny apartment, he said I'm leaving. You can choose—come with me now, or good-bye. She had hesitated for a heartbeat because she had already paid her first year tuition at Simmons, plunked down first and last month's rent. Because she liked Boston—the bookstores, the subway, the funky restaurants—everything that he had hated. And also, in truth, because she was starting to have her doubts about Sam. But a heartbeat was too long, and the next thing she knew his lumberjack boots had clomped down the stairs for the last time. "Maybe I should have said yes."

"Oh, please. You think you would have been happier with what's-his-name than Ed? Honestly, Lucy, Alfred and I agree that you don't appreciate what a cream puff you're married to."

Rosemary favored food imagery. Whenever she really wanted to bulldoze one of her opinions home, she brought Alfred in as a second opinion, although in this case he probably did agree. At the Wheeler bungalows, he and Ed tagged around together like a couple of eight-year-olds. Ed's lanky sunburned body in Hawaiian jams, Alfred's bulldog hirsute one in a Speedo—body surfing, playing horseshoes, scarfing down clam rolls. "So how am I unappreciative of Ed?" Lucy said, feeling like she was being ganged up on.

"Ed adores you. He's thinks you're gorgeous." Her tone implied who-knows-why. "He thinks you're brilliant. No one else but Ed would have believed you could have come up with a best-selling computer game—certainly not me. He dotes on the boys. He humored you when you wanted to buy that wreck in Crowley."

Lucy held up her hand to signal enough. "Okay, I married the perfect man." But not as perfect as you think, she thought meanly. Didn't he tell her not to "dwell on the loss" when she had her last miscarriage? And wasn't his first love Crocker Software—he spent more time there than at home, after all.

"But even Ed is reaching the end of his rope. So snap out of it, okay? Because I don't want to take you out for a divorce lunch."

Rosemary was right, Lucy decided as she stepped into her studio the next morning. Snap out of it, take charge of your life. Today was the first day in her new career as celebrated children's book author. She surveyed the studio—the messy worktable with globs of dried paint and watercolor paper warping in the sunlight, the dusty desk covered with unanswered mail—and considered how shabby it would look in the background of a publicity photo. Not like the photogenic studios of those crusty children's authors with a spinning wheel, bunches of dried herbs hanging from the ceiling, and a hedgehog in a wicker cage.

Time for a makeover. She scrubbed at the worktable with steel wool, then arranged her paint tubes in rainbow order. She dumped Larry's letter and the Camp Kinahwee brochure out of her mail basket and filled it with paintbrushes. The walls needed a face-lift, too, she decided. She ripped down the glossy Maiden's Quest posters and stuffed them into the trash along with the mail, then searched the attic for a replacement. An Amish quilt—too *Country Living*. Photographs of the kids—too maternal. The JFK velvet painting from Ed's MIT dorm room—too self-consciously kitsch.

Finally she found the perfect choice—a stuffed, varnished rainbow trout mounted on a mahogany board with a small brass plaque: CAUGHT BY CYRUS LAMB ON HIS FIFTEENTH BIRTHDAY, AUGUST 28, 1936. 9 LBS., 7 OZ. LITTLE LOST LAKE, WISCONSIN. Her mother had sent it to her along with her father's collection of children's books after he died of lung cancer, horribly, fifteen years ago. The hostility behind this "gift" was unmistakable: *Here's all that peculiar stuff your father was so crazy about. You're the only one who would want it. Certainly Larry doesn't; he's got taste. Good riddance!*

Her father had told her, or at least as best he could with his stutter, the story of the giant rainbow during those endless hours they had spent fly casting from a rowboat along the shores of Little Lost Lake. In 1936, Cyrus's father had a "nervous breakdown"—as a result of either his stock market loses or his fondness for the lunchtime martini, depending on who you listened to—and had been packed off to the Hartford Institute of the Living for an indefinite period to sit in Turkish steam baths and be sent into insulin-induced comas. His socialite wife professed to be too distraught to take care of her two sons—Cyrus, home from his freshman year at Hotchkiss, and Bart, home from his freshman year at Yale. She gave them a hundred dollars and their father's Buick touring car and instructed them to go to the family's fishing cabin in northern Wisconsin for the entire summer and "have a gay time." The boys, who had never made a bed or boiled a pot of water before, and really didn't even know much about fishing because their father had been too drunk to teach them, did as they were told. For a week, they ate stale crackers from a tin in the larder and tried unsuccessfully to catch fish. Then it occurred to them to drive to the logging town of Pembine, fifteen miles away, and buy food from a store. At Dunbar's general store, they stocked up on canned beans, beef jerky, coffee, rice, Lucky Strikes (which started her father on his two-pack-a-day smoking habit), and a jar of hard candies—their one indulgence. Bart mastered the art of crude camp cooking, Cyrus taught himself how to fish, and they did indeed have quite a gay time—lounging around the dock all day dressed in nothing but their skivvies, reading a four volume set of *Lives of North American Explorers* (the only books in the place), playing an ongoing game of pinochle that they tallied in pencil on the wall.

At the end of August—his birthday, the last day before heading back—Cyrus hooked the trout on his final cast, bending the rod double. He fought it for almost an hour, terrified that his ten-pound leader wouldn't hold up and landed it in his raincoat, having forgotten his net. It was gigantic, at least twice the size of any other trout he had caught that summer, primordial-looking with thickened corneas and tattered fins. At Bart's insistence, on their way through Pembine toward home, they dropped it off at a taxidermist. But the punch line came later when he proudly presented it to his parents at Christmas (his father was home from Hartford, still a drunk), as a badge of everything he had accomplished on his solo summer. His parents had torn away the wrapping paper, there had been a pause, and then his mother tilted back her pretty head with its blonde marcelled waves and let out one of her musical, socialite laughs. Lucy could hear her father's voice as he repeated her comment: "Now, wh-wh-what am I supposed to do with th-th-this." She had hung it in the maid's room. When he was married, his wife had hung it in his smoky study along with his collection of children's books.

Lucy gently bathed the fish's flaking gills and hide with a washcloth and hung it over her worktable. She cast her eyes around for something to draw it with and spotted a large tin of Caran d'Ache colored pencils in the corner of the bookcase. The pencils had been Ed's first present to her the day after they had become lovers, bought at an expensive art store in Harvard Square. They had been floating down the sidewalk in that we've-just-done-it-for-the-first-time afterglow, arms twined around each other's waist, and she'd stopped to admire the tin enameled with a reproduction of Monet's waterlilies in the window. "I've always wanted a set like that." He'd been offended that she'd never used them and she'd tried to explain—*they're too beautiful to use*—although she frequently opened the case just for the pleasure of bumping her fingers across the tidy line of sharpened points, from white to black.

Lucy pulled the tin out and snapped open the lid. Sixteen years and at least five moves later, the points were still intact—amazing. She stared up at the trout for a few moments and then picked up two pencils with the colors stamped on the side in silver—burnt umber, raw sienna. She had been saving them for this moment, she decided, this new beginning. To draw her father's trout with Ed's pencils—a convergence of two precious gifts.

She sketched the fish poised in midair above a sparkling stream and a clump of cattails, with a hook in the corner of its mouth, yanking it up. Then she filled in the pattern of speckles along its side; not in the faded colors on this sixty-year-old fish, but the way she remembered trout from her own fishing expeditions, glinting in the sunlight as they flopped around in the bottom of the rowboat. Colors so vivid they looked as if they had been made with dots of enamel paint—red, white, black, green across a golden background. After two hours, she stopped and studied her sketch, her spirits sinking. Her trout looked insipid and limp, like the ones emblazoned on plastic placemats and coffee mugs in the Orvis catalog.

She was still pondering her dismal drawing and wondering what it implied about her future career as a children's book author, when Benjy knocked on her office door to let her know that they were back from their meeting with the Fitchburg personal injury lawyers.

"Is there going to be anything for supper tonight?" he asked. It had gotten so bad that the kids didn't even expect her to feed them anymore.

"I was thinking Swedish meatballs," she said. His absolutely favorite dish—see, I'm snapping out of it. He stayed put in the doorway, bouncing on the tips of his sneakers, until Lucy put down her drawing. "For heaven's sake, Benjy, come on in." It wasn't surprising that Ed and the boys regarded her studio warily, she supposed—hadn't she growled at them, and flipped every drawing over, as if their natural curiosity to see what she was doing were shameful?

Benjy stepped into the center of the room by her worktable and slowly pivoted, giving everything a judgmental once-over. "You really cleaned this place up," he said at last.

"I thought I'd make space for a new project. I was thinking . . . " she paused, feeling oddly embarrassed. "I was thinking of maybe writing a children's book." She cast a sideways glance at his face, half expecting to see a suppressed smirk, but Benjy only adjusted his glasses thoughtfully, as if this seemed like a perfectly normal turn of events.

He leaned over and studied her drawing. "That's pretty cool. It looks like the cover of the L.L. Bean catalog." Then he jabbed a thumb toward the trout. "Where'd you get that thing?"

"Granddaddy caught it when he was about your age." Even though Cyrus had died before Ed and Lucy got married, Lucy had told the boys stories about their grandfather and his cabin on Little Lost Lake.

"What kind of fish is it anyway?"

"Well, a trout, of course." How could he not recognize a trout? Then again, why would he? He had never been fishing, even though she had tried a few times to tempt the boys to try their luck in Crowley Pond with a can of night crawlers. But what if we catch something? Benjy complained, gagging himself with a finger. Like, eat it?

"I don't know why he stuck it on that board. It doesn't look very big."

"It's huge, for a lake trout. Your grandfather was very proud of that fish," she said, trying not to sound irritated as Benjy wandered out of the room without listening.

Ed called a few minutes later. "So, I've been in gamer land all day, talking my butt off about MUDs and cheat codes and BOTs to a bunch of boys with acne," he said airily. Ed was always at his best manning the Crocker Software booth at these conventions, carrying on in a nonstop gush about the wonders of their latest product—the visual feast of the graphics, the sublimity of the Crocker game experience.

"So, how do they like the wondrous Miss 'A'?" said Lucy, her spirits lifting—Ed in his manic mode always cheered her up. She could picture him with his cell phone, pacing up and down in the president's suite of the Trump Plaza. He would have kicked off his Armani shoes by this time and stripped down to an unbuttoned shirt and boxers. Mylar bags of Terra Chips and boxes of Godiva chocolates, raided from the hotel minibar and now empty, would be strewn across every surface.

"I think they were mostly impressed by her big tits."

"Why do boys always find large breasts so impressive?" she asked. Lucy had always considered this a cosmically profound question.

"Dunno, but they sure do. Maybe that should be part of our long-term planning for the twenty-first century. Crocker will implement a higher percentage of female characters with enlarged mammary glands. What have you been up to today?"

She described Cyrus's trout and her possible career as a children's author.

"You know you could write a dynamite book, Lucy." His voice was gentle but persistent, the way it had been four years ago when he nagged her into climbing out from under her bed quilt and trying her hand at a computer game. You can do it, he had said over and over, I *know* you can do it, until she came to believe it herself. Rosemary was right, she didn't appreciate Ed enough. How could she have imagined for a single second that she would have been happier with Sam McCarty? Oh, Ed, I hope I haven't pushed you to the end of your rope.

"Think so?" she said, grinning at the receiver.

"One more thing. Can you check my e-mail and see if there's anything from Russell Mott? He was supposed to get me a draft of our pitch to the Atlantic Group by today, and the modem seems to have blown out on my laptop. Just check E_Crocker@Crocker.com. My password's *Questor.* It's really not that hard," he said in the soothing way that parents use to speak to panicky toddlers.

"Uh, I'll try. Let me put you on hold," Lucy said bravely. She sat down at her new gleaming black P.C., which the Crocker people had installed a few months ago (it had been used only a few times and was covered with a thick film of dust), and consulted the Post-it note she'd stuck on the screen with the rudimentary operating instructions: *Turn on machine (silver button, left hand side), click on WWW globe, type in www.Crocker.com, type in user name and password , click on mailbox, click on read new mail.* She gingerly pushed the silver button and was gratified to see the screen spring to life with icons of filing cabinets and trash baskets. She clicked, typed, clicked and, as usual, was somewhat startled by the cheerful male voice that announced "You've got mail!" Her new mail file usually consisted of two or three items—particularly interesting pieces of fan mail forwarded along by Marla—but Ed's was quite a different story. Lucy scrolled through at least fifty new mail entries—memos from the art director, sales director, gobbledy gook from a researcher at Berkeley, request for an interview from *Salon* magazine—but nothing from Russell Mott scheming to wrangle huge sums of money.

She pressed hold. "I'm not seeing anything."

"Hmm," he said. "Maybe it's under *Atlantic Group*."

"I'll check," she said. She clicked on something marked *MaidQuestII—Urgent!*

To: Ed
From: Ingrid
Re: P.C. Gamer Convention—Trump Plaza
6/23/1998–6/28/1998
I have confirmed our reservation in the presidential suite. Guess what? Found huckleberry massage oil at Bread & Circus. According to the tantric messenger, the lingam is soothed by the juice of the berry. Yum, yum.
I.

Lucy leaned back in her chair, blinked hard, reread the memo, and then let out a low, involuntary moan. "Oh . . . no . . . "

"Lucy? What's the matter? What's going on?" said Ed, along with a muffled clatter in the background as if he'd knocked over a jar of smoked almonds in alarm.

Sound normal, just sound normal, she told herself. "Listen, Ed, I've got to go now. Something's come up with, you know, the boys . . . " she trailed off.

"Oh, all right. I'll call Marla about the e-mail. Talk to you tomorrow," he said.

"If I'm still here," she said, hanging up with a slam.

She lowered her head onto her forearms, the blood throbbing a tattoo in her ears. Maybe you are just jumping to hasty conclusions here, she told herself. Maybe this was part of the interoffice banter—full of sexual innuendo and insults—that everyone at Crocker found so amusing, except her. Ed always accused her of being somewhat thick when it came to jokes and maybe that was true. She raised her head and tried to analyze the memo in a laid-back, Gen X way. The part about *our* reservation in *the* presidential suite sounded bad, she decided—two people, one suite (even if it was a large one). What wife on earth wouldn't object to her husband sharing a hotel suite with a female coworker, especially one with enlarged mammary glands? Now that she thought about it, Ed had brought up the subject of large breasts, hadn't he—as if he were obsessed all of a sudden. Maybe Ingrid with her bionic body and shorn blonde hair was the model for "A"; Ed had re-created Princess Arabella in his publicist's image. Lucy let out another involuntary moan.

But then there was the rest of the memo, which Lucy didn't even understand. Huckleberry massage oil sounded sticky and messy, not erotic. And what in hell was a "lingam." She pulled out her *Oxford Concise,* but the entries jumped from *ling* (an elongated marine fish food) to *lingcod* (a large-mouthed game fish). Then her eyes settled on the "search by word" box on her Internet screen; the hard drive bleeped and whined as millions of files in the World Wide Web were searched for any mention of a "lingam." Suddenly, her screen dissolved into pools of blurry red and peach, then gradually crystallized into a jungle orange Web page of one "Master Ragit" who was a teacher of "tantra." She clicked on the "more information" square and was informed that tantra was "a 5,000-year-old lifestyle philosophy that includes breathing meditation, massage, and practices for making sex sacred." Lucy scrolled reluctantly on toward further knowledge and clicked on a pull-down menu of "tantric terminology."

The tantric way uses special words for sexual organs which honor them. In Western culture, we use derogatory slang—cock, prick, pussy. In tantra, we call the penis a "lingam," which is Sanskrit for "wand of light." The vagina is a "yoni," which is Sanskrit for "sacred space."

She jabbed her finger at the off button until the screen blinked closed, straightened her spine in the gray leather pads of the molded desk chair (a thoughtful gift from Ed when she started having lower back problems last year), raised her eyes above the black rim of the monitor, and stared hard at the Beatrix Potter wall calendar above her desk. The June image was of Jemima Puddle Duck confiding her troubles about finding a safe place to lay her eggs to the sympathetic fox. The caption read, "Jemima Puddle Duck Was a Simpleton."

That is me. I am nothing but a simpleton, Lucy reflected bitterly. For the last few days she'd been lulled into tranquility about Ed and their marriage. Her old Ed was back again, making it home on time to have dinner with her and the boys, complimenting her clothes even if they were picked out by Ingrid, cheering her along in all her little ambitions. Never mind that for the last year their major topic of conversation had been the MQII delays, that he'd fumed, and she'd retaliated with the silent treatment. That he told her not to "dwell" on her miscarriages.

I probably shouldn't be so shocked he's having an affair, she thought wearily. But she was, just the way every woman was when confronted with the hard evidence of flirtatious notes and hotel reservations.

And Ingrid, of all people! Such an obvious choice. The boss' faithful yes-man (yes-woman?) who just so happened to be sexy . . . and single . . . and smart . . . and contemptuous of the boss' wife. Couldn't Ed have come up with someone a little more soulful than Ingrid, with her bottle of huckleberry massage oil and her Sanskrit nickname for his penis?

"Fuck you, Ed," Lucy shouted, hammering her fist down on the keyboard with all her strength. "Take that, and that, and that." The keys clacked in a mournful way, but no matter how hard she pounded, the plastic keys refused to pop off. When the edge of her hand started to sting, she shoved back in the desk chair and rocketed across the floor until it crashed into the edge of her worktable. She jumped up, looking for something else to destroy. She grabbed the tin of pencils, considered breaking each one and stomping the tin flat, but then, even in her rage, couldn't quite bring herself to do it. Why should she wreck her pencils on account of Ed?

She snatched up the trout sketch and tore it up methodically, piece by piece, until it was nothing but a mound of confetti. How could she have thought she could write a children's book? That was pathetic. Everything about this room was pathetic—the basket of brushes and the arty arrangement of paint tubes, the mohair afghan tossed over the overstuffed arm of the chintz sofa. They should have torn the sun porch off the house after all. Maybe if they had bought that deck house in Lincoln like Ed wanted to, this never would have happened. "Oh, shit," she whispered fiercely, staring down at the orange daylily blossoms peeking over the top of the stone wall. "Shit, shit, shit."

She slammed the French door so hard that two panes cracked and strode resolutely toward the stairs. A brisk five-mile walk might clear her head. Maybe as she galloped past the peeling Unitarian church, the lichen-covered mausoleums in the cemetery, the former poorhouse converted into elderly housing, the images of tangled bedsheets and glistening flesh would be pounded away one by one.

As she passed the boys' closed door, she heard a sound that made her stop. Phil's voice, and then the two boys laughing. Not loudly. Gentle laughter, over some small joke. She remembered the first time she had heard them laughing together, when they were only about six months old. She had been driving along Mass. Ave. in Cambridge and the boys were in the back, seated side by side in their car seats. Suddenly she had heard an explosion of tiny, hiccuping giggles, first one, then the other, back and forth. She had pulled over into a parking space and turned around to witness this enchanting sight, but the moment they saw her face peering down at them, they both turned grave and silent. "What's so funny, you two?" she had coaxed, but they had only stared back impassively. So different, even then—Benjy bald and squinting, Phil with a shock of spiky black hair and long-lashed blue eyes. Oh, her sweet baby boys, how she loved them. They would help her survive Ed's betrayal.

She quietly opened the door, hoping she could catch them midlaugh and capture a bit of their mirth before it vaporized at the sight of her. The boys had their backs to her, were inspecting something on their computer monitor. "Look at that one," said Phil, with a soft giggle that made her want to weep. She crept up slowly behind them, until she could see over their shoulders. There, splayed across the screen, was the blurry image of a kneeling woman, her back arched like a purring tabby getting her back scratched, a mane of permed peroxide tossed back, completely naked except for a black leather thong, huge, implanted breasts protruding from her chest like a pair of half-gallon Tupperware containers. Her mouth was hanging open and poking toward it from the left side of the screen was a long lumpy object, like an oddly shaped kitchen utensil. It took Lucy several seconds to recognize that it was an erect penis.

"What . . . are . . . you . . . *doing?*" She hadn't really meant to scream; the sound just burst out of her like a primitive cry, as if she were confronting Ed and Ingrid. The boys jumped, wheeled around in a whirl of gangly limbs, let out a collective gasp, and then Benjy's hand darted behind his back and flicked the off button. He plunked down in the desk chair and peered at the blank screen, as if there were some urgent message he needed to read, but Phil stayed standing in front of her, his spine slumped over with shame.

"Who . . . *is* . . . that . . . person?" *Person* came out like a wet growl. Phil lifted his head enough to cast her a sideways look, flinching with every word as if he expected it to be punctuated by a slap.

Benjy glanced up at her, too, but he seemed only mildly chastened. "How should we know? It's just some picture we found on the Internet."

Of course, Lucy had heard about the horrors of pornography over the Internet; in fact, over the years various journalists and psychologists had sought out her opinion about how to protect children. "I do not think that exposure to pornography is a significant problem," she had said smugly, "because most children, even teenagers, never use the Net unsupervised."

"Did you pay money to see those pictures?" she asked. She had no idea how pornography was purveyed on the Internet. Was it pay-per-view, or did people subscribe by the month, like *Penthouse* magazine?

"We *never* pay for anything," Benjy said dismissively. "We know how to get all the cool stuff on the Internet for free." Phil let out a small groan and kneed Benjy in the back, who jerked his head up in a puzzled way, as if it only dimly occurred to him that this might not be the best point to make with his mother.

"Oh, yeah?" said Lucy, her voice subsiding to mere sarcasm. "Who taught you how? Your father?" This suddenly seemed like an actual possibility—Ed sitting with a boy on either side, guiding their hands with his over the keyboard to type www.pussy.com. The way her father had guided her hand to hitch a dry fly onto a nylon leader.

"Dad? Of course not," said Phil in a shocked tone. "You're not going to tell Dad about this, are you?" He sounded shaky, as if he were about to burst into tears.

Lucy stepped back, wished for a fleeting moment that she could turn around, close the door behind her, go for awalk, and pretend that she had seen nothing. She didn't have the strength to deal with the boys' moral lapses along with Ed's. "I don't know what I'm going to do. I have to think about it," she said in the disappointed tone that always reduced the boys, or at least Phil, to pleading for forgiveness. "I want you to go outside, now."

"Outside? It's time for dinner," Benjy whined. "What are we supposed to do outside?"

"Come on," said Phil, grabbing onto the back on Benjy's shirt and yanking him up. "Just do what she says."

She stood with arms folded across her chest like a sentry, glowering as they clomped down the stairs and slammed out the screen door. Now she was trapped inside because if she left, the boys would simply sneak in and go back to their evil ways. She shuffled back to her studio, leaned her forehead against a windowpane, and spied down on them in the backyard. Phil retrieved an old Frisbee from underneath a peony bush and they made a few desultory tosses back and forth, until Benjy missed and it rolled back underneath the peony again. Next, the boys wandered over to the barn and Phil wheeled out his bike, which hadn't been ridden in at least two years. He squatted down and squeezed the flat front tire, while Benjy fetched an old rusty bicycle pump. They made several attempts to pump up the tire, but the nozzle flew off with every stroke and finally they gave up, leaving both bicycle and pump where they dropped on the lawn. Finally, they lay down on the grass and talked. Every minute or two, one of them would prop himself up on an elbow and squint toward the house to see if she was poking her head out a window, ready to issue a reprieve.

Lucy brushed aside the shreds of drawing paper, sank down in her desk chair, and started swiveling. Now what? she wondered. Sure, she could banish the boys outside for another hour or two, but eventually she would relent. Maybe they wouldn't surf smut on the Internet anymore, but they still would be spending every waking moment in cyberspace, cooking up new ways to expand the BPCC empire. Nothing would change.

Ed would be back from his fun-filled convention in two days and then what was she going to do? She pictured greeting him at the door, tight-lipped and grim as he dropped his suitcase, thinking that someone had died. She would usher him wordlessly up to their bedroom, close the door, hand him a printout of Ingrid's e-mail (if she could figure out how to make a printout) and say, "Could you please explain this?" She considered his possible responses and they all seemed equally depressing. He could say, I am in love with Ingrid, she is my soul mate, I want a divorce. Or he could say, I am such a fool, Ingrid means nothing, you and the boys are all that matters, let's go into couples counseling. Then she would have to sit in some tiny, stale-smelling office in a Fitchburg medical building, while a small, balding man asked her earnestly, "How did it make you feel, Lucy, when you learned that Ed was beingsmeared with massage oil by his publicity director? Can you express your anger to Ed?"

She grabbed the phone and dialed Rosemary's number. Guess what? she would say through her tears, Ed got to the end of his rope. Yes, she needed some of Rosemary's truth telling and bossy suggestions right now. The machine picked up and subjected Lucy yet again to the endless cutesy message by Rosemary's four year old, Gabe. "You have weached the Hoffman-Van Petewson wesidence . . . " "It's me. Just wanted to thank you for lunch," Lucy whispered.

She hung up and spun around toward her father's trout. Why couldn't her life be that simple? If she could only send the boys into the wilderness for two months, away from computers and television and all the other corrupting influences of modern life, they would discover their own inner resources, just as the fifteen-year-old Cyrus had. And what about herself? If she could escape for a few weeks to Little Lost Lake, free from Ed and the Ingrid problem, free from Crocker, free from the boys, maybe she could figure out what she was going to do with the rest of her life.

Her mental whirrings ground to a halt. Wait a second. For the first time in fifteen years she was thinking of going back to Little Lost Lake? Well, there was some twisted logic in there somewhere. A return to the cabin meant a return to her father, who had disapproved of Ed in his own muted way. And the lake also meant memories of Sam McCarty, which she once had considered an act of disloyalty to Ed. But there's no reason to be loyal to old Mr. Lingam anymore, right?

She scooted the chair over to the wastebasket and rooted around under the crumpled-up posters until she resurrected Larry's note and the Camp Kinahwee brochure. It was only 5:15 in Chicago, so she might still catch him at his office. He answered on the first ring, which she took as a promising omen.

"Hi, it's Lucy. I was thinking of going to the cabin for a . . . little vacation, and I was wondering if you could make the arrangements to have it opened up."

There was a pause. "You. Go back to the cabin," Larry repeated. "This place you, like, refused to step foot in for the past fifteen years. That had, as you said, nothing but bad karma. Now you want to have a little vacation there? May I ask why?"

She hadn't expected the third degree. "Well . . . as you always say, I just can't keep running away from my fears." Larry loved shrink talk—he'd been in therapy since he was twelve and had started having gender identity problems, as they now called it. "I think it's time to confront the past, you know? Mom and Dad's weird relationship. Mom being such a control freak, Dad just checking out by going to his fishing cabin. The way we were sucked in as kids, forced to take sides."

"I thought you didn't want to go to the lake because you were afraid of running into your hunk ex-boyfriend." Larry had a sixth sense for divining people's most shameful secrets.

"Sam? Oh, please."

"You and Ed have had a big fight, right? And you're running away."

"Look, I just need a place to get away for a few weeks to finish a project. No more questions, okay?"

"I'm not sure the workmen have completed all the renovations. The place might be a mess." There was a defensive edge to his voice.

"I don't care if there's a couple of paint buckets lying around."

"You can't use a computer, you know. There's no electricity."

Why did everyone, even Larry, assume she was such a techno-ignoramous that she didn't know that computers required electricity? "Yes, I remember, okay?" She started to hang up.

"Ah, Lucy?"

"What?"

"Is everything okay? You sound a little flipped out."

Suddenly, she realized how comforting it would be to confide in someone—even Larry. First, I find this incriminating e-mail about Ed, she would admit, then I catch my kids ogling blow jobs on the Internet. But the grip of pride held her back; she didn't think she could stomach Larry's pity. And then later, he and his partner, Jorge, would have a good laugh about Lucy's travails and who could blame them? It was funny, or at least would be if it were happening to someone else.

"I'm just a little stressed at work and need a break."

"But the cabin isn't a good place to be if you're under stress." Larry's voice sounded almost hysterical. "I think you should reconsider. Please don't go, Lucy." Maybe he really was worried about her, she thought, smiling grimly at the notion that someone might care about her welfare. Maybe after she finally landed at Little Lost Lake, he could drive up for the weekend and she could pour out her woes over gin and tonics on the porch.

"Larry, I'll be fine. Really," she said gently. She could still hear him protesting as she pressed the disconnect button.

Next she dialed Camp Kinahwee. Apparently, modern telecommunications hadn't reached the wilds of northern Wisconsin yet, and the call went through with a series of dim clicks that sounded as if an ancient telephone operator in Green Bay was plugging it through a switchboard. The one phone at Camp Kinahwee had been in the camp "office," a musty brown shed piled high with tubes of fly paper, cases of corroded batteries, yellowing topographical maps, and spools of gimp that were sold by the yard. No one actually worked there, but if the phone rang long enough, some counselor passing by on his way to the dock might pick up. On the twenty-third ring, a gravelly voice barked, between pants, "Keep your shirt on! What do you want?"

"Uncle Bo?" said Lucy, incredulously. Uncle Bo had been the director back when Lucy was a camper in the early seventies. Even then, he had been ancient and legendary—with blue eyes as frigid as polar ice caps, leathery oxen shoulders that could effortlessly hoist and portage a four-man canoe, and a bullhorn voice that bellowed orders to screw-off canoers two miles across the lake. The commands always had a similar theme—shag ass, get your rears in gear, bust your butts, hustle your bustle, fan your fannies.

"Who's this?" he said suspiciously.

"It's Lucy Lamb. I'm sure you don't remember me."

"Oh, Lucy. Of course I remember you," he said, his voice softening. She had been one of his favorites—always willing to carry the heaviest backpack, share a canoe with the most inept paddler, dig the latrine pit, sing the camp anthem, "Kinahwee, You Will Be My Guiding Light Forever." The one who never complained about the rain, mosquitoes, or the Spam. She had won the Bo Thorne Most Outstanding Female Camper Award two years in a row.

"I know this is really last minute, but I was wondering if there was any space for my two sons this summer. They're thirteen."

"We're pretty full up, Lucy. Let me check the ledger." Uncle Bo kept the camp records in oversize leather accounting ledgers. Shelves of them lined one wall of the office, dating back to 1918 when Bo's father started the camp. Any infraction—failing cabin inspection, improper use of a jackknife, not dousing a campfire—was marked in a special column in the ledger, which Uncle Bo implied was as indelible as a police blotter.

"The only spaces I've got are in the six-week senior canoe trip. That's the one that goes up to Hudson's Bay. Your boys pretty experienced paddlers?"

"Ah, well, not really."

"If they're anything like their mother, I'm sure they'll pick it up pretty quick."

Lucy considered this statement. It was true that Benjy and Phil were fast learners; they had figured out how to program in C++ and how to defrag a hard drive in a matter of seconds. They didn't have any athletic skills, but then again, they had never tried to learn any. They were healthy and able-bodied. Why couldn't they become adequate canoers if they put their minds to it? It wasn't as if there was much to it—the j-stroke, the sweep, a couple of hitching knots. Lucy could teach them in an hour on Crowley Pond. Granted, they couldn't swim, but as far as she could remember, she'd never gone in the water at Camp Kinahwee without a life preserver. No one would ever know about this slight failing. "Well, if you think they can handle it, Uncle Bo, I'll sign them up."

"Okey dokey." She heard some pencil scratchings. "The trip leaves in three days."

"We'll be there," Lucy chirped in a can-do, most-outstanding-camper voice.

LEVEL II

The Never-ending Forest

CHAPTER 6

>>

By 6:30, the sun had sunk down behind the line of maples in front of the house, casting a long dark shadow over Phil and Benjy like a monster's claw. Benjy started to shiver and massaged his goose-bumped arms. "She's going to let us freeze to death. I've got two bucks in my wallet. We could get some chips at Smith's." Usually they rejected the local grungy package store, reeking of cigarette smoke. He stood up and waited for Phil to follow. "You coming?"

Phil kept his eyes fixed on the back door. "We better wait here. She's already mad enough." He refused to rub his arms or even reposition himself in the last pool of dim sunshine. When his stomach let out a great churning growl, he felt glad, as if all would be forgiven if he could prove to his mother that he had suffered enough. It was all Benjy's fault anyway. He was always visiting these forbidden Web sites, the ones where you had to swear about ten times that you were over eighteen. Then he downloaded all the most gross-out pictures and made Phil look at them. The ironic thing was that Benjy had absolutely no interest in naked girls or sex stuff; he was just trying to show off what an Internet genius he was.

And now they were going to get in major league trouble, although Phil had spent the last two hours wondering what that might be. His mother could confiscate their computers and make them close BPCC, which Phil didn't think would be the worst catastrophe in the world, even though he wouldn't admit that to Benjy. Maybe she would decide that they were completely psycho, like Zack Rosenthal's parents did after he emptied a gas can all over the floor of their garage and set it on fire. After that, Zack had to visit a lady psychologist over in Groton once a week and go on Ritalin. Phil's body started to feel feverish when he thought of being asked personal questions by someone he didn't even know. Why did you look at those pictures? How did that naked lady with her mouth on that man's dick make you feel? Don't you know what you did was against the law? That you could get arrested and have your name put in the *Crowley Crier* police report, Phil?

Couldn't he just say he was sorry, really really sorry, and that would be the end of it?

Phil stretched himself out flat against the damp, prickly grass and stared up at the Creamsicle orange clouds scudding across the dim outline of a crescent moon. Maybe this would be the view from the inside of a coffin. Maybe if he lay here long enough he might actually starve or freeze to death and then everyone would be sorry. Phil smiled as he imagined spying down on his own funeral like Tom Sawyer, at the pews of bowed, grief-stricken faces. It's all my fault. I should never have downloaded dirty pictures, Benjy would sob. No, no, it's all my fault. I should never have yelled at him, his mom would cry. No, it's my fault. I should never gone to a P.C. gamer convention, his dad would chime in.

Phil heard the warped back door whang open and his mother's voice call out. "Okay, boys. Let's get in the car." He propped himself up on his elbows and glanced toward her. She was holding a Crocker Software tote bag and the car keys in one hand and a folder of papers in the other. She walked down the steps and circled around to the side of the house where the car was parked in front of the old carriage barn.

"Where are we going?" Benjy snarled as she disappeared from view. Phil wished he would at least *try* to sound sorry. Maybe she was planning to take them out to dinner somewhere fun, like the Shanghai Moon in the Leominster Mall where he could order his favorite—sweet and sour pork. The thought of golden brown nuggets of pork swimming in a pretty pink puddle made his stomach yelp again.

"Get in the car and I'll tell you," she yelled back as a car door slammed. It didn't sound like she was planning any surprise dinner treat. Phil stood up, his knees cracking, and ambled stiffly toward the car with Benjy a few foot-dragging steps behind. He was about to climb in the front seat, but when he saw her profile grimly staring out the windshield at the row of garbage cans by the side of the barn, he decided it would be safer to sit in back. Benjy scooted in next to him.

Without turning around, she said, "You guys must be hungry. I made you some sandwiches." She reached into a tote, pulled out two squares wrapped in tinfoil, and handed them back one by one. She started the car, revved the engine with a big gulp of gas, but then twisted around so she could peer back at them around the headrest of her seat. "I've been giving some more thought to your summer plans and we need to have a discussion."

Benjy opened his sandwich, took one scornful glance at the cheddar and sprouts perched on dense slabs of homemade whole wheat, wrapped it back up, and dropped it into the backseat pocket. "What do you want to know, Mother," said Benjy. Phil had never heard him call her *Mother* before and it sounded really hostile. In fact, the only people he knew who talked like that were certain know-it-all tenth-grade girls, who said *mother* the way you would say *stupid idiot*.

"All the time you're spending with computers is unhealthy. I've decided you need to broaden your horizons this summer." She sounded oddly calm, which made Phil uneasy that she had dreamed up an awful punishment.

"Mom, we're really sorry, okay? We'll never do it again," he said, trying to ignore Benjy's disgusted expression. Okay, so I'm a wimp, he thought. It was better strategy than being a wiseass.

"I know you're sorry and I know you won't abuse the Internet again." She reached back and awkwardly gave his knee a couple of pats. "I'm not mad, I just want to be a responsible parent and do what's best for you. So . . ." She retracted her hand, frowned, and raised her eyes above their heads to stare out the rear window. "So, you're going to Camp Kinahwee. I just talked to the director, Bo Thorne, and you're all signed up for the senior canoe trip." She slowly lowered her gaze and studied them cautiously like a doctor searching for telltale symptoms.

They were being shipped off to Camp Kinahwee. On something called the senior canoe trip. Phil repeated these facts a couple of times to himself, trying to figure out his own reaction. Sure, she'd been yammering about old Camp Kinahwee for months now, but he never in a million years thought she'd actually force them to go. He tried to imagine what a senior canoe trip could possibly be like, and the only three words he could conjure up were *wet, cold,* and *gray.*

He tried to think of a bright side. Practically anything sounded more fun than spending his summer with a bunch of Fitchburg personal injury lawyers, even canoeing. At least senior canoe trip sounded better than junior canoe trip, which probably had third and fourth graders. Phil shot Benjy a tentative, sideways look.

Benjy lowered his chin and pursed his lips, an expression he usually reserved for the most dimwitted clients and bug-infested software. "You signed us up for that dorky camp without our permission?" He kicked the back of her seat, hard.

"Yeah," she fired back. "You're thirteen years old. I'm your mother. I don't need your permission to make decisions on your behalf."

Their voices along with the rumble of the engine trapped inside the car were making Phil's head throb. He rolled down the window and hung his head out. Shut up, he muttered to himself, looking down the driveway at the peaceful Crowley green with its Civil War soldier. Shut up, both of you.

Suddenly, her expression softened and she smiled, as if

she'd decided that the encouraging mom routine might work better. "Look, guys, let's not fight. I think you'll like this camp, I really do. Just try it for two weeks. If you don't like it, you can come home. Okay?"

"Okay," said Phil in a whisper. Anything to stop this yelling. Besides, two weeks really didn't sound that bad.

"Well, it's not okay with me. What did *Dad* say?" Benjy sounded like a lawyer springing a surprise witness. Their dad liked to make fun of Camp Kinahwee. On the shores of Kitcheegoomee, he would say, was the camp called Camp Kimono.

"Dad?" she said, as if she found this question surprising. "Oh, right. I called him while you boys were outside. He agrees *totally.*"

Benjy let out a skeptical snort, violently shifting his legs so another foot went straight into the back of her seat.

"I'm sorry this makes you so unhappy, Benj."

"What about our clients? We have contracts, you know. We can't just take off," he said.

"I'll call your clients. They know perfectly well that they can't make binding contracts with minors. I'll tell them you'll be back by the end of August or maybe sooner. So, what's it going to be? Are you willing to try this for *just* two weeks?"

He turned his face away from both of them, toward the side window, and made a noise that sounded like *nff.*

"What?" she said.

Benjy sat up, his glasses hanging cockeyed and his face pulled into an unpleasant sneer. "I said, you win."

"I don't think of it as winning."

"Well, I do. But I still want to talk to Dad."

"He's out tonight at some P.C. gamer symposium. But you can leave him a note before we leave tomorrow."

"Tomorrow?" Now, Phil was the outraged one. Benjy seemed too dazed to say anything.

"Ah, yeah." She sounded defensive. "The senior canoe trip leaves in three days, and it will take us at least forty-eight hours to drive there. I was *going* to tell you." She picked up the folder of papers off the dashboard and started flipping through lists and instructions printed on institutional green paper. "Wow, you guys need a lot of supplies. I think we can make it to Camper's Warehouse before it closes."

An hour later, they were standing in front of an AstroTurf carpet covered with a regiment of nylon pup tents. She squatted down in front of a Day-Glo orange model called "Basic Two-Man Backcountry Dome" and inspected a vinyl-clad information label. " 'Easy two-minute assembly. Reinforced guy-lines. Fly resists rain, snow, and gale winds.' Sounds good." She unzipped the bug-proof mesh door and gestured them in. "Okay, climb in and try her out." Next she was lashing them into waterproof backpacks the size of steamer trunks and zipping them into mummy bags. She even tossed in a backpack and mummy bag for herself. "Who knows? After a summer at Kinahwee, maybe we'll go on a family camping trip. Yellowstone . . . Glacier . . . Mount Rainier. . . . " Her voice trailed off as she hung a right toward footwear.

At first Phil found the Swiss Army knives with sixteen blades and the foil pouches of dehydrated Salisbury steak intriguing, until he contemplated the purpose of all these engineering feats in titanium and Gore-Tex. To make objects as lightweight and compact as possible. So a thirteen-year-old kid could be forced to carry all his food, clothing, and shelter on his back for six whole weeks up to the Arctic Circle. Without once passing a store to buy a Coke, or a Nestlé's Crunch bar, or a bag of Doritos, or a Nutty Buddy, or a Slim Jim. He wasn't a junk food addict, but now the notion of being deprived made his tongue weep with yearning for salt and corn syrup.

After they had been fitted with something called "Whitewater Raftsman Sandals," which Velcroed to the bottoms of their feet like black rubber tire treads, Benjy disappeared. As Phil helped his mother pick out the final items—head lanterns, extrastrength fly dope, and mess kits—he wondered if Benjy had actually run away. He'd looked furious enough in the car driving over; slumped down in his seat with his arms pressed against his body like two planks, swearing under his breath, shitfuckshitfuckshitfuck, but so softly their mother couldn't hear him. In the store when she started piling the cart up with tents and mummy bags, Phil caught another expression on Benjy's face, which he found more unnerving than rage. Benjy looked scared. The person who never got upset about anything—pre-algebra, French vocabulary tests, asshole clients—was scared. Because here at Camper's Warehouse, he was an incompetent. Even if he had a backpack full of the latest camping gear strapped to his back, he would still starve, get lost, get hypothermia, or get mauled by a bear.

Just when Phil was really starting to worry, he spotted Benjy waiting for them at the checkout counter. He smiled pleasantly at their mother and held up a yellow Camper's Warehouse bag. "I bought something with my own money. Is that okay?"

She started unloading shoe boxes and stuff sacks onto the conveyer belt. "Sure. Why not?" The cashier hit the total button, and when the astronomical sum of $1,268.92 lit up in red numbers, his mom snapped down her platinum card without missing a beat.

Figures, Phil thought bitterly. What could Benjy possibly buy at Camper's Warehouse that she *wouldn't* approve of—no dirty pictures or violent Nintendo games here. Over their mother's bent head, Benjy winked at him.

At 7:00 the next morning, she was at them again—snapping up the shades, shaking their shoulders. "Come on, sleepy heads. Rise and shine. We've got lots to do if we're going to get out of here by noon." Through a veil of tangled bangs, Phil groggily gazed out at a towering heap of orange nylon and shrink-wrap packaging. Oh, crap. He had been sweetly dreaming about wandering through an endless mall, had forgotten all about this plot to send him . . . somewhere. Shit, he didn't even know what state he was going to. Or was it Canada? He turned his face to the wall and pulled the comforter over his head.

She managed to tempt them out of bed with the promise of a gourmet breakfast. "Sourdough French toast and bacon," she called up the stairs. As Phil sliced off his first bite of French toast, he noticed her tossing the rest of the loaf and an empty bacon wrapper into the trash. This breakfast had nothing to do with their eating pleasure; she was simply finishing up the leftovers before they took off. She wouldn't let them have five pieces of bacon apiece for any other reason.

"Mom. After a good night's sleep, I've decided this camp idea sucks. I'm not going," said Benjy, his mouth stuffed.

She slowly straightened and folded her arms across her chest, as if she'd been anticipating some renegotiation. "Two weeks. That's all I'm asking. Then you can spend the rest of your life rotting your brain in front of a computer screen. Okay?"

Benjy speared a chunk of French toast on his fork, smeared it around in a pool of maple syrup, and then aimed it toward her. "Bang, bang," he said calmly.

When they were little kids, they used to point their fingers and shoot at people all the time, but now Phil flinched. He didn't poke Benjy the way he usually did to get him to cut something out. Instead, he patted him gently, the way you might calm a skittish horse. "Come on, Benj. We can handle it for two weeks."

After breakfast, she handed them each a permanent black marker and a copy of the Camp Kinahwee packing list. "I don't have time to sew in name tags. So write *Crocker* on everything. Socks, T-shirts, shoes, toothbrushes. *Neatly.*"

It took them three hours to accomplish that task and then

stuff the labeled piles into their backpacks. Their mom seemed to be busy with her own packing chores. Every time Phil looked up, he saw her dragging various loads past his door—a suitcase, a stack of books, a carton of art supplies.

"You need all that stuff just to drive us to camp?" he called out as she scuttled past with the down quilt off the guest bed.

She paused in the doorway and leaned her head against the jamb. Her face was flushed and sweaty, pieces of hair were breaking loose from a messy ponytail. "I'm going to be staying at Little Lost Lake while you boys are at camp."

Even though Phil had been hearing about his grandfather's cabin at Little Lost Lake for his whole life, he had a hard time picturing what this place was really like. The few snapshots he'd seen weren't that interesting—just a semicircle of pines mirrored in black water, a crooked old cabin hidden behind a clump of birch trees. It's the most beautiful, peaceful spot on earth, she used to say. Then his father, who basically hated the outdoors, had chimed in, Don't believe her, boys. The cabin probably smells like mildew and bat shit. The lake is filled with brown slime. The mosquitoes could suck a baby dry in five minutes.

"Is Dad going, too?" Phil asked doubtfully.

"Nope. Just me. I want to see what Uncle Larry's doing to the place, and I might get going on my children's book, too. You know Little Lost Lake is the most beautiful, peaceful spot on earth."

Phil might have said, Yeah, you already told me, but there was something about her mood that made him proceed carefully. You would think she would be thrilled about sending them off to camp and herself to the most beautiful spot on earth, but instead she seemed grim, like she had just discovered a big piece of her back molar was missing. "It sounds really nice," he said. "Maybe Benj and I can come after camp is over. I'd really like to see your dad's cabin."

"You would? That's so-o . . . sweet." She sighed, then

grabbed him around the neck and hugged so hard that his nose got jammed into her damp shoulder. "That means so-o much to me," she whispered wetly in his ear.

"Sure," he said, then wriggled free and went back to his packing. That was the problem with saying thoughtful things to adults. They tended to go completely overboard, which made you sorry that you had ever said anything in the first place.

By one o'clock, he and Benj were wedging the final duffel into the back of the station wagon on top of the box of art supplies. She reached in the backseat and plucked out two large black nylon pouches—one with Phil's Discman and the other with Benjy's Game Gear.

"No electronics, guys. We're going back to nature."

As Benjy let out a groan, Phil grabbed both shoulder straps and sprinted up the stone path toward the back door. "I'll put these inside," he offered. In truth, he wanted to have a final look around. The kitchen counters and floor were scrubbed shiny, the dishwasher was humming. He peeked inside the refrigerator and found the glass shelves almost empty and sparkling. Usually things only looked this good on Wednesday afternoons right after the cleaning lady, Karen, had left. Phil wondered if his dad would come home to this oddly neat kitchen in two days and start worrying. He found a scrap of paper and a ballpoint by the telephone.

Dear Dad,

Sorry I didn't talk to you before we left. I'm sorry about the Internet thing. Camp doesn't sound to bad. Mom bought me a really cool tent and sleeping bag. It is orange. And also some cool river rafter sandles which are black with velcro straps.

Benjy is pised but I think he will feel better later.

See you in 6 weeks, or sooner if we hate it. I will write you.

Please write me. Hope everything is going well at Crocker.

Have a good summer.

Love,
Phil

Phil inspected the note and didn't think it looked too hot. For starters, he hardly ever handwrote anything anymore and his cursive was loopy and uneven, like a fourth grader's. Also, he wasn't a very good speller, and without spell check he was sure there were some mistakes he couldn't spot.

"Phil," she yelled. "Shake a leg!"

"Coming." He dropped the note with a sigh on the kitchen table, then gave the back door an extrahard slam so the old lock would catch.

Benjy and the tent occupied the backseat, so Phil slid in front. She started the engine, then craned her neck out the window as she backed down the driveway. The rear of the Taurus was piled to the ceiling, so high that Benjy would get avalanched on if she had to jam on the brakes. As they headed around the Crowley Common, she handed Phil the road atlas. "I thought you guys could take turns navigating."

"Oh, fun. Then maybe we can win our compass badge at camp," said Benjy's voice from the backseat.

"Shut up," said Phil. He opened the atlas to the first page with the interstates snaking across the entire United States. "Where are we going, anyway?"

She dropped her forefinger on a point at the juncture between Minnesota and Wisconsin. "Right there, on the Saint Croix River. And then . . . " she traced her finger to the right. "There's Little Lost Lake. Three hours to the east. So I won't be far away."

Phil flipped back to the Wisconsin-in-detail map and studied the northern half speckled with tiny blue dots for bodies of water—*Kinahwee Falls, Iron River, Clam Creek*. Little Lost Lake was apparently so small it didn't even get identified on the Wisconsin road map. For the next two to six weeks, depending, he would be traversing from blue dot to blue dot. How many would he canoe across—two, a dozen, fifty?

"Remember *Little House in the Big Woods*? Well, it was set right near your camp," she said gaily as she pulled out onto Route 2 West.

"Neat-o," said Benjy. "Maybe we'll run into Pa with his fiddle."

When they were in kindergarten, she had started reading the Little House series to them. Around the fourth book after Mary goes blind, Benjy had decided for some reason that the Little House books were just for girls and made her stop. After that, she'd stuck to the *Lord of the Rings* and *The Black Cauldron*. Now all those books blurred together, but Phil could still remember the bobcat that watched Laura skate by moonlight and her Christmas presents, which consisted of a tin cup and a peppermint stick.

"So, Phil. Check the map. Should we go the northern way through Buffalo, or the southern way through Cleveland."

He traced I-90 through Niagara Falls and into Canada. "Definitely north."

"What am I supposed to do without my Game Gear," Benjy complained from the backseat.

"Look out the window. Enjoy the scenery."

"What scenery?"

He had a point. The view from the Framingham exit was a cluster of radio towers and the aluminum glint of FIFTEEN ACRES OF SELF-STORAGE.

"Okay, I admit it's lame," she said. "It'll get better in upstate New York."

"In six hours. Great."

"Benjy, I've had it with the sarcasm." She turned around to glare at him, but he was scrunched behind her seat and all she could see was the tent with the headwall of luggage behind. "You can listen to the radio. You can sleep. We can even have a conversation. I went on dozens of car trips with my dad when I was your age and I never got bored."

"Okay, Mom, I'll think of some way to amuse myself."

Phil turned the radio to WRKX, the progressive rock station from Worcester that was already starting to get a little fuzzy. According to the atlas, their route crossed a nub of Canada and then dipped down under Lake Michigan. He heard plastic rustling and paper unfolding from the backseat, and he leaned around to see what Benjy was up to.

He was scrunched next to the door with his legs pulled up, so his mother could not possibly see what he was doing even if she adjusted the rearview. He had the Camper's Warehouse bag across his lap and seemed to be reading an instruction booklet. When he saw Phil's face, he held up a small black gadget covered with buttons, then put a finger up to his mouth and silently made a *shush* sign. It was a global positioning system, which told you your exact latitude and longitude anywhere on the planet Earth. For the last two years, Benjy and Phil had been scrutinizing them in the Brookstone catalog. Benjy had even suggested buying one and writing it off as a BPCC business expense. But why would we need to know our latitude and longitude, Phil had asked. We never go anywhere.

So that's what Benjy had been doing when he went scurrying off at Camper's Warehouse. He had used their BPCC American Express card to buy a two-hundred-dollar toy for himself. Phil scowled at him and turned back in his seat. He didn't care if Benjy was feeling all freaked out about being sent off to camp; that still didn't give him the right to make a major purchase for BPCC without consulting him. Maybe when they came back from this stupid camp, they should just dissolve their business. Just because they were twins didn't mean they had to do everything together. Benjy would probably be happier wheeling and dealing all by himself. The GPS made a soft electronic bleep and Phil turned up the radio so his mother wouldn't hear.

He turned back to the map, wondering what Benjy thought he was going to accomplish with a GPS. Let's say they did get lost in the middle of all those blue specks with no town around for a hundred miles, what good would it be to know your longitude and latitude, anyway, unless you had a topographical map? Probably only the counselors got to carry maps, but then again, if they were with the counselors, they wouldn't be lost.

When they were in fourth grade, their class had to read a book about a twelve-year-old kid who gets lost in the Canadian wilderness with only a hatchet. By the end of the book, the kid has figured out how to make a fire, build a shelter, spear animals and fish—all with his little hatchet. Phil had really liked the book until Benjy had read his book report to the class. The first sentence had said, "This book is completely unrealistic and the author should be sued for making kids think they could survive with some cheap hatchet." Then Benjy rattled off statistics about the amount of calories needed to maintain body heat and how the kid would have died of hypothermia in four days.

Phil found an alternative rock station out of Albany, tilted his seat back, and noticed that the scenery had improved since Framingham. There were now green hilly fields, one after the other, with a few grain silos and clumps of cows. He rolled down his window a crack and took a deep sniff of the cool, sweet air. He glanced back to see if Benjy was noticing the scenery, too, but he was curled up in the guest room quilt fast asleep, his mouth hanging open.

When the sun finally dipped below the western horizon and his mother was able to take off her sunglasses, Phil noticed she looked happier than when she was packing up in Crowley. It wasn't only that she had stopped squinting; it was the way her jaw didn't seemed so tense as she hummed along in her off-tune way to Radiohead. "We can have a conversation if you want," he said.

"Oh," she said startled, like she had forgotten he was there. "What do you want to talk about? Camp?"

He did not want to talk about camp. He had been feeling better in the last two hours because he had stopped thinking about where they were going and concentrated on just the going part instead. "Not especially."

"What then?"

"Let's talk about you."

She laughed slightly and then her smile disappeared. "Me? That's boring. What do you want to know?"

"Let me think . . . okay, tell me how you met Dad."

She looked over at him again, sharply, suspiciously. "That's not very interesting."

"I'm just making conversation, like you told me to," he said.

"Sorry, Phil." Her eyes flicked back to the road, but her hand reached over, stroked his cheek, and then tucked a piece of hair behind his ear. "Well, you know how we met. His apartment was across from mine back when we were both graduate students living in Cambridge."

"That's all I know. What did he look like? Did you fall in love right away?"

She chewed this question over for a few seconds. "Ah, no. Not exactly. I didn't really notice him at first. All I remember is this kid with messy blond hair and a huge fatigue jacket running down the stairs like he was really late for something important. He looked like he was about fourteen years old and he always had a violin under his arm, so I figured he was a child prodigy who was late for rehearsal with the BSO. Of course, it turned out that he was a graduate student at MIT, not a professional musician, but he was late to a rehearsal with the MIT orchestra, so I was right about that part. I did notice that he always seemed to be staring at me, so I guess he had a crush on me right from the beginning. Anyway, one day he knocked on my door because . . . he wanted to introduce himself, I guess. Then he brought me some takeout Chinese food, and played me violin serenades. So that's how I met your dad."

That was it? Granted his dad was pretty awesome on his violin, not that he played it much anymore, but that hardly seemed like a reason to fall in love with a person. Surely there must be some juicy part she left out. "But what made you, you know, want to marry him, have us with him?"

She shot him another puzzled look. It was almost completely dark outside except for a bright pink band outlining the edges of the hills. He wished Benjy were awake to see the sunset.

"I don't know, Phil," she said in a soft, sad way. "I wish I could say there was some moment when the sky lit up with a flash of lightning and I decided that this was the man I wanted to spend the rest of my life with, but there wasn't. We had fun seeing Marx Brothers movies at the Brattle Theatre in Cambridge, we had fun eating roast rabbit in the North End, I loved listening to him practice the violin. He made me laugh. I think those are okay reasons to get married, actually."

"They are?" He thought of a framed photograph on his mom's bureau of his parents hiking in the White Mountains a long time ago, before Phil had been born. Her hair was in pigtails, he had a red bandanna around his head, they were both grinning at a camera propped up on a rock with the timer set. These days his father still looked young and carefree, but his mother didn't, even though technically she hadn't changed that much. She still had long dark hair and skinny legs. Maybe it was because she hardly ever seemed to be having fun anymore.

"Were you ever in love with somebody before Dad?"

"Well, yeah. I was. A long time ago."

Phil perked up, thinking she was about to confess some big secret. "What was his name?"

"His name was Sam McCarty, and his family owned a fishing camp on a pond next to Little Lost Lake. Actually, it was an old Rock Island caboose someone had converted into a camp, but no one had used it for years and years. Then one summer, the summer after I'd graduated from college, I paddled over and discovered, much to my surprise, that this guy had moved into the caboose. He worked as a ranger in the Nicolet National Forest. Anyway, it was love at first sight, for both of us."

Phil shifted uneasily in his seat. He couldn't help thinking that the story about this Sam guy was a lot more romantic and interesting than the one about how she'd met his dad. And she had this little half smile on her face when she talked about this Sam like she was still in love with him, or something. "So then what happened?" he asked, even though he wasn't sure he wanted to hear the rest.

She had to mull that one over for a while. "I was in graduate school in Boston and he wanted to be a forest ranger somewhere, so we went our separate ways."

"But you just said it was love at first sight. I don't get it."

"These things just happen, Phil. You break up with someone you thought you were in love with. You marry someone else you thought you'd never be in love with. Love is unpredictable. Trust me, one day you'll find out for yourself."

Phil wanted to say that he already knew how unpredictable love was. Lila Shea hadn't dumped him, but that was only because she didn't like him enough to go out with him in the first place. Not that anyone really went out on actual dates in seventh grade. They just hung around together after school or at the mall and called it going out.

"So what happened to him?"

"I don't know. I met your dad, your grandfather died, we stopped going to the lake, so I never saw him again. He probably got fat and bald and sells real estate in Chicago. Good riddance. Your grandmother didn't approve of him, anyway."

"Why?"

"She said he was a hick, a ne'er-do-well because he was a

forest ranger." Her voice sounded ticked off, the way it usually did when she was talking to Grammy on the phone.

Phil's grandmother was full of negative opinions about most people. She hated people who chewed gum or wore sneakers when they weren't playing tennis, men who didn't wear shirts, women with nasal voices or painted toenails, boys with rattails or mushroom haircuts. She said all those things were tacky. As far as Phil could tell, she didn't like him or Benjy even though they wore shirts and didn't chew gum. And Dad was pretty much out of the question because of the ponytail, which she said was "icky." But Phil decided he didn't like the sound of this Sam McCarty, either, so maybe his grandmother was right, at least this time.

They reached Niagara Falls a little past midnight and his mom pulled the car onto a scenic lookout perched right above the falls. They tried to shake Benjy awake, but he refused to budge, so she and Phil climbed out by themselves. Phil had heard of Niagara Falls, of course, but he had never imagined anything so huge, or loud. He gripped the slippery wet railing and hung out as far as he dared. Buzzing colored lights made the sky almost as bright as day, the plumes of spray and mist refracting like a thousand stars. He tried to make out the far edge of the falls, but it seemed to wind back and forth without end. When his T-shirt got soaked through and he started to shiver, she wrapped her fleece jacket around his shoulders and rubbed them hard.

"Amazing, isn't it?" she yelled.

He nodded, his teeth chattering. He wished he'd been one of the explorers seeing Niagara for the first time, before it had been wrecked by parking lots and space needles and colored spotlights. A man wandering in the wilderness must have heard the thundering roar of the falls fifty miles away. They had studied the explorers in sixth grade, but Phil couldn't remember which white man had stumbled across Niagara Falls—Henry Hudson, maybe? "Did people really go over in barrels?" he shouted.

They both leaned out to inspect the murky green surf whirlpooling at the bottom around jagged black boulders. "Not more than once," she said, grabbing a hold of the back of his fleece and hauling him back to safety.

A day and a half later, they were winding their way up County Road D toward Kinahwee Falls. Benjy had taken over the front seat after Detroit when he complained that he was getting carsick. At least Phil could play with the GPS in the back, but it wasn't as much fun as he had hoped. Ever since they had turned off I-90 in Eau Claire, a feeling of dread had lodged in the pit of his stomach and grew as the latitude climbed upward from forty-five degrees to forty-six. Phil was sweating so much his shirt was getting smelly, and he hoped he'd get a chance to change it before they got there.

At least Benjy's mood had improved since Niagara, and if he was worried about six weeks of canoe survival camp, he wasn't showing it. At the turnpike rest stop outside of Battle Creek, she had bought them each a giant crossword puzzle book. "That's how I got hooked, on car trips," she explained. Benjy quizzed her about becoming the Under-12 Crossword Puzzle champ, and when he heard that it included a five-thousand-dollar scholarship and a trip to Disneyland, his competitive juices got fired up. Now his nose was buried in the *Great Puzzle Value Book,* determined to finish every word jumble, acrostic, and cryptogram by the time they pulled into Kinahwee Falls.

"Okay, Mom. I need a six-letter word for a Tasmanian city."

"Mmm. Herbert? No, try Hobart."

"Yup. That works. Tom Sawyer's big sister."

"Come on, Benj. You can get that one."

"Four letters. Mary," he tried. "Right. Fool's gold—pyrite. Lazy bird—cuckoo? No, five letters."

"Mazie," said Phil from the backseat.

"Who?"

"The bird in *Horton Hatches the Egg.*"

Since Wisconsin was the dairy state, Phil had been expecting red barns and Holsteins, but County Road D ran as straight as a ruler through endless pine forest. The only signs of civilization were wooden telephone poles flying by and the occasional roadside tavern made of logs, Wisconsin's version of a bar. Little tavern in the big woods, Phil thought. The road dipped and narrowed into a plank bridge over a sluggish stream and there, sunk into the bank, was a tiny tilting green sign: KINAHWEE FALLS, INC. 1906, POP. 41.

"We're here! I can't believe it. Isn't it beautiful?"

With the exception of the dip in the road over what was apparently Kinahwee Falls, the landscape looked no different to Phil than it had for the last forty minutes.

She rolled down her window and hung her head out as they cruised along. "Smell that evergreen. There is nowhere on earth that smells like that except the great north woods, boys."

The road curved slightly and tucked into the indentation was another log tavern. This one had some deer horns tacked to the front and a neon sign of a deer lounging on a barstool with a Hamm's beer.

"Oh, it's the Deer Horn tavern. I can't believe it. It hasn't changed a bit."

Phil could believe it. Even though it was just past noon, there were four cars in the parking lot already. Here were four residents of Kinahwee Falls; where were the other thirty-seven?

"For a special treat, Uncle Bo would bring us down to the Deer Horn for 7-UPs and Baby Ruths when we got in from our canoe expeditions. Too bad we don't have time to stop now. You guys are going to love Uncle Bo. He was like a second father to me." A mile later, she flicked on her turn signal. "Here we are," she said cheerfully, hooking a left onto a rutted dirt path that crossed beneath a wooden archway with Camp Kinahwee spelled out in birch twigs.

The path twisted through a dense forest and into a clearing

by a pine-edged, black-water lake. "Is this Little Lost Lake?" Phil asked, his chest thudding so violently that he wondered if he was having a heart attack.

"No, of course not." She smiled as if this was a foolish question. "That's two hundred miles from here. This is Lake Kinahwee."

"Oh, right." What was the point of paddling from one lake to another when they all looked alike? Phil thought. As they drove closer he could see a row of squat log cabins, several large canoe racks, a dock, a raft, a flagpole. It didn't look much different than the Boy Scout camp on Crowley Pond—hardly something worth driving across country for three straight days, or listening to his mother blather on about for his entire lifetime. An old-fashioned green bus, with rounded edges like it had been inflated, was parked in front of the largest cabin. A trailer with six canoes was hitched to its rear end. A bunch of boys swarmed around a towering heap of backpacks, wooden boxes, paddles, and life vests. They seemed pretty old, like high school juniors or seniors, and Phil couldn't tell if they were campers or counselors. His stomach flipped around again and he definitely should have changed his shirt but it was too late now.

"Oh, look," she said happily. "The green machine. That's the bus that takes the canoe trips up into Minnesota and Canada. The real wilderness."

Wasn't this the real wilderness?

"I thought girls went to this camp," said Benjy.

"They do. But not at the same time as the boys. They take turns in one-week shifts."

Oh, great. Phil had at least been looking forward to canoeing with some girls.

She pulled up behind the canoe trailer. The group of boys stopped their swarming and studied them suspiciously. Suddenly a stocky old guy with a flannel shirt and tufted white hair came plowing out of the crowd. "This must be Lucy!" he hollered.

She jumped out of the car. "Uncle Bo!" He opened his plaid-checked arms and swept her into a big bear hug; she was at least half a head taller. Then he stood back, crossed his arms, and inspected her. "Well, you look pretty much the same. A little pale and flabby, maybe." He tweaked her upper arm and frowned. "You need some hard paddling, girl. Boys, this is Lucy Lamb. She was a Bo Thorne Most Outstanding Female Camper two years in a row." They seemed unimpressed.

Benjy and Phil sheepishly climbed out of the car with Benjy still clutching his crossword puzzle book. Phil pried it out of his hands and chucked it in the backseat.

"So these are your boys, Lucy. Twins, eh? They don't look much alike."

Phil hoped Benjy wouldn't explain that's because they were dizygotes.

Uncle Bo came over and examined them, head to toe. Up close, he seemed frighteningly ancient, his face brown and folded like a Sioux warrior's. With a hand that felt like it was wearing a dried-out work glove, he gave them each a knuckle-crushing shake.

"Well, we almost didn't think you'd make it in time. Grab your gear, boys. The bus leaves in half an hour."

"Geez Louise," his mom said, which must have been an old Camp Kinahwee expression. "Half an hour! I thought the trip left tomorrow." She popped open the back of the Taurus and Phil yanked out their packs. Phil squatted down, tested the bungie cords that lashed on their sleeping bags and water bottles, then slipped the GPS into the side pocket of Benjy's pack. Mentally, he ran over all the items that had been on that green list with a sinking feeling that he had forgotten something really important. Rain poncho, bug goop, a flashlight—something.

He felt the vise grip of Uncle Bo on his left shoulder. "Shag ass, Phil. Load those wannigans into the back of the trailer."

"The what-a-gons?"

Uncle Bo clacked his tongue with disgust. "Didn't you teach them anything, Lucy?"

"Oh, sorry. Wannigans are the wooden chests that hold the food supplies."

Phil bent over one of the green wooden boxes, grabbed hold of the rope handles, and heaved. It did not budge, not even a quarter of an inch. He straightened up, shamefaced, and was relieved to see no one was watching him. Maybe this was some kind of joke—that the box was filled with rocks or nailed down. But all the other boys seemed able to lift a wannigan, although not easily. What the hell, if they could do it, he could do it—they were bigger than he was but not that much bigger. He couldn't wimp out in his first five minutes at camp, especially not in front of his mom and Uncle Bo. He rubbed his hands together, bent his knees deeply, and grunted like a hog. The box rose a few inches off the ground and he staggered toward the trailer. He gripped the rope so hard he could feel the hemp cutting into his hands; if he dropped this freaking thing, it would pulverize his toes.

As Phil dumped the box in the trailer, he felt relieved that Benjy had been assigned to load paddles, not wannigans. Not only would Benjy be unable to lift one, he wouldn't even try. He would probably complain until one of the counselors or Uncle Bo carried it instead. Phil noticed that the other kids seemed to have their own custom paddles, carved with dates and places: 1996, GOD'S LAKE; 1998, BLACK DUCK RIVER.

Suddenly Uncle Bo clapped his hands, the boys loped over to the flagpole and linked hands in a circle. Phil followed along, taking hold of Benjy's hand and some rattailed kid's who was wearing a Canucks hockey jersey. Their hands were all as slippery as seal flippers. Uncle Bo stood by the flagpole and raised one hand like an Indian chief. "May the Great Spirit bring you fair weather and safe voyage. May the weak become strong. May the strong become leaders. I will join you in six weeks at Black Knife Lake at the headwater of the Churchill River. There we will share the many tales of your adventures."

Phil was relieved to hear that Uncle Bo wasn't coming with them. Then if they goofed up, at least he wouldn't know all about it and tell their mom. He hoped the part about the weak becoming strong hadn't been meant specifically for him and Benjy. He looked over at his mom, who was standing outside the circle listening. Her head hung down and her hands were folded like she was praying. Then she raised her head and he saw that her face was all wet with tears.

Geez Louise.

CHAPTER 7

>>

Oh, shit, she was starting to cry—something about the blessing of the expedition just set her off. Maybe it was because Phil and Benjy looked so grown up as they stood hand in hand with the other campers in the big circle, or the way the golden afternoon light kissed the tops of the spruce along the edge of the lake. Maybe it was because Uncle Bo's deep, noble voice stirred primordial memories of her own long-ago canoe expeditions, of her own lost childhood. Maybe it was the realization that once the boys left, she would have to face the wreckage of her screwed-up marriage, her screwed-up life, all alone. Maybe it was just the words—may the weak become strong. Of course, it was only pseudo-Native American mumbo jumbo, but it struck her suddenly as profound. I am weak. Please help me become strong. She better get a grip before she mortified Phil and Benjy. She inhaled deeply and exhaled in tiny puffs, a relaxation technique she had learned in Lamaze class before the twins were born.

After the last trace of Uncle Bo's drone had faded with the breeze and a hand squeeze had been sent around the circle, the campers let out a war whoop and galloped toward the green machine. As Benjy and Phil stood glumly in line to climb aboard, she gave them a wave good-bye and then a thumbs-up. They probably wouldn't tolerate an actual hug and a kiss and besides, she didn't trust herself not to start bawling again. They glanced over and, with the barest flick of a wrist, waved back. Subdued and nervous, she decided, but not *too* miserable. I love you, I know you will be fine, she chanted over and over to herself like a prayer.

The engine fired up, disgorging a black cloud of diesel exhaust, and then the green machine chugged down the rutted road and under the Camp Kinahwee gate, the trailer lurching along behind like a stubborn donkey.

Uncle Bo walked over and slid an avuncular arm around her waist. "There they go. This is my fifty-sixth summer sending off canoe trips."

Lucy could feel her sinuses filling again.

"They'll be all right, Lucy," he said.

She nodded forlornly. He shot her a sideways glance. "What's the matter, sweetie? What are all these tears about?"

That did it. She let out a sob and threw herself into his gnarled arms, shoulders shuddering, soaking his shirt collar with hot tears and snot while he stroked her hair.

"There, there. *Shhh*. It can't be all that bad," he murmured.

"It's . . . " She lifted her head, looked with horror at the mess she had made, and snuffled into a big red bandanna Uncle Bo had produced from his pocket. "It's my husband." She blew her nose loudly. "I just found out he has a g-g-girlfriend." Uncle Bo frowned and tsked-tsked. "So I've left him. But wha—wha—what will my boys do?" Another round of tears. Lucy didn't cry very often, but when she did it was always histrionic carryings-on like this. Why couldn't she cry in a dignified way like her mother—a couple of reptile tears and that was it?

"Well, that's where Camp Kinahwee can help. Every year, we get campers with all kinds of family troubles. Much worse than parents separating, believe me. By the end of the summer, Benjy and Phil will find their own inner strength to handle this." He linked his arm through hers and gently but firmly strolled her toward the waterfront, as if he were exercising an invalid. He lead her to the end of the dock and they stood silently for a few minutes, listening to the water lapping gently against the posts. A loon took off with a furious paddling and croaking and Uncle Bo swiveled her around so she could watch it disappear into the western sky. Suddenly, the old bell above the main lodge clanged a dozen times. Screen doors started slamming and a herd of junior campers, all in bathing suits with towels flapping behind like capes, raced out of the cabins toward the beach. Uncle Bo surreptitiously checked his watch. It was 3:00, of course. Rest time was over, and it was time for the afternoon swim.

Lucy extracted her arm from under Uncle Bo's, made a final snuffle and honk. "Well, I've taken up enough of your time. I better get going. I need to get to Little Lost Lake before dark." She gave him what she hoped was a jaunty grin. "I'll be okay. Really." She patted his arm as a look of relief darted across his face—he had handled yet another overemotional parent successfully.

He escorted her back to the car, opened the door for her to climb in, shut it, and clicked the lock. He bent down to the open window. "Don't worry about your boys. Worry about taking care of yourself and mending your heart, Lucy." He smiled, showing some snaggled lower teeth and the silver loops of a dental bridge. "I bet your husband's going to realize what a fool he's been and come crawling back. A Bo Thorne Most Outstanding Female Camper makes a damn good wife." He leaned in and kissed her forehead. His neck smelled reassuringly of wood smoke and tar soap.

By the time she turned back onto County Road D, the last trace of tears had vanished and she felt sheepish. Why had she told Uncle Bo that Ed had a girlfriend and that she had left him? Is that what she really believed? All right, Lucy, so what do you think *is* going on? I think that Ed is doing something bad with that bleached, pierced slut-bitch. Suddenly, she had an image of discarded clothing and Ingrid's pale thigh. Lucy accelerated until the old Taurus engine raced, then jammed on the brakes and nearly swerved into a drainage ditch. And I am not going to be sitting there in

Crowley twiddling my thumbs, waiting for him to come ambling home from five days of sex games at the Trump Plaza. When he finds his wife and kids gone, then he'll be sorry, *really* sorry. But I will say, Sorry, Ed, you're too late. You've lost this Bo Thorne Most Outstanding Camper for good.

Had she sent poor Benjy and Phil off to the Canadian wilderness just to wreak revenge on Ed? Well, maybe. She glanced down and realized that she still had Uncle Bo's soggy bandanna clutched in her palm.

What she really needed, she decided as she rounded the last bend toward the Deer Horn tavern, was a drink. Maybe a couple. The parking lot had a few more cars than it had at noontime. She pried open the spring-loaded pine plank door and found that the deer motif was continued on the inside, only this time it was stuffed deer heads, Depression-era, with patchy fur and glass eyeballs sinking into sawdust. The pine walls, booths, and bar counter, all covered with thick layers of honey-colored varnish, made her feel as if she were stepping into an amber cave. Five men sat at the counter drinking beer, smoking and paying halfhearted attention to Oprah Winfrey on the wood-encased television. They only barely glanced up when the door banged open, long enough to figure out it wasn't one of their drinking buddies.

Better freshen up from her crying jag first, she decided and headed down a narrow back corridor to the ladies' room. As far as she could make out in the postcard-size mirror nailed above the sink, her eyes didn't look too red or puffy. She wet a paper towel and mopped her face. Then she inspected herself again, this time trying to gauge how she measured up as a thirty-eight-year-old newly single woman who was about to join a bar full of men for some midafternoon drinking. The skin under her eyes didn't look too baggy, she decided; she might even pass for thirty-five. But her eyes could use some jazzing up with mascara and eyeliner, just like her mother had been telling her for years. Too bad she didn't own either. She fished her one and only lipstick out of her purse—pale melon berry, free with a bottle of hand cream. She pouted and wished her lips were as dark as oxblood, then gave the straggly ends of her hair a shake. For the past twenty-five years, her hair had hung five inches down her back; definitely time for a more sophisticated look. She peeled off her sweatshirt, tucked her shirt tight into her jeans, tightened her belt, and then ran an appraising hand down the front of her body—over a breast, down the flat of her stomach, along her thigh. Pretty damn good. Not much in the way of boobs, but at least the women in her family were leggy and not prone to middle-age spread. She wished she'd packed those chunky black sandals that Ed had brought her from Palo Alto; they would definitely enhance her legs as they dangled off a barstool.

She sauntered back to the bar, trying to put attitude in every step, but as she drew nearer, her confidence wobbled. Did she really have the nerve to sidle in between the two lumberjack types with beefy deltoids rippling under grimy T-shirts? It would be so much easier to hunker down in one of the booths and hide behind a wall of hair and the latest Martha Grimes mystery in her bag. She inhaled deeply. May the weak become strong.

"Excuse me. Mind if I have a seat?"

The blond one to her right swiveled around and cocked his head sideways so he could inspect her from underneath the overhang of his Bass-O-Mania baseball cap. "Shoo-are," he said, finally smiling. She'd forgotten about *shoo-are,* that northern Wisconsin twang with a Swedish lilt. She'd forgotten about that Swedish look, too, the big square teeth, the perfect pale blond features. Handsome in an insipid way, like a speed skater.

She sat down and perched her feet awkwardly on the metal hoop around the bottom of the bar stool. She folded her hands on top of the slippery counter and glanced over at Oprah, who was leaning empathetically toward a small woman who was dabbing at her eyes with a crumpled up Kleenex. A caption flashed across her: "Husband Killed by Grizzly Bear in Front of Couple's Three Small Children."

Lucy started to laugh, one of those unhinged out-of-nowhere laughs that crazy people make on subway cars. Then she forced herself to stop, so suddenly that the silence seemed deranged, too. "I suppose that's not very funny," she said.

The speed skater's expression was serious. "Well, you got to feel bad for those poor, little kids, seeing their dad killed like that."

Lucy nodded in what she hoped was a sober and repentant way. "Tragic," she murmured, trying to catch the eye of the bartender, who was swabbing beer taps with a spray bottle of blue cleaner. A tidy man in a polo shirt ambled over, a cigarette dangling from the lips. Everyone else seemed to have a butt smoldering away in one of the yellowed plastic ashtrays that dotted the bar, including the rosy-cheeked Swede. Apparently, smoke-free hadn't reached northern Wisconsin yet. "Can I help you, miss?"

How sweet. When was the last time anyone had called her *miss*? She was about to order white wine, until she spotted a twist-cap gallon jug of New York's finest behind the bar, the bright yellow type that gave her headaches. Hamm's didn't have enough alcohol to provide the buzz her present emotional state required. "Double shot of Jack Daniel's on the rocks, please." This was her mother's lunchtime cocktail when she was playing bridge with the ladies at the club.

The speed skater and the lumberjack on her other side each gave her a long second look. Clearly they had been expecting an order for Diet Pepsi. When the bartender smacked down the glass, she straightened her spine and took a showy swig. As a jolt of liquid fire raced down her throat and up her nose, it took every shred of self-control not to gag. How could her seventy-five-year-old mother drink this stuff in the middle of the day and not topple off her chintz-covered bridge chair? Lucy wondered, not for the first time, if her mother had a serious drinking problem.

The lumberjack to the left shifted his attention from the grizzly bear widow. He was wearing a black T-shirt and an orange nylon hunting vest; his thick, dark hair was roguishly long, parted in the middle, and brushed back. Definitely not the polite, bland Swede type. He was about her age, she guessed, and handsome in a swarthy, hard-living kind of way. In ten years, Marlboros and Hamm's would turn his face fleshy and flushed. "You from around here?" he asked innocently, as if so many of the Kinahwee Falls women popped in for Jack Daniel's at 3:00, that it was hard to keep them all straight.

"Well, no actually. I was just dropping my sons off at the camp. I'm from Massachusetts."

"You're a long way from Kennedyland."

"I'm from here originally." Okay, Libertyville, Illinois, was not "here," but you were allowed to tell white lies about yourself in a bar, weren't you? "I even went to the camp myself, back in the Stone Age." Back in the Stone Age—that was the sort of thing her mother said when she flirted with the lawn service boy. Lucy was going to have to work on her pickup lines.

"Don't know much 'bout that camp except when I take my outboard up there once a summer and poach a few trout. Then the old guy paddles over and threatens to turn me into the ranger." He gave a withering smirk.

"That's Uncle Bo. He doesn't approve of motor boats." She'd meant to be irreverent, but it came out scolding, as if Uncle Bo really was her uncle.

"I figured that out. So, what took you out east?" He seemed to think as highly of the East Coast as he did of Uncle Bo.

She considered saying graduate school and then figured she'd better steer clear of that stereotype. "Work," she said. "My husband and I started a software company." Appearances to the contrary, I'm not an unemployed, alcoholic loose woman on the make.

"Oh, yeah?" He leaned back and studied her face with a newfound interest. "What kind of software?"

Over the years, Lucy had observed that the term *software* was sort of a gender test; women got nervous and changed the subject when they heard the word, while men turned aggressive, demanding specific details, as if their intelligence had been challenged. "We design computer games. Pretty dumb," she said with a modest shrug.

"Games? My son loves computer games. Which ones do you make?'

"You've probably never heard of it. It's called Maiden's Quest," she admitted bashfully. Ed had come up with the name Maiden's Quest, but Lucy always thought it sounded like the title of a romance novel, the type with a busty, disheveled woman getting fondled by a pirate on the cover.

He seemed to find this news exciting. "You mean the one with the princess who's, like, lost in the catacombs and has to find the key, the scepter, and the magic mirror? That one?" When she nodded, he slapped the counter. "Awesome. Wait till Bart hears I met the lady whose husband designed Maiden's Quest."

She swirled her ice and then polished off the rest of her drink in a single gulp. "Actually, I'm the one who designed the game. My name's right on the box—Lucy Crocker." Her usual perverse reaction—she never took MQ seriously until someone gave all the credit to Ed.

"Well, I'll be. You don't look like a software designer. Then again, I don't know what a software designer looks like."

"Neither do I."

"Hey, George. This is the lady that designed that Maiden's Quest thing," he said, leaning back so he could address the speed skater. George, who reluctantly turned his attention from the children of the grizzly bear victim, seemed confused.

"It's a computer game," Lucy offered.

"Like Doom?" he said, brightening. "You know the cheat codes for the fourth level of Doom?"

" 'Fraid not."

"She doesn't need cheat codes, asshole."

George looked chastened. "So, what kind of computer do you use?"

Uh-oh. Sooner or later, any conversation with guys about computers took a technical turn. Having just billed herself as a software innovator, she had to come up with some better geek-speak than, It's a big black box. "We get them custom built so it doesn't have a name." That sounded plausible, didn't it?

"It must have a three hundred megahertz Pentium Two, right?" said George.

The lumberjack let out a disdainful snort. "Of course it does. Even my Dell's got that."

Now, the rest of the men were leaning across the bar toward her, as if they were expecting her to spout some definitive opinion on RAMs and megahertz.

"You ever meet that Gates guy," the tidy bartender asked, refilling her glass.

"Yeah, once," she said, hoping they wouldn't probe much further. She'd seen him at a summit where all the great minds were gathered to discuss the future of technology, but her only memory was of a slope-shouldered guy with smudged glasses. Ed had offered to make the Crocker presentation so she could spend the day at the local botanical garden. At the time, his willingness to take over boring chores such as schmoozing Bill Gates seemed thoughtful. Now, sitting on a barstool at the Deer Horn tavern, it seemed diabolical. Right from the get-go, he had been plotting to appropriate her ideas, silence her, supplant her with . . . Ingrid.

The conversation quickly moved from Bill Gates to everyone's favorite Web sites. You seen the one for Makko's? one man asked. Then there was the one for freshwater fishing lures that George said was tops and the men passed a ball-point around so they could jot down the Web address on their cocktail napkins. Lucy didn't want to seem standoffish, so she jotted it down too—http//www.joeslures.com. The lumberjack, whose name turned out to be Roland, admitted that he'd designed his own home page about his favorite singer, Sheryl Crow. "That Roland. He loves foxy ladies," said the bartender.

At least Lucy had heard of Sheryl Crow. Once, she had heard an interview on NPR with some down-and-out poet, whose verse about hanging out in a bar had been turned into a pop hit. At the time, the line "All I want to do is have some fun" had seemed merely proof of why the poet's chapbook was out of print; now it seemed prophetic. Lucy scribbled Roland's home page address on her napkin, too.

By the time she'd finished her second drink, she noticed that the afternoon light filtering in past the beer sign had turned salmon. She unsteadily dismounted her bar stool. "Well, I better hit the road," she said to no one in particular, half expecting her departure to go unnoticed.

Roland spun around. "Sure you have to go?" he asked. Lucy was gratified that he actually seemed wistful. "George and I are going up to Annie's Steak Chalet in Eau Claire. Want to come?" He gave George a little nod for support.

"It's all-you-can-eat surf and turf night. T-bones, jumbo shrimp, king crab legs," George chimed in, obediently. It probably wasn't the first time Roland had tried to pick up a dinner date at the Deer Horn.

Roland climbed off the bar stool, sidled next to her, and gave her upper arm a friendly nudge with his knuckles. "You can tell us all about your next computer game."

Sitting down, Roland had only been a pleasant-enough male face. Now she felt his barrel-chested body next to her, insinuating. I could do this, Lucy thought. Over bacon-stuffed baked potatoes and steaks smothered in A-1 sauce, I could hear about their broken marriages and screwed-up kids, and they could hear about mine. Then later, I could go back with Roland to one of those low stucco bungalows on County Road D. He would take me into the tiny back bedroom with gold wall-to-wall carpet and a gold chenille bedspread and we would fall down together on a bed with bouncy box springs, and he would slip off my clothes with his rough hands, and tell me I had a beautiful body and make love to me. Under his soft, weathered flesh, the muscles down his back will feel as hard as metal cable. This man is not some sicko—he's just lonely, like me.

I am a thousand miles from home. For now, I have no husband, no children. I could do this.

"I better not. I've got a three-hour drive. My mother's expecting me." Just as she had expected, the mention of an old waiting mother seemed to settle the question. I am such a coward, she thought.

Roland escorted her out to the parking lot and chivalrously held the driver's door while she climbed into the station wagon. In the dusky evening, his face looked younger and sweeter than it had in the glare of the color TV. "Hey. You almost forgot this," he said and handed her the cocktail napkin with his home page address. "Check it out. It has a place for visitors to leave comments."

"Okay, I will," she said, glancing over at the dashboard and passenger seat strewn with Coke bottles and empty chip bags for a safe place to put this offering. Finally she folded it and tucked it underneath the visor. Of course, she wouldn't be near a computer for weeks. It was possible that she would never log onto the Internet again, but she needn't tell Roland that.

He leaned in the window and kissed her hard. He must be as drunk as she was. He tasted pleasantly of beer and cigarettes, his stubbly face rubbed her chin. "Stop by when you come to pick up your kids. I'll probably be here," he called, as she backed out onto County Road D.

She set off, accelerating recklessly, punching at the radio

buttons until she hit static-free Madonna. "I'm alive," she whispered. "I'm alive, I'm alive, I'm alive." A man, a very attractive man, at least she had thought so after a couple of Jack Daniel's, had invited her to dinner at a steak house in Eau Claire. She reached up and adjusted the mirror so she could see her face. Two hours of flirting with strange men at the Deer Horn had transformed her from the weepy cheated-on wife who had pestered poor Uncle Bo. Her cheeks were flushed, her eyes were white and sparkling. She gave herself a mischievous, lopsided grin. No wonder Roland had desired her.

He had kissed her, she had tasted the inside of his mouth. If she let him, he would have kissed her more, on her breasts, between her legs. Suddenly, her whole body turned moist and tingly with lust. How could she have said no and driven away? What was she driving to, anyway? A lonely cabin with a single lumpy bed where she could stew on all the blunders of her life. The rows of spruce trees were whizzing by so fast it made her dizzy. She glanced down at the speedometer edging toward eighty. She slowed to forty and pondered turning around at a rest stop and heading back. If she really stepped on it, she could catch them just as they were climbing into their pickup to head off for Annie's Steak Chalet. She tried to picture Roland's face as he saw her hell-bent Taurus round the bend. Would he tip his head back with a laugh, maybe grab her around the waist and twirl her off her feet, like they did in those wartime romance movies? Lucy's heart faltered. It seemed quite possible that he had forgotten her in fifteen minutes, just the way she was now having trouble recalling the exact features of his handsome face. She reimagined Roland's formerly ardent expression—eyes averted, hands jangling the change in his pocket if she returned to take him up on his invite.

Once it's over, it's over, someone had once said to her. Who, she tried to think. Ed? No, he never thought anything was final. He wouldn't think their marriage was over, not even after he discovered his wife had disappeared into the wilderness. Who had said that? Suddenly, she remembered. It had been written down, not said, in blue ballpoint on cheap lined tablet paper by Sam McCarty, in his farewell letter mailed from the Badlands. *Dear Lucy: When you hesitated, when you chose the squalor of the city instead of coming with me, I knew that our relationship was finished. You are not the person that I thought you were. Please do not try to contact me. Once it is over, it is over.*

A good souvenir in case she ever forgot Sam McCarty's principle flaw—self-righteousness.

What had she said to poor Phil when she gave him the dispirited version of how she met, was courted by, and married Ed? See, son, love is unpredictable—I dumped/got dumped by my true love and married a barely visible nebbish, your father, instead. She should have told her son the unexpurgated story of how she ended up sharing her life with Ed Crocker rather than Sam McCarty, even if it leaked a few family secrets along the way.

Let me start at the beginning, before I met your father, before I even met Sam McCarty. It was the summer of 1982 and the entire Lamb family was in disarray. Your Uncle Larry had just finished his freshman year at Northwestern where he'd come out of the closet big-time, was spending the summer haunting gay bars in Chicago somewhere, he didn't exactly say. Your grandfather Cyrus had been forced into early retirement at the Newberry Library for some reason, he didn't exactly say, either. My guess is that he was too much the old-school bibliophile—the type that still smoked at his cluttered desk, took a week to catalog a single volume, had a couple of cocktails at lunch, scoffed at computer technology.

And me, I was at loose ends, too. I'd just graduated from Madison in a desultory way as an art major, where I'd mostly been ridiculed for my Maxfield Parrish-esque landscapes. When I worked up the nerve to ask my advisor for a recommendation to grad school, he suggested library school instead, because I was really an illustrator, not a painter—the ultimate insult. So for lack of anything more inspirational to do, I'd applied to Simmons Library School for the fall and thought I'd spend the summer living rent-free at home, busing tables at Uno's pizzeria at the Old Orchard shopping center, maybe resurrect a high school boyfriend or two.

But Corky had other ideas. She wasn't about to have Cyrus and me underfoot all summer. Now that he was retired, Dad said he was going to finish up his collection of lumberjack folklore he'd been assembling for the past twenty-five years. So now that you have unlimited vacation time, Corky said, never able to resist a dig, why don't you go up to Little Lost Lake for the summer and do some original research. Who knows, there are probably some real Paul Bunyans nearby, you can do an oral history. And to me, she said, I'm worried about your father, his color is poor. So she proposed that I go along to keep him company, make sure he ate enough, didn't drink too much. It's your last summer at home, Corky said, it's the least you can do. And before I could say no way, Cyrus put in his oar. I need a re-re-research assistant, he said. It'll be fu-fun. Like the old da-da-days with my brother Ba-bart.

So off we went to Little Lost Lake for the summer, me with my paints, Cyrus with his legal pads of lumberjacks notes, a case of Dewar's, five cartons of Tareytons. After the first rainy day I realized that this was a disastrous plan. When I was a little girl I hadn't minded the cramped quarters with the single bedroom and the sleeping loft over the living room. But now there was no privacy, I felt invaded by my father's presence—his smoker's cough, his dental bridge in a glass by the kitchen sink, his stacks of messy notes littering the couch. And my mother was right, he didn't seem well. He dozed off over his writing desk, got winded walking up from the dock, stuttered more than ever, which derailed his train of thought. So I discouraged conversation, never asked a question that required more than a one-syllable answer, looked impatient when he tried to tell me about Ole the Big Swede or the winter of the blue snow.

Every unrainy morning, I fled out the door with my paint box, sketch pad, a sandwich—up an old lumber road, off in the canoe, away. One day I decided to bushwhack the narrow inlet over to Twin Pond. Back in the lumber camp days, they'd built a railroad spur down to the shore and left a Rock Island caboose, which later was turned into a funky fishing camp that Cyrus said belonged to a family named McCarty from Appleton who never used the place. When we were little, sometimes Larry and I paddled over and played house in the louvered cupola until the yellow jackets drove us out.

It was late afternoon by the time I scooted the canoe under a blowdown, broke free of the inlet, and glided into Twin Pond. Then I noticed the caboose was slightly less dilapidated than usual, the shutters hung straight, the grass around it had been mowed, a towel and a pair of jeans flapped on a clothesline. And there was a man standing at the end of the dock, backlit by a blast of western sun—I was so startled that I nearly spun the canoe around and hightailed it back to Little Lost Lake. Then I made out brown pants with a stripe, a brown shirt with patches—a Wisconsin Forest Ranger uniform. He cupped his hands around his mouth and helloed across the water to me like a loon.

I figured a forest ranger was pretty safe bet, so I paddled over, and there stood the most handsome man I had ever seen. His uniform made him look like a Civil War soldier in an old tintype, with a craggy profile, somber expression, dark hair parted in the middle and hooked behind the ears. As I pulled up, he bent down and offered me a hand. "So, you must be from the Lamb place at Little Lost Lake," he said, smiling in a way that seemed cordial but not frivolous.

He told me he had a seasonal job as a ranger at the Nicolet National Forest, was camping out at his uncle's cabin for the summer, invited me in for a cup of tea even though the place was a mess. I followed him up an iron staircase into the caboose, a shoebox-shaped compartment all in varnished tongue and groove—ceiling, walls, floor. The place looked like a kid's clubhouse with a toy galley kitchen in one corner, a little table with built-in benches, a ladder leading to a loft, which I guessed must be where he slept. As advertised, the place was a wreck—clothing mounded in the corners, dirty dishes piled in the sink, books stacked everywhere. New Age, Save the Earth titles—*Zen and the Art of Motorcycle Maintenance, Black Elk Speaks, A Sand County Almanac.* I nursed a grimy mug of Red Zinger tea and listened to him hold forth on everything from his nomadic college career to his various ecology missions.

"So after two semesters at Reed, I transferred to Antioch because they had a mentoring program in environmental law, which turned out to be totally bogus, so then I went trekking in Nepal for six months.

"The forest service is totally corrupt, drops its pants to the lumber industry. So I took a ranger job to do a little industrial spying, expose some of their clear-cutting schemes before they happen." His voice actually trembled with indignation.

Finally he thought to ask me a couple of questions, but seemed dissatisfied with the answers. "Why would anyone want to go to library school? The only thing libraries do is encourage publishers to cut down more trees and make more paper. If you really want to go to art school, go to art school. What's holding you back?" But I was scarcely listening to either him or myself, felt my lust ricocheting off the walls like a squash ball. A possible romance with this Sam McCarty offered everything—a little sex, a little adventure, an escape from my summer baby-sitting job.

The next day, Sam paddled over to Little Lost Lake and took me fishing and I admired his hands, which seemed to know what they were doing as they handled a canoe or tied a dry fly in the dusk, or cast out twelve feet of line with barely a flick of the wrist. I had dressed up strategically for this out-ing—in a red bikini with one of Cyrus's buffalo plaid shirts tossed over my shoulder—and was wondering what else Sam could do with those know-it-all hands.

He caught a big brown, fourteen inches or so, but he was strictly a catch-and-release man. When he reeled it close enough, I bent over and scooped it up with the net. And then as he watched, admiring my technique, I gently worked the barb off the trout's springy jawbone and tossed it back.

"Nicely done," he said.

"I do a lot of things nicely," I said, staring at the crotch of his cutoffs. He stowed his paddle, crawled over the gunwales to face me. Now, any other boy I'd been in a similar situation with would have then kissed me, but Sam McCarty bent forward and licked the salty sweat off the top of my breast. I don't think you need to know all the particulars of what happened next. Suffice it to say that I lunged forward to lick him back, spilling Cyrus's tackle box into the lake in the process. We then paddled over to the island in the middle of Little Lost Lake, had soon shed the bikini and the cutoffs and were covered with pine needles, and spent most of the next two months in the caboose's hide-a-way bunk bed.

And what did my father do, left on his own? I'm ashamed to say I don't really know. After I moved my paints and clothes over to the caboose, I hardly ever saw him. The blue bourbon glasses and ashtrays piled up, the groceries I bought him never got taken out of the bag. The notes on lumberjacks multiplied onto more legal pad and index cards, but never got themselves collected.

When Labor Day rolled around and it was time for me to head to Boston for library school, Sam insisted on coming along, because he couldn't bear for us to be apart, he said. But in truth, it was because he had gotten in a scuffle with his boss over the Nicolet selling off logging rights that had ended with Sam spending a night in the Eagle River lockup and losing his job.

So Sam came to live with me in Cambridge for a while, but he was like one of those tigers that turns psychotic in a small cage. His constant questions about my goals and motives in life had a way of escalating into tirades. Sometimes he would grab me—I couldn't tell if it was in anger or passion—hard enough to leave bruises. Once he hit a guy in an Irish pub in Central Square and ended up with a fractured jaw. Then the man I abandoned my father for abandoned me. He said not to bother writing, but I tried anyway, sent three letters to his parents' house in Appleton with *Please Forward* scrawled urgently under the address. I begged him to forgive me—I'm not sure for what—to give me a second chance. A couple months later they all came back in a manila envelope with a note on Welsh corgi stationery from his mother: "Sorry, dear. We don't have a forwarding address for Sam at the present time."

Now here is the part where your father comes in. I was in my little Cambridge apartment, crying over my lost love, when there was a knock on the door and it was your dad, the fourteen-year-old prodigy, in his army fatigue jacket and with the violin tucked under his arm. "Um, are you okay," he asked in this voice that was definitely not a little boy's. "I heard you crying." Then he dropped his eyes and turned red and I realized that all I was wearing was underpants and a turtleneck.

The story has a few footnotes. At Christmastime we found out the reason why Cyrus had been looking so gray—he had lung cancer and a year later he would be dead. Neither he nor I ever went back to Little Lost Lake again. A couple of years later, Corky, in one of her whiskey-soaked confessional moods, admitted why she'd been so keen on banishing me and Cyrus to the lake that summer. She was having a fling with my newly divorced orthodontist, Dr. Bartholomew. When she conveniently became the widow Lamb eighteen months later, she hoped he'd make an honest women of her, but he married his receptionist instead. And as for Sam

McCarty, he was true to his words that once it's over it's over, and I never heard from him again.

County Road D came to a four-way stop at the intersection of County Road GG. As Lucy slowed to a gratuitous stop—she hadn't passed a car since she'd left the Deer Horn—it suddenly occurred to her that she had no idea where she was going. She had a vague memory of a County Road D somewhere near Little Lost Lake, but perhaps this was not the same one. She dug around the litter in the passenger seat—Benjy's crossword puzzle book, a half-eaten bag of Cheez Doodles, an empty can of A&W root beer—until she found the crumpled remains of the Wisconsin road map. She flicked on the feeble overhead light and smoothed the map across the steering wheel. Just as she had feared, this County Road D had no relationship to the one a hundred miles east at Little Lost Lake. A worms' nest of county roads lay between her and the cabin and they started to dart and blur in the dim light.

She stared out at the tiny ribbons of pavement disappearing into the pine forests and tried to blink back her panic. Sober up, Lucy, she thought, twisting a piece of flesh on the top of her hand hard enough to make herself wince. Think of it like the dragon's maze puzzle in MQI, where Arabella has to memorize the runes on the castle wall. Okay, D to Winter, then left on W, which becomes H past the Jump River State Forest, then take scissors right onto 70 before Tripoli, then left on County D past Squirrel Lake. Got it.

"Ed," she said out loud, flicking on the high beams and gripping the steering wheel so hard it turned slippery, "where are you now?" The rattle-trap Crowley Airport Limousine van was probably dropping him off at their doorstep at this very moment. She smiled meanly as she imagined him frowning up at the dark house, his voice echoing through the empty rooms "Lucy? Benjy? Phil? Where is everybody?"

She hadn't left him a note. At midnight before she left, she had decided that a mere note couldn't contain her mushroom cloud of rage. Instead she had left him—what poetic justice—an e-mail! Under subject, she had typed *youfuckingingrid*, then she had cut and pasted in the text of Ingrid's incriminating e-mail, and in the reader's comments box she had put:

> *Ed: Have gone on research trip. Please tell Ingrid she does not need to make my hotel reservations. Boys decided to go to camp for summer. Hope your lingam enjoyed the huckleberry massage oil, and MQII keeps on the upward swing. Have a great summer.*
> *Lucy*

It had taken her more than an hour to master such e-mail pyrotechnics but the final product had been worth the effort. She had even found a menu with instructions on how to make smiley and frowney faces to punctuate her e-mail, so she had closed with a line of faces that reminded her of the figure from *The Scream*: =:o, =:o, =:o, =:o. Then she had figured out how to have it delivered two days hence, so it would be zapped into Ed's e-mailbox at the exact moment he arrived back from the gamer conference. Which was right about now, come to think of it.

As she stared into the wedge of headlights plowing through the gloom, she tried to imagine Ed's reaction when he scrolled down his list of incoming e-mail and hit *L. Crocker: youfuckingingrid*. Would he be sick with shame or burned up? Suddenly she wished she hadn't tried to be snide; a plain note on her cream stationery with the deckled edges would have been more honest. She should have spoken the simple truth—*you have hurt me*.

She zipped past a sign that announced WINTER—SPEED LIMIT 25 and jammed on the brakes. That's all she needed—getting pinched, having a cop catch a waft of whiskey on her breath, and ending up in the Winter slammer. That would be a humiliating end for the runaway wife. Ah, hello, Ed? It's me. I've run into a slight problem.

County Road H ran like a chute between the towering red pine walls of the Jump River State Forest. By now, she was dead sober, straining to make out the sandy edge of the road. She'd passed a single car since Winter, a Jeep filled with teenagers with the windows rolled down and a scratchy radio blaring. Lucy could only think of disastrous destinations for joyriding teenagers in these parts—collisions with massive trees, canoes swamped in the middle of desolate lakes, unprotected sex in boarded-up summer camps.

She almost missed the scissors right to Route 70—another dim road heading off past a bunker-style elementary school and a darkened quick stop. By now, she was almost woozy with hunger. Why hadn't she thought to bring a box of food supplies from the gourmet store in Concord before she left—a plump focaccia garnished with fresh rosemary, a pound of the Tanzanian espresso blend, a dozen fresh ginger snaps. Where was she going to find good food around here, even if there was a store that was open? This was the land of iceberg lettuce, Wonder bread, and Wisconsin's gourmet treat, brick cheese and summer sausage on a Saltine. She groped blindly around her feet for another one of Benjy's leftover snacks. There must be something, she thought desperately; he'd munched and sucked steadily all the way from Niagara. Finally, her hand lighted on a pile of Cheez Doodles on the seat and a cellophane wrapper filled with something slippery. She held it up to the windshield and the headlights illuminated a bag of gummy worms the color of a stained glass window. Some dinner—packing peanuts and bait.

At midnight, she passed the public beach at Squirrel Lake and headed east on the correct County Road D—home turf at last. The turnoff to the cabin was only a few miles away and at least it was going to be well marked. Larry had billed her $1,000 for a hand-painted sign. It had been the only one of his many extravagant renovations that she had actually questioned. A thousand bucks for a sign, she had said. What's it made of, plutonium?

He's a very important sign artist, Larry said earnestly. There was a big article about him in *Chicagoland* magazine. The sign's made of Honduras mahogany and has *Lamb* painted in maroon italics, with a landscape of Little Lost Lake, covered with three coats of marine varnish.

She drove another ten miles searching the scrubby roadside for a tasteful hand-carved sign. When County Road D intersected the County N to Dunbar, she knew she'd gone too far and made a U-turn. She finally spotted the dim outlines of a roadside picnic table and trash barrel, a tourist amenity that no one, to her knowledge, had ever used. The turnoff to the cabin was an eighth of a mile beyond. She dropped her speed to five miles an hour, her eyes staring so hard they started to burn and water. Finally she spotted a small gap in the undergrowth and a tilted sign post, but when she turned in, the headlights did not bounce off the gleam of fresh polyurethane. She stopped the car and set it in park. The post was the old one, which once held the original family sign. Lucy made it herself one summer—smashed 7 UP bottles and set the shards in tar smeared on a board with saw-toothed edges. So where did my thousand-dollar investment go, she wondered. Vandalized, of course, just like all the fancy duck mailboxes in Crowley got flattened with baseball bats by marauding teenagers, while the standard aluminum models from the hardware store never got touched. Impractical Larry, she thought fondly.

She set the car in low gear and maneuvered it down the narrow drive. It was slow going—the strip of grass down the middle had grown so high it whapped against the muffler, the overhanging branches scratched along the car doors like giant claws. Why hadn't Larry's contractor at least kept the road cleared? Finally, the gloomy outlines of a cabin loomed into view and the car rolled to a stop against a spongy stump, its headlights shining on a cockeyed staircase leading up to the front porch. The porch railing was warped like a roller-coaster track, a screen door hung drunkenly by a single hinge, its twin panels of rusted screening sprung loose and flapping in the breeze.

Lucy craned over the steering wheel and tried to make sense of what she was seeing. Where was the new screen door for $700, the pressure-treated porch railing and custom-cut balusters for a whopping $1,300, the battery-operated, motion-sensitive security lights for $400 that flicked on automatically if a vehicle pulled up? Slowly, panic gave way to rage. Vandals again, probably crossing the lake in January on Ski-doos, clumping up from the shoreline, smashing a window with a porch rocker, using the balusters as firewood to toast weenies and marshmallows.

She climbed over the back seat and rummaged through a duffel until she found the flashlight she'd been clever enough to pick up at Camper's Warehouse. She opened the door, timidly stepped out, and flashed the beam up the stairs, along the porch and around the door. Toppled furniture, overturned trash cans, more busted screens, but nothing living, nothing lurking. Now that she was outside she could feel the lake, down there somewhere. A breeze off the water carried a medley of peepers and lapping waves, the fragrance of pine pitch. She made her way up the front steps, circumnavigating the rotten spots, carefully wedged open the screen door so it didn't pop off its hinge, and turned the corroded doorknob. Locked. By instinct, she opened the wooden chest by the door, reached under a pile of stiffened flotation cushions, lifted out a rusted Hills Brothers coffee can, and shook out the key. She pried the door open with a hip check and stepped into the large vaulted living room, stinking of mold and piss.

Taking sips of breath through her mouth, she danced the beam around the room, across the pine board kitchen counter, the gateleg table, the field stone fireplace, the saggy green couch and Morris chairs. The only sign of vandalism was by animals—a couch cushion reduced to a heap of horsehair and cotton batting where a mouse family had happily spent the winter, plumes of cobwebs hanging from the log beams. A coffee mug, an ashtray, and an unfolded *Chicago Tribune* perched on the table, as if a ghostly reader had stepped away and would be back any moment. She directed the beam across the headlines: PRESIDENT REAGAN WARNS SOVIETS. The date was August 28, 1982, their last summer at the cabin.

The truth struck her so suddenly that her knees buckled and she settled weakly down on the reader's pulled-out chair. No one had been in the cabin since then, sixteen years ago.

She surveyed the room with the flashlight to confirm her suspicions. There on the trout-patterned couch, a stack of yellow legal pads covered with a thick layer of soot. Not a single item had been reupholstered, replaced, repainted, or reanythinged. For five years, Larry had been sitting on his skinny rear end in his fancy Chicago architecture office, billing her for bogus renovations, while this place slowly, slowly sank into the earth. How much had he cheated from her—it must be close to twenty thousand. God, that treacherous creep! She would sue him, she would put him in jail, she would tattle on him to their mother. Guess what your little favorite did, Mom?

And then, a totally unexpected emotion seeped over her, pushing out all the rage. How grateful she was that not a single thing had been touched. She'd spent years avoiding the memory of her father and this place. Now here he was with his lumberjack notes and coffee and cigarettes, as if he had never left. She lifted one of the butts from the ashtray and examined it. Smoked right down to the filter, as usual. A Tareyton—who in the world still smoked Tareytons, even back in 1982? God bless him and his filthy, fatal smoking habit. "Hey Dad?" she said out loud. "It's Lucy. I've come back." She cocked her head and listened hard, half expecting to hear her father's stuttering voice answer back: "Lu-lu-lucy, I'm so gl-gl-glad."

A scrambling sound came from under the floor boards, as if a fat raccoon were trying to wedge itself through a small hole, followed by a soft *cheep cheep cheep* from behind the fireplace. I'm not spending the night in here, she thought. At least not tonight.

She made her way back down the porch stairs, her foot half sinking through a spongy tread this time. She'd left the car lights on and the car door open, the chime dinging away to warn that the key had been left in the lock. Stupid, she thought, climbing in and autolocking the doors, she could have killed the battery and had to walk ten miles over to Dunbar. She rolled the new sleeping bag across the backseat, climbed in, lowered the last two gummy worms into her mouth, wadded her fleece sweatshirt into a kind of pillow, and closed her eyes with a deep sigh that was almost contented. Why am I happy, she thought, when my life is a complete mess? My sons are huddled together in a flapping pup tent somewhere up in the Canadian wilds. My husband is probably in our antique sleigh bed at this very minute with his publicity director's legs wrapped around his waist. My baby brother has swindled me. My only shelter is a shit hole, literally. Because I am home, she thought, worrying a bit of cherry gummy worm off her back molar with her tongue, at last.

Lucy sat sprawled across the stoop of Dunbar's general store, holding her hands out like a cup to absorb every feeble ray of morning sun, when the girl came at 7:00 A.M. to open up. She pulled her shiny black pickup next to the Taurus, swung her long blue-jeaned legs around and down with a single athletic jump. She scrutinized Lucy's face while she adjusted a pile of curly red hair under a complicated goldtone clip. "Trouble?" she asked.

"Hungry," Lucy answered.

"Oh, we can do something about hungry," she said, opening up the passenger door and sliding out two long cartons tied up with white string. "Like donuts? These are the best in the state, Darcie's donuts up to Eagle River. Drive over there every day at six."

A talker—Lucy didn't think she had the strength to deal

with a talker. The girl handed her the donut boxes to hold while she fished a key ring out of her leather sack. Lucy clutched the warm boxes against her chest and took a deep whiff of yeast and sugar. “Love ’em,” she said. Actually, she had always despised donuts, especially the novelty ones from donut shops covered with pastel frosting or filled with goo. Well, no donut snobbery for me, she thought. Not now, not ever again. I am a new woman.

She set the boxes on the counter and it took every shred of self-control not to rip off one of the lids and dig in. While the girl set a pot of coffee brewing, Lucy busied herself with a slow stroll around Dunbar’s general store, marveling at all the changes. Back when it had been run by foul-tempered, sour-smelling Mr. Dunbar, the boxes of Ritz crackers and Fig Newtons were stale, the popsicles were covered with half an inch of frost, the packages of bologna were a suspicious color. But her father had shopped there anyway, because any place better was another sixty miles away. Now the old wooden shelves were freshly painted and bursting with groceries and hardware supplies, a stand-up dairy case held eastern amenities like Ben & Jerry’s and Snapple. There was even a rack of polar fleece sportswear, a lunch counter with four stools, a magazine rack, and oddly enough, a hairdresser’s chair and sink in the back corner.

Lucy picked up a copy of the *Land O Lakes Ledger,* sat down at the lunch counter where the girl placed a cup of coffee and an entire box of donuts in front of her. “Help yourself,” she said.

Lucy did—first a plain, then a jelly, and finally a chocolate creme-filled, washed down with two cups of coffee. “Mmm,” she grunted.

“When’s the last time you ate?” the girl asked.

Suddenly, it occurred to Lucy how outlandish she must look—dirty, disheveled, stuffing her face like a bag lady. “Breakfast yesterday. But it’s not like I usually skip meals. I dropped my kids off at camp and by the time I got back on the road, all the stores were closed." The girl still looked vaguely worried, as if she suspected Lucy might not be able to come up with the three bucks for coffee and donuts. Lucy decided to try another tactic. "This place sure has improved a lot. Back when I was a kid, it was a complete dump."

"Right. Back when my dad ran the store," the girl said, smiling pointedly.

Her dad? This girl was old enough to have creepy old Mr. Dunbar for a father? Lucy studied her face again—it was the freckled type that can look deceptively young. Her mouth was edged with the beginnings of grooves; she was probably more like thirty. "Ah, sorry."

"That's okay. It was a dump. My husband and I had to put in lotsa elbow grease when we took over six years ago."

The only other person Lucy had ever known who said *elbow grease* was her father—probably learned it from old man Dunbar. The woman closed up the donut box and slowly mopped the counter with a Handi Wipe, ready to share more tales of her transformation of Dunbar's, but Lucy was too distracted. Now that she was no longer famished, she had some pressing business—first give that skunk Larry a piece of her mind, then figure out how to make the cabin habitable. "Is there a pay phone?" The woman nodded to one by the magazines. Lucy had hoped for something a little more private, a phone booth out on County Road D, so she could yell freely.

Larry answered groggily on the eleventh ring. Probably out late, buying a posh meal with Lucy's latest installment. "Fuck you, Larry." The woman stopped wiping and straightened. Lucy gave her a helpless shrug, as if to say this, like wolfing down three donuts, was a tiny aberration of an otherwise well-behaved person.

"Don't be mad at me, Lucy. I can explain everything," he said, suddenly clearheaded.

"I'm listening," she growled, although she could already feel her righteous anger dribbling away. She was never able to resist Larry's wheedling for very long.

"Okay, okay," he said slowly, as if he were gathering his thoughts. She could picture him sitting up in his pickled beech platform bed, groping for his glasses, raking his cowlicky hair back with his fingers. Was Jorge in bed beside him, his sculpted, bronzed arm dangling over the side? It was hard to keep track of what Larry formerly called his lovers, now his partners, although partners did not seem to be much more permanent than lovers. Jorge had been around for almost two years, seemed to live with Larry officially, but usually wasn't there. The last partner, Rolf, had always been there, answering the phone "This is Rolf," until the day he suddenly was not there anymore. "I didn't plan for this to happen, honestly. It wasn't premeditated. A contractor up at Eagle River did give me an estimate five years ago. But then when you sent me the money to have the work done I . . . sort of . . ."

"Kept it."

"More like borrowed it. I had all these expenses for my new office. Rolf and I were redoing the apartment. Then we were both totally stressed, so we needed ten days in Martinique. The Clemintine Inn, with these bamboo cottages right on the beach. So great. You and Ed should go sometime. Unfortunately, Rolf tried to get a tan and got sun poisoning instead. I was always *planning* to get the work done and it wasn't like you were ever going back there, right? It's really unfair to stick me with all the blame. You need to take responsibility for your part in this mess, Lucy."

She almost burst out laughing. Larry could make excuses for anything, including embezzlement. "How is it my fault that you stole twenty thousand dollars?"

"You're the one that said we couldn't let Dad's little shrine fall down, right? But were you willing to take charge of it yourself? No, of course not. You were too busy making a zillion dollars with your computer company. So why not get Larry to do all the work?" His voice rose with indignation.

She was too weary to point out that he hadn't done any actual work. "Look, Larry, you are my baby brother. For some stupid reason, I really love you. If you needed money, you should have asked me."

"I'll pay you back. Soon."

"Just forget it." God knows she'd made enough with Crocker Software to afford a couple of permanent loans to Larry.

"I can come up this weekend and do some of the work myself," he said halfheartedly. "I won't charge you."

"I can handle it. Don't worry."

"Is Ed there?" he said, sounding nervous. Cheating his sister was one thing. Cheating his brother-in-law the software mogul who probably had a pack of mad dog lawyers on retainer was another.

"No."

"The boys?"

"No. Actually, they're going to Camp Kinahwee this summer. I dropped them off yesterday."

"Camp Kinahwee! Oh, God, Lucy. How could you do that to them?"

That's right, Larry had gone to Kinahwee, too, but his camp experience had been less positive, as she recalled. He certainly had never been a Bo Thorne Most Outstanding Camper. "I think they'll have fun," she said.

"Remember that sadist, Uncle Bo? Well, at least he must be six feet under by now. The worst was the senior canoe trip. It was like this death march up to Hudson's Bay where . . ."

"Listen, I've got to go."

"Forgive me?" he said in his meekest baby brother voice.

She let out a loud sigh. She needed all the allies she could get, even Larry. "I forgive you."

The woman was standing statue still when Lucy hung up, as if she were expecting some kind of explanation, but Lucy wasn't sharing this sordid sibling squabble with strangers. She busied herself in the hardware section, filling a shopping cart with every supply she could think of—mop, broom, dustpan, bucket, scrub brush, rubber gloves, Lysol, matches, ant hotels, wasp spray, mouse traps, branch clippers. She threw in a hammer even though she suspected there was more to fixing rotted-out porches and splintered doors than a handful of nails. She filled another cart with groceries, in the remote event that she could somehow get the propane refrigerator to work.

"Looks like you're planning to stay a while," the woman said as Lucy handed her two hundred-dollar bills. She extended her hand, smiling broadly, which caused the lines around her mouth and eyes to furrow deeper. "April Dunbar, now Myette."

"Lucy Lamb, now Crocker," she said, taking hold of the woman's thin, calloused hand. "I'm going to be here for the summer."

"Not in the old Lamb cabin up to Little Lost Lake?" April said, her mascaraed eyes bugging wide. "When we snowmobiled by that place last winter, it looked like it was about to cave in."

"Not yet. At least, I don't think so." Lucy's voice trailed off uncertainly. At sunrise, she had inspected the cabin and grounds to scope out just how bad the situation was. Oddly enough, the cabin had looked both better and worse in daylight than it had the night before. The shit (mouse, raccoon, bat, you name it) and grime that covered every inch of the floor and furniture could be cleaned up with elbow grease—lotsa elbow grease. But then there were certain structural problems—the places in the roof where you could see six inches of daylight, the spot in the bedroom floor under the armoire that sagged. Those weren't so good, she guessed. The other problems—the path down to the beach that had reverted to brambles, the leaning boathouse, the sunken rowboat—those would have to wait.

"How you going to fix that roof?" April asked. When Lucy held up her little shiny hammer, April scoffed. "Look here, Lucy—mind if I call you Lucy? You climb up on that roof and you'll fall right through a rotten beam and break your neck. You don't want to do that, do you?" Lucy shook her head. "My husband, Hank, just got laid off at the lumber mill down at Buck's River. He does carpentry, painting, landscaping. Charges fifteen dollars an hour plus materials. He can be there by ten." April picked up the phone, poised to give Hank his marching orders.

Lucy remembered April now. Bossy little brat, always lecturing them for not wearing shoes in the store or keeping the freezer door open too long.

"At least he's not going to cheat you like your own brother," April added.

I need a Rosemary surrogate, a truth-teller, Lucy thought, someone to give me *my* marching orders. "It's a deal," she said.

By 7:00 that evening, Lucy was tilted back in a porch rocker, her feet perched against the newly fortified railing, gazing down the freshly mowed path at the green Old Towne canoe bobbing against the dock and the sun setting in crimson and orange streaks over Little Lost Lake. In one hand, the first volume of *North American Explorers* opened to the chapter on Pierre Radisson, and in the other, a chilled bottle of Hamm's. Something called "Rizzo-toe! Italiano style"—made from a boxed mix at Dunbar's—slow cooked on the single functioning gas burner. It had been, as Pierre Radisson wrote in his journal, a hard day of paddling. While she had swept up three garbage bags of shit and dirt, Hank, April's bearded hippie husband, patched the roof with tar paper, braced the sagging floor, and replaced the screening on two windows. She had even paddled out to the channel that once led to Sam McCarty's cabin at Twin Pond, but found it covered over with a fifteen-year-old thicket of deadfall and hedge. Just as well—she'd revisited enough old haunts for one day.

Lucy stepped back inside the main room to give the risotto a stir. The cabin still stank of piss and decay; she would have to sleep on the porch for at least a week. The legal pads had been gathered up, dusted off, filed in a neat stack on the bookshelf next to the moldering leather volumes. The ashtray and newspaper had been left in its still-life arrangement on the table. Now, she carefully folded the brittle paper and placed it on top of the lumberjack notes. Then she sealed the red glass ashtray—butts, ash, and all—into a Ziploc bag and set it on the mantel. A relic, as precious as an Ojibwa basket, to be preserved for always.

CHAPTER 8

>>

Ed, staring out the back window so he wouldn't get car sick, reminded himself never to take Crowley Airport Limousine again. First of all, *limousine* was a euphemism for a meals-on-wheels–type van—every bolt rattling, reeking of smoke, with the door handles knocked off and the heat set permanently on full blast, even in summer. The driver, who was probably an ex-con, was taking some circuitous shortcut from the airport through the warehouse districts of Revere and Somerville—all the while accelerating to the beat of Herb Alpert's Tijuana Brass.

It wasn't like the rest of his trip had gone so great, either. The reaction to the new and improved Princess "A" could only be described as lukewarm. The questionnaires filled out by their focus group—fifteen-year-old boys with piercings and Ted Kaczynski T-shirts—had said things like "Thumbs-up for the big boobs, but what's with the chemotherapy haircut?" and "You call that wimpy laser job a gun? Gimme plasma rifles, dudes."

When he had suggested that maybe Crocker should reevaluate its approach to MQII, Ingrid had said, "Oh, not now, Ed." It probably hadn't been a very good time to bring up his reservations—he had been giving her a foot massage, kneading his fingers deep into the sinewy flesh under her high, bony arch. A flood of shame—titillated shame, but nevertheless shame—washed over him as he thought of all the gyrations and positions he'd assumed over the last three days in the Trump Plaza presidential suite. One would have to admit that his relationship with his tantric masseuse had achieved, in Ingrid's words, a new plateau of mutual pleasuring. Or as his mom would say, he was doing the big uh-oh. A list of lame excuses scrolled through his mind—I didn't mean to do it, I was powerless to stop her, to stop myself.

Ed let out a moan and clapped a hand over his eyes. Forget about getting carsick, he had to shut out all the sordid images leering up in his face. Oh, he missed his little family, Lucy and the boys. How soon before he'd be back to them? He peeked through his fingers to get his bearings—the limousine was just weaving past the Alewife subway station, another forty minutes at least. He pressed his eyes shut again and tried to visualize the home scene that awaited him. Ingrid had been the one who had taught him about visualization, but no matter. Benjy and Phil, not holed up in their room with their goddamn computers for once; no, in the kitchen playing a board game—Monopoly, maybe (they must have a Monopoly set somewhere), while Lucy stirred a copper pot on the stove, something warm and comforting that would soothe his upset stomach, her risotto with porcini mushrooms. Yes, that would be nice. He was grateful she was back into cooking again, after a year of all those organic frozen dinners. Had he told her how much he loved her cooking, how much he loved her recently?

He had bought her a spectacular pair of earrings when he was in New York—teardrops of carved jade set in filigreed gold. He had seen them spotlit on a black velvet pillow in the window of a fancy boutique in the Trump lobby and bought them on impulse. They were ridiculously expensive, of course, everything was in those hotel boutiques—no one but an Arab sheik would actually shop there. He dreamily imagined the green lobes swinging into her dark hair, accenting the blue of her eyes. Then he wondered what she would make of such a gift—it wasn't as if he were in the habit of bringing gold jewelry back from gamer conventions. Would she suspect that he was trying to relieve a guilty conscience? Maybe he'd better save the earrings for their anniversary at the end of July. They would really celebrate it for a change, have a big party with a swing band, a clambake catered by Legal Seafood, a tent in the backyard, maybe even renew their wedding vows.

I swear that I will never touch Ingrid again, I swear that I will never allow Ingrid to touch me again, he vowed. He had a flash of Ingrid's hands, with the long palms, the short red nails, the stack of silver rings on her right index finger. The way they looked so white and strong against his shoulder, his chest, cupped inside his own hands. Yes, well, this wasn't going to be easy, it wasn't supposed to be easy. That was the point of vows—to suppress your own base desires for the welfare of others.

He would explain his resolve to Ingrid on Monday, call her into his office, shut the door. On second thought, if there was going to be a big scene, maybe it should be at a less intimate spot, like the terrace of Au Bon Pain in Harvard Square. He would say, I can't do this anymore, I love my family, I love my wife, I can't betray them like this. She would understand his love for his kids, if not his love for Lucy, who she said was a dingbat. He tried to imagine her face as he broke the news—her pale complexion flushing in blotchy red patches, her cupid's bow mouth pinching tight, a plucked, bleached eyebrow arching up with dismay. Would she be relieved, brokenhearted, enraged? He swallowed hard at the thought of being the target of Ingrid's full-blown wrath. No doubt about it, she could make things very sticky for him and telling all to Lucy was just the least of it. He himself had written the Crocker sexual harassment policy: "Crocker employees are forbidden from engaging in any sexual contact, consensual or otherwise, with subordinates." Uh, oh. Maybe he could give her some stock options or find her a really great job somewhere else, maybe Dragon Dreams Software. Roth owed him one, didn't he?

The Crowley "limo" bumped to a halt and Ed opened his eyes to see the marble path leading up to their fortress-size house, now pitch black. It was probably just as well that Lucy and the boys were off somewhere, he thought, as he climbed out and handed the driver a completely undeserved ten-buck tip. He needed some time to settle his stomach, change his clothes, shake off that I-just-spent-four-days-in-bed-with-another-woman aura.

He stumbled over a pile of newspapers and mail on the dark porch. Had Lucy said something about going off for a few days? Probably, and he'd been too distracted to listen. That would change, he would change, he thought, as he groped his way down the long unlit hallway to the kitchen. He flicked on the overhead. Yes, spotless counters and empty sink definitely meant they were away, but at least Lucy had left him a note—it would be embarrassing to have to admit he'd forgotten where they'd gone to.

He had to read the squiggly, smudged words twice before he fully understood that the note had been written by Phil, not Lucy. He sank down onto a chair, fighting back a panicky sensation that Phil must be in danger. Why else would he resort to pen and paper instead of e-mail? Ed tried to analyze its meaning phrase by phrase: *Sorry about the Internet thing, some cool river rafter sandals, see you in six weeks or sooner if we hate it.* Well, apparently, the boys had done something so horrendous on the Internet that Lucy had sent them off to her stupid canoe camp, but what?

Ed leaned back in his chair and scrutinized the tidy kitchen, trying to imagine the knock-down, drag-out scene he'd missed. Benjy with his shoulders twisted at a stubborn angle and his glasses skewed while Lucy tried to pry the mouse out of his clenched fist. Then Phil jumping in, his long hair falling over his face, his fretful eyes darting back and forth between his mother and Benjy. We'll stop now, right, Benj? Always the peacemaker who would agree to do anything, just to smooth over any friction. Maybe he had been the one to suggest camp and had badgered Benjy to go along, just to please his mother.

Ed reached over and punched the blinking play button on the answering machine—Lucy would have left him a phone message, of course, from the road. But no, it was the usual sundry messages for members of the Crocker family—from the lawn service, from his mother, from BPCC clients, from Rosemary about next weekend's flea markets, from the neighbors inviting them to a Fourth of July barbecue. No one else seemed to know that his family had fled, much less where.

Now the trickle of panic gave way to a deluge. Ed jumped up and paced through the rest of the house like a nervous red setter, searching for more notes or clues. The boys' floor was littered with wrappers, boxes, and price tags. He picked up a glossy instruction brochure: *Congratulations! You are now the proud owner of the Basic Two-Man Backcountry Dome!* A color photograph showed a smiling blond couple effortlessly setting up the two-man by the edge of a mountain lake—she popping the frame together one-handed while he hammered in a tent stake. Ed dropped the brochure with a shudder. The first time Lucy had taken Ed camping back in their courting days, it had taken them a full hour of squabbling to erect the WW II-vintage pup tent. Later, either to make up or to show him the erotic pleasures of camping, she had insisted on making love and he had bruised his tailbone on a rock. He had suspected that she'd been comparing him the whole time to that ex-boyfriend of hers.

Ed tried to blink away the image of Phil and Benjy with something called an "Allagash Waterproof Pack" strapped to their backs, ankle-high lug-soled hiking boots tied to their feet, their heads swathed in mosquito net hats. How could Lucy dress them up in something so clownish and cruel?

Lucy's office had been mysteriously rearranged. The MQI posters were crumpled into the trash and in their place was that grotesque stuffed fish that Lucy's father had caught when he'd been sent off to Little Lost Lake when he was something like twelve. Just looking at its peeling gills and crooked yellowed teeth made Ed's flesh crawl. He picked up the torn fragments of a watercolor and pieced them back together like a puzzle. It was that damn fish again. Maybe Lucy had a new career illustrating fly fishing manuals.

In their bedroom, Ed made another search for a note from Lucy—under his pillow, inside the drawer of his night table, on top of the toilet. If she had flown out to Michigan or Minnesota or wherever the hell Camp Kinahwee was to drop the boys, she should be back any minute. Unless she was planning to drop by Libertyville to watch her mother get crocked and make snide comments about him and the boys. What is it that Ed does again, something with computers? I keep forgetting, Corky would say, pouring out Jack Daniel's with a withered, spotted hand, the platinum and diamond rings jangling up to an enlarged knuckle.

He opened Lucy's closet, a big walk-in with shelves and lights that flicked on automatically, and tried to figure out what she had taken with her. The row of dresses seemed undisturbed. He lifted the hem of a long, filmy green skirt with pale yellow roses, rubbed it against his cheek, then inhaled. A faint trace of Miss Dior. Ingrid disapproved of perfume or aftershave, said it covered up your body's natural musk, and he had to admit Ingrid did smell pretty goddamn delicious. But he loved Lucy's perfume, too, which she dabbed behind her ears and along the side of her neck with a long glass stopper right before she went out at night. And even though Ingrid said Lucy's clothes were dowdy, he admired the way the thin material clung to her slim hips and long thighs. He noticed a gap in the neatly lined-up shoes along the wall. Her hiking boots, he finally guessed.

He closed the closet and checked out the rest of the room. Hairbrush from bureau gone. He dropped to his knees and peeked under the bed skirt. There was his violin and a dust-free rectangular spot where her old canvas rucksack had lain. Now, where would his wife go with her hiking boots, hairbrush, and rucksack?

After another prowl through the house, including the attic and the basement, he was back in Lucy's office with a bowl of Frosted Flakes in one hand, checking his e-mail—the last place to look. When he spotted *L.Crocker: youfuckingingrid,* his arm flinched so violently that milk sloshed over the mouse and down his pant leg. His first reaction was indignation—We never actually fucked, he thought. Ingrid insisted on the purer tantric methods of "mutual pleasuring" rather than "intragenital contact," which in fact seemed much naughtier, much more adulterous, than plain old fucking. When he read Lucy's e-mail, he had another odd reaction—surprise that she'd figured out how to cut and paste Ingrid's e-mail into hers. To make matters worse, she'd thrown back at him all the sordid details—the huckleberry massage oil, his lingam. Christ, how embarrassing.

Then the reality struck him like waves breaking against a seawall—she'd found out, she was furious, she'd split, and taken the boys with her. His family was gone.

He carefully set down the cereal bowl and mopped up the milk spills with one of Lucy's paint rags. As he bent down, he caught his reflection in the blackened window glass and half expected to see his degradation imprinted across his face—sagging jowls, warty nose, eyes narrowed to shifty slits. But here he was, Ed Crocker, the adulterer who had just been caught by his wife en flagrante, still as boyish and innocent as ever, hair blond and unreceding, stomach flat. Surely it was a character flaw, that he could do such evil and still look so unblemished.

He felt as if he were playing the lead role in some clichéd farce about a philandering husband who gets his comeuppance. What was the next scene, where was his script? He wanted to grab the phone and call Lucy, say something that would magically undo what had been done, restore her and the boys to the kitchen with the Monopoly game and the porcini risotto on slow simmer. But for starters, he had no idea where she was. He considered the possibilities—at her mother's, at Rosemary's, dead in a motel room. He stopped, chilled. Was she desperate enough to attempt suicide? Nah, forget it. That feisty e-mail was written by someone who was homicidal, not suicidal. No doubt she considered his transgressions with Ingrid too puny and pathetic to kill herself over.

Then another unpalatable truth slowly dawned on him—he would have to call someone and ask, Do you happen to know where my wife is? He decided on Rosemary—she would be the friendliest, the least judgmental. She might even find it amusing—men are so predictable, incorrigible, hopeless. Ha, ha, ha, he would laugh along, always the good sport.

Rosemary picked up groggily on the tenth ring. Ed checked his watch—only 10:30—but then remembered that Rosemary and Alfred always turned in by 9:00, so they could get the requisite ten hours suggested by the AMA for maximum mental acuity.

"Hi, Rosie. It's me, Ed."

"Ed," she said, suddenly awake, worried. "What's the matter?"

"Nothing. I just called to say hello, see how you guys are doing."

A pause. "Oh, come on, Ed. Cut the bullshit. You've never called me in all the years I've known you. I always call you. Something's wrong."

"Not wrong exactly. I just got home from a computer conference and Lucy and the boys are gone. I'm sure Lucy told me they were going off for the weekend and I've just, you know, forgotten." He tried to say this airily. More silence on the other end; Rosemary was not going to make this easy. "So, you don't happen to know where she went, do you?"

"I just had lunch with her four days ago. She didn't say anything about going anywhere." Rosemary sounded more indignant than alarmed. How dare Lucy make plans without consulting her first. "Did she leave a note?"

"Not a note, an e-mail." Uh oh, that was a strategic mistake.

"An e-mail . . . *from Lucy?* That's strange. What did it say?" Her voice took on a worried edge.

"She sounded a little stressed."

"Stressed," she repeated back at him.

"I think she might be mad at me."

"Might be."

A big sigh wheezed out of him. "She's really ripped. She thinks I'm having some kind of relationship with this woman at work."

"Thinks."

"Okay, okay, Rosemary. Maybe there was something, but it wasn't as bad as she thinks. And besides, it's all over now. I want to call her up and explain."

"Oh, I see. Explain."

"Will you stop repeating everything I say. So, where is she?"

"I don't know, Ed," she said, her voice a mournful whisper as if someone had died. Why couldn't Rosemary be her usual bossy know-it-all self? "Maybe you should try her mother."

First, she worms a confession out of him and now she's telling him to try Corky? "Thanks for your help," he said unpleasantly.

"Ed, I am trying to be helpful. Okay, first you find her. Then what are you going to say to her?"

"That I'm sorry?"

"That's a good start. Anything else?"

"That I want her to forgive me, that I want her to come back. That she and the boys are the most important things in my life. That I couldn't survive without them. That I'm a complete jerk. Does that about cover it?"

"Look, Ed. This isn't just about you having an office fling. You and Lucy have been drifting apart for a long, long time.

The more she got lost in her sadness about the miscarriages, the more you buried yourself in your work. Even when we were all together at the Wheeler bungalows last August, it was as if you two lived in separate time zones. When you were bobbing the waves, she was doing her one mile of laps. When you went to the video arcade with the boys, she pedaled off on the bike trail. You've got to do better than saying you're sorry. You've got to figure out what's been pulling you away from her, and her from you. And I really hope you do, because you two are our best friends." The pep talk came out polished, as if she and Alfred had spent considerable time analyzing the fault lines in the Crocker's marriage. "Remember the Preston Sturges revival at the Kenmore?" she added.

"Yeah," he said, his voice wavering. During Lucy and Rosemary's first year at Simmons Library School, they had gone on a double date. Rosemary and Alfred, Lucy and Ed, both couples living together but not married. It was the first time Ed had met Rosemary's nerdy economist boyfriend, who had insisted on going to some triple feature by a director no one had ever heard of because it worked out to be the best deal, only seventy-five cents per movie. When he suggested that they also bring their own popcorn, citing statistics about movie theaters making ninety percent of their profits by overcharging on concessions, Ed was about to blow his stack. Then Lucy jumped in, saying her popcorn was much better than that stale stuff anyway. Always the peacemaker, just like Phil. She made them each brown paper sacks of popcorn, drizzled with so much butter that the paper turned translucent. Oh, my, how they had laughed—at Rex Harrison plotting to murder his wife, Barbara Stanwyck scheming to entrap Henry Fonda. Alfred especially, with one of those high-pitched, maniac brays that makes everyone else in the theater join in. Afterward, on the sidewalk, he and Alfred had replayed a couple of the hysterical moments, then fallen weakly into each other's arms, friends forever.

"Why don't they have triple features anymore?" Rosemary said, sounding shaky, too.

"Why don't we laugh like that anymore?" he said, choking up. She answered with a sniffle and he snuffled back. They went back and forth for a few minutes, like dueling banjos.

She offered to take him out to lunch at Buddy's rib house after he'd found Lucy. "I always take my friends out to lunch when they've been fired or get divorced. I took Lucy out last week. Now it's your turn."

"I'm not getting divorced yet."

She hung up saying, "I love you, you asshole."

The call to Corky was far less cathartic, thank goodness. "Lucy? No, I have no idea where she is," she said, far too sloshed to be alarmed that her daughter was missing. "Got to run. *ER*'s on, and I'm dying to find out if Dr. Ross is going to get back together with that Carol Hathaway. Too bad her hair is so long and messy, sort of like Lucy's. Why can't you get Lucy to cut her hair, Ed? A short bob, like Audrey Hepburn's, would be so becoming."

All right, that left Larry, but Ed hesitated. He was in no mood to put up with Larry's cozy chatter and it didn't seem very likely that she would tell him, of all people, where she was bolting off to.

"Oh, Ed," Larry said, sounding suspiciously ingratiating. Ed steeled himself to get hit up for another renovation bill. "I've been expecting your call. I'm ashamed, just ashamed of myself. I'll repay every last penny, I promise. Just as soon as we get paid for the Merchandise Mart job."

"What are you talking about?"

"You haven't talked to Lucy?"

"You have?" he said, his voice rising hysterically.

"Yesterday morning."

She was safe and sound, thank God. He would make it up to her, he would repent every day for the rest of his life. "Where was she?"

"Dunbar's."

"Where?"

"Dunbar's general store. It's about ten miles from the cabin."

Lucy had gone to Little Lost Lake? Ed's fuzzy brain struggled to make sense of this information. Here was this place that she had been avoiding for all the years he had known her. Then she discovers her husband, um, misbehaving and where does she flee for safety, solace, whatnot . . . Cyrus's fishing shack up in the old north woods. There was only one way to look at it—Lucy had gone off the deep end, literally. "When's she coming back? Did she say?"

"She's planning to spend the summer there. What's with you two, anyway? Having troubles?" There was an unmistakable note of pleasure in his voice.

Confessing to Rosemary was one thing, confessing to Larry, who would see their marital woes as nothing more than juicy gossip, was another. Let him draw his own conclusions. "What's the phone number at the cabin?" He was impatient now—a man with a mission.

"There is no phone at the cabin. That's why she was calling from Dunbar's."

Ed had a hard time picturing a spot in the civilized world unattached by an umbilical cord of cable or wire. "So, how can I get in touch with her?"

"Mail her a letter at Dunbar's." He was enjoying this.

"FedEx?"

"That would probably work."

"By the way, what are you so ashamed about?"

"Never mind."

Ed carefully replaced the receiver, then started swiveling back and forth in Lucy's desk chair, ruminating. He was going to have to write a letter that was so inspired and articulate that she would come scurrying back from Little Lost Lake, into his arms, into his bed, forgiving and forgetting his transgressions forever. A tall order—Ed had problems enough writing a persuasive interoffice memo. He studied the oddball stuff tacked to the wall above Lucy's computer for a hint on where to begin—a Beatrix Potter calendar with a picture of a duck confiding to a fox, two ticket stubs from the MIT orchestra's performance of the Bruch violin concerto back in 1983 (Ed had been the soloist, the pinnacle of his music career), a Baggie of snippets of the boys' hair from their first trip to the barbershop (Benjy's curl almost white), a snapshot of her father with waders, creel, and cigarette. Lucy, Lucy, he thought hopelessly, I will never understand how your mind works. Rosemary had it only partially right. Lucy had always inhabited her own time zone.

Dear Lucy, he tapped out on her keyboard and then stopped. A letter of abject repentance should be handwritten, not word processed, he guessed. He rifled through Lucy's desk drawers until he found a few sheets of stationery and a fat black Waterman fountain pen nested in a leather box, which he had bought for her at Dunhill's on a business trip to London. She had acted pleased, had made a few calligraphy doodles on the wrapping paper, but he had never seen her use it. Another mysterious Lucy reaction, like that tin of colored pencils she'd never used. He glanced around to its usual spot on a bookshelf, but it was gone—how strange. Add tin of pencils to hiking boots, hairbrush and rucksack.

He tried the pen on a piece of scrap paper and it still worked, much to his surprise.

Dear Lucy, he began again. His handwriting was small and elegant, but he used a pen so infrequently that his hand would start aching after a couple of lines. Well, no one said this was going to be easy. *I am so sorry*. About what—the affair, relationship, thing? Better stay nonspecific, no reason to go into tawdry details—*I am so sorry I have hurt you.* Okay, what next?

Ed tilted back in the chair and closed his eyes. He remembered an article he had read in *American Way* magazine about a woman who taught writing workshops in an adobe hut in Santa Fe. It had been called "Sucking Out the Marrow," or some such. There had been a picture of her, round as a Buddha and decked out with big turquoise slabs of Indian jewelry, surrounded by a coven of female disciples all hunched over their leather-bound journals, writing furiously. Her method had been to write for half an hour without stopping or lifting the pen—just write whatever pops into your head.

Ed set his stopwatch—on your mark, get set, go!

Lucy, first time I ever saw you. September 2, 1982—see, I even remember the date!—and it was the day every student in Boston was moving, streets were clogged with U-Hauls. I stepped out of my apartment, late for orchestra rehearsal as usual, and I see this cardboard box of squashed paint tubes propped against the door to your apartment. Then hear this melodious voice, stick my head over railing to look down stairwell and there's yours staring back. Those huge blue eyes, the dark hair swinging to one side. Oh, is my stuff in the way? you asked, smiling your smile. And I thought, fate has sent me a beautiful artist to fall in love with. Then that hairy forest ranger sticks his maw in the way. What do you want? he snarls.

I am looking at the ticket stubs for the Bruch violin concerto tacked above your desk. Bless you for keeping them. I was so nervous I was trembling before we went on stage. You, in a long velvet skirt and lace blouse, led me into a broom closet and gave me a hand job to help me relax, then afterwards straightened my tie and tucked in my shirt. What a thoughtful thing to do. And I played better than I ever had in my whole life, than I ever will again . . .

Our boys, our twins. Do you remember that first ultrasound? The technician rolling the tracking ball across your already puffed-out belly, saying, "Here is the baby's heartbeat, and here is the baby's heartbeat." "Right," I said, thinking he was showing us two views of the same baby. "Ed, don't be dense," you cried, jolting upright in your johnny. "He's saying it's twins." You looked upset, but I was filled to the brim with joy. Because, you see, I always wondered if you loved me, if you'd married me for lack of better options. And now here were two babies, not just one, to bind us together . . .

When I was riding home tonight, getting carsick the whole way as usual, I was picturing the scene waiting for me at home. You and the boys in the kitchen—them playing Monopoly by candlelight, you cooking something on the stove with a delicious aroma. When I found a cold, dark house, I felt so empty and alone. I cannot survive without my family, without you and the boys. Even though I have no right to ask, I am asking anyway. Please come home . . .

By the time his throbbing hand forced him to stop, he had covered seven sheets of paper and had been at it for fifty-eight minutes. He considered reading what he had written, but then remembered the fat lady's proclamation—never edit, never self-censor. Okay, he would pop it into a FedEx envelope tomorrow, send it off to the Dunbar's general store, wherever that was, and see if it got a rise out of Lucy. This writing stuff was fun—he would try it again tomorrow, start a daily habit. Maybe he would even get one of those tooled leather journals they sold in Barnes & Noble next to the cash register.

Now it was almost one in the morning. He stumbled down the dark hallway back to their bedroom, too exhausted to consider brushing his teeth or undressing. He threw himself, shoes and all, across the bedspread and shut his eyes. The letter danced through his head, line by line. Lucy in the dark closet, pressing him against a barrel of industrial cleaner, his hands smoothing down the soft nap of her skirt, while she unzipped his fly and reached inside. Then her on a table, draped, her stomach slit open, as the doctors lifted the twins out, first Benjy, then Phil, slippery, angry blue color, their cords tangled. Ed hammered the heel of his hand against his forehead to knock these images away. He tried to think of something else—the Bruch concerto. He pictured himself standing in front of the orchestra, head bowed as the soft roll of the timpani wafted over the audience, nervously tightening his bow, then lifting the violin to his shoulder as the woodwinds started in on their melody—finally drawing out the first long open G and letting the instrument send its mournful arpeggio soaring into the hushed expectant stillness of the concert hall.

CHAPTER 9

>>

When Lucy strolled into Dunbar's at the dot of seven for her daily fix of watery coffee and Darcie's donuts, April greeted her at the door, holding a FedEx envelope by one corner at arms length as if it were a wild chipmunk that might whirl around and bite her. "This came for you yesterday," she said. "It's from some man who says he's your husband. He called asking if we could get a FedEx to you. I said maybe." She gave Lucy a conspiratorial wink.

In three days, Lucy had already been gathered under April's wing—another Dunbar customer to be protected from IRS auditors, parole officers, game wardens, abusive ex-husbands. And why wouldn't she think Lucy was hiding out from something? She had vaguely mentioned having two sons at camp, but nothing else about her personal life—where she was from, where she was heading, certainly nothing about a husband. She had shed her wedding ring the first day of cabin cleaning with the excuse that the heavy-duty detergents would make it chafe, then had never put it on again because her finger had felt so naked and free.

So Ed had tracked her down, through Larry, she supposed. "Thanks," Lucy said, taking the envelope and settling on the sunny front step with a large coffee and a butter crunch donut. She was gradually working her way through all of Darcie's varieties, and so far Boston creme pie was her favorite.

A sheaf of handwritten pages was hardly what she expected when she tore open the envelope, although it was difficult to say what she did expect her estranged spouse to FedEx to the Wisconsin wilderness—a Crocker Software memo, maybe. She read it leisurely, with butter crunch crumbs punctuating each page. She had forgotten what stylish handwriting Ed had, and it even looked as if he had used a fountain pen. *I am so sorry I have hurt you*—infuriatingly vague, not owning up to anything. The backstage broom closet—now there was a scene she hadn't thought of in years. She shut her eyes, tipped her face up to the sunlight—Ed's ragged breath against her neck in the darkness, the smell of ammonia, a can of Borax clattering off a high shelf, dusting her satin pumps. But his description of her and the boys in the kitchen awaiting his return from New York was infuriating—as if he could remember the last time the boys played Monopoly. How dare he be wistful when he had chucked their marriage, their family life out the window. And then his final paragraph:

> *Please, let me come to the cabin. I can charter a plane and be in there in twelve hours. Maybe with some time by ourselves away from Crocker and the boys and all the other distractions, we can figure out why we have been drifting apart.*

Boy, did that burn her up! Away from all the other distractions—you mean like Ingrid. And you did the drifting, buddy, not we. Suddenly, she had a sickening feeling that he was already on his way, about to barge into her safe haven. No, she would not allow it. She stuffed his letter back into its cardboard envelope, jumped up, and stormed toward the telephone on the back wall.

"Got to make an important call," she blurted.

"Go ahead," said April. As usual, she had been standing with arms crossed behind the counter, watching, drawing her own conclusions.

Ed picked up on the first ring. "Lucy?" he said.

Had he been standing in wait by the telephone for the last two days, answering every call "Lucy?"

"Yeah, it's me, Ed," she said tonelessly.

"Did you get my letter?" he asked, his voice relieved, eager.

"Yes. And no, you cannot come."

A pause. "Why not?" He sounded surprised.

"Why not? You've been screwing your publicity director, that's why not. End of discussion. Period." She swiveled around to see what April was making of Lucy's latest telephone drama. April grinned and gave her a thumbs-up—give him hell, girl.

"You mean you're not going to give me another chance?" he said softly.

Is that what she meant? Ever since she had discovered Ingrid's e-mail, her thoughts had been focused on fleeing—Ed, their marriage, Crocker, Crowley. Her plan thus far was to stay at Little Lost Lake until the boys were finished at camp. Beyond that, her future was a swirling void. "I don't know. For now, I just need to be at Little Lost Lake by myself."

"Doing what?"

"Not much. Taking hikes, going through Dad's research notes, paddling on the lake, working on sketches for my book." In truth, her drawing supplies hadn't made it out of the car, but why did she have to justify her activities to Ed, of all people?

"So, what did you do with the boys?" The tone of his voice had suddenly shifted from contrite to accusatory.

"Just like I explained in my e-mail, they decided to go to Kinahwee for six weeks." Her self-righteousness was evaporating.

"Oh, come on, do you expect me to believe that Benjy and Phil out of the blue said, Gee, Mom, we've changed our minds, camp sounds like more fun than running BPCC. You must have blackmailed them somehow. That's what Phil implied in his note."

A note—God knows what Phil could have said. Mom totally flipped out and started shrieking. You have done nothing wrong, she reminded herself. Your children were at risk and needed to be protected. Any responsible mother would have done just the same thing. "They were looking at blowjob photographs on the Internet." The word *blowjob* ricocheted off the walls like it had been fired out of a gun. Lucy didn't have the courage to turn around and check out April's reaction this time—maybe the term *blowjob* hadn't made it north of Madison yet. "I suppose you think that's an appropriate thing for thirteen year olds to be doing," she added, her voice frosty. That's right. Who's got the moral upper hand here, anyway?

Ed let out a long, sobered sigh. "Of course, I don't approve. But they're thirteen, you know. It's normal to be curious about sex. They shouldn't be punished, like they've done something disgusting or bad."

Lucy clenched her eyes tightly so she wouldn't have to see her distorted reflection on the chrome coin return. She hadn't made the boys feel ashamed, had she? Well, maybe a little bit, but why was she being turned into the transgressor? "Going to Camp Kinahwee is not punishment, Ed. It is a healthy and constructive way for teenage boys to spend their time. It certainly is a better alternative than surfing porn on the Internet. I do not think that I have done anything that I need to apologize for." The words came out with a drumbeat of conviction. What a fraud I am, she thought.

"No, no, you're right," he said, back to his groveling self. "I just worry about them at some macho wilderness camp. What if they can't cut it or the other kids pick on them?"

What had Larry called the senior canoe trip—a death march? "They'll be . . . just . . . fine," she whispered.

"All right. I trust your judgment. I always have."

She didn't have the stomach for one more word of this conversation. "Someone needs to use this phone. I've got to go now."

"Will you call me?" he pleaded.

"No. As I said, I need to be by myself to sort things out."

"Will you write me?"

"No."

"Can I write you?"

"Sure. But no FedEx, please. Just stick on a stamp."

"I love . . . " he began as she hung up.

"I'm not going to explain what that was about," said Lucy, turning around to face April.

"Your phone conversations are private. None of my business."

Lucy made a slow perusal of the magazine rack, trying to figure out what she should do with the rest of the day now that she had already discussed adultery and divorce over breakfast. Maybe she should buy a stack of women's magazines and a tube of coconut suntan oil. Now that she was officially single until the middle of August, she could read up on beauty and dating tips, lounging on a deck chair at the end of the dock. She checked out a few headlines: NEW YORK'S TOP MADAME SHARES TEN SECRETS FOR PLEASING A MAN, DON'T MAKE A FIRST DATE INTO A LAST DATE, SHAPE YOUR THIGHS FOR SUMMER. Then again, preparing for the perfect date in the middle of nowhere did seem a bit pointless. She spun the carousel of romance novels. Maybe she should forget about reality and lose herself in a tale of perfect love instead.

"You ever read any of these?" she asked April.

"Oh, sure. Hank likes me to read the love scenes out loud."

"Any particular one you might recommend."

"Let's see." April ambled over and bent down, giving Lucy a nice view of her slim, blue-jeaned rear end and curly red ponytail hanging over a freckled, bare shoulder. Yes, she could see April and Hank having a fine old time reenacting the racy parts of *Love's Splendid Fury.* She considered a few, then handed Lucy one called *Prairie of Passion,* with a voluptuous pioneer woman standing in front of a sod dugout, staring out into a fiery sunset. "Try this one."

Lucy perused the jacket blurb. Boston school marm Samantha Savage thought she was destined to become a spinster, until she saw the advertisement for a mail-order bride! But her mail-order husband, Seth Adams, with his crude manners and dug-out cabin on the lonely prairie was not what she had expected. Seth was ruthless, barbaric, and yet he ignited within her a passion that Samantha had never dreamed existed! "Great. I'll try it," she said, not quite ready to banish herself back to the cabin. She pointed toward the hairdressing chair and sink in the corner. "What's that for, anyway?"

"Oh, that's mine. I went to beautician's school up in Iron Mountain before I married Hank and took over the store. So now Dunbar's even has a little beauty parlor."

Lucy leaned over so she could inspect herself in the mirror hanging in front of the aqua blue chair. Since there was nothing more than a hand pump at the cabin, she had made do with bathing and hair washing in the lake. She'd given up trying to brush out the tangles and had taken to simply pulling the mess back into an elastic. "I think I need a new look," she said, climbing into the chair.

April shrugged noncommittally and slipped a pink cape over her shoulders. "What did you have in mind?"

"You're the expert. You tell me."

April snipped the elastic with her pointy haircutting scissors, tried to fan out the matted strands, then scrutinized Lucy in the mirror. "What if we bring it up to here to accentuate your nice jawline," she said, making an imaginary cut with her fingers. Did they teach hairdressers to talk this way in beauty school? "Then blow-dry straight, with a slight flip under. The Courteney Cox look."

"Who?"

"You know, that girl on *Friends,*" she said, ushering Lucy over to the sink and lowering her head.

"Oh, right." She should probably pretend she knew a little about popular culture or April might really get suspicious, think she had spent the last five years in jail. "Hot water. You don't know how good that feels."

"I can guess," said April, squirting on what seemed like an extralarge dose of shampoo. "Now, shut your eyes and relax. You've had a rough morning."

I *have* had a rough morning, thought Lucy as she let her head loll back and submitted. Maybe it was the gentle hiss of the water nozzle or the sensation of April's fingers massaging suds into her hairline, but she found herself slipping into a lady-at-the-beauty-parlor confessional mood. "I was talking to my husband on the phone."

April let out a tiny laugh. "I kind of guessed that."

"I found this e-mail from his publicity director. We run this software company together. Believe it or not, I'm this pretty well-known computer game designer. You probably didn't think I did anything for a living and I suppose now that I'm here, I actually don't. Where was I?"

"The e-mail?" April said as she rinsed off the back of Lucy's ears.

"Oh, right. Here she's telling him in an e-mail that she's reserved the presidential suite at the Trump Plaza for them and she's bringing along some flavored massage oil. Well, I freak out. So while he's off in New York getting massaged, I jump in the car with my two sons and take off. You probably didn't know I had thirteen-year-old twin sons, either. I guess I've been kind of secretive. I dropped them off at camp in Kinahwee Falls and then I came here."

"*Mmm,*" said April in the same empathetic tone used by a therapist, or Rosemary, who Lucy suddenly missed with a pang. Maybe this was something else they taught in beauty school—how to act like your customer's best friend so she spills out her guts and leaves a big tip.

"Do you ever wonder what would have happened if you had married someone else? If I'd never met Ed, I never would have ended up designing computer games. I might have had twins, but at least they wouldn't be complete clones of their father." Lucy was shocked to hear herself describe her boys so dismissively, as if they were defective merchandise that needed to be exchanged for a better model. Maybe she could imagine herself married to a different man than Ed—at least one that was faithful—or with a different career. But she couldn't imagine different kids than her oddball boys.

April's hands slacked off slightly, as if she couldn't shampoo and consider the full weight of Lucy's cosmic question all at one time. "I guess I never thought I'd end up with anyone but Hank. Then again, I never really knew any other boys 'cept Hank 'cause we've been going together since tenth grade. Never thought about having any other kids but Hank Junior and little April. Never thought I'd do anything else but go to beauty school and then eventually run Dunbar's store. Not that I think that my husband or my kids or this store are jim-dandy. Just never considered any other possibilities."

"My boyfriend before Ed was his polar opposite. Antiurban, antitechnology. Totally committed to his causes—stop logging, stop commercial fishing, whatever. Ed doesn't have any causes, except maybe bust up Microsoft."

"So why didn't you marry your tree hugger."

"Well, we talked about getting married. We were going to be homesteaders in the Yukon. Build our own shelter, hunt our own food. Some really realistic plan like that." Her voice took on a sneering tone, but who was the target—Sam McCarty for painting such preposterous dreams, or herself for believing them? "But then . . . it didn't work out." Her voice trailed off sheepishly.

April wrung her hair out like a washcloth, then wrapped it in a turban and straightened her up. Lucy blinked as if she were just waking up from a long winter's nap. Here she was back by the magazine rack and stand-up cooler in Dunbar's store. The four formerly empty stools at the lunch counter were now occupied by a UPS man, a postman in his summer shorts and blue kneesocks, and a couple of nonuniformed old geezers. She hadn't even heard the screen door whap open. Had they been eavesdropping on her dopey musings about true love, marriage, and homesteading in the Yukon? When she glanced over, all four simultaneously dropped their eyes as if they'd discovered something interesting floating in their coffee. Well, it's probably good for them to hear what women talk about when they are by themselves.

April pumped up the chair and then with three brisk swipes of the scissors, whacked one side of Lucy's hair up to her chin—before and after, all at once. "You may even have known this guy," said Lucy, dropping her voice to a near whisper that she hoped was out of range of the coffee klatch. "His family had a camp north of Little Lost Lake on Twin Pond. It was a Rock Island caboose. The McCartys?" She felt ashamed even asking April about her old love, but curiosity had gotten the better of her.

"McCarty," said April slowly. Clearly Sam McCarty had not been a regular customer of Dunbar's rancid meat products the way the Lambs had. "That lanky guy who worked as a ranger at the Nicolet one summer? Looked kind of like Pierce Brosnan in a flannel shirt and without an English accent?" Lucy nodded, wondering if Pierce Brosnan was on the same show as Courteney Cox. "He had these hazel eyes that just, you know, kind of smoldered. Didn't he end up getting in some kind of trouble?"

"Not trouble exactly. Just a fistfight. With the head ranger, trying to stop a logging road. He was kind of an idealist."

"That was him? That was the guy you wished you'd married?" April paused her scissors and studied Lucy in the mirror as if she now questioned her judgment. Lucy nodded faintly. Then April ducked down and started vigorously on the back of Lucy's hair. "Good-looking guy, of course, but doesn't strike me as husband material exactly. Anyway, I haven't seen him since he hightailed it out of town after socking Ranger Wilcox. Twin Pond's silted up, you know. Camp's probably been abandoned."

Lucy liked the idea of Twin Pond gradually filling up with slimy weeds until it disappeared into the earth. Maybe the McCarty cabin had gotten swallowed up along with the lake; all that remained was the caboose cupola inhabited by field mice. "I guess that's kind of a relief," she said. And it was, despite all of her foolish reminiscing. "I wouldn't want to run into him when I was skinny-dipping."

"How'd you like to run into me?" yelled one of the codgers from the lunch counter. April drowned him out with the dryer as she shaped the sides of Lucy's hair into sleek wedge-shaped wings. Then the chair sank with a gentle hiss and she twirled Lucy's cape off like a matador. "What do you think of the new you?"

The two prows of hair pointed like road signs toward her pale lips and the bags under her eyes. She looked at the coils of dark hair strewn across on the gray linoleum and wished there were some way to reattach them. After all the upheaval of the last five days, she wasn't compos mentis enough to have undertaken anything so radical and irreversible as a haircut. She stood up, shook her head gamely, and stroked her naked neck. "Wow. It feels so, um . . . " Bald, she thought. "Liberating." She didn't think she could face the scrutiny of the lunch counter, so she ducked down the personal hygiene aisle, grabbing a lipstick, a tube of piña colada-scented suntan oil, and a pair of Foster Grants shaped like mirrored insect eyes along the way. She slapped a fifty on the counter, grabbed up Ed's letter and the romance novel, and sprinted out the door. "Thanks for the new me," she yelled toward April. "I think I'm going to love her."

Chapter 8 of *Prairie of Passion* was getting so interesting that Lucy flipped over onto her stomach into a more comfortable reading position. Three towels protected her from the splintery dock as she slowly rotated herself in the midday sun like a chicken on a spit. She was wearing her father's gray felt fishing hat with dry flies hooked into the band, the new Foster Grants, and the old red pique underwire bikini she'd found jammed in the back of a bureau drawer. Gratifyingly, neither her stomach nor thighs bulged too badly around the sprung elastic edges.

It was pretty pathetic that she was getting so turned on by Seth having his way with Samantha right there on the earthen floor of his sod hut. If one analyzed the text objectively, the scene was quite implausible. First of all, since when did homesteaders have the free time to do a lot of midday sporting? Secondly, if you lived in a place with no indoor plumbing or bathing, wouldn't the bed or the hay loft be a much tidier place to do it than the floor?

Maybe her lusty state could be blamed on the bathing suit itself. She'd been wearing it the first time she and Sam McCarty had paddled out to the island in the middle of Little Lost Lake, after he licked her and she'd licked him back. The second the canoe bumped into a leafy cove, Sam leapt out, grabbed Lucy by the arm, and scrambled up the slope to a woodsy spot out of sight of the cabin. He leaned her up against a tree and then as he stared so intently into her eyes that she wondered if he were angry, his hand fumbled with the hook of her bikini top until it fell open. Just like that, urgently, without a single preliminary kiss. He bent down formally, as if he were a knight bowing to his queen, and kissed the tips of each breast, then dropped to his knees, pushed the bottom of her suit down low enough to kiss her stomach and the bottom of her triangle of pubic hair. Gazing out through the trees at the horizon of water, she rested her hands on top of his head for support lest she swoon. The actual sex that followed, of course, was not nearly so delicious and was chafing, too, what with those dried pine needles working themselves into every exposed crevice.

Lucy jolted upright, shaded her eyes with a hand and

squinted toward the island. It was only a few hundred yards away, nothing more than a knob of rock with a clump of pine trees. How could it have taken on such epic dimensions in her memory? "I'm boiling," she said out loud, jumping to her feet with a force that sent *Prairie of Passion* sprawling into the water. It slowly swelled, then turned on end and sank like the *Titanic*.

She adjusted the underwire cups against her sweaty breasts—maybe she should paddle out to the island. But twigs would cut into her tender feet and the mosquitoes would feast on her white bottom. Besides what would she do there—lay a bouquet of wildflowers at the site where she and Sam McCarty first did it? How about bushwhacking through the channel over to silted-up Twin Pond and inspecting the ruins of the caboose—that sounded like much more fun.

Adding hiking boots to her bikini and fishing hat outfit and armed with hedge clippers, work gloves, and a can of Cutter's, she nosed the canoe into the mouth of the channel and set to clearing. As she hacked and slashed, her thoughts drifted back to Ed. Self-serving, stupid, gutless letter. Never apologizes, never owns up to a thing, then takes her on a trip down memory lane. "Groping in a broom closet," she muttered as she snipped a crawl space under a bramble hedge. Why am I supposed to care? She bent double and pushed the canoe through the hole, getting bloody rake marks over both shoulders in the process. He had sounded like such a sad sack on the phone, so maybe he truly was sorry. Strange to say, she had felt a tiny burst of tenderness at the gravelly hum of his voice.

Suddenly, thunderous footsteps crashed through a stand of birches and she straightened with a gasp. The white-tailed rump of a deer bobbed and weaved until it disappeared from view. She rested a trembling hand over her heart and waited for the thumping to slow down. What am I doing here, she wondered, gazing up at the withered spires of half-dead pine trees.

If only I'd let Ed come, I'd be picking him up right about now at the Iron Mountain Airport. Sure it would be awkward at first. We'd suffer through a silent meal at the Fountainbleau steak house—the T-bone with béarnaise for him, a wilted Caesar salad with gooey dressing for me. Then later back at the cabin, after he'd complained about the dust mites and Larry's thieving, we'd sit at either end of the lumpy couch and start working through our woes, bit by bit. Sure he was a cheat and a liar, but right now glowering at his sweet boyish face would be a lot more pleasant than hauling a canoe through the forest gloom.

She picked the clippers up from where they'd dropped in the bottom of the canoe and tested the springy handles. Get a grip, Lucy. Maybe you eventually will patch things up with Ed, but not now, not yet. Make him suffer. This separation is a test to prove his love, his remorse. Yes, the little bad angel in her head answered back, but what if he decides not to suffer all by himself? Then he's worthless scum, and I'm well rid of him.

She clipped and shoved for another hour, the rays of sun now filtering through the branches at an ominously low angle. She almost lost heart when she discovered the channel ahead was blocked by a toppled spruce, its dead branches poking out in all directions like spears. It was like the impenetrable forest around Arabella's castle. Just when Lucy was about to give up and turn back, she spotted a thin spot in the woods ahead. Only a little farther, she thought, as she stepped out, heaved the canoe onto the spongy moss shore, and scraped it inch by inch over the log. I can make it.

Climbing back in and dusting the pine bark off her chafed stomach and arms, she looked up to find herself heading down the open mouth of the channel toward the smooth black surface of Twin Pond. She poled the canoe forward a few feet and rubbed her eyes hard to make sure this was not an optical illusion. Yes, there was the elbow shape of Twin Pond that looked, if anything, more pristine and weed-free than it had twenty years ago. At the crook of the elbow was the McCartys' dock and green Old Towne canoe, and perched above on a grassy slope the caboose cabin, formerly a sad peeling brown but now cherry red enamel with bright white trim. No silt, no decay—how could know-it-all April have gotten it so wrong?

Her canoe was drifting toward the center of the lake into full view of the cabin and Lucy considered what to do next. The McCartys had probably sold the cabin years ago—it had never looked this spruced-up during their tenure—and what would the new, possibly gun-toting owners think of a trespasser? This is Wisconsin, she reminded herself, where even gun nuts invited you in for a cup of Maxwell House. And besides, as long as she stayed on the water, technically she wasn't trespassing because no one owned the water in this state, only the land around it—a pedantic point her father used to make when fishermen came floating into Little Lost Lake on rubber rafts.

She was now close enough to notice that the row of square windows across the caboose front was shut—no one appeared to be home. At least they would be spared the sight of their new neighbor in a twenty-year-old Jantzen bikini. Suddenly a door at the end of the caboose slammed and a man stepped out on the iron porch, pausing for a moment with hand over brow to inspect the trespasser, and then trotted down the slope toward the dock. Lucy lifted her paddle out of the water and held it like a shield across her tummy, which now that she was sitting looked slightly like the Saggy Baggy Elephant's.

Should she yell hello and paddle forward, or start backtracking furiously, even though she could only get as far as the logjam at the mouth of the channel? She floated silently, squinting into the setting sun as she watched the backlit silhouette of the man stroll down the dock. All she could make out was long rangy legs in ragged jeans mended with duct tape, and a halo of dark curly hair and beard. No reassuring forest ranger uniform this time. He came to a stop at the end of the dock—now she could see work boots capped with duct tape—and hunkered down below the sunset. Now she could make out the face—narrow and bronzed as a mountain climber, with faded hazel eyes edged by deep crow's-feet, a shaggy beard, and hair grizzled with wiry gray. A face weathered and worn by years of adventuring, but one she would have recognized anywhere. Sam McCarty. After all the years of her wonderings, here he was, the apparition made real.

"So, Lucy," he said. She'd forgotten the soft intensity of his voice, as if it were whispering an urgent secret. "I've been expecting you."

She hugged the canoe paddle close to her chest. "I wasn't expecting you," she said, sounding as mumbly and sullen as Benjy at his worst. Although a psychiatrist, or Rosemary, would surely say she had been. At least those silly sunglasses hid the startled, mortified look in her eyes.

"You weren't?" He smiled, showing the hairline gap between his front teeth that she'd forgotten about. "Who were you expecting?"

"April down at Dunbar's store said that Twin Pond was silted up and the caboose had caved in." The canoe was making lazy circles and had rotated her face away from his.

"You sound disappointed that it's still standing."

She let that remark hang in the still of the evening.

"Well, your source was right. When I moved here five months ago, the lake was choked with water chestnuts and the caboose was half-gone. So, I got rid of the weeds, restored the lake, fixed up the house." How Sam-like, to reel off a list of Herculean tasks with a manly shrug. "Lucy, I'm getting dizzy talking to the back of your head." He reached out a thick forearm with the kind of well-defined muscles you get from restoring lakes. "Let me pull you in."

She sighed and held out the paddle blade, glancing up at the caboose for evidence of any other residents. Surely Sam must have a tan, fit helpmeet, who had homesteaded and kayaked across glaciers and skinned Kodiak bears with him, taking a day off here and there to give birth with no more complaint than a few grunts. "You live here by yourself?" she asked as he tied up the canoe, then grabbed both of her hands and hoisted her onto the dock.

"Yup," he said matter-of-factly, as if his solitude were preordained. He kept a grip on her hands in his sandpapery paws, insinuated his body closer, and then gave her goose-bumped flesh an unabashed once-over, slowly down and then back up. "Have I seen that bathing suit before?"

And to think that three hours before she had been recalling those once-keen eyes ogling her once-firm flesh in this very suit. "Nope. Just got it last year. It's the retro seventies look." She jerked her hands away, grabbed the orange life preserver out of the canoe, and clipped it on.

"Don't think you're going to need that. You're on dry land."

That's what you think. "I'm cold." She took off her glasses and hat and combed her fingers through her bobbed hair, startled all over again that ten inches were missing.

He was still staring at her, in that slow, intense way that she had once found impossibly sexy, still found impossibly sexy. "You look just the same, except the hair." What a fib, she thought, wishing she'd at least brought a towel to wrap around her middle-aged middle.

"So do you," she lied. One could hardly say the truth—you look the same only better. Why was it that a sprinkling of gray hairs and age lines made women look haggard, but gave men's faces character and virility? Life was so unfair.

"Come on up." He grinned at her, the creases around his mouth folding stiffly like dried leather, as if he hadn't smiled in a long time. Maybe he hadn't. "Let me give you the grand tour." He loped up the hill toward the caboose with Paul Bunyan strides.

The grand tour? Am I really going to stand here half-naked, making polite chitchat about home improvements with the former love of my life? The sun had already dipped behind the tree line and the mouth of the channel had disappeared in shadow. I'll give him fifteen minutes, she thought, and then I'm out of here. Even if he asks me to stay, she told herself sternly.

He paused in front of a series of crude but well-tended flowerbeds and waited for her to catch up. "This is my first year, so the perennials look a little puny. Should be enough basil for a few quarts of pesto, if the deer leave it alone. The peppermint is Adam's sweet, the best for tea." His words came out in a rush, as if he hadn't spoken to another human in six months, which he probably hadn't.

At the edge of the caboose, he opened a gate made of woven branches lashed together with twine and ushered her into a huge vegetable garden. "Here is my pride and joy. Lettuce, arugula, spinach, cabbage, five different kinds of tomatoes, three different kinds of squash, pole beans, bush beans . . . " he boasted as they walked down one perfectly weeded, mulched row after another. At last, a man who truly loved a garden. For years, she'd been waving exotic seed catalogs under Ed's nose, dragging him outside to show off the first tender shoots poking through the rich, black earth. After an uninterested glance, he would say, "Uh, I guess that's kind of neat."

Tucked behind the garden in a small clearing, she spotted a fairly new pickup with a camper back, up on blocks, half-buried in weeds. Twin Pond was fifteen miles from Dunbar's. How could he get food or supplies in here without a truck? Okay, time to cut the *Victory Garden* bullshit. "What are you *doing* here, Sam?" The word *doing* came out with four beats and echoed across the surface of the pond like a drumroll.

He stopped weeding a corn row, straightened, and brushed his hands against his pants. The forced smile faded back. "You always were able to cut to the quick of things, Lucy. What I'm *doing* here is kind of a long story. Let's go sit down."

She followed him up the iron stairs into the tongue-and-grooved shoebox interior of the caboose. The place still had the kid's clubhouse look with the galley kitchen in one corner, a table covered with a blue-checked oilcloth, a naked forty-watt bulb swaying at the end of a shredded cord. And that ladder leading up to the hideaway cubbyhole bed underneath the cupola. Lucy took one furtive glance and felt her face turn hot at the unbidden image of Sam's naked body, ghostly white except for the tan neck and arms, lying back across a tangle of blankets and sleeping bags. She plopped herself down on the built-in bench by the table and wedged a boat cushion behind her back, eyes roaming about for clues to the secret life of Sam McCarty. He'd mended his sloppy ways. The caboose was as stripped down as a monk's cell—a topo map of the Nicolet National Forest tacked to the wall, a mandolin dangling from a hook, an ancient Underwood typewriter, a thick accordion file sealed shut with a rubber band, a gadget for tying flies, a jar of Teddy Bear all-natural peanut butter, half a loaf of lumpy homemade bread on a crumb-dusted counter. No photographs or letters from loved ones in view. "I'm listening," she said.

Since there was no other place to sit, he perched at the other end of the bench by her feet. After an awkward pause he shrugged. "I don't know where to start. Why don't you ask me a question? You were always good at getting me to open up. I didn't know until I saw you tonight in the canoe how much I've missed that."

"All right. Did you ever make it to the Aleutians?" He squinted with confusion. "Don't you remember? When you fled from Cambridge, you said you were going to the Aleutians to live with the Inuit."

He flinched at the word *fled* as if it were an unfair blow. Had he ever thought of her over the years, and if so, what did he recall? Some soft-focus image of breasts and tongues, pine needles and loon calls? Or was it her fist, her fist going *thud thud thud* with impotent rage against his chest, when he announced in the Cambridgeport apartment that he was leaving for a better, more spiritual life—without her.

"I said that? God, I was such an asshole. I made it as far as Seattle and worked a lot of alternative jobs. For a while, I ran an Outward Bound program for troubled city kids. I started a community garden project with a homeless shelter. I edited the newsletter for an environmental organization. Filled in along the edges with carpentry jobs. Never had health insurance or a pension plan. Never wanted them."

"Is that all?" she asked in an almost accusatory way. All these years she had pictured Sam in a crude log cabin nestled into the side of a jagged, snowcapped peak, living off the land.

"I like to think that I haven't sold out. That I've done my part to help make the world a better place to live in." His voice took on some of the sermonizing tone of the old Sam. Now, with the wild hair, he even looked like an evangelical preacher. And who was she, the designer of the world's most popular fantasy computer game, to pass judgment on anyone else's life choices?

"Do you have a wife or children?" Might as well cut to the chase.

"A wife. I was married to a programmer at Microsoft, believe it or not. Microsoft is this immoral software conglomerate outside Seattle."

"I know what Microsoft is," she said testily.

"Oh, right. I guess everyone does. Anyway, I was married to Heidi, until she decided last fall she didn't want to be married to me anymore." He raised his eyes from his lap and gave her another one of those fragile smiles.

"Do you have any kids?"

"No, we never did. I felt that it would be irresponsible to bring children into such a toxic world, so Heidi found someone else to have kids with. I can't say I blame her. I'm not the easiest person to live with." Did he sound mournful because she had left him for another man, or because she had refused to go along with his bleak worldview?

Even if he didn't want to have kids, how could this Heidi have left such a soulful man, Lucy thought, her heart fluttering. Especially one who looked so dashing in a tortured, Heathcliff way under the feeble glow of the forty watts?

"What made you decide to come back to Twin Pond?" she whispered, barely resisting an impulse to reach over and give his broad shoulder a reassuring squeeze.

The spark reignited in the forlorn eyes. "The day Heidi kicked me out, I went to the Elliot Bay bookstore because I couldn't think of any other place to go. Picked up a copy of *Walden* that they had on display next to the cash register and then sat in the cafe for about two hours reading the part about Thoreau deciding to spend a year in his own backyard. Suddenly, I was on I-90 heading east, back here, back to Twin Pond. All I had was my Toyota pickup, thirty bucks, and a Visa. At Spokane, I bought a sleeping bag and a tent at an army/navy store. Called home and left a message on the machine for Heidi. I'm not coming back, you can get rid of all my stuff. When I got here, I stocked up on lumber, paint, tools, food, seeds. Everything I would need to be self-sufficient for a year. Then I put my truck up on blocks and I've been here ever since. I'm even trying to write my own version of *Walden,* which I guess I'll end up calling something original, like *Twin Pond.*" So that explained the typewriter. He hooked his hands around one knee and leaned back, waiting for her reaction.

Lucy uneasily shifted her spine against the lumpy boat cushion. Ah, yes, deciding at a moment's notice to flee the wreckage of a troubled marriage, heading off across the country with nothing more than a sleeping bag and a charge card, back to the family's decrepit cabin on a remote lake in northern Wisconsin. One could say the story rang a certain bell, but she didn't have a Thoreauvian vision like Sam's. She wasn't honing carpentry skills or living off the land—she was hiring Hank at fifteen bucks an hour and shopping at Dunbar's.

"But I haven't asked you anything about yourself." He looked chastened, as if the notion had just occurred to him that it might have been polite to show a bit of curiosity about his guest. Well, that was Sam. Back in the old days, he'd monopolized the conversation, carrying on about the latest environmental outrages—trout dying from acid rain in the Adirondacks, Amazon tribes having their habitats destroyed by clear-cutters, the shrinking polar ice caps—while she sat at his feet, staring up with a Nancy Reagan expression. "How's your father doing? Every time I see an old bamboo fly rod, I think of him."

"Dead. Fifteen years dead," she said, more brutally than she intended. "Turns out the summer I was hanging out with you, he was showing the first symptoms of lung cancer. If I'd been paying better attention, maybe they could have caught it sooner."

Sam seemed shocked, his eyes scanning the ceiling as he pondered a suitable response. "I'm sorry," he said finally.

"It's not your fault. It's mine." The doctors had said the tumor was too aggressive to be stopped even if it had been diagnosed earlier. But there it was, her malignant lump of guilt. The specter of Cyrus squashed the impulse for any more flirting, at least tonight. "I've got to head back up the channel before it's totally dark," she said, standing up, straightening her life jacket, and striding toward the door fast before he could try to stop her.

"But you haven't told me what you're doing back at Little Lost Lake."

"Another day, when I've got more light," she answered cryptically, marching down the path to the dock. Maybe that would give her enough time to dream a slightly more dignified life story. Doing an article for *Audubon* on the flora and fauna of a north woods pond, or something.

He jogged after her and caught up at the end of the dock. She stopped and there was an awkward pause as she tried to figure out how to say good-bye. A kiss on the cheek, a hug, a hand-shake? Finally she settled for a formal bow that came out more like a curtsy, climbed into the canoe while he untied the painter and shoved her off. "Will you come back?" he called out plaintively.

"Maybe," she said, her head already turned toward the channel. She tried to sound blasé and tentative, but of course she would come back. Properly dressed, with enough time so she didn't have to worry about nightfall, maybe loosened up with a couple of glasses of wine (although Sam probably didn't drink), she could finally take care of unfinished business—so why did you desert me, you shit? And maybe start some new business.

"Tomorrow, for dinner? My first eggplants are in so I'll make ratatouille." His voice echoed across the inky water.

"All right," she answered, glancing back at the lonely figure on the dock with hands shoved in his ragged jeans. "Hey, Sam? How did you know it was me in the canoe?"

"I've been waiting for you for six months. You're my destiny, Lucy," he yelled, as she nosed her canoe into the channel.

Now I understand, she thought, easing her bare legs into the chilly water to hoist the canoe back around the deadfall. I did not come back to Little Lost Lake because of Ed or the boys or because of my own whims. I was pulled back by destiny.

CHAPTER 10

>>

Here the Senior Canoe Trip hits civilization for the first time in, like, two weeks, but instead of letting the campers thunder across the road to Larson's trading post and tavern which had pictures of ice-cream bars glued across the front window, their Nazi counselors made them write letters home! Kids aren't allowed in Larson's, said Chris, because they serve liquor. He pointed at a couple of neon beer signs hanging next to the Good Humors. Right, said Dave winking at Chris, we might lose our jobs if we let you guys come with us. Sorry. So tell you what, Chris offered, everyone who writes a letter home will get a treat from the store. Then he ripped off sheets from a spiral notebook and handed them around, along with a ratty collection of pencil stubs and chewed-up ballpoints. Have fun, they said, strolling across the road and into the tavern side of Larson's.

Phil and the rest of the Kinahwee "team" were left in a buggy little clearing by a splintery dock that poked out into the murky water of something called Lake Winter. With six canoes pulled up and flipped turtle and wannigans strewn around, there wasn't much place to stand, let alone find a flat surface to write a letter.

"They're trying to ditch us so they can get wasted," said Brandon Fiske, a loudmouth from Winnetka with body hair and the grimy shadow of a moustache, who was by far the most obnoxious kid on the "team." "I'm not writing any fucking letter." He scrunched his paper into a tight ball.

Wasted—Chris and Dave? Chris, the head counselor, was

a Dudley Do-Right kind of guy who wore wire-rim glasses and a black felt hat with an eagle feather stuck in the band, and had been going to Camp Kinahwee since he was about eight. He was a nature fanatic who liked to quote some guy named John Muir about tiptoeing through the woods without leaving any mark of human presence. So it seemed pretty unlikely that Chris would pollute his own body with alcohol, because as the DARE officer at school had explained to them during their fifth-grade substance abuse awareness program, you should think of your body as a sacred temple. But now that Phil considered the evidence, Chris and Dave had high-tailed it into the bar pretty quick, so Brandon was probably right. Benjy was always telling Phil he was gullible, but how did a person go about becoming less gullible?

Brandon's two sidekicks, Zack and Trevor, had balled up their sheets, too, and were playing hacky sack, bouncing them back and forth off knees and ankles and managing to shove their stinky feet into everyone else's faces in the process—how typical. The assholes could goof off all they wanted, but Phil was actually glad to have a chance to write down some of his experiences over the last ten days, although already it seemed like he'd been gone about a month. He searched around for a flat surface and spotted Benjy in a far corner, his paper spread across the humped bottom of a canoe. Phil strolled over and squatted down at the other end.

"Do you mind?" Benjy said prissily, shielding his paper with both arms. "I'd like a little privacy."

Christ, no wonder everyone thought Benjy, or Crocker as they all called him (within two days Benjy had been reduced to Crocker, while Phil for some inexplicable reason still got called by his first name), was a total jerk. Phil tried to peek over his scrawny, sunburned arm to see what in hell he was writing but could only make out a couple of lines of messy scribble. Was he complaining about Phil? Nah, if anything, Phil had stuck up for his twin more than anyone, even his parents, could reasonably have expected. No, probably Benjy was just feeling sorry for himself, whining about how much camp sucked and how unfair his mom had been to send him there.

Phil walked out to the end of the dock, found the least warped plank, and started writing.

Dear Mom and Dad,

I am sitting on a dock in Lake Winter. My councilers who are Kris and Dave say that if we write letters to our parents we can have candy bars so I am writing you a letter. Brandon says that they are really in the bar getting drunk but I don't think so.

Phil nibbled on the end of his Bic and considered what to say next. The bumpy dock made the letters look all quivery, like the birthday cards written by his Grandmother Crocker who had had Parkinson's. He probably shouldn't have mentioned that his counselors were off getting hammered, but if he crossed it out that might look even more suspicious.

You were right, Mom. This camp is a very educational experience. I am learning a lot about how to canoe a canoe. I think I am getting much better.

Phil flattened out both palms and studied the rows of blisters, which were still red but at least weren't oozing pus anymore. If Chris were writing this letter, he probably wouldn't use the word *better.* He'd say at least Phil hadn't paddled like a feeb, swamped the canoe, or dunked any wannigans—this week. And as for the first week, well, let's just forget about that.

Our councelors who are Kris and Dave know a lot about nature and the outdoors and are very patient about teaching us stuff. The other kids are nice and I am making friends.

Phil glanced up to make sure none of the guys were close enough to read this last line. Most of them had now crumpled up their papers and were chucking them full force into one another's nuts. Not one of them could even remotely be described as "nice." They were from places like Minnesota where they played hockey and went ice fishing and did gross-out things with girls. The best you could say was that a few of them, like Harris and Richard, who were sitting over on the wannigans writing their letters, were not as big assholes as the rest. But even Richard and Harris weren't particularly nice, much less friends, at least not to Phil and Benjy.

I don't think Benjy likes camp as much as I do, but he is learning a lot of camping skills too.

That was a complete whopper but not quite as big a one as saying Benjy was having fun or making friends. So far, Benjy had resisted learning any actual canoeing or camping skills. After that first humiliating day when they capsized a canoe and sent a wannigan with the breakfast cereals and pancake mixes to the bottom of a lake, and then flailed around so helplessly in the water that it was obvious to everyone they couldn't swim a stroke, Chris had made a special effort to, as he said, bring them "up to speed." He didn't bother with the swimming, only said tactfully, out of earshot of the rest of the guys, that from now on they'd have to wear life preservers all the time, even during free swim. Then he took them out in the canoe while the other guys set up camp, placing Phil and Benjy at either end and himself in the middle with his long hairy blond legs pressed flat along the ribbed bottom. And in the same kind of ultrapatient way you teach retarded kids to zip their parkas, he demonstrated the various canoe strokes and the proper way to grip a paddle so you didn't get blisters. See, Chris said, it's not so hard.

Phil stared so intently that he could see the individual muscles pop up and tighten along Chris's arms. He figured he had no choice—get better at this canoeing stuff, or be the butt of Brandon Fiske's jokes for the next six weeks. But not Benjy—no, of course not. Benjy kept his eyes on shore where a cook fire was now blazing, sniffed hard at a breeze carrying the tantalizing aroma of Chef Boyardee. "Are you done yet?" he said, his back to Chris. "I think supper's ready."

"Don't give up so easily. You can do it—just give it a try," Chris coaxed. It still hadn't dawned on the guy that Benjy was just a bone-lazy genius with major attitude, not a retard.

Phil decided nature was a safer letter topic.

I have seen a bunch of mooses and some big birds but I don't know what there called. One night I saw something called northern lights, which looked like spotlights criss crossing across the sky. Sure is a lot more pretty than Crowley except when its raining, but I still like Crowley better! Well I guess that's all I'm doing. How is your summer? How are things going with MQ2? I miss you a lot but I am mostly having fun so don't worry.

Love,
Phil Crocker

p.s. the food isn't too gross and I am learning to cook it.

He read it over a couple of times, just like his English teacher Mrs. Chadwick had lectured him. The problem was that he never had any idea on how to fix the things that looked wrong, so all proofreading seemed to accomplish was to make him feel stupid. Oh, well, at least it looked better than Benjy's, he thought, folding it up into quarters.

The tavern door slammed and Chris and Dave came lurching back, looking a lot more carefree than they had in the last two weeks. Chris was waving a handful of Canadian airmail envelopes and Dave had an armful of strange red-and-white candy bars.

"Everyone finished?" Chris asked cheerfully, but when he saw the wads of paper flung all over the ground, his face darkened into its disappointed expression. "No letter, no candy bar," he added.

The nut bashers looked kind of embarrassed and picked up the litter pretty quickly, all except Brandon. "So what. The candy bars look nasty."

"They're Cadbury Caramellos. Fine English chocolates. I guess Phil, Benjy, Richard, and Harris will all get two," said Dave, his happy-go-lucky grin melting away.

Benjy scrawled across one of the envelopes, stuffed in his letter, and then walked over to Phil. "Give me your letter. We can share an envelope and save on postage."

Phil hesitated—Benjy had written their address so sloppily it would probably never get there. But how could he refuse when Benjy was actually being thoughtful for once? "Okay," he said, but when he handed over his letter, Benjy got one of his I'm-up-to-something-sneaky looks, which made Phil suspect he'd been suckered.

Phil saved his Cadbury bars until he'd crawled into his sleeping bag for the night—he'd already brushed his teeth, but what the hell. All afternoon, as they did the last leg of the trek up Lake Winter into a head wind and set up camp in the rain, he'd imagined the delicious feeling of chocolate melting all over his teeth and tongue as he fell asleep. Holding the flashlight under his chin, he unwrapped the gold foil only to discover the squares of chocolate had turned frosty white with old age. He flicked off the light—maybe they'd taste all right in the dark, he decided philosophically—and they did.

CHAPTER 11

>>

It was the twenty-seventh day since his family had abandoned him, thought Ed as the alarm clock beeped him awake at six o'clock. Actually, now that he counted on his fingers, Lucy and the boys headed off to Wisconsin a full thirty days ago, but he had only found out about it twenty-seven days ago, when he returned from what he had come to think of disingenuously as "that gamers' convention." So the fact that he dated this cataclysmic event not from the moment that it occurred, but from the moment of his knowledge of it, probably indicated something disturbing about his character—that he was a narcissist incapable of remorse or empathy, or whatnot. One of those ominous red flags of social deviation, like torturing small animals or using the chemistry set you got from your grandmother for Christmas to build bombs.

Come to think of it, when Ed was eight he'd used the Mr. Wizard chemistry set he'd gotten from Granny Crocker to implode a galvanized watering can that their cat, Gingersnap, had been sleeping next to. He'd meant to scare the cat, not harm her, of course, but she'd gotten the end of her tail singed. Later the denuded spot turned into a stinking, oozing abscess and two inches of her tail had to be amputated. Most parents would have been alarmed that their kid was turning into a sicko, but not Harry and Marion. They had called up his grandmother to brag about the boy genius. He's going to go to MIT, you can bet your sweet bippy, his father had said.

For the past twenty-seven mornings in the hallucinatory

state between sleep and wakefulness, he had dredged up other shameful scenes from his past. The time in fourth grade when he farted while reading his term paper on J. Edgar Hoover aloud to the class, straight into the face of Maxwell Peters, class clown, sitting in the desk behind, who pretended to faint from the stench. Or that time when he had been making out with his tenth-grade girlfriend, Mandy Pomeranz, one night nestled in a sand trap on the eighth hole of the Marshfield municipal golf course. Things had progressed for the first time past dry humping through their clothes. Mandy had unbuckled his web belt and thrust her hand boldly down into his jockey shorts, and that first sensation on his penis of a human hand besides his own caused him to ejaculate immediately. She had let out a gasp of disgust, yanked out her hand, and held it up to scrutinize the pearly liquid in the moonlight. Who knows what she expected semen to look like, but she seemed unpleasantly surprised. She jumped to her feet and attempted to wipe her hand clean in a clump of tall grass by the edge of the trap while he fastened up his fly, diminished.

He let out an anguished groan, flipped over on his stomach, bent one of Lucy's snake-shaped neck pillows around his head to block out the morning glare, the truth. Compared to the likes of O. J. Simpson and Newt Gingrich, he was probably not a truly evil man, and yet why did he feel like one?

He clambered out of bed, hitched up his boxer shorts, smoothed down his MAIDEN'S QUEST II NOW! T-shirt, yanked his hair back into a messy ponytail and started his morning ritual. The only way he had been able to stumble through the past three weeks was to adhere to a strict schedule. He stepped over to the bay window, and went through a modified version of the "Tai Chi for Busy People" workout he'd found on the Internet—Wild Horse's Mane, Repulse Monkey, and Snake Creeps Down, six repetitions each, all the while concentrating on his breathing, in through the nose and slowly out through the mouth. Ingrid had taught him about the value of rhythmic breathing, admittedly during more strenuous activity. As his head jabbed up and down in front of the window, he reminded himself to observe the view of the Crowley Green. One of the revelations from his journal writings was how blind he had become to his physical environment. Sun muted by a light gauze of gray clouds, he noted, low bank of fog, will probably burn off by eight. A chirrup, chirrup sound coming from the copper beech tree. Listen to Lucy's backyard birdcall tape and try to identify; possibly a chipmunk. Long stalks covered with some pink lily of the valley–type flower in Fairbank's front yard that wasn't blooming yesterday. Try to identify in Lucy's perennial flower book. There was that old guy again, humped back, dingy yellow cardigan, tripod cane. Every day, same walk at same time, across green, along Harvard Road, back on Spring Street, into back ell of brown Victorian on corner. About a quarter mile, which took at least twenty-five minutes in halting, shuffle steps—his doctor or his wife probably makes him do it. Should know who he is. Lucy would.

Next, Ed ambled down the hall, purposely averting his eyes from the ghostly disarray of the boys' bedroom to the kitchen. He had decided to reform his diet along with his exercise routine and sexual behavior. He had chucked out the Alphabits, Sugar Smacks, and Lucky Charms—his breakfast since he was old enough to express an opinion—for a sack of nut-and-dried-fruit Muesili he'd picked up at the local health food store. As he dutifully masticated apricots and filberts with the consistency of wood chips, he tried to figure out his schedule for the rest of the day.

Ed was now on an indefinite leave of absence from Crocker Software. Twenty-six days ago, the morning after his life had imploded, he had fired off an e-mail to the troops that he hoped came off as visionary rather than deranged.

To: All Crocker Software Employees
From: Ed Crocker, CEO

The past few months have been very difficult in the life cycle of Crocker Software. As we have struggled to come up with a sequel to Maiden's Quest II, I think we would all agree that we have lost our way, both as a company and as a family. We are too quick to criticize others' ideas, even though we lack the energy and commitment to come forth with original ideas of our own.

I hold myself entirely responsible for not providing the leadership to steer us through the shoals of our malaise. I, too, have lost my way. I can't remember why I started Crocker Software. I can't remember why people have fun playing our games. I am taking an indefinite sabbatical to rediscover what Crocker Software is all about, and then maybe I can lead us forth into the future.

Who knows what any of them made of this bullshit—he hadn't had the courage to check his phone messages or e-mail to find out. It was probably irresponsible or even illegal for the CEO of a medium-size software company to disappear without a trace, but Ed figured drearily that they could manage perfectly well without him. Daria the accountant could issue the paychecks right on schedule cosigned by Russell Mott, the Maiden's Quest II task force headed up by Ingrid and Ralph would roll merrily along with their plans for "A," oblivious to the fact that she'd been panned by the focus groups.

He had sent Ingrid a personal e-mail where he admitted the truth—that Lucy had found out about "our relationship" (whatever that meant) and had bolted, that his precious sons had been banished to hell, in part because of the sins of the father.

And so here I am, Ingrid, alone in this house of horrors in Crowley, feeling that I have betrayed everyone I ever loved. Most of all I feel that I have betrayed you and your generous love.

Of course, Lucy was the betrayed one, not Ingrid, but complete honesty was not exactly called for when you were worming yourself out of a messy love affair. *Generous love* was a bit over the top, too, especially when applied to Ingrid, who in her daily interactions with coworkers was neither generous nor loving. *Generous lust* was more like it—lusty and very generous. Ed tried to dress up the romp at the Trump Plaza with some flowery language—*I will always remember our few days together, how could I ever forget them?*—and then closed with abject apologies and pleas for eventual forgiveness.

When he had aimed the cursor at send, he knew at the very least that he had handed Ingrid the implement for perfect revenge. She could either turn his note over to some pit bull sexual harassment lawyer to pick his carcass clean, or, a much more likely scenario, keep the note to herself and simply take over Crocker Software in his absence. Either way, he deserved it.

Ed limped back upstairs to Lucy's studio and deposited his still unwashed, boxer-shorted body in front of her computer to commence the work of the day. First, he wrote his daily letters to the boys, which was a challenge since he barely had enough news to fill one letter let alone two. For Phil, he painted droll anecdotes of life in Crowley.

> *Mr. Farwell was backing his Lincoln Town Car into Spring Road, just in time to get barreled into by Carlson's septic pump truck . . . I am getting used to cooking for myself, but I'm afraid I don't measure up to your mom in the culinary department. Last night I ate some prickly greens and a strange white squash from the vegetable garden, and they turned my tongue black, so I guess they must be good for me.*

He kept it technical for Benjy, listing every check mailed to BPCC, explaining how he had unplugged the BPCC computers during a lightning storm in case there was a power surge. With Scotch tape, he carefully stuck two pieces of Juicy Fruit gum wrapped in tin foil on the bottom of the boys' letters.

Gum letters had been one of the few thrills back in Ed's two wretched summers at Camp Tomahawk in the Poconos. The mail mistress sniffed and fondled each letter and any boy who managed to get a gum letter slipped through the lines had a certain cachet—particularly a smelly type like Juicy Fruit. He wondered what gave a boy cachet at a boot camp like Kinahwee—probably surviving for a week on nothing but roasted june bugs or treading water for hours fully dressed in the middle of an arctic-cold lake, not a measly piece of contraband gum. Every day at eleven he sprinted down to the mailbox in vain hopes of a crumpled envelope covered with their beloved misshapen scribble, but nothing. What did the silence of a thirteen year old portend—too busy to write, or too miserable?

After he finished his letters to the boys, he tackled a much more difficult task, his daily letter to Lucy. No Crowley newsbreaks allowed, just a headlong leap into the entrails of their marriage.

Rosemary says that the more you grieved over the miscarriages, the more I buried myself in Crocker Software. I've been thinking about that a lot over the last few weeks, and of course she's right (then again, when is Rosemary ever wrong?). I remember when you had the last one a year ago, you said you would never get over the feelings of sadness. And I said something I've always regretted. "Why do you have to dwell on the loss?" And you said—angrily—"How can you not *dwell on the loss?"*

I guess what I was trying to express was that to dwell on the loss of an unborn child seemed disloyal to Benjy and Phil. It was if I was saying to them, you aren't enough, there is a hole in my fatherly love that you can-

not fill. Because you see, Lucy, you and the boys are all the family I have ever wanted or needed. I feel no lacking.

But that is me, not you, and I was insensitive to your pain. And so if you decide to forgive me and give our marriage another chance, we can try again. Go back to the fertility guy, adopt, whatever path you want to take.

After he'd finished his daily correspondence, Ed tried to be true to his memo and think visionary thoughts about computer games and Crocker Software. Every day for exactly forty-five minutes, measured with the chicken-shaped egg timer on Lucy's bookshelf (another flea market treasure), Ed popped in the Maiden's Quest I CD and played, to "rediscover the computer game experience." The first few times he played, his skills were pretty rusty. He'd forgotten most of the mazes and puzzle solutions; at every turn he seemed to steer Arabella into a deathtrap. There were dozens of gruesome ways to die in Maiden's Quest—falling into a vat of hot oil, being slowly flattened in a shrinking catacomb or elongated on a rack, being hoisted up the flagpole in a tiny cage and left to parch in the sun. And then Ed made a miraculous discovery that made his old hacker's heart soar like an eagle—he figured out how to cheat.

It was just like those countless all-nighters in the MIT computer lab when he'd figured out how to disembowel someone's computer program and rewrite it. He hadn't done any real programming in years, and what an adrenaline rush to tinker with a few lines of code and voilà—Arabella would leap over obstacles, illegally jump from Level I to Level IV. Ha! God, I'm good, Ed thought, pounding away at the keys. That's right, that's why I started this stupid company, because it made me feel like a freewheeling eleven year old again, snitching money from my mother's purse and then tearing off on my banana-seat bike for penny candy and Sno-Kones.

Now, he'd made it past the gnomes' labyrinth and the great lizard swamp to the most dastardly part of the game, Morgan's castle. Ed guided Arabella carefully up the tower's slippery stone steps—one false step and it was a two-hundred-foot plunge into the crocodile-infested moat—to the sorceress' lair. All Arabella had to do was tiptoe in and grab the magic crystal before Morgan returned. Suddenly Ed's mouse hand paused as he leaned in close to study the screen. Funny, he'd never noticed the stone frieze carved along the ceiling of Morgan's lair—pairs of giraffes, nose to nose, drawn art deco style.

Rosemary and Alfred gave the boys stuffed giraffes for their first birthday—covered in nubby terrycloth, one yellow and one blue. Benjy and Phil had dragged those giraffes around for years, until they both turned the same soiled gray color, until the necks had stretched out like they'd been wrung. The boys called them blue Giraffy and yellow Giraffy, only they pronounced it "yewwow." Ed had found other Crocker family totems hidden throughout Maiden's Quest—his violin, Lucy's crossword puzzle trophy, Granny Crocker's silver teapot. He'd never noticed them before. He sighed, wishing Lucy were here, right now, so he could tell her he'd finally discovered the clues she'd left behind, scattered like a trail of bread crumbs, leading him back home.

He had paused too long. Without warning, a scorpion skittered out from behind the crystal and bit Arabella's hand; she slumped over, dead. Well, no matter. Just enter the cheat code, and lo, Arabella is resurrected, the scorpion scampers away. If only the sordid events of his own recent past could be undone so easily. Type in the cheat code, and *poof*—Ingrid's e-mail was unsent, the Trump Plaza tryst never happened, Lucy was back painting trout in her studio down the hall, the boys in their room designing a Web page for Kleenit cleaners. Tomorrow, they would pack up the car and head off, as planned, for Wheeler's bungalow colony for their annual two-week vacation with Alfred and Rosemary. And by dinnertime we would be having steamed lobsters on the picnic table in the shady pine grove behind the cottages, Ed thought, almost weeping. Our arms covered with deep woods Off!, our chins slick with lemon butter. If only, if only.

The chicken timer dinged and he clicked on quit. After forty-five minutes of computer games came forty-five minutes of violin practice, also timed with the chicken. He positioned his music stand back in the bay window where he had done his morning exercises, tuned up, and then attacked the opening bars of the Bruch concerto. He grunted and sawed his way through the first two movements, trying to ignore the out-of-tune octaves and his vibrato that had taken on the tight whine of a mosquito's hum, then stopped to wipe his sweaty hands and chin on yesterday's T-shirt crumpled at his feet. Well, at least it sounded slightly less shitty than it had the day before. He hadn't practiced seriously since the birth of Crocker Software eight years ago, so it would have been far more logical to start with scales and études, but a masochistic streak had made him attempt the Bruch right from the get-go, a daily reminder of how far his talents had withered. He gave the strings a quick tuneup, repositioned his bare feet at ten and two o'clock, hummed an approximation of the orchestra's introduction to the finale, and dove in once again.

Outside on the street came a grinding of gears and a screech. Ed caught a flash of metallic red through the maple canopy and lowered his violin in time to see Ingrid's Subaru Outback pulling up at a crooked angle in front of the house. He jumped back from view and watched covertly as the door popped open, one pale, muscled calf shod in pink platforms swung around and then another, and the top of Ingrid's bristly, lemon-colored head bobbed its way up the path to the front door. Ed's heart hammered as he considered the possible reasons for a visit—to serve him with legal papers or a vote of no confidence signed by every Crocker employee, to hurl angry or tearful accusations at him. Whatever the reasons, it was going to be an ugly scene of some sort. The brass doorbell trilled three times imperiously. Well, he didn't *have* to answer it; she didn't know for sure that he was lurking inside. He caught sight of his reflection in the bevel-edged mirror above Lucy's bureau—hunched over with guilt like Rev. Dimmesdale, six days of stubble darkening his face like a shadow of shame, his boxer shorts and T-shirt sagging in mournful folds around his middle. What a pathetic excuse for a . . . well, what am I, anyway? Not a husband, not a lover, not even head of a medium-size software company anymore. If I'm going to jilt my lover, at least I can have the guts to do it face-to-face.

The bell screeched again—one long, angry blast this time. "I'm coming," Ed yelled toward the window as he made a quick stab at presentability. He pulled on nylon running shorts and black rubber flip-flops, tried to straighten his ragged ponytail, and gave his tonsils six sprays of Binaca. "Coming," he cried, whapping down the stairs two at a time, lopping down the long hall, and pulling the front door open with such force that he practically catapulted through it. And there stood Ingrid, gotten up in an ill-considered baby doll dress. The last time he'd seen her, clad only in a neon green thong, lounging in a nest of rumpled sheets, she had seemed as languid and regal as an Egyptian princess. But now, with a good portion of her freckled breasts peeking out of a gaping ruffled neckline, she looked as tentative as a ten year old impersonating Courtney Love. Her eyes were blotted out by cat's eye glasses, her maroon lipsticked mouth an inscrutable straight line.

"Ingrid," he said, overwhelmed by an unexpected rush of tenderness for her neat, compact body and the heart-shaped curve of her face. What was the proper way to greet a spurned lover? A peck on the cheek, a stiff-armed hug, surely both would be resented, misinterpreted. He tilted back and gripped the door handle.

She slipped off her sunglasses, cocked her head to one side, and squinted at him as if she were studying a mildly disgusting zoo exhibit such as maggots feasting on a chipmunk carcass. "You look like shit," she said after a pause. A matter-of-fact observation without a trace of concern, not that he expected any.

He knew better than to say, So do you. "You look great. As always. That's a really great dress. Not that I'm saying you *are* feeling great, of course. But if you're feeling great, well, that's great."

"Shut up, Ed. You're babbling. Is Lucy back from Wisconsin?" She leaned forward on her pink, spangled platforms and peered past him down the gloomy hallway. "Do you think maybe I could come in for a minute?" Ed was unsettled by this new hesitancy—the old Ingrid would have demanded to be invited in or simply stormed in uninvited.

"Yeah, of course. Come on in," he said, trying to sound welcoming as he sidestepped to make room for her. Inviting your former lover into your house when your wife was out of town felt like a greater betrayal than the adultery itself, but he could hardly say no to Ingrid's meek request. He checked over her head to see if the old guy with the tripod cane was hobbling over to bear witness.

She wandered slowly down the hall, ogling like a tourist—the giant Canton ginger jar used as an umbrella stand by the front door, the faded Heriz runner on the stairs, the curly maple trestle table in the dining room, a primitive portrait of twin girls over the mantel. "My grandmother had creepy old stuff like this. Did you buy the house furnished, or something?" she asked, her shoulders in their powder blue puffed sleeves shuddering slightly.

"Lucy collects antiques. She's got a really good eye," he said, trying not to sound irritated. He considered giving her a brief primer on early American decorative arts, but then figured why bother. Ingrid's apartment was decorated in grad student Pier One/Pottery Barn style. "Let's sit out here." He steered her through a side door to the screened porch, which seemed like the most aboveboard spot for a tête à tête.

Ingrid settled down into an oversize wicker armchair with bamboo print cushions. Now she directed her scrutiny to the buildings along the common. "This seems like kind of a funky town to live in."

"What's so funky about it?" he said, propping himself on the armchair at the opposite end of the porch from hers.

"Well, you've made a lot of money with Crocker. You could buy a nice house anywhere you wanted—Cambridge, Lincoln, Weston. So why live way out here? The town's a dump, the commute into Cambridge is a nightmare, the schools probably stink."

True, true, and true. But in the last three weeks, the place had wormed its way into his heart—the airiness of the high-ceilinged rooms, the tranquil hum of the occasional car looping around the Crowley Common. For the first time, he found all of Lucy's clutter—from the row of dachshund salt and pepper shakers that stared at him when he brushed his teeth to the Dale Evans tin lunch box that held the coffee filters—comforting and homey.

"Crowley's got its charms, even if they're not obvious to you. There's Mount Monadnock in the distance," he said, pointing out the back field toward a hazy bump. "Can't see that in Cambridge."

"I guess," said Ingrid doubtfully. "If you like old houses and mountains, but. . . . " She stopped and shifted her gaze to a swarming yellow jacket nest tucked under the eaves outside the porch door. She toyed nervously with the stack of silver rings on her index finger set with garishly colored, ersatz gemstones—acid green, bilious orange, Pepto-Bismol pink. *Click, click, click* off into her lap, *click, click, click* back on to her finger.

"But what . . . " he said, not quite sure he wanted to hear the answer.

"But I don't think you like old houses or mountains. I think you'd probably rather have a view of Storrow Drive and the BU bridge than some mountain. I think . . . " She stood up, straightened the drooping pink bow of her dress and started walking toward him, slowly, " . . . that you're living here because Lucy wanted to, not you. That this house was another one of her screwy ideas that you were forced to go along with, just like she tried to make everyone at Crocker go along with her screwy ideas for Maiden's Quest II." She sat down on a wicker footstool by his feet, pressed her bony knees into his.

"Just remember, Ingrid, that if it weren't for Lucy's screwy ideas, Maiden's Quest wouldn't exist and neither would Crocker Software," Ed said evenly, dislodging his knees.

Ingrid seemed to realize she had misplayed her hand. "Lucy may have all sorts of special talents. But you can't tell me that in the two years I've been at Crocker, she's made you very happy, Ed." Her black mascaraed eyes fixed him with a hard stare, daring him to contradict her.

"I don't think I made Lucy very happy, either."

"But you deserve happiness," she whispered, reaching forward to grab his wrist and give it an urgent squeeze.

Ed shifted uneasily under her grip. "I don't know what would make me happy, Ingrid." What a lie. Lucy and the boys home again, everything back to normal, back to the way it had been, that would make him happy.

"*I* can make you happy." Her eyes slowly filled until her turquoise-colored contact lenses started to drift up and down, two mascara-tinged streams trickled down her cheeks.

The sight of Ingrid, who had never showed a shred of emotion before, huddled over and weeping, undid him. "*Shhh.* Please don't cry. I'm not worth crying over," he mumbled, wiping away the streaks of tears with the back of a hand.

"I can't help it." A pause for a few hiccuping sobs. "I . . . love you." The words had a strangled, foreign sound as if she had never said them before.

Of all the possible scenarios for a confrontation with Ingrid, this was one he would never have figured. As his hands patted hers in a fatherly way, he leaned his body back as far as possible to let in a little oxygen. "I admit I'm really surprised to hear you say that. You never acted, you know, um, in love with me." No, she had been too in charge of the situation, putting him through his paces like a dog trainer with a choke collar.

"I'm really surprised, too," she said, fishing a wad of Kleenex out of a pink patch pocket and blowing her nose. "I enjoyed all the physical stuff with you. And it was a power rush getting it on with the boss. But I never thought I'd fall in *love* with you." She lowered her head for another round of sniffles. "It wasn't until after the conference, when I was back in my apartment, that I realized how much I missed you. Just talking to you about Crocker and our strategy for Maiden's Quest, and all your dumb jokes. I used to think nice guys were just wimps and losers. But you made me understand that maybe it's not such a bad thing to be nice, you know?" She looked up at him beseechingly.

Ed studied the yellow jackets lowering their hind quarters into the hexagonal holes of the nest and tried not to appear offended. Is that what all his Generation X employees thought of him—that he was nothing but a wimp and a loser? He turned back to Ingrid and smiled wanly. "I don't think Lucy would agree that I'm such a nice guy."

"*Phhh,* Lucy!" Ingrid said dismissively, adjusting the huge neck hole of her dress so it draped properly across her chest. She was getting a grip on herself. "She takes you for granted. I mean, we all thought you were a saint to put up with all her screw ups and excuses."

No, not so saintly. Instead of being empathetic when she'd gotten stuck, he'd been furious, fed up—he'd turned to Ingrid to punish her. "She's not taking me for granted anymore. She doesn't want anything to do with me." He let out a bleak sigh.

Brightening, Ingrid sat up straight. "So much the better. Then she won't mind if you decide you want to be with me instead." She rushed along as if she were ticking off goals in

Crocker's long-term planning strategy. "I promise, I will work really hard to make you happy, Ed. We'll be a team, and together we'll put Crocker back on its feet. I'll develop a good relationship with your sons. I've got a fourteen-year-old brother, so I understand what boys like." She smiled knowingly—yes, Ingrid knew what boys liked all right. "I'll be the best decision you ever made. You won't be sorry."

All he had to do was say yes and this would be the last decision he ever made—the rest of his life would be directed for him. "No, Ingrid. I'm sorry, but no," he said softly. "I know my relationship with Lucy doesn't make any sense to you, just the way this house doesn't make any sense to you. But this is the life I've chosen and I don't want to change it. I am still in love with Lucy and I want her to take me back if she'll have me. Me, my wife, and my sons, together in this house. That is what will make me happy." Ed Crocker's manifesto—it felt oddly cleansing to say it. He glanced warily toward Ingrid. She was staring over his shoulder out the back field at something, her hands had fallen away from his and hung limply at her sides.

"What's that brown thing running along the wall out there?"

Ed squinted at a ragged dog-shaped animal that skulked along the edge of the wall for a few feet and then dipped behind a blackberry thicket. "A coyote." A pack of coyotes had taken up residence in the woods behind their house. Mostly they were quiet, but on occasional nights they kicked up an otherworldly racket—single dogs yipping followed by the baying of an entire choir. One could only guess with a shiver the reason for their joy—a stray cat, a wounded fawn. Whenever they started, Lucy would throw open all the windows and then coax him to make love to the rhythm of their howls.

"A coyote? You're right. I don't understand." She stood up and then staggered slightly, as if dazed from the shock of not getting her way. Then she slipped on her sunglasses, smoothed back the platinum tresses, reapplied the maroon lipstick, headed out the side door and across the lawn as fast as her platforms could navigate the bumpy terrain.

"I'm sorry, I'm so sorry, about everything," said Ed, trailing along behind.

She climbed into her car, started the engine, and waited for Ed to catch up. "If Lucy doesn't come back, then what?"

His stomach clenched as he glanced back at the house—the tiger lilies that needed deadheading, a huge Staples carton for BPCC that had been deposited on the front porch—everything in wait for Lucy and the boys to return. "I don't know what I'll do."

"Think about what I said. I'm not giving up, because I know I'm right." Her perfectly shaped lips turned upward in a loving smile, confident that eventually she'd bring him around, make him see the world through cat's eye glasses. She revved the engine and rocketed off with Paula Cole blaring full tilt from the CD player. He watched as the perky rear end of her SUV with its bustle-shaped spare tire screeched around the green at sixty and disappeared from view. He walked dejectedly up the path, pulled open the tin letter box, and peeked inside. There, on top of the L. L. Bean catalog and *Information Age* magazine, was a small envelope addressed in Benjy's ax-murderer scrawl.

At last, thank goodness, he thought, admiring the Canadian Mountie stamp and the Ontario postmark. Some postal worker had stamped DELIVERY DELAYED DUE TO INCORRECT ZIP CODE across the zip code which was indeed incorrect. He pulled out a torn, blotted scrap that looked as if it had been written inside a sleeping bag under the wobbly glow of a flashlight.

Dear Dad,

This camp sucks. The kids are a bunch of sychos. Yesterday I nearly drowned. The counsilers are complete jerks. The food is like barf. Mom said I only had to stay two weeks so come get me or I will run away.

Please, Dad.

Benjy
p.s. I am not kiding

When Ed lifted his eyes from the page, the world seemed to have stopped. The orange lilies against the shiny white clapboards and the persistent snore of a lawnmower shrank and faded away with a *whoosh* of hot blood in his ears. The bumblings and musings and torpor of the last weeks vanished, along with any guilty residue of the showdown with Ingrid. His boys were lost in the wilderness, calling out to him for help. Hold on, guys, he thought loping up the path to the front door. I'm coming, I'm coming as fast as I can.

LEVEL III

The Lumberjack's Lair

CHAPTER 12

>>

The next evening, Lucy was dressed more appropriately as she hauled her way over to Sam's caboose—a pair of faded but clean jean shorts, a bulky gray Crocker Software sweat shirt with a slinky plum tank top underneath, black satin bra and bikini underpants, sports sandals showing freshly polished toenails, moussed and styled hair, tweezed eyebrows, mascara, lipstick, two spritzes of Lancôme citrus splash, and earrings with dangling silver eagle feathers. Armed with a sack of every cosmetic, nail, and hair product available at Dunbar's, she had spent most of the afternoon jumping up and down in front of the tilted bureau mirror to put together this ensemble.

The logic went as follows: I am going on a wilderness date with my ex-boyfriend, who is living like a hermit à la Thoreau. I want him to find me attractive, but I don't want him to think I dolled myself up on purpose since Sam, as I remember, disapproves of female vanity. So first I wear sensible clothes that you can paddle and portage in and not get too sweaty or chilled. The Crocker sweatshirt has many textures of meaning—even though Sam disapproves of technology, I have made my fame and fortune designing software. So lump it, Sam, Crocker Software, *c'est moi.* Probably disapproves of makeup and nail polish, too, but a woman of a certain age needs all the help she can get. Native American-themed jewelry is politically correct, environmentally sensitive, and might distract the eye from the crow's-feet. Outfit also has interesting layering possibilities. If things get too toasty in the caboose, I can always strip down to a more comfortable tank top, and if things get really steamy, there's always the black satin underwear to fall back on, so to speak.

When she burst out of the channel onto the now choppy surface of Twin Pond, she spotted Sam's rangy figure waiting at attention at the end of the dock. Even from halfway across the pond, she could see that he'd made a stab at sprucing himself up—jeans without duct tape patches, a work shirt that was probably the most respectable one he owned, the dark gray-tipped hair parted and slicked back. A sudden flash of teeth through the now neatly trimmed beard. "I was afraid you weren't going to come," he yelled out.

Had he been standing there all afternoon, she wondered, answering back with an eager wave. A man waiting for her, fretting that his hopes might be dashed—there was a flattering thought. Now that Sam was watching, she propelled the canoe forward with her neatest Kinahwee-style j-stroke until it glided alongside the dock with nary a bump. He stooped down to grab the painter, fixing her body with one of his smoky stares in the process. "You're wearing clothes this time," he said.

"I was wearing clothes last night."

"Could have fooled me."

Well, this evening was getting off to a good start. She handed over her party offerings—a giant bottle of Merlot and a loaf of prefab garlic bread from Dunbar's—which he inspected quizzically. "Oh, right, booze and store food. Haven't had either in a while but I'm willing to give them a try."

He led her up the path to the warped, moss-covered deck off the caboose. It was set up with a pair of battered aluminum chairs and an orange crate wedged between as a crude coffee table. He gestured toward the chair with the least amount of plastic webbing missing and Lucy gingerly eased herself down. "I'll open the wine, that is, if I can find a corkscrew," he said.

"Always be prepared," she said holding up her Swiss

Army knife with the corkscrew extended. She had no intention of trying to get through this evening sober. His work boots clanked up the caboose's iron steps and she heard the cupboard doors in the galley kitchen bang open and shut. Sweet, really, that he was so attentive to a dinner guest, not that he'd had any before her.

After another round of kitchen clatter (their supper being prepared?), Sam reemerged with two chipped coffee mugs, the opened bottle of wine, and a plate of tiny carrots with stalks still attached. She took a carrot and munched it with as much enthusiasm as she could muster. Why hadn't she thought to bring dip? But then again, her stomach was so jangled that it probably couldn't handle anything more complex than carrots straight.

Passing on the other deck chair, he stretched himself out on the warped decking—which made his body seem even longer and sexier than when it was vertical. "I'm not much of a cook, I'm afraid, so don't have any high hopes for the ratatouille. It's the first time I've made it."

Yes, she remembered Sam's cooking abilities—the Boston baked beans charred to the bottom of the pan. On second glance, maybe the sharp collarbones and angular face looked more underfed than lean, the result of six months of bad cooking. She'd have to fatten him up. "Nothing like a fresh carrot," she said stupidly, washing it down with a big gulp of wine.

"I felt like such a jerk when you left last night. I just carried on about myself and my garden for half an hour and didn't ask you a single question about your life. So, tonight you're going to do all the talking and I'm going to do all the listening." He propped himself up on his elbows and folded his leathery hands expectantly. "Tell me everything."

Sam, listening—and who said men never change? Too bad her mind was suddenly such a yawning void. "What do you want to know," she said, taking another slug of wine.

"Why don't we pick up where we left off? You start with when I left Cambridge."

Pick up where we left off—he made their parting sound so jaunty and carefree. Maybe men don't change so much after all. "You mean after I stopped crying," she said quietly, narrowing her eyes to slits.

This wasn't the answer he'd been anticipating and his bushy eyebrows pushed together in a perplexed peak. "Why were you crying? You were the one who called it quits."

"I didn't *call it quits,* as you say." The words came spitting out. How dare he have a version of their breakup that was different from her own. "You were the one who laid down the ultimatum—leave now or else. I just wasn't ready to pack up and go with twenty-four hours' notice." Her spine stiffened with indignation and she glared out over his head at fresh hatch teeming over the surface of Twin Pond, punctuated by the sharp splash of a rising trout. Her father always had his smelly canvas creel, rod and waders set by the door, like firemen's boots, so he could gallop down to the stream at a moment's notice. At least until the summer he got sick.

Sam's shoulders slumped and he turned his calloused palms upward, as if he were waiting to get thwacked by a ruler. "The point is, I've regretted losing you ever since. But I can't undo it—what's done is done."

What's done is done. Once it is over, it is over, as he wrote in his final letter. A very black-and-white thinker, Sam was. If he'd missed her so goddamn much, couldn't he have tried a little harder to undo the past—answered her three letters, come crawling back a month later begging for a second chance? She crossed her arms, unmollified. "Remember that kid violinist who lived next door, the one you said was a twelve-year-old prodigy?"

"*Mmm.* Yeah, maybe." He followed Lucy's gaze toward the hatch. "What about him?"

"He came knocking on my door after you left. He'd heard me crying and wanted to know if I was all right. Turns out he was twenty-five not twelve, and a graduate student at MIT. So eventually, I married him."

"You're married?" Sam said, sounding almost indignant.

"Yeah. Why is that such a surprise?" She grabbed another carrot and took a defiant chomp.

"Oh, I don't know. You came paddling up here all by yourself dressed in nothing but a skimpy bathing suit. You weren't wearing a wedding ring. There was no mention of any husband waiting back at the cabin. You just didn't look married," he concluded.

Lucy didn't dare ask what married looked like. Not half-crazed, half-clothed? She glanced down at her left hand. After a few days without a wedding ring, the indentation had plumped out, the pale flesh had reddened in the sun. All the telltale signs of marriage were disappearing one by one. "Well, in truth, I'm not one hundred percent married. My summer at Little Lost Lake is kind of a trial separation."

"You're separated?" he asked, his glum tone lifting.

"Yup. Have been for about a week."

"I can't say I'm sorry."

"I'm not asking you to be sorry," she said, giving her head a roguish tilt. There was an awkward pause as if no one knew what came next in the flirtatious, newly single, on-the-loose script, and she dropped her eyes back to her naked ring finger.

Finally, Sam reached over with the wine bottle to refill her mug and top off his own.

"You're not done yet, you know. You've told me about meeting the violin player and about leaving him last week. That leaves a fifteen-year gap, so keep going."

"I'll do my best." At first, her voice sounded oddly formal as it carried out across the quiet hush of the lake, as if she were giving a speech in an outdoor amphitheater. But eventually, she got caught up in the grandiosity of explaining her life to a rapt audience. The only other times she'd been asked to explain herself was to those twenty-something writers who interviewed her for gamer magazines, but they were only interested in pixels and RAM requirements and gamer strategy. Here was someone who wanted to know the answer to how Lucy Lamb Crocker had come to be sitting in front of a derailed caboose by a half-silted pond in Forest County, Wisconsin, at 6:35 P.M. on July 6, 1998.

She described her Corky-directed wedding reception under a pink-and-white striped tent at the Libertyville country club, the birth of the twins fourteen months later, Ed's first Tandy computer, the early days of Crocker Computers with Victor, Vlad, and Laszlo in the two-family on Spruce Street, the meteoric success of Maiden's Quest, the August bungalow vacations with Rosemary and Alfred. Then the saga of all her woes—the miscarriages one after the other, the growth of Crocker into a soulless corporation, the move to the wreck in Crowley, the twins' retreat into the cyberworld, her struggles with MQII, Ed's growing estrangement, and finally, betrayal.

By the time she finished, the hatch had died, the sun had dipped from view behind the far side of Twin Pond leaving only an orange-tinged glow, the brown bats had started swooping for mosquitoes, the peepers had cranked up their nightly chorus, and the bottle of wine had been polished off—mostly by Lucy. She had given up on the sagging lawn chair and now sat crouched on the deck next to Sam, the Crocker sweatshirt pulled down over her legs to fend off a suddenly nippy breeze. The outline of her canoe was about to be swallowed up by the deepening dusk, but she was past caring how she was going to find her way back to Little Lost Lake.

"So, you've got two thirteen-year-old sons. You've designed a computer game that's so famous even I've heard of it. You've accomplished a lot."

"No, I haven't," she said, shaking her head so hard that the tendrils of her newly shortened hair dropped into her eyes waifishly. Now that she had summarized herself, she felt oddly deflated. Is that all her entire adult life amounted to? "I have no husband. I have no job. My boys are on their own, at least temporarily. Right now, I don't even have a home, just my father's old fishing shack." She let out a self-pitying sigh.

"Don't you get it, Lucy?" Sam said, suddenly lunging forward and placing his giant hands over her sweatshirt-covered knees, as if he were steadying her so she wouldn't topple over. "Coming to Little Lost Lake isn't a retreat, it isn't a failure. It's a triumph."

"It is?" she asked meekly.

"You're just like Thoreau. You're taking the time to stop and reevaluate your life. Sure, you could have designed another stupid computer game and made another undeserved million. You could have let your kids rot their brains and destroy their souls in front of a computer monitor. You could have let your husband screw around and pretended that it didn't matter. But instead, you drew a line, you said no more. I am going to stop being a sellout and start leading a life that has some integrity to it. That's what brought you back here. Back to me." He delivered this speech in the same intense, passionate voice that he had once used to extol the beauty of timber wolves and peregrine falcons, but instead he was talking about her, Lucy. And coming from his lips, her flight to Little Lost Lake didn't seem feckless and pathetic. It had integrity, goddamn it. She liked the sound of that word, especially when it was applied to herself. His grip around her knees tightened, he tilted his head slightly and leaned toward her.

"Ah, Sam?

"Mmm."

"What's that smell?'

He leaned back and sniffed the night air. "Oh, shit. It's dinner." They both jumped to their feet and staggered drunkenly up the iron steps to find a smudge pot of smoke pouring out of the oven. Her garlic bread resembling a charred log, the ratatouille a tar black lump. They ferried them down to the lake and chucked them in, where they hissed, burbled, and sank.

"Sort of pretty. Like watching fireworks," she said, her legs now naked and trembling.

"Speaking of sparks," he said, grabbing her around the waist with one arm and carefully smoothing her hair back off her forehead with the other. He gazed down at her with one of his soulful the-world-is-all-in-a-shambles stares, then broke into a smitten grin. "You are so lovely. I can't believe you came back to give me a second chance." And then as a foul cloud of scorched ratatouille and garlic bread oozed up from the pond to surround them, he kissed her.

Instead of fogging over with lust and booze and smoke fumes, Lucy's mind suddenly took an analytical turn. For the first time in eighteen years, I am kissing someone other than Ed Crocker, it thought. In fact, I am kissing the man that I sometimes wished I had been kissing instead of Ed Crocker. So now that I am kissing Sam McCarty, what do I think? Not sure about this beard, liked it better when he was clean shaven. At least it's not as bristly as it looks and smells like Ivory soap, but it feels a bit like kissing a boiled wool sweater. And I'm having to bend my neck back at a funny angle—that's what you get for kissing someone who's six inches taller instead of one. But these hunky shoulders are nice, Lucy thought as her hands traveled up his ripply torso. Just shows what can happen if you drain lakes and double spade garden beds instead of push a mouse around all day.

"You're shivering," he said, rubbing his hands hard along her backside to get the blood flowing. He had once showed her techniques on how to prevent hypothermia that he'd learned at the National Outdoor Leadership School. That they had both been buck naked in the caboose bed on a sweltering August day didn't matter. She'd discovered that she needed to be warmed up after all.

"I'm cold," she said, pressing her goose-bumped legs hard up against his thighs.

"It's probably warmer inside." Warmer was an understatement, oven hot was more like it, although the smoke had thinned out. She peeled off the Crocker sweatshirt to the tank top, he shed the button-down to a waffle weave undershirt. When he grabbed her around the waist again, they bumped into the table and the dangling lightbulb whacked hard into his skull. It was problematic getting intimate inside a caboose. Undaunted, Sam kept trying to warm her up, his hands roaming up her bare arms and across her shoulders, up the tense muscles of her neck and combing through her hair, his fingers all the while doing some king of vibrating, pummeling action.

"Is this part of your hypothermia training," she murmured into his neck, also smelling sweetly of Ivory.

"Massage training actually. Tantric massage," he informed her, pushing the tank top off one shoulder and sliding his lips along her collarbone.

Lucy stiffened and stepped back, the lightbulb smacking her this time. "What did you say?" Her voice came out loud and petulant in the shoebox space. She would think he was kidding if she'd included all the tawdry details of Ed and Ingrid's union in her disquisition, but pride had held her back.

"It's an ancient form of spiritual and erotic massage. I met this tantric expert who gave me, uh, kind of a private workshop."

So maybe that's what Ed had been getting—his own private workshop, she thought, staring hard at her feet with their silly red toenails. When Sam hooked his thumbs into the waistband of her shorts and tried to coax her back, her feet remained immovable as if they were bolted to the tongue-and-groove floor. "You're so tense, Lucy. What is it?"

Don't analyze, she told herself, allowing her body to go limp, be pulled against his. "Maybe I need a tantric massage," she muttered.

They both glanced around for a plausible location for such an activity—the floor underneath the table, the built-in bench with the lumpy boat cushion? He took her hand, pressed it to his wildly thumping heart, and then led her up the ladder.

> > >

She'd forgotten about the morning light, the way it slanted in through the louvered slot at the top of the cupola and left three strips of sunshine across the jumble of discarded clothes and bodies and blankets strewn across the cubbyhole bed. She sat up, tried to smooth down the moussed spears of hair, and wrapped a scratchy Hudson's Bay blanket across her naked breasts. She studied Sam, sleeping like Phil used to when he was a toddler, on his back with one hand thrown poetically over his head, as if he were dreaming of King Arthur's round table. Even though she had lost all of her clothes early on, Sam had managed to hang onto the olive drab waffle weave shirt, now twisted and disheveled in a Lawrencian way. Oh, Sam, as gorgeous in the flesh as he had been in soft-focused memory (the one that filtered out the scuffle with the forest ranger and the bar fight and his tirades at her). She bent down, felt his moist breath on her cheek, gently touched his sweaty temple with her tongue. Yes, this was not a dream.

Her gut rumbled crossly and she placed a hand on a stomach that hadn't been as flat since the birth of the twins. That's right—she'd forgotten to eat last night, not that there had been anything edible. She managed to locate the tank top and the black bikini balled up under the covers, dressed, crept down the ladder to the galley kitchen. Surely, Sam must have something besides raw carrots in his larder. She pried open the warped cupboard doors and found the kind of austere, vegan supplies a Thoreau wannabe would lay in for a one-year solo—twenty-pound bags of soybeans and brown rice, a carton of whole wheat pasta, a quart bottle of tamari. She finally came up with a couple of herbal tea bags, a jar of honey, and a lump of homemade bread. As she padded around the caboose, straightening the table, wiping up the charcoal remnants of dinner, the strangeness of the situation struck her full force. Here she was doing breakfast chores as if this little playhouse were her home, as if the man upstairs were her husband or even her lover. But he was neither, he was a stranger. Her real home and her real husband seemed as distant and fairy-tale as Fogbound Isle in Maiden's Quest. Suddenly, the tongue-and-groove walls started to ripple and bow, and she sank weakly onto the bench, lowered her head between her knees.

She opened her eyes and found herself staring underneath the bench at an old typewriter and an accordion file where they had been shoved out of sight. That's right, they had been sitting on the table the first night she dropped by. Yes, she was right to feel woozy—she knew nothing about this man. After checking to make sure she was out of view of the loft, she sank stealthily to her knees, crept under the bench, unsnapped the elastic, and expanded the file, divided into three compartments. If Sam climbed down and found her two bare feet poking out, she could say she was looking for an earring. Just to be on the safe side, she unhooked one of her earrings and dropped it on the floor. The first compartment contained a stack of photographs. She slowly pulled out a gruesome color glossy of a wolf caught in a trap, its leg chewed down to a bloody bone trying to work itself free. Her stomach heaved, the taste of bile rose up in the back of her mouth. She flipped through the rest quickly—baby calves hemmed into tiny pens to be fattened into veal, clubbed baby seals, dolphins caught in tuna nets—the full repertoire of animal rights atrocities. The second held a stack of clippings on the derring-do of animal rights activists—"Green Peacers Dye Baby Cub Pelts," "Timber Spiked to Protect Spotted Owl Habitats," "Eco Nuts Torch Ski Lodge." She quickly scanned the first one, dated 1994.

Extremist Group Suspected in Provo Mink Farm Raid

Hans Jaeger, owner of Jaeger Mink Farm fifteen miles west of Provo, reported a breaking and entering on March 23. Accord-

ing to Mr. Jaeger, over five hundred cages were opened, freeing approximately 1,000 mink into the surrounding countryside. Efforts are underway to recapture the animals.

A fax received by the Provo city police claimed that a group calling itself the Animal Free Frontline was responsible for the crime. The group states that illegal actions are justifiable to prevent inhumane treatment of mink, including euthanizing the animals in gas chambers. The group's call to arms is, "Free the mink nation! Open the cages now!"

Well, Sam always had been a big fan of eco-outlaws. The last compartment contained dozens of typed drafts on onion skin. The top one was entitled "My Woodchuck." Ah, this was more like it—the beginnings of Sam's Waldenesque masterwork, *Twin Pond.*

"Lucy. Are you down there?" a voice called out from the loft, sounding slightly alarmed. She slammed the file shut, set it back by the typewriter, and wriggled backward out from under the bench. She scrambled to her feet, brushed the coating of dust off her front, and slipped her earring back on.

"I'm making tea," she yelled back, stepping out from under the loft to be greeted by Sam's sleepy face beaming down at her, sending a jolt of electricity straight down her spine.

"I was afraid you'd slipped off in the night."

"No such luck. You're stuck with me." She crossed her arms in front of her gaping, braless tank top, suddenly embarrassed by her nakedness in the harsh light of day. God only knows what her face looked like—the mascara had probably worked its way down to raccoon circles. "You stay there. I'll bring you tea in bed." While the tea steeped, she checked herself out in the tiny dime-store mirror over the sink, wiping away stray makeup with spit, restyling the hair with her fingernails. Now that Sam was awake, all her misgivings were washing away with a fresh wave of lust. There was probably some perfectly reasonable explanation for an animal rights clip file lurking under Sam's furniture; she'd ask him about it when an appropriate moment presented itself, but right now he was waiting for his tea.

She crawled up the ladder balancing two mugs in one hand and found Sam, now without the T-shirt, his chest hair a shocking black against his milky white skin. He took the mugs from her, set them down on the board shelf above the bed, then pulled her back in under the Hudson's Bay blanket. "I haven't been a very good host," he said, sliding the tank top over her head and chucking it down the ladder. "You must be hungry."

"But not for food," she said, pulling him back under the bright bars of sunlight.

Two hours later, when starvation had finally driven them down the ladder and Sam, with Lucy's assistance, had actually produced something suitable to eat—powdered scrambled eggs and hash browns with onions—and they had settled on the deck to savor a perfect cerulean-skied, pine-scented morning, Lucy decided the appropriate moment had come to probe his political leanings. As she watched him wolfing down his eggs, discussing his gardening and carpentry schemes for the day, she felt confident that there were no dreadful secrets to discover.

"So, Sam," she asked, oh so casual. "Are you still as fervent about all those environmental causes?"

"Not like I used to be when I slugged Ranger Wilcox in the snoot over the National Forest Service's logging policy, which he had absolutely nothing to do with, and broke his dental bridge. Remember that?"

"Hard to forget it. I bailed you out of jail," she said. And you didn't pay me back, come to think of it, she thought.

"Christ, I was such an intolerant asshole. Anyway, I hooked up with a couple fringe groups out on the West Coast. I even edited one of their newsletters for a while. But I got kind of turned off. They didn't care about the welfare of animals, they just wanted to burn down buildings and destroy logging equipment for the thrill of it. Now I'm strictly a twenty-bucks-to-the-Sierra-Club kind of guy."

"Got any new cause?"

He turned around to survey his self-created universe—the vegetable garden with its picturesque sapling fence, the snappy red boards of the caboose, the silt-free, slate blue pond water. "Yup. I do"

"What's that?"

"Help Lucy Crocker née Lamb get her life together. That's my new cause."

She tried to smile in a grateful, pleased way. This was what she had wanted after all—someone who shared her vision of how the world ought to be. Stripped down to its bare essentials, at one with nature, not enslaved to soulless technology. She closed her eyes and rubbed an aching spot over the bridge of her nose, trying to banish the image of Sam's last cause, a haunted-eyed wolf with its leg caught in the jaws of a spring-steel trap.

CHAPTER 13

>>

Tonight, Phil was on wash-up duty, which was worse than tent stake or food prep duty, but much better than latrine digging, so on balance, it was a wash—ha, ha. He carried a chipped enamel basin down to the lake's boggy edge, tipped it until it filled up with scummy brown water, then staggered and sloshed back up to the campfire, and plunked it down in a bed of red coals. While he waited for the water to boil, he gathered up the dozen tin plates and forks strewn cockeyed in the sandy dirt around the fire. The guys could have at least stacked their dishes in the washbasin like they were supposed to, he thought, scrapping half-chewed chunks of potato, onion, and Spam into a shallow compost hole.

Come to think of it, his mom always used to yell about how inconsiderate it was when he and Benjy ran off after dinner, leaving their dirty plates on the table for her to clean up. These days, Crowley seemed so long ago and far away that it was hard to believe he'd ever again open the pantry cupboard and help himself to an entire canister of sour cream-flavored Pringles, play online Command and Conquer, dream of excuses to walk by Lila Shea's house about five times a day.

Tonight they had had his second-favorite meal, Hudson's Bay hash. His first-favorite meal was called grizzly gravy, which was Knorr brown gravy mix dribbled over instant mashed potatoes and slices of spongy, white bread with margarine, which you had to admit sounded disgusting, but was really pretty tasty.

When the water started to steam, Phil dropped in the stack of plates and forks, squirted in some dish soap, and gave everything a stir with a long handled brush until bits of greasy food floated to the top. Then he carried a second washbasin down to the lake to get rinse water, pausing to admire a fireball sunset exploding behind a bunch of really tall pine trees. Tonight's was a medium-size lake. So far, he had identified three different lake types—huge lakes with dozens of islands and white-capped waves, medium lakes with maybe a couple of islands and large ripples with no white caps, and small lakes that probably were ponds that you could paddle across in about three minutes. Crossing the huge lakes scared him shitless—the way the wind sent the canoe skidding sideways no matter how hard he tried to keep it pointing straight, the waves splashing over the side and forming a brown puddle that sloshed back and forth until everything and everybody was soaked through.

But these medium lakes were just about perfect to paddle across or camp next to, Phil decided. On the far shore was a patch where the bushes and cattails were trampled flat. A watering spot, he had learned, and sure enough, a doe and fawn tiptoed down for a few slurps that he could actually hear, then fixed him with a suspicious stare. I won't hurt you, deer, he muttered softly. He slip-slopped the pan back up the bank and dumped the water over the quasiwashed dishes. Then he wiped each one against his sweatshirt and dropped it back with a clatter into the wannigan box. Not a great job, but at least he hadn't left any visible food chunks.

"Crocker, you're such a spaz." The voice was Brandon Fiske's, and he was speaking to Benjy, not Phil. Brandon's beefy arm with its wish bracelet made by his girlfriend Kyla, who he Frenched with back in Winnetka, was tugging at a wobbly tent line. Phil stood up and squinted over at the six orange tents in the clearing and realized that every one was lopsided, with tent poles poking out at crazy angles and untethered tent flies flapping in the breeze, like they'd been set up by Dr. Seuss. Unless someone took them down and set them up again properly, they would all cave in by midnight. Benjy was on tent stake duty—Uh oh, Phil shuddered, here we go again.

Benjy was leaning against a birch tree with his nose buried in a formerly waterlogged copy of *Dune*. "If the tents don't meet your high standards, Fiske, feel free to fix them," he said without looking up.

"Why should I do your job for you?" Fiske snarled, crossing his arms across his chest.

"Suit yourself," said Benjy, lowering his book and giving Fiske a screw-you smile. "Sweet dreams." By this time, all the other boys had stopped their latrine digging and canoe tying and wood gathering and waited nervously to see what would happen next.

Last night, Chris and Dave had gathered them round for something called "campfire dialoging" to discuss "bad attitudes." Chris had said in a soft, sorrowful voice that in his ten years at Camp Kinahwee—six years as a camper and two years as a CIT and two years as a trip leader—he had never seen such a bunch of "drag asses." He reeled off a list of their slacker infractions—doing chores in an incomplete or slipshod way, dawdling in the morning while packing up camp so the group made a late start, not paddling hard enough to keep up with the rest of the group, always picking the lightest loads during portages while leaving the canoes and wannigans for others to carry. Despite Chris's touchy-feely attempt to make it sound like they were all equally guilty, everyone knew that there was only one drag ass in the group—Crocker. So Chris had finally figured out Benjy was a slacker, not a retard.

"What should we do to someone we think is being a drag ass?" asked Fiske, who wasn't about to get blamed for Crocker's goofing off.

"Suggestions?" Chris asked, letting his eyes sweep around the circle, resting on everyone's face for an equal amount of time so that they knew he wasn't singling anyone out. This was something Chris called "consensus," which theoretically meant kids got to decide for themselves, but which in reality meant that decisions took about ten times longer than simply having a grown-up tell you what to do.

Phil kept his eyes fixed on the snapping pine boughs, not daring to make eye contact with anyone, especially not Crocker, who was sitting on the other side of the circle, thank goodness. At times like this, Phil tended to think of Benjy as Crocker, too, which was probably really disloyal, but he couldn't help it. Crocker just pissed Phil off. Crocker seemed to be deliberately weaseling out of his chores and paddling so pathetically that now he always had to share a canoe with Chris so he didn't hold the whole group up. Crocker didn't seem to mind that everyone thought he was a wuss. He didn't even care that if he acted like a wuss, everyone would assume that his twin was one, too.

"Why don't we form a court with judges and then when someone starts fucking—I mean screwing up, we can put him on trial and give him a sentence," said Trevor, a buzz-cut kid from St. Paul who wore camouflage army surplus clothes and bragged that he went bow hunting every fall with his uncle who'd been in jail, even though Phil didn't think that was anything to brag about. The rest of the guys shouted, "Yeah, a court, put him on trial!" Unlike Chris, they were all staring straight at Crocker.

"So what kind of sentence do you think would be fair?" Chris asked in a neutral way, like he couldn't take sides.

Brandon jumped right in, as if he had been hatching this plan with Trevor. "If a kid doesn't do cook duty right, he doesn't get to eat. If he doesn't carry a wannigan or canoe during a portage, he has to carry a double load the next time, and everyone will sit and watch him *sweat.* If he doesn't set up the tents right, he sleeps outside, even if it's *raining.* If he doesn't dig the latrine, then everyone gets to watch him take a dump." Brandon seemed to get more and more excited thinking of new punishments, and all the other kids nodded along, except Crocker and Phil.

"That sounds kind of punitive to me," said Chris, his voice heavy with disapproval.

"Well, it's *supposed* to be a punishment," Brandon whined.

"Here's another idea. Why don't we just help the drag ass become more motivated. If we help him understand how he's letting the team down, he'll try harder," said Chris, using a motivating voice. That was the other problem with consensus, if the grown-up thought the kids were coming up with the wrong decision, then he just told them what to do anyway.

All the kids groaned, including Phil. Get Crocker motivated to try harder? Fat chance, even if Trevor had brought along his uncle's stun gun.

"Chris and Dave," Brandon now yelled over to the counselors who were sitting on a log down by the lake. "Can you help me motivate a drag ass?" Every evening after supper, they made mugs of herbal tea and wandered off as far away from the team as they could possibly get. After a whole day of yelling at drag asses, they seemed pretty fed up and needed a break. Dave would play jigs on his penny whistle while Chris wrote long letters—probably complaining about Crocker—to his girlfriend, who was leading a bunch of Kinahwee girls across Lake in the Woods.

Chris wearily set down his writing tablet, swiveled around, and summed up the situation—the every-which-way row of orange tents, Crocker unbudging behind his book. Phil could hear Chris's worn-out sigh all the way over at the campfire—Crocker had really gone too far this time. Phil dropped the scrub brush and sprinted over to the clearing before Chris could get there.

"I'll help Benj fix the tents," Phil piped up. Rather than seeming relieved or grateful that Phil was saving his ass, Benjy leaned lazily against the tree and gave him the same screw-you look he'd given Brandon.

By this time, Chris and Dave had walked up from the lake

along with a clump of kids who smelled blood in the air. "It's not your chore, Phil. That's what the campfire dialoging was all about. *Individuals* need to take *responsibility* for their own *stuff*." Chris pronounced *individuals* and *responsibility* and *stuff* very carefully and quietly, through clenched teeth—this was as close to pissed off as Phil had ever seen him get.

"That's okay. We'll do it together. Right, Benj?" Phil said, delivering a sharp kick to Crocker's bony butt. The message was hard to miss—you stand up and help me set up these tents right now . . . or else. I'm not going to share a bedroom with you when we get back home, I'm not going to be your partner in BPCC, I'm not going to hang around with a loser like you in eighth grade. Got it?

Everyone fell so hushed that Phil could hear a big animal—probably a moose or a bear—lumbering down the embankment to the watering spot. Then Benjy shrugged, closed his book, clambered up, pushed his glasses back up his nose, and headed off toward the most cockeyed number. Together, they made quick work of removing the poles, most of which had been jammed in the wrong pocket, pulling the four corners square and tight, reinserting the poles in the proper place, pounding the stakes deep in the hard-packed dirt with ten-pound rocks. For once Crocker managed to do a halfway decent job, which made Phil even more annoyed because it meant he was just pretending to be a spaz.

Meanwhile, Dave and Chris and the rest of the guys had gathered around the campfire to roast marshmallows over the last glowing embers. Their voices floated up on the cold north wind—Brandon's obnoxious bray probably bragging about Frenching Kyla, everyone busting a gut, including Dave and Chris, then Dave playing "Light My Fire" with the others singing along off-key. Even after Phil and Benjy were clearly finished, no one yelled over, Come join us, they're a couple of marshmallows left. No, the tide had turned completely and permanently against both of them—they were outcasts, lepers, Crockers.

When it was time to pair up in tents for the evening, it was unspoken that no one would pick the Crocker twins, that they were stuck with each other for the rest of the trip. After they'd peed in the bushes, crawled into their tent, rolled out their sleeping bags, and were finally about to put an end to this cruddy day, a flashlight beam zigzagged across their faces. "Mind if I come in for a little dialoging?" Chris's voice whispered from out in the darkness. Without waiting for an answer, he unzipped the mesh flap, crept in, and sat cross-legged at the end of Benjy's sleeping bag. "I was pretty disappointed in how you guys handled things tonight," he said, shining the flashlight police interrogator fashion, first in Benjy's squinting face, then in Phil's.

"Me!" Phil yelped indignantly. "What'd I do?" Usually he wouldn't ditch Benjy when an adult took to spreading the blame around, but this was totally unfair. Crocker was so clearly guilty, and he, Phil, was so clearly innocent.

"When I told you that individuals needed to take responsibility for their chores, you went right ahead and did Benjy's job for him anyway," Chris lectured. "I know you were just trying to help out your twin, but on this trip, he's a fellow team member, not your brother. We decided as a team that individuals had to be responsible. So when you covered for Benjy, you let everyone else down."

Ah, what a bunch of crap. If Phil hadn't jumped in, they'd still be trying to "motivate" Crocker to set up the tents so they could get some sleep. Phil held up a hand to fend off both the flashlight and the faultfinding, but then Chris switched the spotlight onto Benjy.

"And you. What was that little performance with the tents all about?"

"What performance?" Benjy said coolly. You had to admire Crocker for never backing down no matter how out of line he'd been. Although, come to think of it, Crocker refusing to act sorry when their mom caught them surfing porn on the Internet was what got them in this mess in the first place.

"Don't be a wiseass. You just thought you'd stick it to me and everyone else by putting the tents up wrong. Well, guess . . . what . . . Crocker?" Chris said this slowly and ominously, like one of those Nazis in old World War II movies interrogating a French resistance fighter who refuses to talk.

"What?" said Benjy, for once sounding slightly intimidated. Chris had never called him Crocker before.

"You know how Brandon suggested that we put drag asses on trial. Dave and I've decided that's not such a bad idea. Next time you screw up, you'll be tried, and if you're found guilty, you'll be punished." Chris rocked forward onto his knees and lowered his flashlight from Benjy's face to the door.

"You mean, like, get sent home, or something?" Benjy said hopefully.

"I know that's your scheme. You're going to make yourself such a pain in the ass that we'll send you home." He shone the flashlight in his own face this time, so that they could see his expression, which was pretty scary. "Trust me, Crocker. Whatever punishment we choose for you, we are not going to send you home early. You're staying with us right to the end. That goes for you, too, Phil." With that, Chris crawled out and zipped the flap shut as if he were locking a cell door. Outside in the night from a dozen different directions came the sound of muffled snickers. Of course, "the team" had enjoyed Chris chewing out the drag asses.

Phil lay back on his sleeping bag and stared up at the moonlight blasting through the orange tent roof. How could he have been so dense? Benjy had been slacking off and screwing up because he hoped that they'd just give up and send him home. Phil flipped over on his side so Benjy wouldn't see the tears streaming down his face into the balled-up sweatshirt under his head. Well, maybe Benjy was right. Who'd want to be on a team with those fart faces who were still out there laughing their butts off. Phil let out a strangled sigh and then found himself wondering if they would have grizzly gravy tomorrow for supper in the last second before he drifted off to sleep.

There was a scuffling, then a crinkling of paper, and Phil pushed himself awake thinking maybe that a raccoon had gotten into the tent. But it wasn't a raccoon, it was Benjy—fully dressed, his sleeping bag rolled, his backpack loaded up and strapped shut. He was sitting cross-legged, holding the flashlight under his chin and pressing buttons on that stupid GPS—*bleep, beep, bleep*. A topo map was spread out on the ground. Benjy checked his watch—3:08. "Isn't it a little early to be getting packed up?"

"*Shhh,*" Benjy hissed.

"What the hell are you doing?" Goddamn, Benjy. Now he was going to be exhausted all day.

Benjy dropped the GPS and scooted over so his face was two inches away from Phil's. "I'm running away." His voice was as soft as a falling leaf.

Phil bolted upright, wide awake now. "What?" he whispered urgently.

"You heard me."

"You can't."

Benjy turned his back to him and zipped the GPS into an outside pocket. "Yes, I can." Again the voice soft but determined, much scarier than a shout.

Phil lunged out and grabbed Benjy's elbow with both hands. "I'm not letting go until you tell me where you're heading."

"Okay," Benjy whispered, jiggling the map in front of Phil's face. "I've been planning this for about a week. According to the GPS and this map, we're about seven miles away from a town called Beaver Falls. If I paddle across this lake, up something called Mud Creek which flows into something called Lake Hazard, then paddle across that and walk out a couple of miles, I'll be on Canadian Route 15A, straight into Beaver Falls. Piece of cake."

Phil almost burst out laughing. "*You?* Paddling across two lakes and hiking out to a highway. Get serious."

Benjy silenced him with a look that Chris would call "motivated." "Sorry to disappoint you, but that's what I'm doing."

Now a cold stab of fear shot straight down Phil's spine at the thought of klutzo Benjy heading off all alone into the wilderness. "What if you get lost or the canoe tips over or you run out of food? Come on, Benj. It's not safe. Chris and Dave will go ballistic if you run away."

"Oh, right, they're really going to be worried about me. What are you going to do? Tell on me?" It was the same go-suck-eggs voice he'd used with Brandon.

Phil was just showing a little concern for Benjy's safety—was that such a crime? He wished he *could* tell on Benjy, maybe make some loud noise right now and wake Chris up. But then another shiver zapped through his body when he considered what Chris would do if he caught Benjy trying to run away, especially after the warning he'd just delivered. A trial with Trevor and Brandon and all the other buttheads as judges, sentencing Benjy to some sicko torture, like having to portage a canoe naked. Phil would probably be put on trial, too. Oh, shit.

Benjy folded the topo map and stuck it in his pocket along with the GPS "Okay, I'm out of here. See you back in Crowley."

Suddenly, their mom's face popped into Phil's head, with her eyes squinting and her dark eyebrows pushed together with worry. What was she going to say when she heard that Phil had let Benjy run away? And what if something really, really awful happened, what if he did drown? Phil would be blamed for the rest of his life that he'd killed his twin. "Wait. I'm coming, too," Phil whispered, grabbing his smelly damp sneakers and jamming them on. He was no ace canoer, but together they had a lot better chance of making it across a huge, wind-whipped lake than Benjy solo.

"You are?" said Benjy, actually smiling. Well, at least the little creep was grateful. Phil rolled up his sleeping bag and stuffed it in his pack, then squashed the rest of his reeking clothes on top. Whew—maybe he'd get a hot shower at Beaver Falls. "Should we take down the tent?" he whispered.

Benjy shook his head. "Too noisy. I packed a tarp. We won't need a tent."

Slowly, slowly, Phil unzipped the tent an inch at a time, then poked his head out to see if the coast was clear. Five mountainous shapes, silver in the moonlight. Not a creature was stirring, except Trevor's snores as loud as a foghorn. First they slipped their packs out through the tiny flap door, then themselves. Hugging the packs tight to their bodies, they crept along the edge of the clearing—step, pause, step, pause—down to the shore. Thankfully, the wannigans were stored by the canoes, as far away from the tents as possible in case of marauding bears. They rummaged through for supplies, being careful not to clank any pans—a pot, matches, a jackknife, two forks—and then went wild in the food boxes. Benjy grabbed the two remaining packages of Campfire marshmallows; Phil the last four packages of Knorr beef gravy, a box of instant mashed potatoes, and a whole loaf of bread. They would feast on grizzly gravy and toasted marshmallows for breakfast, lunch, and dinner until they hit civilization!

They crawled on hands and knees down the row of overturned canoes and as gently as possible, flipped the last in line over. Benjy loaded in the supplies while Phil grabbed a couple of paddles and life vests. He threw a vest toward Benjy and gestured for him to put it on, which he actually did without protest. At least Phil could tell his mom that if he hadn't come along, Benjy would have probably forgotten to wear one. With Benjy at the bow and Phil at the stern, they hoisted up the canoe as high as they could by its gunwales and staggered drunkenly over the boggy ground into the water. Benjy lost his footing and let his end go with a resounding *smack, splash*. Spotlit by the full moon, they stopped dead, knee high in the freezing water and bent double over the gunwales, waiting to be discovered. Ten seconds passed, ten more, but no stirrings from the tents. They exchanged shrugs, clambered wetly aboard, and then with two swift strokes launched the canoe out across the inky water.

Like Daniel Day-Lewis trying to outrun an Iroquois war canoe in *The Last of the Mohicans,* they paddled hard and deep, in perfect unison, four strokes then rest so they could glance over their shoulders to see if shadowy forms were rushing down to the shore, waving frantically for the escapees to come to their senses and return. But all they saw were the six luminous, tranquil tents and five overturned canoes shrinking smaller and smaller. Panting openmouthed and ragged like dogs, they kept paddling at a fierce pace until they were swallowed up by a cloud of early morning fog. They rested long enough to give each other high fives, their faces dotted with dew, then started up again at the same heart-hammering rate. This was the first time Phil had been allowed to be the sternman; Trevor and all those other jerkoffs always said that he was too much of a spaz to handle it. Too bad they weren't here to see how competently he corrected direction and kept the canoe pointing straight for the stream outlet. Benjy wasn't doing half-bad, either, putting so much elbow grease (his mom's words) into every stroke that Phil could see his pecs and biceps bulge. Why hadn't he bothered to paddle like that before, why had he been willing to sit back and let Chris drag his lazy carcass across half the lakes in Canada?

But if Benjy hadn't been such a wuss, then they wouldn't have needed to run away. Now that a sharp early morning wind was plastering back his hair and filling his nose with the scent of pine and damp earth, Phil was quickly changing his mind about Benjy's moron scheme. This was the coolest, coolest thing he had ever done in his whole life. He could hardly wait to tell his parents all about it, and Lila Shea and all their friends back in Crowley. Maybe he'd even write a book like *Hatchet,* only without the plane crash.

They scooted past the watering spot where a couple of raccoons were busily washing their paws and nosed the canoe into the mouth of the narrow outlet. "Are you sure this is the right way?" Phil asked, still whispering.

"Yup," Benjy whispered, pulling the GPS out of his pack and giving it a few pokes to confirm his data. "The main way out of this lake is up north. They'll never figure out in a million years we took Mud Creek over to Lake Hazard. Trust me."

The sky was lightening now, just barely, a gray gloom darker than the moonlight. Phil checked his watch, only 4:22—the "team" wouldn't wake up for another hour and a half. By that time he figured they'd be on the far shore of Lake Hazard and long gone. He gave a final backward glance to the distant clearing in the woods, the tents and canoes shrouded in a haze of morning fog. "So long, suckers," he muttered softly.

Soon Phil understood why this body of water was called Mud Creek. Creek was the part it didn't deserve—ditch or puddle was more like it—but mud hit the nail on the head. They poled, they waded, they dragged, they portaged—the only thing they didn't do for an hour and a half was paddle. "Are you sure this shit hole leads someplace?" Phil whined every five minutes.

"Trust me. The map says it's only half a mile so we should be there any second," Benjy answered in his new confident, Joe Woodsman voice.

Here's a guy who can't even tie his shoes properly so they stayed tied, and I'm trusting him to guide me with some map and some plastic gadget through the Canadian wilderness? That map was probably drawn up twenty years ago, before

Mud Creek had dried up to a trickle. A hot ball of sun was poking its way above the cattails, half blinding him. He checked his watch—6:10. Chris and Dave and the rest were getting up now, stoking up the campfire to cook breakfast. What were they having, he wondered, his stomach churning at the awesome memory of Carnation hot chocolate mix and instant oatmeal with powdered milk. But no, they wouldn't be having a nice campfire breakfast today, because they had just discovered the Crockers' empty tent and the raided food boxes. With whoops of rage, the "team" would be climbing into the war canoes and heading after them. Catch the Crockers, try them, punish them!

"Let's haul ass, Benj," Phil shouted, jabbing at the murky bottom with his paddle. As if the god who watches over runaway campers had been listening, Mud Creek gradually filled with water until the trickle became a creek and then a stream became a river with a mind of its own, carrying them somewhere. Poling turned to actual paddling, and after ten minutes they burst onto a lake.

Squinting across choppy whitecaps toward a distant mist-covered shore, Phil revised his list of different lake types. There was huge, medium, and small. And now there was this—so gigantic that you couldn't even see the other side, that there were easily hundreds of islands and waves so large that they seemed to actually roll in like they did on Nauset Beach at the Cape. "Are you sure this isn't Lake Superior or Hudson's Bay or something?" he asked, trying to keep the shakes out of his voice.

"Trust me," said Benjy holding up his GPS now hanging by a dinky red lanyard around his neck. "This is Lake Hazard."

Lake Hazard, that name should tell you something shouldn't it, Phil? He remembered as if in a long-ago dream his first night at Camp Kinahwee when Chris had explained some of the fundamental laws of canoe safety. He said how the senior canoe trip would mostly avoid the biggest lakes because even an experienced paddler could get swamped and capsized by a rogue wave, and lightning storms came on so quickly that there was no time to reach shore before they hit. In other words, lakes like this one.

Last year a Crowley police officer had lectured the seventh grade about how to resist peer pressure. When a friend wants you to try something dangerous, you need to make eye contact and say, I think this is a bad idea, no. And if paddling across Lake Hazard with Benjy wasn't a bad idea, what was?

"Hey, Benj?" Phil said, resting his paddle across his lap. He had to shout to make himself heard over the whistle of the wind and the roar of the waves. The morning sky, which had seemed so rosy and cheerful a moment ago, was suddenly looking soupy gray in the distance. When Benjy turned his head, Phil tried to make eye contact through his foggy glasses. "I think this is a bad idea. The lake's too big. We're going to flip over. No."

Benjy glanced over his shoulder, his shirt and hair already half-soaked with spray, and frowned in a puzzled way, as if this thought hadn't crossed his mind. "So, what do you want to do? Turn back?" he snarled.

The idea of slogging back up Mud Creek so they could slink back to camp with their tails between their legs and be put on trial wasn't very appealing, either. "Maybe we can just paddle around the edges," Phil suggested.

Benjy pulled out the map and studied it as best he could with the wind billowing it out like a sail. "Obviously, that would take about twice as long as crossing the middle. The circumference of a circle is three-point-fourteen times the diameter, right? That's the definition of pi," he yelled back.

"I don't need a freaking math lesson, Crocker."

"Okay, sorry. If we go around the edge, they'll catch us for sure. Let's hop from island to island instead." He held up the flapping map for Phil and jabbed at a stepping-stone row of islands straight down the center of the lake. "See? Squirrel to Blueberry, to Hermit, to Otter, to Snapping Turtle. Looks easy."

Squirrel, Blueberry, Hermit, Otter, Snapping Turtle—the names made Phil think of happy woodland creatures having a picnic. And it was a lot less scary to think of six or seven short crossings than one enormous one. He checked the map and then aimed the canoe toward a rock and spruce bump that didn't seem too far away. "Okay," he called, dragging his paddle hard through the chop. "Squirrel Island, here we come."

Phil didn't do so well as sternman this time. Even though he yanked until every muscle in his back and arms screamed, the canoe kept veering off to the right, where it wobbled back and forth between the troughs of waves. Benjy was back to his old wuss self, too. His strokes were either so shallow that they barely glanced the water, or so deep that Benjy nearly threw himself and everything else overboard. "Take even strokes and pull harder!" Phil instructed.

"Why don't you point us where we're supposed to be going instead of over there!" Benjy shouted back. What was the use of trying to explain that he was aiming the canoe toward the island, but the wind kept slapping it sideways?

After almost an hour—with every one of his strokes wrestling against Benjy's until sweat soaked his shirt and his stomach heaved with hunger—Squirrel Island seemed only a fraction closer. "Whoa," he yelled, bending double to catch his breath.

"Don't stop," Benjy whined.

"We're pulling against each other. I'm the sternman, so you have to follow my lead. One, two, three, *stroke!* One, two, three, *stroke,*" he bellowed until his throat rasped raw. With each semicoordinated stroke the canoe pointed slightly straighter, and wonder of wonders, Squirrel Island inched closer until half an hour later they bumped into a tiny rocky inlet. "Let's pull up," Phil said. If he didn't stand on firm ground for a few minutes to eat something, drink some water, pee, and stretch out his back, he'd puke or faint. Benjy didn't even complain for a change. Phil nosed the canoe against a toppled spruce stump, the most unrocky mooring spot he could see, while Benjy scrambled out with the line and pulled them in. "Make sure the line is securely tied or the canoe'll drift away," Phil warned.

Benjy stopped to give Phil one of his superior, over the top of his glasses looks. "Thanks for the tip. I never knew you had to tie up a boat or it would float off."

"Okay, sorry," said Phil, lowering himself into the choppy water and dragging off the two packs. But he wasn't sorry, not when every other canoe that Benjy had tied up in the last four weeks had come unhitched. Benjy had to realize that Chris and Dave weren't around anymore to fix his mistakes, that there could be life-or-death consequences to screwups. On his way past the line, Phil tested the knot. Well, okay, maybe he had tied a bowline right—this time.

Phil propped his pack against a birch and rummaged inside for the box of instant potatoes and a gravy package. "I'm making us grizzly gravy for breakfast," he announced.

"We can't stop long enough to boil water," Benjy said, fishing the marshmallows out of his pack.

"We can make it with cold water." Phil filled the pot with a couple of waves. He put a pile of potato flakes on a tin plate, then dribbled some water over it and stirred with his jackknife until he'd made a doughy lump. That didn't look right, so he added a much bigger splash and mashed until it looked like Elmer's glue. Then he dumped the gravy mix in a mug and added water until it turned into something the consistency of brown poster paint. He dropped a clump of gravy on top of the puddle of potato and offered some to Benjy, who stuck a finger in his mouth like he was going to barf.

"I'll stick with marshmallows," he said.

"Suit yourself," Phil said, scooping up a clot of grizzly gravy with his knife and shoveling it in.

"Tasty?" Benjy asked, as Phil made a gagging sound and lunged for the water.

Phil studied the flotilla of islands and the misty, darkening far shore of Lake Hazard. Even if the weather stayed good, which it probably wouldn't, it would take them a whole day of haul-ass paddling to cross this mother. And if a storm came up, they'd just have to hole up on one of these islands till it blew over, maybe in a day or two. It was now 8:20—the "team" had discovered them missing two and a half hours ago. With luck, they were still searching for them south of Lake Hazard. Phil looked down at the red Kinahwee canoe pitching back and forth against the line. It would be pretty conspicuous even far out in the lake, or if they sent a search plane over. A search plane—now there was a sickening thought.

"Let's get moving," said Phil. He spread the remains of the grizzly gravy on a piece of bread like extrachunky peanut butter and made himself eat it. He couldn't paddle for eight more hours on an empty stomach.

Using Phil's new and improved sternman techniques, they managed to stroke, stroke, stroke over to Blueberry Island in a respectable twenty-five minutes. This time they didn't pull ashore. They merely caught their breath, grabbed a couple of marshmallows and a swallow from their water bottles, and shoved off again. They passed close to a third treeless island that Benjy identified as Hermit and a tiny rocky fourth one which he said was Otter. As Phil chomped another marshmallow, he nervously studied the black storm front brewing on the far shore, even though there were still puffy white clouds overhead. Curiously the storm cloud that had once been directly in front of them now seemed to have moved off to the right. "Hey, Benj? Are you sure we're heading in the right direction? All these islands look alike."

"Of course I'm sure."

"Don't you think you better check?"

Benjy pulled out the GPS, started pushing buttons, and then took his bearings against the horizon. "Oh," he said. "I guess we kind of got off course. We should go thataway." He pointed forty-five degrees to the right, straight into a rising headwall of nimbus clouds.

"Which one's Otter?" Phil asked, but Benjy shrugged. Well, maybe it didn't matter if they identified every island, if they were at least heading in the right general direction, Phil told himself hopefully, even though they seemed to be paddling full steam into the eye of the storm.

Suddenly, the air took on an electric charge and Phil felt the hairs on the back of his neck rise. A sharp wet wind picked up and the stagnant storm line started marching toward them fast. There was a distant rumble of thunder followed by another. The water turned dirty-gray and murky, then the rain started. They stopped long enough to fish their rain jackets out of their packs, stow the water bottles and marshmallows, and strap the waterproof packs tightly shut. Benjy reverently wiped the raindrops off the GPS and zipped it into the pocket of his rain jacket.

Ah, screw that thing, thought Phil as he paddled resolutely into the storm. Benjy never would have come up with this harebrained scheme to run away if he hadn't gotten the GPS. It made him think he actually knew what he was doing; that he wasn't a spaz, wasn't Crocker. Phil yanked the drawstring of the rain hood tight around his head and squinted through the deluge. All around him, there was nothing but choppy gray water broken only by the needle pricks of raindrops. They should head for the nearest island, but suddenly there were no islands, only a rocky bump with a couple of pine trees, and even that was still a few hundred feet away. The waves were coming faster now, bigger, taller, rocking the canoe crazily back and forth. Don't panic, thought Phil, panicking.

Suddenly, a huge bolt flashed across the sky. Benjy jumped, wheeled around so Phil could see the terror in his face, and then in slow motion his body leaned sideways, farther and farther across the water, until over he went, taking a whirling jumble of paddles and packs with him. The canoe is capsizing, Phil realized. I am going to die in some lake in Canada, he thought. Mommy, he heard himself yell, then the shock of freezing cold water against his body, a big gulp of water, a distant thud as the canoe smashed against his skull. Now he was under water, black water, his arms and legs and feet heavy with jackets and shoes and life vests. He thrashed and kicked until his head poked up into air, spitting out a squirt of putrid water. He opened his eyes only to get pelted by another face full of rain and waves. "Benjy," he spluttered. "Benjy," he tried again, a little louder this time. "Benjy," he shrieked. Nothing. Oh, shit, shit, shit, this cannot be happening, he thought, flailing around to see the overturned red hull of the canoe, the paddles, the outline of Benjy's pack bobbing in the waves.

Then a splash and a strangled voice. "Phil . . . sorry," Benjy wailed. His sad wet head, now missing its glasses, bounced up next to his pack. Well, you should be, asshole, Phil thought, kicking over to him.

"You okay?" Phil asked.

"Co . . . co . . .cold," was all Benjy could manage through chattering teeth.

Hypothermia, Phil thought. Chris had warned them about hypothermia, along with big lakes and lightning storms. All right, it's up to me, thought Phil, his mind suddenly becoming clear and calm, the frigid wetness on his body and face receding until it seemed like no more than a minor discomfort. He kicked his legs hard to push his head high enough above the waves to get his bearings. Yes, there was that island not too far away, a few hundred feet, a brisk swim, they could do it. But first things first—save Benjy, canoe, packs, paddles—in that order. He was grateful that Chris had spelled out the emergency procedures step by step in the event of a capsize. Don't think, just do.

He splashed over to Benjy, grabbed him by the shoulders, and shook him hard —get that blood moving. "Benjy. Don't panic. You'll be all right. Swim to the island but first help me flip the canoe back. Got it?" Phil was yelling; Benjy seemed dazed, as if he'd just been startled awake from a nap. He's in shock, Phil thought. "Got it?"

"Yeah," he coughed out, without making any movement toward the canoe.

"Come on! Kick your legs! Move!" Phil started swimming toward the canoe, dragging Benjy by the strap at the back of his life vest. Oh, shit! He wasn't strong enough to pull Benjy and the canoe and himself all the way to that island. "Kick," he shrieked, taking in another mouthful of water, and Benjy, thank you, thank you, started to kick.

Phil dropped Benjy on one side of the bobbing hull of the canoe, then paddled around to the other side and hung onto the metal rim. This was as much of Chris's instructions on how to flip a canoe as he remembered—now what? "You pull, I push," he yelled. And that's what they did, with grunts and thwacks against the aluminum hull for what seemed like five minutes, until suddenly Phil's side popped out of the water and the canoe smacked onto its back, still a third filled with water but floating. They hung on either side, kicking and gasping for breath, checking to see if any of their other gear was still floating. At least Benjy's teeth weren't chattering as hard and he didn't look half-dead. Phil grabbed first one paddle and then the other, tossing them in the bottom of the canoe. He kicked over to the bouncing hulk of Benjy's yellow pack, towed it by one of its straps over to the canoe, and together they were able to hoist it into the canoe with a thud and a splash. Then Phil spun around trying to spot his green pack poking above the chop, but nothing. Must have gotten waterlogged and sank. A list scrolled through his head—sleeping bag, knife, grizzly gravy, dry clothes. He lunged at a piece of plastic drifting by and pulled up Benjy's glasses, which had washed off his face. When he held them up, Benjy actually managed a slight smile.

"Swim to the island, I'll pull the canoe," Phil shouted at him, but Benjy hung on the edge of the canoe, unmoving as if he didn't want to ditch Phil but didn't have the strength to help him. "I can do it. *Go!*" Benjy released his grip, sank down into the water, and then headed off, wallowing like a wounded Saint Bernard until he hit the island, then crawled up the bank and collapsed on his back.

Phil floundered round to the end of the canoe and tried to propel it with kicks toward the island. The sludge in the bottom sloshed back and forth, but the canoe, heavy as a barge, didn't budge. His rain slicker scooped in more water with every move, dragged against his arms. Cold, wet everywhere, he thought, shivering hard now, his teeth chattering like Benjy's. Maybe he should give up and let the canoe drift off. He noticed the Day-Glo orange coils of the safety line, still jammed under the metal ledge of the bow. One more try. He wrestled the rope free and dog-paddled to the island, unwinding the line as he went. Yes, I got lucky, he thought, gaining a slippery toehold with the line still in his hands. With the water neck deep, he tried to stand and haul at the line, but the canoe jerked back, dragging him face first into the water. "Need help, Benj."

It took a while for Benjy to stir, but eventually he splashed back in and together they reeled the canoe in a foot at a time up to the shore, then with the final ounce of their strength, hauled it up the bank. Phil leaned back against the overturned canoe hull and for the first time, scoped out this island that had just saved their hides. It was mostly a big pile of rocks, with three crooked spruce trees surrounded by a clump of bare blueberry bushes—nothing that offered any protection from the steady drizzle or lightning. Another flash of light, clap of thunder, but more distant. They might freeze, but probably wouldn't get struck by lightning. Now that the thrill of hitting solid ground was wearing off, Phil started trembling violently in his sopping clothes and noticed Benjy's lips had turned blue. They had to rig some kind of shelter fast, strip, and find something to change into in Benjy's pack.

Whispering a little prayer, please be dry, please be dry, Phil loosened the straps of Benjy's pack and peeked inside. Top layer damp but not too bad, and a few other miracles—the loaf of bread and the marshmallows had gotten stashed in Benjy's and not Phil's pack, the sleeping bag was dry, and at least Benjy had packed a tarp. They stretched the tarp on top of the blueberry bushes and tied two corners to the spruce trees, making a prickly but fairly dry shelter. Then they peeled off their soaking clothes, the blast of wind hitting their bare flesh like a slap, and put on every item in Benjy's pack—two pairs of socks apiece, long underwear, turtlenecks, shorts, hats, sweatshirts, polar fleece vests, bathing trunks—and pulled the unzipped sleeping bag over them. They rubbed their arms and thumped their legs, blowing warm air into their hands until slowly the quivering and chattering stopped.

For the first time, Phil noticed that he had a throbbing pain on his forehead. He reached up and touched a bump that felt as big as a Ping-Pong ball. It must be from the canoe smacking against his skull. His fingers were covered with a sticky film of blood.

Benjy stared over, his eyes getting huge with alarm. "You okay," he asked sounding scared, which didn't help matters.

"I guess so," Phil whispered, wiping his hands on a spare dirty sock. His mom would know what to do, of course. Wrap ice cubes in a dish towel, make him lie down on the couch, give him two Advil. Who's going to take care of me now, he wondered, a sour taste rising up in the back of his throat. Benjy?

"Better eat something," Benjy suggested. They each had two pieces of bread and three marshmallows, washing it down with the water left in Benjy's bottle, which made Phil feel better. At least the bump had stopped bleeding.

"Now what?" Benjy asked, staring out at the endless wet gray which seemed to have swallowed up the far shores of Lake Hazard.

"We wait for the rain to stop," Phil said, yawning.

"Then what?" Benjy said, his voice demanding like a little kid's.

"Then we wait for someone to find us."

"No one's going to *find* us. No one knows we're on this *stupid* lake."

"They'll probably send out a search plane when it stops raining," said Phil, trying to sound confident, but now Benjy was getting him worried. He suddenly remembered all those movies where the survivors in the life raft hear the roar of a search plane. Oh my God, we're rescued, we're rescued, light the flares, wave the red flag! The sound of the plane comes closer and closer, then is overhead; the survivors flap their arms, shrieking, Down here, down here. Then slowly, the engine sound gets fainter and fainter until it disappears, forever.

"No food, no tent, only one sleeping bag . . . " Benjy's voice choked and he lowered his head on his sleeve and started to cry, big hoarse sobs.

"Don't cry," said Phil, feeling helpless. He reached over and awkwardly patted Benjy's skinny arm. The only time they touched anymore was when they slugged each other. Please, please stop, thought Phil, because if you totally lose it, I'm going to totally lose it. "Look. We've got the canoe and the GPS. Tomorrow we'll paddle over to Beaver Falls and call someone."

"I'm not getting back in that canoe," Benjy wailed. "And besides, the GPS is probably wrecked. I got the cheap model that's not waterproof."

Oh, great. He gets the cheap model. "Let's just go to sleep, okay?" Phil said, yawning again. God, he was pooped even though it was only 4:30. But then again, he'd been awake since three in the morning, more than twelve hours ago, when he thought the worst problem in his life was maybe being put on trial by that butthead Brandon Fiske. They spread a couple of garbage bags on the wet ground, used the backpack as a lumpy pillow, huddled side by side so the sleeping bag covered most of them. He gingerly touched his lump and was relieved to find it had shrunk down to mere cherry size. "Good night, Benj," Phil said, shutting his eyes and trying to ignore Benjy's spiky back pressing into his and the smell of his greasy wet hair. The drumbeat of raindrops against the tarp and metal canoe was slowing now, the wind turning soft and sweet.

"I know I act like a real jerk sometimes," said Benjy, still tearful, to the back of Phil's head. "I know other kids think I'm a loser and you stick up for me."

Granted, Benjy was a loser, but an island in the middle of Lake Hazard hardly seemed like the place to discuss his social problems. "That's okay. I don't mind."

"I guess you kind of saved my life today. So, like, thanks. You know I really, um, do love you. I love Mom and Dad, too. Think we'll ever see them again?" He said this like it had never occurred to him before that he might actually love the members of his family.

Of course, Phil loved Benjy, too, but it would feel weird to say it out loud, and he didn't want to speculate on whether or not he'd ever see his mom and dad again because then he really would start crying. He wondered what they were both doing right now. Dad was probably in some meeting with Ingrid with the big boobs, hammering out the final details of Maiden's Quest II. Mom was sitting at an easel by the edge of Little Lost Lake, wherever the hell that was, making watercolors for her new children's book. Hopefully neither one would ever find out that Benjy and Phil had run away from Camp Kinahwee. "Things will probably look a lot better in the morning," he said, not believing a single word, but Benjy was already softly snoring.

At sunrise, when their empty stomachs grumbled them awake, things really did look better. All traces of the storm had blown away in the night. Their island seemed scrubbed clean, a steamy sun beat down on the glassy surface of Lake Hazard, which today looked smaller and less hazardous. The lump on Phil's head was sore, scabby, but a lot flatter. They spread their soggy gear over rocks to dry out, including the waterlogged, nonfunctioning GPS, which had been rescued from the pocket of Benjy's rain jacket. When Phil went down to the water's edge to refill the water bottle for their bread and marshmallow breakfast, he spotted the green corner of his half-sunk backpack, which had come to rest in the roots of a tree. Phil waded out and was able to drag it to shore, even though it had picked up at least fifty pounds of water. They opened it up and found the gravy packages and box of potatoes wet but still edible. Using crumpled pages of Benjy's Kinahwee Camper's Manual and pine needles for kindling, they built a fire and had grizzly gravy for breakfast. Three helpings apiece—so much that their stomachs bloated out like they were pregnant. Then they stretched themselves on a rock in the sun and waited for a search plane.

"What'll we do when the plane flies over?" Benjy asked sleepily.

"Throw some more wood on the fire. Wave our arms. Yell."

After three hours with no more sounds out of the sky than a stupid osprey diving for a trout, they decided they needed a fallback plan. They scanned the horizon in every direction but couldn't spot a single canoe, black puff from a campfire, ramshackle hunting camp, or a fisherman in waders. "We could still hike to Beaver Falls, you know," said Phil. "The lake doesn't look so scary today."

Benjy examined the GPS, punched a few buttons, and managed to get a bleep or two. "The display is fogged but it's working," he announced, pulling out the soggy remains of the topo map that had dissolved into eight pieces. Benjy studied the map to figure out the best possible route while Phil jammed the damp clothes and unwashed dishes back into their packs. Sure, Chris would probably disapprove of the stray wrappers left here and there, but who was ever going to visit this dinky island again, anyway? They loaded the canoe up, shoved off, and soon all the terror of the night before was burned away by the morning sun as they skimmed over the flat water with neat, efficient strokes.

He wished his mom could see him now, and Chris and Uncle Bo—dressed in cool wraparound canoer shades and bandanna headband, with all his slick sternman moves. And they'd be pretty blown away when they heard how he'd kept his head when the canoe flipped over in the middle of a lightning storm. Benjy was right, he had saved his life, Phil thought, sitting straighter and squaring his shoulders.

Even with a GPS and a topo map, the trail head to Beaver Falls was invisible. What was supposed to be the proper location turned out to be a big bog with no landing, so they paddled up one side of the shore for about a mile and then back the other way for another mile, but all they could see were pine trees, pines trees, and more pine trees so thick that not a single ray of sun could shine through. Phil thought he would rather cross Lake Hazard back and forth ten times than get lost in the middle of some pitch black forest no human had ever stepped foot in before. "Now what, Einstein?" he panted.

Benjy pulled the goddamned GPS out again and scowled at it through his glasses, aiming it at the shore and then at the sky, taking readings. "Well, according to my calculations, we were right the first time. Let's go back," he said, pointing toward the boggy spot.

According to my calculations, Phil muttered to himself as he steered the canoe into a 180. Benjy lashed the canoe to a tree stump and they sloshed through the soggy moss along the perimeter of the woods in search of clues. A hundred feet along, they found a fire ring with a few cigarette butts (clearly not Kinahwee campers), behind that a vaguely trampled and indented path leading straight into a spooky forest.

"Well, that must be it," said Benjy doubtfully, as if he'd been expecting something more official—a visitor's center with a ranger dressed like Smoky the Bear and a snack bar, perhaps. "According to the map, it's less than a mile to Beaver Falls, so let's leave our stuff here."

Ah, Benjy, any excuse to avoid a portage, but this time, considering Phil's waterlogged pack weighed about a hundred pounds, maybe he had a point. Benjy pulled out the map and a small nylon pouch which he Velcroed around his belt.

"What's in there?" Phil asked.

"Phone card, Visa, American Express, my personal organizer, and twenty bucks," he said, heading off into the wild.

It was a path all right, but one that seemed to have been laid out by a blind man or a drunk—zigging left for no reason, then zagging right. Not only was it chilly and damp under the trees, but every exposed piece of skin was set upon by a swarm of mosquitoes. After half an hour, Phil halted and grabbed the map pieces from Benjy "This can't be right." Yes, there was the well-marked, straight trail leading from Lake Hazard to Beaver Falls. But then north of it was a random half-dotted line that seemed to loop back and forth for miles before it hit pavement. According to the map key, half-dotted meant "trail may be unmarked, partially cleared, or abandoned." Phil held the map under Benjy's nose and pointed at it with his thumb.

"Oh,"said Benjy meekly, willing to admit for once that he might have made a mistake. "I guess we better go back." Phil set the pace back at a jog. This wilderness survival stuff was starting to get really, really old. He wanted his jacket, the bug spray, his water bottle, and the rest of the food. They burst back onto the shore to discover the stump where Benjy had moored the canoe to be rope-free.

"Maybe it's the wrong stump," Benjy wheezed hopefully. Phil pointed toward a red canoe drifting lazily a half mile out in the lake.

What was the point of saying the obvious? I told you to tie the canoe tightly. Neither of us can swim well enough to go get it. Now we don't have any food or our sleeping bags.

Hear that thunder—too bad we don't have our rain jackets. He bent down and cupped a handful of water for a last drink. "We better hustle if we want to make Beaver Falls by dark," he said, wiping his mouth with the back of his hand.

Like his mom used to say, you should be grateful for small things. In this case, Phil was grateful that half-dotted meant partially cleared rather than abandoned. The trail was marked, sort of, with faded red dots of paint, probably put there by Henry Hudson with Injun blood. Every time the trail seemed to give up and die, or was totally blocked by a fallen tree, if you looked hard enough you eventually found one of those stupid marks hidden under a branch, or on the wrong side of a tree trunk. It was like a scavenger hunt and might even have been fun if they hadn't been starving, weren't being sucked dry by insects, their faces hadn't been scratched into mush and their shins bruised black, if it hadn't been pouring. Phil wasn't even speaking to Benjy anymore, not that it mattered much because Benjy didn't seem to be speaking to him, either.

They hit hardtop by dark, which was not to say that they had hit civilization. A quick check of the map in the last flicker of twilight showed that the half-dotted trail landed them about three miles south of Beaver Falls. If he were speaking to Benjy, he might have discussed several things as they trudged single file down the road. He might have pointed out to him that this road was not really hardtop—it was more tar-covered rocks without a top layer. He might have asked him if they should try to hitchhike if a car came by, even though their mom had told them about all the perverts that drove around looking for kids to pick up and murder. He might have asked him who they should call when they got to Beaver Falls—their dad, Camp Kinahwee?—and what they should say.

According to his watch with the glow-in-the-dark display, they plodded for over two hours without seeing a vehicle, a house, or any signs of civilization besides a sign on a bridge over a dinky waterfall, which probably would have said Beaver Falls, if there had been light enough to read it. Phil had a terrible thought—what if this was all there was to Beaver Falls? He had started looking for a good spot on the road to lie down and die when they rounded a turn and there, like the star of Bethlehem, was a tiny electric light, way off in the distance, guiding them to safety. They both broke into a run, the light slowly getting closer and closer until they could make out that it was attached to a building by the side of a road. Not any building, a store—a closed store.

The sign that the light was beaming down on said OGILVIE'S VARIETY STORE, and in smaller letters underneath, BEAVER FALLS, ONT. It was the kind of old-fashioned store his mom would like, Phil decided, standing on the front porch and pressing his nose to the big plate glass window. It had a big long counter with a crank cash register and cartons of candy bars—Mars, Oh Henrys!, Kit Kats. A rack with bags of chips, Canadian types he'd never heard of, like Old Dutch cheese puffs. He rattled the funny brass knob with the pathetic hope that it had been left unlocked. Could they tell the Canadian police that they had to toss a rock through the plate glass window because they were starving to death? Did not eating since breakfast constitute starving to death? Phil turned his attention to the Coke machine on the porch. "Got some change?" he asked, hammering at it with his fist and poking at the empty coin return.

"Just a twenty," Benjy snapped. "But there's a phone." He walked around to an unlit pay phone hanging on the edge of the building. Which will probably be out of order, Phil thought glumly. Then he heard Benjy using his BPCC voice with a telephone operator—husky and businesslike, which made him sound a lot older than thirteen.

"I'd like to use an ATT credit card to call the United States, please . . . Crowley, Massachusetts . . . no answer? Okay, I'd like information for Little Lost Lake, Wisconsin. Try the name Lucy Crocker . . . no listing? Try the name

Lamb . . . no Lambs? All right, I'd like information for Kinahwee Falls, Wisconsin. Camp Kinahwee . . . can you connect me? . . . no answer? Oh . . . " Benjy hung up, chewed things over for a moment or two, then gave it another shot. "Can I have the Yellow Pages for Beaver Falls, Ontario? . . . Do you have any listings for taxi cab companies? . . . All right, what about limousine services? . . . How about transportation? . . . I guess trucking will work. Can I have that listing? . . . Hello, my name is Benjamin Crocker. My brother and I have gotten stranded on a camping trip and we need a ride back to the States . . . yes, I know you're a trucking company but there's no other kind of transportation around here . . . Beaver Falls. It's off Route 15A . . . yes, I know that's seventy miles away, but you're the closest thing . . . yes, our parents know where we are . . . My father told me to call you . . . yes, we have money. Sure, we can pay in advance . . . yeah, cash, just get me to a cash machine . . . Massachusetts? . . . Okay, okay, how about Wisconsin? . . . Little Lost Lake, Wisconsin . . . sure I know where it is . . . we'll be waiting on the porch of Ogilvie's variety store. Oh, and one more thing. Can you pick us up some food? We're really hungry. Let's see, cheeseburgers, extra-large fries, large Coke, fudge brownies for dessert. Two of everything. And some ketchup, too. Lots of ketchup. Thanks."

CHAPTER 14

>>

Of course, Ed should have known that to get from Crowley to Camp Kinahwee was going to be like something out of *Mission Impossible*. When he got the suicidal letter from Benjy yesterday, without thinking he just ran inside the house and called those felons at Crowley Airport Limousine, even though he had sworn only three weeks earlier never to use them again. "Get me to Logan. It's a family emergency," he had said. Emergency meant that it only took them an hour to get there instead of the usual three, long enough for Ed to pack a bag. He brought clothes for a couple of weeks, because a scheme had taken form in his head that after he'd rescued the boys from Camp Kinahwee, they'd pop in on Lucy at Little Lost Lake. She might want to slam the door in Ed's face, but the boys were a different story.

Then they'd have their August vacation, as planned, only at Little Lost Lake rather than at the Wheeler bungalow colony. Ed even dared to imagine how it might go. He'd put on Cyrus's vest and waders and let Lucy teach him how to fly fish. Even though the notion of hooking a trout through the lip seemed barbaric, he would give it his best shot, work hard to perfect his cast, to tie a fly, even to clean a fish with a pocketknife if he had to. He would learn to see Lucy's world through her eyes, and then with luck, she would accept him back into her arms, her bed. He'd even brought along his violin so he could serenade her with Elgar's "Salut d'amour," just like the old days.

When Ed had finally gotten to the American Airlines

counter at Logan, he'd been told, "Sorry, Mr. Crocker. The best we can do for you is an eight-thirty flight to Chicago tonight, then connect with a Northwoods Air nonstop to Eau Claire, departing at nine-thirty tomorrow morning. You should be able to rent a car at the Eau Claire airport."

So here he was, twenty hours later, in the best vehicle available from the Eau Claire Mr. Rent-A-Car, a sub-sub-compact Chevrolet, trying to find Wisconsin County Road D on the two-inch-square courtesy Mr. Rent-A-Car road map.

Just past something called Jump River, Route 73 came to a four-way stop with County D and Ed turned north on a ribbon of frost-heaved blacktop. Lucy had made the north woods of Wisconsin sound as spectacular as the Swiss Alps, but the scrubby pine trees and straggly birches, punctuated here and there with some dreary settlement consisting of two trailers and a water tower, gave Ed the heebie-jeebies. Every now and then, a dirt driveway disappeared into the underbrush, leading no doubt to some militiaman's hideout complete with plywood shack, pregnant wife, conspiracy pamphlets, rottweilers, and enough assault weapons to win the Seven Day War. Come to think of it, hadn't Timothy McVeigh built his fertilizer bomb around here?

Now that he was on County D, how was he supposed to find this Camp Kinahwee? It was probably too much to expect that it might be right on the road, identified with a helpful sign. He pulled up to a squalid log building, a tavern with rows of deer horns tacked over the door, to ask directions. Even though it was only 2:00 in the afternoon, he found eight men sitting at a bar under the murky yellow glow of a Pabst Blue Ribbon sign, smoking cigarettes and drinking scotch from shot glasses. Isn't anyone employed around here? Ed edged just inside the doorway and asked, "Does anyone know where a place called Camp Kinahwee is?" He wasn't sure how to pronounce Kinahwee, so he tried keen-ah-*whey,* which sounded the most authentically Native American to him. They all swiveled around in unison and stared openmouthed as if he had some hideous deformity, even though he was a lot better dressed than he had been in the last three weeks in his black travel outfit—black jeans, black Gap T-shirt, black Reeboks, black elastic on his ponytail, black Oakleys hanging around his neck with a black cord. Finally someone said, "It's up the road 'bout a mile."

"How will I know when I get there?" He thought he heard a few sniggers, even though it seemed like a perfectly intelligent question.

"You get to a driveway on the left, see? It's got this tall wooden gate and on the top of the gate is a wooden sign, see? On this sign are some big wooden letters which spell out *Camp Kinahwee*. That's how you'll know you're there," the old guy behind the bar said in a sarcastic fashion. The name of the camp seemed to be pronounced kin-*ow*-wee. Rhymed with *rowdy.*

"You're not from around here, are you?" said a swarthy guy at the bar with a smirk.

"No, I'm not. I'm from Massachusetts," said Ed politely. Okay, boys, have your fun.

"There was a lady in here about a month ago. She was from Massachusetts, too."

"What a coincidence," Ed said, although they seemed to expect a more thunderstruck reaction. Europeans were the same way—if their cousin lived in Massachusetts, they figured you'd know him. "So what was her name?" he finally asked.

"Dunno, but Roland here had the hots for her," said the man behind the bar. Ed shrugged, mumbled thanks, and backed out the deer antler door before they could start asking him if he'd ever been to Hyannisport to visit the Kennedys.

He turned in under the admittedly hard-to-miss Camp Kinahwee gate and bumped down the rutted road, his heart starting to race as he imagined Phil and Benjy's overjoyed faces when they saw their dad had come to the rescue. Benjy's perpetually cockeyed glasses and slumped thirteen-year-old posture, Phil's beautiful face, so much like Lucy's, with its worried expression, that mop of dark hair always flopping over his forehead—how he yearned to hug their knobby, recalcitrant shoulders. He pulled up in front of a deserted-looking log lodge with a faded red Kinahwee banner flapping out of a peaked roof over the door. The only other vehicle in sight was a beat-up pickup with an equally beat-up canoe slung in the back—Ed certainly hoped the boys were out in something a little more seaworthy. The sound of very young children jumping off a diving board wafted up from the waterfront. An ancient, lizard-skinned man banged out the lodge's screened door and eyed him suspiciously. "What do you want?" he asked in an unpleasant tone. He was wearing a faded flannel shirt and baggy loden wool pants held up with frayed leather suspenders; thick white hair stuck out in unkempt tufts over his leathery pate.

"I'm Ed Crocker. My sons, Benjamin and Philip, are campers here." He couldn't remember the last time he'd used the boys' full names and it felt unnerving, like he was filing a police report. He offered out his hand to this guy who seemed to be in charge, but when he made no movement to take it, Ed let it drop at his side.

"So, you're Lucy's husband, eh?" the man said, inspecting Ed from head to toe with those preternaturally blue eyes that only old Yankees seem to have and scowled with disapproval. "We don't have parents' visiting day at Camp Kinahwee. I'm surprised Lucy didn't tell you that."

"I'm not here to visit my sons. I'm here to pick them up," Ed fired back. He was not going to let himself be intimidated by some sanctimonious old geezer. He pulled Benjy's letter out of his pocket and waved it like a subpoena. "I received this letter from my son. I think it will explain why I've come."

The man snatched the letter out of Ed's hand, then held it at arm's distance to read it. "Your kid writes you some whiney, candy-ass letter and you come running? Ah, for crying out loud. If I had a buck for every kid who'd written a letter halfway through begging his parents to pick him up, I could buy a condo in Vail. What next?" He smacked his withered lips with disgust.

"Listen, Mr. . . . I'm sorry, but I didn't catch your name."

"You didn't catch it because I didn't say it. I'm Bo Thorne. My father founded this camp in 1918. I took over for him in 1942. Everyone calls me Uncle Bo. You can, too." This was not a friendly offer, it was a command.

He wasn't calling this guy "Uncle Bo," not now, not ever. "My son has made some serious allegations. He says that he is being mistreated, he says that the other boys are psychos."

"Yeah, right. Spelling psychos s-y-c-h-o-s. Listen, Crocker, if you're going to worry about something, why don't you worry about your son's spelling and penmanship. They're god-awful. Don't they teach kids anything in school these days? He even got his own zip code wrong."

Ed had had the same thought when he'd read Benjy's letter, but he wasn't about to admit it to Uncle Bo. "I'd like to see my sons now, please."

Uncle Bo poked at the stamp on the envelope with a yellowed nail. "What is that, Crocker?"

"A Canadian stamp?"

"Right, dimbulb. That's because the letter was mailed from Canada. The senior canoe trip is up in northern Ontario. They won't be back for another two weeks."

Ed shifted from one Reebok to the other feeling foolish, diminished. Of course he should have called first to check if the boys were at least in camp before he came charging out a thousand miles to Kinahwee Falls, Wisconsin, with six-shooters blazing.

"So come back in a couple of weeks. Hopefully your kids will have stopped acting like cowering dogs by then." With that, Uncle Bo turned his back and started to load three hundred-pound wooden chests stacked on the porch into the back of the pickup, his gnarled brown arms hoisting them as if they weighed no more than an empty cardboard carton.

Ed felt his arm draw back and fought back the urge to pop Uncle Bo one, right in the kisser. Brains will conquer brawn, he reminded himself, and reverted to his menacing, don't-screw-with-me CEO voice. "I resent the pejorative way you're talking about my children. I'm not leaving here until I speak with them and am reassured that they are not in an abusive or dangerous situation." Ed reached into his brief case for his cell phone and flipped it open. "The counselors must have a cell phone for emergencies. What's the number?"

Uncle Bo gave Ed's cell phone a this-world's-going-to-hell-in-a-hand-basket sneer. "Your kids are on a wilderness trip, Crocker. There's no phone. No fax, either."

"I need to talk to them," he said, sounding desperate as he imagined the return drive to the Eau Claire airport in his tin can sub-sub-compact, another jolting ride from Logan via Crowley Airport Limousine, and two more lonely weeks rattling around Crowley.

Uncle Bo suddenly softened, the eyes looking more rheumy than glacial. "Sorry if I offended you. I'm not criticizing your boys in particular. I think all kids are too soft and too spoiled these days. They say *boo* once and their parents bail 'em out. I'm going to see Benjamin and Philip in four days, so why don't I take them a message from you, okay?"

"See them? Where?"

"I'm heading up to Ontario right now to resupply the senior canoe trip. I'm meeting up with them at Black Knife Lake." He threw a dinged-up paddle and a WW I-vintage canvas rucksack in the rear end of the pickup beside the canoe and the food chests. They fell into an awkward silence as Uncle Bo battened down the canoe with wide nylon straps and Ed returned the scorned cell phone to his briefcase. "You can join me if you want to, Crocker. It's a lot easier to paddle a canoe with two people, even if one of them's you. And frankly, I wouldn't mind the company." The offer actually seemed genuine and Uncle Bo's voice quavered, sounding for the first time like the old man he was.

"Gee, not sure I can spare the time," Ed stalled. Now there's an attractive offer—spend four days paddling through black flies with a crackpot. But then the empty spot in his gut clenched again. He couldn't endure another two weeks without a glimpse of his straggly boys. And besides, Lucy would be pleased that he'd taken up canoeing, wouldn't she? "But, if you really need me, I guess I could do it," he added.

"I didn't say I needed you, I only said I wouldn't mind you. Well, hustle your bustle. I haven't got all day. Pull out your gear and transfer it to a pack," said Uncle Bo, tossing a huge rubberized sack with shoulder straps on the ground. He supervised as Ed opened up his suitcase, approving swim shorts, running shoes, a Red Sox baseball cap, and nixing a button-down shirt, blue jeans, a laptop computer, and deodorant. "Attracts mosquitoes, and bears," he explained.

"Oh, right," said Ed, wondering about the bears part, and what he was going to smell like after four days. Or was it eight days because there was the return trip, wasn't there? Uncle Bo fetched a few missing items from a storage closet—a sleeping bag and pad, a rain poncho.

"Play that thing?" Uncle Bo asked, pointing at the violin case in the sub-sub-compact's trunk.

"A little," said Ed modestly.

"Bring it along. Music sounds kind of sweet played next to a campfire."

As instructed, Ed dropped it in the pack, wondering if he was crazy to be bringing a hundred-year-old Silvestre violin, one of his prized possession, on a canoe trip. He doubled over the waterproof flap, tightened down the straps, and hoisted it into the rear end of the truck. "Okay. Let's hit the road," he said gamely. The more he thought about it, the more he liked this plan. Four days of back-breaking paddling and hauling, no decision making, just following Uncle Bo's orders. Falling in bed at night too exhausted to cogitate about his screwed-up life or to dream about his failures.

But instead of climbing in the truck, Uncle Bo stood with

arms crossed, still dissatisfied. "One more thing, Crocker. Your hair."

"What about my hair?" Ed asked, fingering the tangled ends sheepishly.

"That ponytail's going to get snarled up in your backpack and life vest, it'll be hot, it'll catch bugs. And besides, it makes you look like a jackass."

Ed gave a sullen teenaged shrug, as if to say, So what are you going to do about it? In truth, he had long been considering lopping his ponytail off because he suspected it did indeed make him look like a jackass, although no one had ever said so before—not Lucy, not Ingrid, not even Phil or Benjy, who were never shy about pointing out their dad's blemishes.

"Let me get the supplies. Don't sweat, Crocker. I've been giving campers haircuts for fifty years. I won't scalp you." He clomped inside and came back carrying a shoe box with scissors, a tapered black comb, and electric shears. He sat Ed down on a porch rocker and made quick work of it—snipping his ponytail off in two whacks that fell in four-inch hunks all over Ed's Reeboks, parting his hair on the side, layering the back, and trimming around the ears with clippers, then brushing away the stray hairs with a small towel. He stepped back and assessed the final product through narrowed cobalt eyes. "That's an improvement. You're not a bad-looking fellow, Crocker. You should take more pride in your appearance."

Ed rubbed the back of his naked neck, admiring Uncle Bo's professional technique, feeling as if he'd just slipped off a disguise. "Thanks for the suggestion, Bo," he said affably. I have entered the realm of the absurd, no point getting my hackles up about this or anything else.

"That's Uncle Bo to you."

"Shall we get going, Uncle Bo?" Ed asked in a pleasant tone, gesturing toward the truck.

"Not so fast. We need to perform the blessing of the expedition first."

Ah, the blessing of the expedition, of course. How could we forget that? Ed obediently trotted over to the flagpole, grasped Uncle Bo's leathery paw, dropped his head reverently as the quavery voice intoned, "May the Great Spirit bring us fair weather and fair voyage. May the weak become strong. May the strong become leaders." Climbing into the passenger side of the truck, Ed wondered if that weakling part had been thrown in for his benefit.

As they pulled out onto County Road D, Uncle Bo called over, "I don't believe in stopping unless you got to take a leak. Got it?" With that he rolled down the window to hang his left elbow out, turned the radio to a scratchy all-news station full blast so it could be heard over the roar of the rattle-trap engine, and didn't say another word.

Ed didn't mind the lack of conversation. Hiding behind his sunglasses as the sun set over the blasted landscape of stunted trees and stunted towns, he tried to make sense of this flight. In theory he was going off to save his boys from the forces of nature and the taunts of bullies, but even Uncle Bo could see through that lame pretense. I'm not running to Benjy and Phil, he thought, I'm running away from the rest of my life. My love for my boys is the only bedrock fact I'm certain of—everything else is quicksand. Do I love Lucy? Yes, but I don't love my closed-mouthed, shut-down relationship with her. Do I love Ingrid? No, but I loved my illicit relationship with her before it imploded the rest of my life. Do I love Crocker? Yes, I used to love my little company, our candy factory office, our logo, our cool games, being Ed Crocker, CEO, but just thinking about working there again makes me want to puke. Do I really think that four days hauling canoes with some screwball who probably has a more dysfunctional life than I do is going to solve anything? Nope, but it will be four days of distraction, numbness, biding time until Lucy and the boys come back to Crowley and we figure out what's next. And at least I won't be alone.

They passed a sign welcoming them to Minnesota, the

gopher state. Whaddya know, Ed thought dully, first the badger state and now this, two new states for my life list in less than twenty-four hours. He had no idea how Wisconsin and Minnesota hooked together, much less how they attached themselves to Ontario; there was probably a Great Lake or two shoved up between them. He had been to Ontario once, a gamer's convention at an airport hotel in Toronto, but that part of Ontario had been over by Buffalo, so who could explain why he was now halfway across the United States and still heading for the same province. Ah, the mysteries of geography. He could probably rummage around the glove compartment for a map, but why bother when Uncle Bo seemed to know exactly where they were heading. Ed scooted down in his seat, jammed a wadded-up sweatshirt between his head and the window, and shut his eyes, the last sight being a darkened expanse of water as vast as an ocean flickering by.

Uncle Bo's hand on his shoulder, jiggling him awake. "What? Where?" Ed mumbled, trying to knead a screaming crick out of his neck.

"Put in at Two Sister Lake," Uncle Bo answered curtly, but Ed's question was cosmic, not geographic. What am I doing here, where have you taken me? Ed climbed out, stretched his arms, wobbled his neck back and forth, and admired how the sunset turned the misty, pine-rimmed lake a luminous peach color. He sniffed deeply but something was off about the damp air, and he checked his watch—5:15. It took a moment or two for him to register that this was a sunrise not a sunset, that he had slept for nine hours while Uncle Bo had driven through the night.

Uncle Bo lifted the canoe onto his shoulders, carried it down a dirt path to the water, and lowered it in without a splash. "Get the wannigans off the truck, Crocker. That's what we call the food boxes." There was a new tone in Uncle Bo's voice now, the patient teacher. My education is beginning, thought Ed.

He grabbed one and inched it back and forth across the truck bed until it crashed off the back, pinning the tip of Ed's sneaker in the mud. An inch more, and it would have crushed his toes. "Careful with those wannigans," Uncle Bo's voice warned from behind a clump of grass. "If one falls on your foot, it'll crush it." Ed carried it as nimbly as one could manage something the size and weight of a tree stump and hoisted it into the canoe without making a gouge or a puncture. He hesitated for a moment, waiting for a word of praise from Uncle Bo, who was building a campfire in a fire ring along the lake's edge. "Don't just stand there, Crocker. Get the rest of the gear and lock up the truck."

Breakfast was a bowl of oatmeal and powdered milk garnished with raisins and a cup of cold black coffee from a Thermos that he had to share with Uncle Bo. If there was one thing Ed hated more than oatmeal it was raisins; if there was one thing he hated more than raisins, it was cold coffee. But of course it tasted somewhat delicious, because it was his first meal since lunch yesterday. "Okay, finish up. I want to shove off," said Uncle Bo, studying the water and sky of Two Sister Lake with an appraising eye.

"You've been up all night. Don't you want to have a nap first?" Ed asked.

"When you get to be my age, you never sleep anyway. You feel like crap all the time, awake or asleep, so what's the point?"

For the first time, Ed scrutinized Uncle Bo, hunched over the campfire trying to warm his gnarled hands, his wrinkled face highlighted in the harsh morning sun. Under the ruddy tan skin, there was a hollowness to his cheeks, a pinched look of pain in his cataract-fogged eyes. "May I ask how old you are?"

"Seventy-eight, almost seventy-nine." Slightly older than Ed's parents, Harry and Marion, who now lived in a retirement community and had recently given up their weekly nine holes of golf because it was too strenuous. What would he do if Uncle Bo keeled over at the helm of their canoe—fashion a stretcher out of two birch saplings and drag him two hundred miles through the forest to the nearest hospital? Ed didn't even know CPR, for Christ's sake. Why hadn't he at least brought his cell phone to summon a handy helicopter, if he could figure out where he was?

They washed and loaded up, Ed was instructed to put on his life vest and sit in the bow, and Uncle Bo, with a gut-wrenching grunt launched them into Two Sister Lake, then with the grace of a gymnast, vaulted over the side into the stern without causing the canoe to bobble once. "I don't suppose you've ever done this before," he said.

"Nope." Of course not, why do you even have to ask? By the time they were halfway across Two Sister Lake, Uncle Bo had instructed him on the basic bow strokes, and Ed felt rather pleased with himself that he had been such a quick study, that perhaps he might even have a natural talent for the sport. But then again, after fifty years, Uncle Bo could probably teach even the biggest dolt, maybe he'd given Ed the special Paddling for Dummies version.

"The canoe's fully loaded and riding low, which means it can swamp, so don't do anything stupid, Crocker. No shifting your position, no sudden moves, don't even turn around to look back at me. Just keep making those simple strokes I showed you, nice and easy."

Now that Uncle Bo had pointed out how low they were riding, Ed couldn't peel his eyes off the lip of the canoe skimming a mere three inches above the midnight blue water, stretching miles in all directions and a mile deep. Probably ice cold, with giant fish snoozing along the bottom. He forced himself to pry his gaze upward and keep it fixed on the distant shore. Try to appreciate the landscape so you can describe it to Lucy. He had seen the rolling hills and lakes of New England before, not happily or willingly of course, but the colors two hundred miles to the north seemed more intense, the greens of the trees almost black, the sky bigger and grayer, as if someone had taken a photograph of Maine and played with the negative to make the colors take on an eerie, unreal cast.

At the mouth of the next lake, a huge swollen one appropriately called Madonna, Uncle Bo allowed them to pull ashore for a quick lunch break of stale sprouted wheat bread (the type Lucy liked), American cheese, and another shared cup of cold black coffee from the Thermos. As they ventured forth into the onyx expanse, Ed fought back another wave of panic and forced himself to pick a focal point, this time an island because the shore was too distant to see.

"So, Crocker," said Uncle Bo behind him, his paddle making tidy, almost soundless dips in the water. "Now that you've got your strokes down, you're ready for the next step of big lake canoeing. Good conversation."

"Like what?" Ed asked suspiciously, whirling around in his seat to check out Uncle Bo's expression. The canoe bobbed, then Ed overcorrected and sent it into a head-spinning wobble.

Uncle Bo steadied it with two swift draws. "I told you not to do that. You can talk without turning around. So let's talk about you, Ed."

Ed? Suddenly, he preferred Crocker. "What do you want to know?"

"When Lucy dropped the boys off she said you two were having some problems. She seemed very upset. Don't turn around, Ed."

"Ah, did she give any specifics?" Ed asked, the words *tantric, Trump Plaza, huckleberry massage oil* jolting through his head.

"That you had a girlfriend. So why don't you tell me your side of the story." Uncle Bo's voice was curiously nonjudgmental, but that was probably the tactic he used for campers who had really screwed up—stolen food, sunk canoes, started forest fires. The give 'em-enough-rope school of interrogation. What *was* the story anyway, and what *was* his side of it? He paddled straight ahead, his strokes suddenly becoming quieter, smoother.

"Ed?"

"All right. Let me start at the beginning. September, 1982, before I ever met Lucy Lamb. I was finishing grad school at MIT. I'd started out in math, but right off I switched to computer science, because that was clearly where the action was."

Uncle Bo harumphed behind him.

"So I guess you'd call me a hacker, a programming geek. I spent about fifteen hours a day pounding away at one of those old Digital mainframes, trying to program this little tank game for my master's thesis."

"Sounds challenging," Uncle Bo scoffed.

"Actually, it was pretty complicated—making the tanks look three-D, move over variable terrain, and have turrets that rotated—all with this model-T software. But I wasn't completely one dimensional. I was concert master for the MIT orchestra, I even had a girlfriend." Sasha Goldfarb, fellow hacker. After punching code side by side for a few hours, they'd go back to her squalid dorm room for a perfunctory screw on her pizza-box-littered bed, then back to the lab for another all-nighter. But Uncle Bo probably didn't need to know every detail. "I'd had lots of girlfriends, ever since tenth grade. For some reason, they found me attractive."

"Even with that asinine ponytail?"

"It was preponytail."

"I rest my case. Go on."

"My girlfriends were all just like me, math-whiz types. So it never felt special, like love. Until this beautiful girl moved into the apartment next door with a backpack and a carton of art supplies."

"That's my little Lucy," said Uncle Bo appreciatively.

"Except there was one problem. She had this boyfriend."

They were halfway across Madonna Lake by the time he'd finished up with his wooing campaign. "Finally, I managed to win her over. She actually agreed to take me back to Libertyville to get the once-over from her parents, Cyrus and Corky. Did you ever meet the happy couple?"

"Just the father, who used to drive Lucy up to camp. A fine outdoorsman. Sometimes he'd stay for the afternoon and fish the inlet to Kinahwee Lake. Used an original Abercrombie rod. What's the mother like?"

"Jack Sprat's wife. He stuttered, she yammered. He read de Tocqueville, she read Harold Robbins. When he went to his fishing camp, she went golfing in Boca Raton. He drove a fifteen-year-old Pontiac, she had a brand-new Audi. He had two left feet, she was the Over-Fifty Tango champ at Arthur Murray. She thought she was marrying a future bank president. He decided to switch careers and become a rare book librarian at the Newberry."

"So, how'd they like you?"

"That was one of the few things they agreed on. They both thought Lucy could do better. Cyrus wanted her to marry someone bold, adventurous, Sir Edmund Hillary, for example. What he might have been himself, if he hadn't been imprisoned by his wife, his stutter, and his demons." In other words, someone like Sam McCarty. "Corky's only complaint was that I wasn't a few inches taller, didn't have chiseled features, and wasn't head of arbitrage at Solomon Brothers. Small stuff."

"But surely Lucy stood up to them?" said Uncle Bo, sounding alarmed that his prize former camper might have showed a lack of spine.

"She said she didn't care what they thought." *Fuck 'em* is what she'd actually said, several times, on the flight home to Boston after a couple of Beefeaters, crunching smoked almonds loudly with her back molars. *As if they're the experts on conjugal bliss.* "I always wondered if Cyrus would have come around, but he never had the chance—he died of lung cancer eight months later. So his disapproval, or maybe a better word would be disappointment, always hung over our marriage like an asterisk."

It took the whole afternoon, all the way across Madonna Lake and something called Great Grasshopper Pond to tell the rise and fall of both the Crocker family and the Crocker business. As he told the woeful final chapters, how he wished he'd done things differently—been more sympathetic about the miscarriages, the Crowley house, Lucy's creative block with MQII.

"So I'm afraid Lucy's found our life together a big disappointment, just like her father predicted she would," Ed said into the silence. That was the legacy handed down to Lucy in equal measure from both her parents. A discontent with what is, an unquenched yearning for what might have been. The late afternoon had turned brisk; a sharp wind from the north dirtied the water, made his sweaty arms goosebump. Suddenly he was overcome with a spooky sensation that he was no longer speaking to Uncle Bo, but to Cyrus's apparition.

"So if Lucy had been a little less faultfinding, maybe your marriage wouldn't be in such a shambles, right?" Uncle Bo observed dryly. Ah, the old grouch was still there after all. "There's just one thing you left out of this sad tale of an unappreciated husband, Ed. Your girlfriend."

"Oh, her." How to make Ingrid comprehensible to an eighty-year-old man? "She's the publicity director at our company. She's twenty-seven, young but not too young, has a nice body, wears the latest fashions. It started innocently. We worked side by side, lots of out-of-town conferences, lots of late-night discussions about programming glitches and marketing strategy, the kind of stuff that bored Lucy to death. Then one night Ingrid gave me a massage when I had a rotator cuff problem, and it kind of evolved into a more physical relationship. But that didn't last long, one long weekend actually, and now it's over, over, over." He left out an explanation of tantric techniques, Ingrid's exquisite breasts. Ed waited for Uncle Bo to make some pronouncement, felt his frigid eyes boring neat holes into his sweat-soaked back.

"You sure made a hash of your life for a few cozy chats and shoulder massages," he concluded at last. "So, now that your fling is over, how are you going to get Lucy to forgive you?"

"I don't know." After four hours of simultaneous paddling and soul searching, Ed was wrung out and started to think longingly about cold coffee and processed cheese food. "Any suggestions?"

"Nope. I'm not a marriage counselor."

Nope? He weasels a confession out of me and then all he says is you sure made a hash of your life. Where was the wisdom of the ages, the ponderous solution to how Ed could set everything to right again? No fair, false advertising as a sage, or something.

Uncle Bo nosed their canoe into a cleared campsite at the far end of Great Grasshopper Pond. A ring of sooty stones, a mound of ashes, six fat log seats arranged in a circle around the campfire. A chill prickled up Ed's spine as if he could see the ghosts of five generations of Kinahwee campers.

"So your dad founded this camp ninety years ago. He must have been quite a guy," Ed said over Kraft macaroni and cheese dinner and cold Taster's Choice. It was time for a little quid pro quo storytelling from Uncle Bo.

"He was a son of a bitch, I hated his guts," Uncle Bo said fiercely, as if he were suddenly face-to-face with a long slumbering giant who had just awoken. "Lucius Thorne, the great outdoorsman. He was a drunk, a mean drunk, hit my mother, paddled us kids with a cricket bat. Started this camp so he didn't have to have a real job to support his family, so he could be half-tanked all the time and disappear for weeks on canoe trips. Whipped the boys with a leather belt, didn't feed them enough. When boys would beg not to go back because they were beaten and starved, parents figured Lucius Thorne was making men out of their sons, and sent them summer after summer. Not like parents today," he added pointedly.

Ed tried to think of a more congenial topic than Lucius Thorne. "Do you have a wife and family, Uncle Bo?"

"Had a wife once," he said, his eyes fixed on the soothing flames. "Grace Whittey from Saint Paul. Not a pretty girl, but spirited. Loved fly fishing. Her mother played canasta with my mother, they set me up with Grace because I was too backward to court a girl on my own. For a couple of years, she helped me run the camp, managed the kitchen girls, seemed happy enough. But then she divorced me to marry my old best friend from grammar school, George Donnelly." Uncle Bo threw another pine branch on the fire and watched as the dried needles combusted, shooting a flume of sparks into the night sky. "Never understood why. Grace didn't even bother to explain. Just too backward, I suppose. They had three daughters and sent them all to Kinahwee."

Better steer clear of any more personal questions. "Well, you've run this camp for fifty years. That's a real accomplishment." Ed tried to muster an enthusiastic tone.

"Don't know about that," Uncle Bo said bleakly. "Done a better job than my old man, I guess. Don't drink, don't hit anybody, but I'm not sure kids like me any better than old Uncle Lucius. No, Camp Kinahwee is going the way of the dodo. Now kids want tennis camp, theater camp, lacrosse camp. Camps today are supposed to be fun, not rigorous." He pulled out a pocket handkerchief and honked his nose loudly with disgust.

Ed felt chagrined that he'd dared to criticize Kinahwee's methods—at least the boys hadn't had Lucius Thorne. "I'm sorry," he murmured lamely.

"Don't worry about me. My life's not so bad. I've figured out how to keep myself busy in the off season when everyone's gone. In the fall I repair the buildings and the docks. In the winter, I snowshoe the trails and chase away those goddamn snow mobilers. In the spring I paint the canoes and varnish the paddles. When I kick the bucket, my sister's kids can bulldoze the place and build condos."

"How about a tune?" Ed said, rummaging through the rubberized canoe pack and pulling out his violin, which seemed mercifully dry. Maybe it was the crisp Canadian air on the strings, or his fingers limbered up by eight hours of paddling, or the acoustics of the great outdoors, but Ed played better than he had in the last month. He kept it light, playing every tune he could remember from Suzuki Book I—"Twinkle, Twinkle, Little Star"; "Oh Come Little Children"; "The Happy Farmer"; "Long, Long Ago"—finishing off with "Go Tell Aunty Rhody." Uncle Bo's off-key, wavery voice made the final line, "the old gray goose is dead," seem as poignant as a widow's dirge.

The night was clear enough to roll out their bags next to the campfire and sleep under the stars. Ed tried not to stare when Uncle Bo stripped down to his antique bloomer underwear with a button fly and drawstring waist, his wiry naked legs tattooed with blue spider veins. Uncle Bo unzipped his lumpy khaki cotton bag and eased himself in gingerly as if every bone ached. "Good night, Ed. You did a good job today. You should feel proud of yourself."

"Thanks." Ed's cheeks flushed with childish pleasure. He lay on his back and studied the canopy of stars, picking out Orion's belt and the Big Dipper, the only two constellations he knew. How could a former math major at MIT be so ignorant of the natural world? The fire turned one side of his face milky warm and he fell asleep without dreaming.

Three days, eight lakes, four class-2 and one class-3 rapids later, they pulled into the Black Knife Lake campsite and hauled theirs into the row of overturned red canoes with KINAHWEE stenciled in yellow across the bow. Ed shook his legs out and loosened up with a few shoulder shrugs, noting with satisfaction that his arms were dark bronze and, he thought, more buffed. The boys would be pretty proud of their old dad, coming all this way.

They walked up an embankment toward the campsite, which seemed oddly nonshipshape. Even though it was suppertime, no one had built a campfire or opened up the wannigans, no one had set up the tents. Long-faced campers stood around in shiftless clusters not doing much of anything—no chatting or horseplay. As Ed searched for Benjy's blond head with the glasses and Phil's dark one, two college kid counselors and a man in a Canadian Forest Ranger uniform stepped out of the pack and stood waiting, hands folded like penitents, eyes lowered to the ground.

Uncle Bo stopped short, swept a surmising glance over the scene. "What's happened?" he asked in a hushed tone that Ed hadn't heard before.

A baby-faced man wearing a pretentious felt hat with a turkey feather stuck in the brim opened his mouth to speak, then noticed Ed and raised his eyebrows at Uncle Bo in question.

"This is Ed Crocker. He's here to see his boys." The campers' and counselors' faces went pale and slack with panic, all taking giant steps backward as if they suddenly learned he was contaminated with E. coli.

"What *is* it?" Ed said, not meaning to yell.

"Um, the boys . . . Benjy and Phil," the baby-faced one said in gulps, as if he were talking through the hiccups. "They took a canoe and ran away two nights ago." He stopped and looked beseechingly toward the ranger.

"What aren't you telling us?" said Uncle Bo in the same eerily calm, soft voice.

"They found the canoe this morning, empty." Babyface was talking to his Tevas now. "In Lake Hazard. Half-swamped. Packs, paddles, and life vests still in it."

CHAPTER 15

Twenty-seven days had passed since Lucy had spent that first fateful night with Sam. She knew because she had made a tally mark with a pencil stub for every night they'd spent together since, on a wall in her cabin right underneath where her father had kept a running score for the summer-long pinochle game with his brother, Bart. Sam was most definitely a lover, even though he was still a bit of a stranger.

Their days together had taken on their own peculiar routines. After the night at the caboose, they never spent another under the cupola—too cramped and uncomfortable, they agreed, to be inhabited by two people no matter how intimate. But the unspoken truth was that Twin Pond was Sam's Thoreauvian turf and she sensed he didn't want it trespassed upon, so their budding romance migrated over to Cyrus's cabin on Little Lost Lake.

A typical day with Sam went as follows. He paddled over around five in the afternoon, bearing the meager bounty from his garden, which served as garnish for the real dinner Lucy prepared. Now that she had Sam to fatten up, she let her gourmet talents run as wild as the slim pickings at Dunbar's would allow. Fettuccini à la porcini made with canned button mushrooms, enchiladas verdes made with canned Old El Paso jalapeño peppers and Wisconsin brick cheese. They ate supper at the battered wicker table on the lopsided porch with rusted screens. Lucy drank more Merlot, but Sam had reverted to his abstemious ways and stuck to well water from the hand pump in the kitchen.

Dinner conversation with Sam was unpredictable. Sometimes he bubbled over with tales of his day's labors—how he'd figured out a way to outwit the woodchuck clear-cutting his pole beans, built an outdoor oven to bake bread, fashioned a writing desk out of bent birch. But frequently working with his hands and contemplating simplicity seemed to leave him brooding and distracted. Lucy did her best to draw him out. "How's the firewood supply coming along?"

"It's coming." He sat slumped over his enchiladas with barely enough energy to lift his fork to his mouth.

"Did you do anything else?"

"Like what?" He rubbed his sunburned neck while his eyes nervously scanned the horizon.

"I don't know. Take a hike, go bird watching. Write in your journal," she said, getting defensive.

"I don't have time to fool around, Lucy. See that?" he pointed to a clump of birches on the far side of Little Lost Lake.

"See what?"

"An orange leaf. Winter's coming. I need to get prepared."

At times like this, Lucy missed Ed's easy banter, his nightly riffs about the ridiculous goings-on at Crocker. The computer software industry might be immoral and mercenary, but it was a lot more fun to hear about than aerating a compost heap.

Sam became more loquacious when the conversation turned to his new favorite cause, Lucy's Quest for a Meaningful Life. The course of these conversations was hard to predict, as well. Sometimes he found everything she did a marvel—her ingenious meals, the arrangement of black-eyed Susans and foxglove in a cracked delft teapot, the way she was calligraphing Cyrus's lumberjack tales onto parchment bond. At other times, he seemed to think that she needed spiritual reeducating from the ground up. "Didn't it bother you that your so-called computer game was being used to control the minds of impressionable children?" he asked, his fingers setting imaginary quotation marks around the word *game*.

"I guess I didn't see it that way," she said, hackles rising. "Maiden's Quest is just a form of entertainment. Kids have fun playing it. What's so bad about that?"

"Everything," he proclaimed, pounding the wicker table so hard that the verde sauce sloshed over the rim of his plate. "Kids start thinking it's just a game, but after a while they're brainwashed. It becomes their only activity. They give up reading, they give up talking to other human beings, they give up going out into nature. Their minds are completely controlled by a little beige box. You said so yourself about Benjy and Phil."

Lucy hated it when Sam turned her own words against her. "I said they spent too much time with computers. I didn't say my kids had been brainwashed."

"But that's what they want parents to think. That it's normal for children to be obsessed with computers. That's it's even educational, helping kids get a leg up in the cyberworld. It's a conspiracy. Don't you get it, Lucy?"

"Who is they, Sam? Who are these conspirators?"

"Bill Gates, Steve Jobs, cyber philosophers like Evelyn Dyson and Nick Negroponte. Ed." He ticked the list of sinners off one by one on his calloused fingers.

The vision of her rumpled husband as part of an evil empire made Lucy burst out laughing. "Ed? Oh, come on."

"No, I'm serious. It wasn't your idea to give up being a librarian and design computer games. It was Ed's, right? Did you ever consider what his motive was?"

"His motive was kindness," she said in a warning tone, tossing a balled napkin onto her plate and straightening her spine. "I was deeply depressed after my latest miscarriage. Ed thought that if I did something creative, it might lift me out of the black hole I'd fallen into and he was right. Ed may have many flaws, but he is not evil."

Sensing that once again he had gone too far, Sam reached

for her hands and dropped his shaggy head onto her lap. "I'm just jealous that you married Ed instead of me, so I like to think that he's one of the bad guys."

Lucy combed her fingers through his hair, traced the rim of his tanned ear with a finger, and bent down to kiss him, trying to banish the niggling worry that someday Sam might think that she was one of the bad guys, too. And then they adjourned, as they always did after dinner, to make love in some off-beat place—the island, the end of the dock, right there on the porch floor under the wicker table—in some original, east-meets-west way. Later, they fell asleep in Cyrus's sprung cast-iron bed with the prickly horsehair mattress, Sam's powerful arms wrapped around her waist making her feel protected, cherished. By dawn, before Lucy had stirred, he would be gone.

The rest of Lucy's day as she waited for Sam to return also came to have its own rituals. When she woke two hours after he had slipped away, she headed off to Dunbar's for donuts, bad coffee, and the mail. First she would sit at the counter and write postcards to each of the boys. At first she tried to pick out a new one from the carousel of Wisconsin scenes—starting with the funny ones of gigantic trout hanging off the end of a pickup tuck, working through local sites ("Visit Oldest Mine at Iron Mountain," "Monster Muskies Featured at Fishing Hall of Fame"), and finally onto sentimental wildlife ("Mother Deer Protects Her Fawns"). Lucy tried to be as truthful as possible in describing her summer—*turns out Uncle Larry hadn't fixed up the cabin very much after all, so I am mostly busy repairing screens and sweeping up raccoon poop*. She didn't have the heart to ask probing questions, so she tried the wishful-thinking approach instead—*I'm sure by now you're both real canoeing pros and having the time of your lives!* Before she dropped the postcards in the outgoing mail slot by the post office window, she bent down and gave each one a tiny, surreptitious kiss over the words *Phil* and *Benjy*. "Be well, sweet boys," she whispered.

Then she moved on to Ed's daily letter. Although it was a little stomach churning to deal with lovelorn pleadings from your husband only hours after you'd been in bed with your old boyfriend, Lucy made herself sit down on the front porch of Dunbar's every morning and read them—twice.

I'm on an indefinite leave of absence from Crocker, so I spend my days wandering from room to room, looking at your collections of salt and peppers shakers on every surface, at the framed photographs of the boys waiting with backpacks for the school bus on the first day of kindergarten, in their robot Halloween costumes you made out of liquor cartons and duct tape, at the straggly geraniums that are about to burst right out of the Chinese urns, everything in waiting for your return.

Ed never mentioned Ingrid, but the message was clear—he wasn't going into work at Crocker anymore, and was left to his lonesome back at Crowley. See what a good boy I'm being, Lucy? Considering her own tantric indiscretions of late, it was hard to muster too much indignation over a few days at the Trump Plaza.

And then Ed would tackle some thorny problem of their marriage, as if they were sitting face-to-face on a therapist's couch. That's right, she had been enraged when he'd told her not to "dwell on" the miscarriages, had always held it against him. Now for the first time, he was apologizing, offering his own logic that bottomless grief over the loss of a baby seemed a rejection of Benjy and Phil. In a way, he was right. Even though she adored her boys, there was some void in her maternal yearning that they couldn't fulfill. But why weren't Benjy and Phil "enough," as Ed had said? She had no words to explain.

The most wrenching part of Ed's letters were his speculations about the boys.

I worry about Phil and Benjy every minute of every day. When it rains, I wonder if they are out in the middle of a storm-tossed lake. When I'm eating my breakfast, I wonder what they're having, and where. How do you think they've changed in the last month? Has Phil grown another two inches, has his voice started to drop? Has Benjy learned to stop being such a know-it-all and started getting along with other kids better? So far, no letters, but I'll let you know as soon as I get one.

Ed's right, she'd think, they must be miserable. Why didn't I just bring them to Little Lost Lake with me instead of banishing them off to camp? Because if I had, I never would have reunited with Sam, that's why.

No doubt about it, Ed's daily letters were a painful dose of reality. Yes, there was an astral plane out there that contained a house back in Crowley, Massachusetts, and two thirteen-year-old sons and a remorseful husband, and this present astral plane that contained a fishing cabin on Little Lost Lake and a hermit lover. In two weeks' time when the boys finished with camp, the two planes were going to intersect in some way she couldn't quite envision, but suspected would be cataclysmic. But until then, she decided philosophically, better not dwell on it too much.

Sam had made her promise not to mention his residence back at Twin Pond to anyone at Dunbar's. "You know how these busybodies are around here. They'll be dropping by to do a little fishing and then expect a fresh cup of coffee and a tuna fish sandwich on toasted rye," he said. Lucy had her own reasons for keeping mum. After hearing Lucy wax on about the man she should have married, April would draw the obvious conclusion if Lucy reported that—what a coincidence!—Mr. Right was living one pond over and romantically unattached just like her. But April seemed to have figured out that something was up without any clues.

"So, what are you doing with yourself these days," she'd ask.

"I'm collecting my dad's lumberjack tales into a children's book and illustrating them. I told you I was going to work on a book, remember?" Lucy said, avoiding April's skeptical, pale-lashed gaze by turning her attention to the remaining varieties in the Darcie's donut carton on the counter.

"You want Hank to stop by this afternoon? He hasn't finished replacing the shingles on the boat house yet."

"That's okay. They can wait." She took a bite of a lemon-filled and dabbed a dollop of yellow goo off her chin. Goddamn April and her sixth sense for what would be exactly the wrong time to send Hank over.

"You must be getting lonely out there night after night. Want to come for dinner tomorrow? It's Thursday, you know, *Fraiser* and *Seinfeld* reruns back to back. Reception's good—we've got a dish."

"Thanks for the offer, but I like being alone. Really."

April turned her back and started to clean out the grease trap on the grill, her flaming ponytail swishing indignantly at having her favorite TV shows dissed by an East Coast snob.

Lucy hadn't been entirely lying to April—she had been illustrating Cyrus's lumberjack tales, in her own idiosyncratic way. From the moment she got back from Dunbar's at eight until Sam paddled up the channel at five, she was hard at it, covering the log trestle table with sheet after sheet—fine detail watercolors and dashed-off sketches—too busy to clean the brushes or cap the paint tubes.

The first set of sketches were about the Winter of the Blue Snow, which according to Cyrus's squiggly fly-specked notes, was one of the most famous lumberjack tales of all.

One of the worstest winters we ever put in with Paul Bunyan was the winter of the blue snow. It was so cold that the snow all turned blue—came down blue in the first place, and then turned bluer when it touched the ground. It was so cold that the words froze in our mouths when we tried to talk. Broadaxe Bill, a fellow that talked a lot, the words froze so thick around him that Paul finally had to get Babe the Blue Ox to pull him out. And then in the spring when the words began to thaw out, they came out in different combinations, so that lies turned into bald truths.

She painted Broadaxe Bill, a bearded lumberjack in red plaid and wool knickers, trapped in an ice cave of blue frozen words. Then she illustrated a second of Cyrus's tales, Broadaxe Bill and the Moving Forest. When Bill raises his ax to cut a giant fir, it pulls up its roots, scoops up the baby trees in its outstretched branches, and runs away.

But after a while, Lucy went off on her own tangents. The images kept swirling up, as if she'd tapped into an underground cavern of the subconscious—many stories or one story with many chapters, it was impossible to tell. There was a castle controlled by fantastical clockwork gears. A dark-haired woman searched for her beloved, a handsome fair-haired man. Gradually the woman figured out that all the castle's inhabitants were clocks, as well, wearing human face masks. Then she made a horrifying discovery; her beloved had been turned into a clock by the evil clockmaker who was a temptress. The woman fled into the wilderness with the aid of two gnomes. The next series of watercolors was a cabin on a remote lake, much like Cyrus's cabin on Little Lost Lake, but with a few magical touches—the inhabitant was a mute wizard who communicated only through codes, the furniture was fashioned from carved wooden creatures.

Every night on their way to the horsehair bed, Sam stopped by her table to riffle through the day's work. "The wizard guy looks like your dad," he said. She held up a yellowed snapshot of Cyrus in his fleece band fishing hat and waders, smiling at the camera, cigarette dangling. What a pleasure it had been to try and capture that smile, joyful rather than merely polite, which he only made fly casting at Little Lost Lake. She'd left out the horn-rims and Tareyton.

"And I guess we know who inspired the gnomes," he said, pointing toward the row of photographs of the boys she had propped along the bookshelf. One gnome was tall with a coxcomb of tangled hair, the other small and peevish, a pair of cockeyed spectacles perched on his long nose. The boys would probably be offended by her portraits, in the unlikely event that they ever saw these scribbles.

"And the lumberjack guy kind of looks like me."

"You may have noticed there's a shortage of models around here. Besides, I think you make a pretty good lumberjack."

He surveyed the drawings strewn every which way across the table and spread his arms with dismay. "Where's all this stuff coming from?" She tapped her skull. "Don't you think maybe you're getting a little too, you know, out there?"

"You're a forty-year-old man holed up in a caboose who spends his time hoeing turnips, and you ask me if I'm getting too out there?"

At a quarter past ten, as Lucy put the finishing touches on a sketch of Broadaxe Bill giving himself a shave with his silver-headed ax, Sam's hello echoed across the water. She leaned over her worktable, raised the screen, and poked her head out the window to see Sam with a canoe full of camping gear hitching up to her dock. "What are you doing here," she called. "You're six hours early."

"Time for a road trip." Road trip—the words sent a prickle of nervousness down her spine. Once, when Lucy had suggested a jaunt to Iron Mountain for dinner and a movie, her treat, Sam had refused rather self-righteously. A ride in a car would dilute his Thoreauvian sojourn, he'd said, making her feel shallow for thinking *Deep Impact* and a bucket of buttered popcorn might be fun. Next time I climb into the driver's seat, he'd said, it means I'm leaving for good.

She jogged down to the dock to find him off-loading a backpack and tent roll. "What's up?"

"Cabin fever. I was about to pick up an ax to split a stack of logs into kindling and suddenly I thought, Screw this, I deserve a vacation. So how about a little camping trip?" He stooped down and expertly hitched a dented aluminum frying pan to the top of an ancient Kelty frame pack, the same one he'd had when they'd gone on camping trips way back when. He'd changed out of his ubiquitous jeans and work boots into cargo shorts, a canvas baseball cap, and a pair of hiking boots the same vintage as the pack. He tossed the pack over one shoulder and walked up to the cabin with a jaunty swagger, the cargo shorts showing off his sinewed calves nicely. Biker's or rock climber's legs, one would guess to see them now, not gardener's legs. Yes, Lucy had forgotten how much more easygoing the footloose Sam had been than the new dour earthbound one.

An hour later, after she'd packed up her gear and a few meager provisions in her larder—four eggs, tea bags, and a hunk of Wisconsin brick cheese—they were in the Taurus heading north up scenic Route 55.

"You drive, I'll navigate. Wow, this speed—I'm feeling dizzy," he said, foraging in the glove compartment for a road map. The Taurus was only poking along at forty but he didn't sound as if he were kidding.

"Where we going?"

"Well, I thought we'd head up to the north end of the Nicolet at Tippler. Then we can hike into Porcupine Lake and camp there."

"Can't we go a little farther away, over to the Apostle Islands or up to the UP? The Nicolet is so boring," she whined, stretching the first syllable of boring into a three-beat nasal bray, just like Benjy. For years back in boring old Crowley, she had been thinking of this landscape as the most exciting, the most exotic on earth. How could it have become humdrum after only four weeks?

"This isn't just a hike through the woods, Lucy," he said, sounding more cheerful and carefree with every high-speed mile. "I'm taking you on a panther hunt. An eastern panther was spotted there a few years ago. I thought we could hunt for tracks."

"Okay," she said, trying to muster enthusiasm for panther tracking—at least that was something you couldn't do back in Crowley, Massachusetts. As they looped past decrepit lakeside cottage "resorts" and raw bald spots where gigantic skidders were in the midst of clear-cutting, Sam gave her a detailed history of the panther in northern Wisconsin. Population originally numbered in the tens of thousands but declined sharply as forests were settled after 1850. Last panther, also called catamount, was hunted in 1910; the stuffed specimen was still on display at the Nicolet ranger station, moth-eaten but still with cute little tufted ears, as Lucy recalled. Found panther tracks on a sheep farm near Tippler in 1992, which meant that the panther population might be migrating down from Canada now that northern Wisconsin is reforesting. "That is, if the Feds don't spread their legs for the lumber companies," Sam said, rapping his knuckles against the window in disgust as they drove past another jagged skidder track leading into the tender underbelly of the forest.

She pulled up at the Tippler general store, the last outpost of civilization before they hit the trailhead, for an extralarge takeout coffee and a Snickers. The more she heard about stumbling through the forest in search of invisible tracks left by an invisible animal, the more she felt the need of fortification—too bad Tippler general didn't sell gin. Sam opened the hatchback, pulled out a manila envelope covered with a hodgepodge of stamps, and shoved it into the blue mailbox bolted next to the front door. "I thought you didn't do mail," she said, taking a greedy gulp of scalding coffee and regretting it.

"Not usually. But Heidi's been bugging me to sign a separation agreement."

"Since when have you been communicating with Heidi?"

"Like, eight months ago or something. It takes me a while to get around to paperwork. You're not jealous, are you?" He bent down, gave her cheek a peck, then bit off half her Snickers and chewed it noisily. "*Mmm,* tasty. Forgot about candy bars."

Two hours later, after an eight-mile hike through an unremarkable second-growth forest with nary a panther in sight, Lucy was sitting on a stained, pressure-treated log, courtesy of the National Forest Service, next to the regulation fire pit with grill, staring forlornly out across the ripply surface of scenic Porcupine Lake. She tried to catalog its unique features, but found none. Bigger than Little Lost Lake or Lake Kinahwee, but the same tea brown water with a blue-green cast, the same blasted spruce stump that had been struck by lightning, the same washed-up chub carcass, the same red-winged blackbird warbling on a cattail. Same old, same old. I want to go home, she thought for the first time. I miss electric lights, my subzero refrigerator/freezer, Pima cotton sheets on my Sealy Posturepedic, my pulsating shower head, central air, the *Boston Globe, Mystery!,* my Loreena McKennitt CD, traffic, sushi, stacks of Day-Glo T-shirts at the Gap, my kids, and Ed. In that order. She slipped on her sunglasses and let out a big snuffle.

Sam dropped a pile of pine brush and birch bark into the fire ring. "Why so glum, Lucy?" He sat next to her on the prefab log.

"I miss my kids," she said, suddenly paranoid that Sam could peer into her heart and divine her yearning for consumer products.

"They'll be back soon. Meanwhile, they're having the time of their lives."

"I'm not sure about that. They're pretty unathletic. What

if they can't hack it? What if the other kids are picking on them?"

"Well, then, a little hardship will be good for them. Make them discover they're more resourceful than they ever realized." He nonchalantly layered the kindling in the fire ring—first the birch bark, then the dried pine needles, then a tepee of larger boughs.

Good for them—that's the kind of thing people who didn't have kids said. It was so easy to inflict hardship on someone whose dear face you'd never laid eyes on. She suddenly conjured up Phil's expression when she had dropped him off at Kinahwee—the large eyes turned toward the ground so that all she could see were the rims of long lashes, the lips moving against each other as if they'd become painfully chapped, the shoulders slumping down so far that he looked like a hedgehog curled into a ball. Yes, Sam had never seen a boy look like that when he said hardship was good for them.

But come to think of it, hadn't she said the same thing—that Camp Kinahwee would be good for Benjy and Phil, help them discover their inner resources. Ed was the parent who was tenderhearted enough to worry about them. I am such a bad mother, she thought, stomping on an iridescent-shelled beetle that was about to scuttle under the log.

"So, have you decided what you're going to do when the boys get out of camp?" He pulled out his Swiss Army knife and whittled away at the log end—never miss an opportunity to deface government property.

Oddly enough, in all their time together, he had avoided asking this obvious question. At last, the two astral planes were about to collide. "I'm going to pick them up, and then . . . " She paused as she considered the options. Bring them back to Little Lost Lake, introduce them to Sam? Here's Mom's old friend, I mean new friend, boys. "I guess we'll head back to Crowley." There now, she had decided. She shrugged, as if to say what other answer could there be.

"So that's all this has been—a little fling in the wilderness and then back to suburbia." He now started jabbing the knife full force into the log, sending wedge-shaped chunks flying.

"What did you expect, Sam? That the boys and I would stay on at Little Lost Lake permanently, that it could all be that simple?"

"Why not? Why can't it be that simple?" He plunged the knife into a rotten spot all the way up to its hilt and raised his eyes. Not angry, just weary bafflement that once again someone did not follow the obvious and correct path.

She rested a hand very gently on top of his. "Crowley is my home. It's the boys' home. I can't just run away from my life and never go back, Sam." Her voice was slow and patient, as if she were explaining something complex to a small child, and in a way she was. Sam was clueless about the compromise-ridden, justification-laden emotional terrain of the average adult. "Even if Ed and I do eventually separate, I still have to go back there and face him. Together, we have to decide what's best for our family." As long as she was sharing hard truths, she might as well go the rest of the way. "And frankly, even if I decide I don't want to live in Crowley any more, I'm not sure I want to live year-round at Little Lost Lake in a cabin with no plumbing or electricity. Sorry if that disappoints you."

"Disappointed but not surprised, I guess." He let out a resigned sigh, as if this weren't the first time he'd been let down by the shortcomings of his fellow mortals. "I just hoped that you really were ready to make the big step. Go off the grid."

If she wasn't ready to go off the grid, what was she choosing instead—to stay on the grid? Couldn't she be half on and half off? She gently pried the knife free, shut it, and slipped it in his breast pocket. "Let's go hunt for panthers, okay?"

"We can't leave until nightfall. They're nocturnal, remember? That gives us two hours to kill."

They spread the sleeping bags out on the tiny muddy beach by the shore of Porcupine Lake, covered themselves with

Cutter's deep woods spray to fend off the cloud of evening mosquitoes, and made love in a slow, wistful way. Lucy touched the hard creases over his mouth, the lopsided tilt to his nose, the dark line of hair down his white belly, the heart and head lines across his broad calloused palm as if she were seeing them for the very first time, or the last. Then after a cheese omelet cooked over Sam's expertly laid fire, it was time to head off in search of panthers.

"We'll leave the big packs here. All we need is flashlights and water bottles." He dug a battered daypack out of the Kelty, loaded it, then held a flashlight up to the map and checked his bearings with the compass. After a few moments of figuring, he tucked the gear back in the pack, grabbed Lucy by the hand, and lead her out of the clearing, past the blazed trail, right into the heart of the forest. He headed off at such a swift pace that she had to jog to keep up, fallen logs barking her shins, aspen branches whapping her in the face.

"Sam. Wait a sec. Why are we going this way? Isn't there a trail?" she panted, bending double to massage her scraped shins.

"Nope."

"I don't get it. If no one's seen one of these panthers, then how do you know where to find one?" This almost sounded like one of those conundrums that Benjy liked. If a tree falls in the forest and no one is there to hear it, does it make a noise?

He stopped and handed her the map. "We're going to the sheep farm where one was supposedly sighted in 1992." He flashed his light on a spot circled in yellow highlighter and then Porcupine Lake, which appeared to be several significant inches away. They'd be hiking all night.

Lucy danced her light across the map. "Look. There's a road that goes right up to the farm. Why don't we drive there tomorrow instead of bushwhacking." Okay, so she was wimping out.

"Because this is much more of an adventure, don't you agree?" There was an ironic edge to his voice. Was she being subjected to some kind of high-stress wilderness test, like those hikes at Kinahwee where the leaders deliberately got them lost and disoriented, and then ditched them. Without waiting for a reply, he grabbed the map out of her hand, jammed it back in the daypack, and headed off. Oh, what the hell, she thought lumbering along behind, a little hardship never hurt anyone. Maybe I'll discover some inner resources. Every fifteen minutes or so when Sam stopped to check the map and get his bearings, Lucy scanned her flashlight up into the looming cathedral of trees, searching for the tufted ears of a perching panther.

After three hours, or was it four—she was too bruised and exhausted to reckon—a constellation of high-wattage electric lights glinted through the tree trunks. Sam waited till she caught up, grabbed her arm, and held his fingers to his lips. "This is it," he whispered.

They crept closer until she could make out a farmyard illuminated by buzzing vapor lights strung on poles and the wire mesh of animal pens. Suddenly, her nose was assaulted by a musky stink like cat spray. "Whew. What's that?" she asked loudly.

"*Shhh.*" Sam gave her upper arm a hard squeeze. "It's sheep."

Their neighbors in Crowley kept a couple sheep in their back field, which smelled rather pleasantly of grass and dung, not like this. "No, it's not," she whispered.

"Come on," he ordered, apparently not interested in a further discussion of animal odors. He grabbed her arm and pulled her along, creeping along the shadowy perimeter of the farmyard, stopping to unbolt a wire mesh farm gate and tugging her into a cavernous animal pen.

"You think the panther's in here?" Now the stink was overpowering. With sweat dripping down her back despite the chill night air, she halted in her tracks and slowly spun around. There was not a sheep in sight, in fact there were no animals in sight, just low cages like dog crates, rows and rows of them, stacked three high. "What is this place?"

"Oh, gee. I think it might be a mink farm," said Sam unsurprised.

Oh, gee, I think it might be a mink farm? Lucy's brain repeated dully. But where's the panther, it asked. She watched as Sam set down his pack, pulled out a pair of leather welder's gloves, slipped them on, and started to unlatch the cages, quickly but soundlessly, swinging the doors wide. Then long brown creatures leapt out, shaped like weasels. No, not like weasels. They *are* weasels. Three and four at a time, until the ground was covered with them, wiggling and oozing, beady black eyes bobbing, their minky soft bodies swarming around her legs. "*Ahh!*" she screamed, leaping back, kicking out with one foot hard, then another as the mink puddle flooded after her. She grabbed a rake and tried to sweep them away. "Go! Scat! Shoo!"

"Good, Lucy. Herd them out of the pen."

Slowly she backed up until she hit the sharp prongs of the wire gate, reached behind to pull the bolt and creaked it open, jabbing with her rake until the squirming furry mass redirected itself out the gate into the darkness. Brown sausage bodies, soft beige ones, some with pink noses and some with black ones. When one stopped to sit up on its back legs, paws grabbing, tiny mink-covered ear at attention, Lucy lashed out savagely. "Out. Out." Much, much later, long after the sound of unlatching cages had stopped, long after the last mink had scurried to freedom, she was still flailing until Sam finally pried the rake from her hands. "It's all done. Come on. We've got to run." His urgent voice was like a slap in the face. She gave one hurried backward glance at the dozens of emptied cages and ran. Out of the pen, around the pools of glaring light, back into the woods, the flashlight beam bobbing wildly with each step, her breath rasping in her throat, the smack as branches, logs, rocks hurled themselves against her body.

After another long while, longer than it had taken to unlock the cages and sweep the teeming mink into the woods, Sam finally let them stop. She fell on a pile of leaves, crying as she rubbed her mangled, bleeding legs. He kneeled down beside her. "Lucy, I'm sorry."

Of course, she should demand an explanation, but she was too exhausted to listen or to care. Then she considered slapping his deceitful face but decided it might hurt her hand, and she was in no mood for any more pain. "Fuck you."

"I'm sorry I lied to you, but I had to. Those poor creatures were being butchered and skinned to make coats for rich women. I had to do something." His face was flushed, his eyes shining like a little boy who had just taken his first run down a steep hill on a Flexible Flyer.

"Not with me, you didn't. I just committed a crime."

"They're the criminals, not us. And the farm is on land that they lease from the federal government. That's what makes liberating the minks morally justifiable." His voice rang out with indignation, the way it had when he justified slugging a paunchy Nicolet ranger to defend the spotted owl nesting grounds. He's the criminal, not me, Sam had said.

"I don't think the police will see it that way. How much are those animals worth?"

"Oh, I don't know. Half a million or something. It's one of the biggest mink farms in the country," he said airily. "But don't worry. They're not going to catch us."

Catch us—for the first time Lucy wondered if an irate band of mink farmers and local police were following their tracks through the woods, trying to lift prints off the rake handle. "I don't want to go to jail for a bunch of weasels," she hissed.

"Well, that's where you and I are different, Lucy. I value a mink's hide as much as my own." Then again, maybe she could stand a little pain. She stood up, took a deep breath, and kicked him hard right on a hairy shinbone. "Ow!" he yelped, loud enough so a grouse darted out of a bush with alarm. Good.

They didn't say anything more on the trudge back to Porcupine Lake. Now that the sun was up and she didn't have to worry about barking her shins, she had renewed energy for fuming. How long had he been planning this? Days, weeks, before she even paddled blithely down the channel to Twin Pond. What other felonies had he committed on behalf of Bambi and Thumper and Jimmy Skunk? She tried to reconstruct the clippings in the accordion file—a burned ski lodge, spiked trees, toppled power lines. That would have him all over the globe. But these eco-animo-terrorists must all be in cahoots, she thought, whoever they were. Sam, still rubbing his wounded calf in a bemused way, paused to smile back at her beseechingly. She gave him the finger.

Why had he dragged her along on this escapade—couldn't he have gone by himself? Was it just because she had a functioning car, or did she serve a more sinister purpose, a cover story, perhaps? No, Officer, I don't know a thing about any mink ranch raid. My friend and I have been here camping all night and haven't seen a thing, isn't that right, Lucy? This is Lucy Crocker, Officer, famous software designer, spotless record, check her out if you don't believe me.

No, Lucy thought bitterly, this had been another one of Sam's tests—like when he demanded that she flee Cambridge with him—to prove that she was high principled enough to deserve his love. And once again, she had failed.

Then her musings took a more practical turn to minks. Her grandmother had worn a string of them around her neck, the type with the heads biting the toes of the next, the eyes made of black glass. Lucy still had them coiled in a hatbox with a pile of mothballs. The absolute first thing she would do when she got home was to chuck it straight into the trash barrel. Corky used to have a mink stole that she wore over her evening dresses when she managed to get Cyrus to take her to the dances at the country club. It had a luscious navy satin lining with her initials embroidered in emerald silk. How many pelts went into that little garment—five, a dozen, several dozen? Lucy had no idea, not that she could muster an ounce of sympathy for those repulsive, slithering creatures. Surely there could be no good end for two hundred mink bolting into the Wisconsin woods—roadkill, coyote chow. Or more likely, they'd all skulk around the outskirts of the mink farm, waiting to be ushered back to their safe, cozy cages and two squares a day.

At Porcupine Lake, they stopped long enough to roll up the sleeping bags that had been left on the mud slab beach and clean up the crusted remains of dinner. An omelet cooked over an open fire and eaten straight out of the frying pan, making love in the middle of the afternoon—could she have shared these domestic rituals with this lunatic a mere twelve hours ago? By 7:30 they were in the parking lot of the trail-head and there were no state troopers waiting to slap on the cuffs. Sam was probably right, by God. They were probably going to get away with it.

They tossed the gear in the back of the Taurus and climbed in. "Where to, Mr. Kaczynski?" she said, smiling poisonously as she backed the car between the Smokey the Bear sign and the Plexiglas-covered trail map and headed toward Tippler.

"That's not funny, Lucy."

"Who says I was joking? I want to know what other lies you've told me. Did you ever run a community garden for a homeless shelter in Seattle?"

"That's true."

"Were you ever married to a woman named Heidi?" She checked the rear view for flashing blue lights as they crawled past the Tippler general at a very law-abiding twenty-five.

"That's true, too. But we got divorced a long time ago. That's not why I came back to Twin Pond."

"Why did you come back?"

"I'm not sure you want to know. Let's just say I was

involved in some extralegal activities and I needed a place to be inconspicuous for a while." He leaned out the open window to check the side mirror, the wind plastering back his shaggy hair and making him look rugged and purposeful, more Captain Courageous guiding his ship through a tempest than a crackpot who'd spent the last twelve hours staggering through the underbrush.

"So, you're on the lam." He was right, she didn't want to know the specifics. "What was in that envelope you mailed?" A mail bomb? No, even Sam at his nutty, zealot best wouldn't kill someone, at least she didn't think so.

"I was informing the media about the liberation of Swenson's mink farm."

"How thoughtful. All right, one more question. Where do I fit in? Was all the destiny stuff for real, or was I just a cog in the wheel."

He turned back from the mirror, reached over, and stroked her arm with a hand blackened by mink farm grime. "That was for real, Lucy. Some things are kind of hard to fake." She thought of his ardent dark face, staring out across Twin Pond for her canoe to make its way up the channel. Yes, some things were hard to fake—she believed him. "I know you're probably sick of doing favors for me, but can I ask one more thing?" He was using his low, coaxing voice on her, the one that had made her shimmy up the ladder to the cubbyhole bed and herd minks with a rake.

She actually laughed. "Sure, Sam. What?"

"Do you think you could give me a lift to the Iron Mountain Airport? It might be better for you if I disappear for a while."

"What about your garden?" she asked. A stupid question considering the circumstances, but after providing her with a daily report on everything from leaf mold to cabbage slugs, how could he leave it to fend for itself?

"Frankly, I stink at gardening, in case you hadn't noticed." He grinned, for once able to poke fun at himself. "I probably would have starved to death by January. Tell the woodchucks to help themselves, I surrender."

When she pulled up in front of the terminal and parked illegally in a handicapped space, they fell into an awkward silence. How do you say good-bye to someone you made love with every day for almost a month, who you committed a felony with? She pulled her wallet out of the side pocket of her backpack and handed Sam all her cash—a couple hundred dollars at least. "Here, take it. I don't want you to get caught." His strong brown hand opened and accepted it without hesitation or qualm—it probably wasn't the first time a woman had given him money.

"I'll be back. Probably in the spring." He said it like a question, waiting for her to fill in the blank.

"I'll be long gone." She didn't add, but drop by anyway, stay in touch. He leaned over, gave her a chaste kiss on the cheek, pushed back a tangled lock of hair from her eyes, reached back for his pack, and climbed out. She watched him as he swung the backpack onto his broad shoulders and ambled off through the double glass with the frying pan swaying to and fro. Yes, any ticket agent or flight attendant or fellow seat passenger would find this grungy but cute guy in the cargo shorts and hiking boots perfectly unremarkable. On vacation? they would ask. Hiking up in the UP for a couple of weeks, he'd say. They'd nod, relieved at this healthy, legitimate reason for the sweaty smell—not some weirdo, after all. Going back home? Yup, he'd say. Seattle, Portland, Boulder—someplace out west where he'd get back in touch with his fellow AFFers. That is, if he'd ever been out of touch with them, which seemed unlikely, on second thought.

Several minutes after the last trace of Sam McCarty had disappeared inside the terminal, she moved the car into a legal space (she would never commit an illegal act again for the rest of her life) and found a pay phone by the baggage claim. Pick up, Ed, she thought, pick up, but she got the machine. "Hi, Ed, it's me. Thank you for your letters. I really enjoyed them." In the mirrored surface of the phone, she inspected the haggard, crusty eyes, the tears that started to roll down her dirty face. "Listen? Do you still want to fly up to Little Lost Lake, because I miss you a lot. Come as soon as you can, okay? Ah, I guess that's all. I love you. I always have. I always will."

LEVEL IV

Return to Mink Cottage

CHAPTER 16

>>

The truck driver was a lady named Bea, not a man like Phil had expected, and her truck was a hot four-door extended Chevy Silverado pickup, midnight blue with orange detailing, not a Peterbilt eighteen-wheeler hauling a bunch of chickens. She was a medium-old lady, with half-gray, half-black hair pulled into a ponytail and glasses that hung on a chain around her neck. Unlike most old ladies, she wore white Nike Airs and blue jeans, even though it was pretty amazing she could find jeans to fit, because she was, as his grandmother Corky would say, "broad in the beam."

Under the puny lightbulb of Ogilvie's variety store at midnight, she seemed to be checking them out, too. "I expected you boys would be older," she said finally, like those no-nonsense teachers in elementary school who always got disappointed instead of mad.

"We're fifteen," said Benjy, in a tiny, squeaky voice like a chipmunk. She didn't even bother to say he was lying. "So, did you bring us any food?"

She reached over the front seat and pulled out a large paper bag spotted with grease and a cardboard carrier with two giant soda cups. Benjy scowled down at the bag through his crooked glasses. "You didn't go to McDonald's?" he whined.

"Aren't any McDonald's around here, son. Be glad the

diner at Saxon's Falls was still open when I went through. As it was, they'd already turned off the grill and I kind of had to beg them to fire it up again."

"Thank you, ma'am. We really appreciate your thoughtfulness," said Phil, grabbing hold of the bag, which was still warm. The odor of cooked hamburger and melted American cheese and warm ketchup drifting out the top made his knees get wobbly and he had to sit down fast on the front steps before he keeled over with starvation. It had been over forty-eight whole hours since he'd eaten a real meal and it was kind of a miracle that he hadn't lapsed into a coma by now. With trembling hands, he pulled out a boat of fries, soggy like the ones under the heat lamps in the school cafeteria, and ate them in gulps, like the Talmadges' golden retriever, Chester, gobbling his Eukanuba.

"I'm supposed to be taking some John Deere parts for a busted bulldozer up to a logging camp at Big Trout Lake," she told them. "But I decided when you boys called that someone should keep an eye on you, 'cause you never know. There are a lot preverts up in these parts."

That must be how they say "pervert" up here in Canada, only Phil couldn't guess why there would be a lot of them up here or why they would be particularly interested in him and Benjy. Being a grandmotherly and responsible kind of person, Bea made them call home to let their parents know they'd been picked up. Benjy dialed on Bea's truck phone, but he got the machine again so he left a message. "Hi, Dad, it's Benjy. That trucker that you instructed to pick us up is here." Phil wondered what his father would make of all this until he noticed Benjy's finger on the disconnect button—the little sneak was just pretending to leave a message! "We'll probably get to Mom's cabin sometime tomorrow morning. We just had a big bag of burgers and everything is great, so we'll talk to you, um, you know, soon."

As Phil climbed into the backseat of Bea's extended

pickup, which was blue velour and still smelled new, he started worrying that maybe they would eventually get in more trouble for not leaving a message than for leaving one. But their dad was probably spending twenty hours a day at Crocker debugging MQII and wasn't even bothering to check his messages, Phil told himself. Benjy sat next to Bea, talking her ear off with some crock-of-shit story about how they had to leave camp early to go to their aunt's wedding and how their camp counselors had dropped them at Ogilvie's variety. Phil stretched himself across the backseat, luxuriating in the bouncy foam cushion, the nubby velvet rubbing against his bare arms, the vinyl smell and the well-tuned hum of the V-8 engine gently lulling him to sleep. He didn't care where he was heading or when he got there, just as long as he never again had to bed down in a saggy, nylon tent or eat anything that had formerly been dehydrated flakes.

Phil woke up to the sounds of a heated discussion between Benjy and Bea. "Thought you boys said this was an old family place and you knew right where it was," Bea said, her soft pink face furrowing as she watched Benjy wrestle with a midwestern United States road map like it was an octopus.

"It is an old family place, my mom's family, but we haven't been there exactly. I know what it's near."

"So what's it near?" she asked, her patient kids-are-so-cute former-first-grade-teacher voice wearing thinner by the minute. It was dawning on her that she might be stuck with a couple of runaway thirteen year olds for a while.

"My mom said it was about three hours from Kinahwee Falls, which is where our camp was."

"I don't call that very near," Bea said, now actually starting to sound mad. She pulled off into the Mobile minimart and shoved the Silverado into park. "Run in there, Ben, and find yourself a better map. Get me a Yodel and an extralarge black coffee. I think I'm going to be driving for a while." Benjy opened the door and hesitated, his eyes fixed on Bea's big trucker wallet chained to her jeans. "And you can use your own goddamn money. See. There's one of them Cirrus machines."

He came dragging out of the minimart a few minutes later with a folder-shaped north Wisconsin-in-detail map tucked under his arm. "This cost me seven bucks," he complained.

"Just figure out where we're supposed to be going, okay, Benjy," said Phil. The sky had suddenly turned pea soup green and big drops of rain started falling until the truck's windows blurred like an out of focus camera. In a mere eight hours, Benjy had pushed Bea over the edge, just like he had Chris and Dave.

Benjy unfolded a map the size of a double bed. "Well, here's something called Little Lost Lake, but it looks kind of puny and there's no road to it."

"Maybe I should let you boys off here . . ." Bea started.

"But it's near a town. Can you take us that far? Um . . . please?" said Benjy, in a polite way followed by a semigrateful smile. Talk about too little too late. He held up the map and pointed at a dot that was a mere inch and a half away.

"Well, as my old dear mother always said, no good deed goes unpunished," she said, flooring it. By the time she lurched into something called Dunbar's general store an hour and a half later, Phil was about to puke. He didn't care if Bea ditched them here, or if they found their mom at Little Lost Lake and she yelled at them worse than when she caught them looking at blow jobs. Hell, he was even ready to give Camp Kinahwee a call and turn themselves in to Uncle Bo.

"Okay boys. Here we are. Time for a final accounting. Let's call it five hundred miles at twenty cents a mile, plus a hundred for picking you up, gas, and the sack of burgers. That'll be two hundred." She held out a leathery palm.

Benjy opened up his wallet, counted out the money in twenties, then recounted it like a bank teller. "I need a receipt for tax purposes," he said.

Phil didn't even wait for Bea to tell Benjy to take a hike.

"That's really not necessary," he said, jumping out into the drizzle and sprinting over to the front porch of Dunbar's general store. Benjy had no sooner stepped out and slammed the door than Bea had whipped the truck around and pulled out with no more good-bye than two blasts of the horn. "Thank you," Phil yelled after her.

"Wow, she sure took off fast," said Benjy. "What was her problem?"

"You," said Phil.

"Me? What'd I do?" His eyes bugged out wide with astonishment.

"You treated her like she was our chauffeur. You complained about the burgers. You pulled your usual cheapskate act about paying up. Face it, Benj. You're totally obnoxious and you drive people crazy." Benjy for once didn't have some smart-ass answer. His head drooped and his sneaker poked at a line of ants that was heading for cover under the store stairs, as if he'd become interested in insects all of a sudden. "So, listen. We're going to go into this store and try to find someone to help us get to mom's cabin, so try to act like a normal thirteen-year-old kid, okay? Say please, say thank you, smile, don't act like you're smarter than everyone else. In fact, why don't you let me do the talking for a change?" Benjy kept his face down so Phil couldn't see it, and shrugged. Well, so what if he was upset—it was the truth.

Phil pushed open the screen door to Dunbar's general store and looked around for someone who might be useful, but unfortunately the place was empty except for a skinny, red-haired girl behind the lunch counter who was washing up some dishes. "Can I help you?" she said, without even turning around.

"Um, I'm not sure," he stumbled, pushing a clump of wet hair out of his eyes. What if she started asking a lot of questions, like how come they were there without any car or any grown-up, and then when he couldn't explain, she called the police. The back of his shirt got wet with sweat, even though it was still pretty chilly from the rain. He probably should have let Benjy handle this after all, he was always so much better at making up bullshit, even if eventually he ticked everyone off. "I'm looking for my grandfather's cabin up at a place called Little Lost Lake, which you've probably never heard of." He was rambling like a complete idiot.

Something he'd said made the girl drop her scrub brush, whirl around fast, and squint at him like she was supposed to know him. "You Lucy's boy? Of course you are. You're a spitting image."

It took a few moments for this information to process through Phil's carsick, rain-soaked brain. This girl, who was probably more of a woman than a girl now that he got a closer look at the wrinkles on her face, seemed to be good enough friends with his mom to know not only that her name was Lucy but also that she had a couple of kids. These were the facts, but he had a hard time believing that his mom actually shopped in this store, had made some brand-new life for herself near Dunbar, Wisconsin, in the four weeks (or was it now five?—he had completely lost track of time) since he'd seen her last. As for being called a spitting image, he had no idea what that meant, but it sounded nasty, like he had a string of drool hanging out of his mouth. Suddenly he realized the woman was waiting, with a big broad grin spreading across her face, for him to say something. "Um, yeah. Lucy Crocker's my mom, I guess."

"Knew it," said the lady, smacking her palms triumphantly down on the counter. "But I thought she said you weren't done with camp for another couple of weeks. Anyway, where is she? Out in the car?"

Uh oh, here it comes, the hard questions. "Well, no, not exactly, not yet. Actually, she doesn't know that we got out of camp early. So you think we could use your phone to call her." Already, he could hear how lame his voice would sound—Oh, hi, Mom, it's me, Phil. You'll never guess where we are.

The lady seemed to think the idea of a phone call was pretty funny. "You know there's no phone at your granddad's cabin." She circled around the counter, wiping her hands against her jeans and started toward him fast, like she was planning on grabbing him.

"Oh, right," said Phil, backing away and wondering if he should break into a run. "I forgot."

"Where are you going? I'm not going to hurt you." She rushed toward him, not to grab him after all, but to rest a hand gently on his upper arm like she was steadying him so he wouldn't fall over, which he thought he might actually do because his heart was pounding so hard. "Christ, you're a jumpy kid. I was about to offer to drive you over to Little Lost Lake right now. There aren't any customers with this rain. I can close up for an hour."

Drive him to his mom, just like that. "Um, that would be great."

"Are you hungry? You look like you're about to faint or something." She selected a donut covered with pink frosting and colored sprinkles out of a box on the counter, the kind of gross-out donuts that grown-ups think kids like, wrapped it in a paper napkin, and handed it to him.

"I can pay you. We've got money." The idea of taking a bite made him gag, so he held it politely, being careful not to dent the frosting.

"It's on the house. What did you say your name was?"

"Phil Crocker. Pleased to meet you," he said with a small bow, shifting the donut to his left hand and offering his right, the thumb smeared with pink frosting.

On the ride over to Little Lost Lake with the three of them jammed into the seat of a nonstretch pickup, the woman named April yakked on and on about her long history with their mom. "I first remember seeing her in our store when I was about five, so I guess she was about thirteen or so. Same age as you guys. She was as tall as she is now, with long black hair pulled back in a braid, and she was carrying a sketch pad under her arm, a fancy kind that you'd have to go all the way to Green Bay to buy at an art store, so I thought she was big-city sophisticated. She was with her dad, your grandfather, who even then seemed like an old man with thick glasses and an old flannel fishing shirt, stuttering so bad you could hardly understand him. I remember thinking that she deserved a younger, handsomer man for a father. Funny, huh?"

His mom had never mentioned his grandfather's stutter. Before, Phil thought of his grandfather as this simple guy who loved to fish, but this stutter thing was changing the picture, even though he didn't know what a stutter sounded like exactly. It was like that movie where Mel Gibson's face had been burned off, so he had to hide out in a shack in the woods because no one could stand to look at him. Only in his grandfather's case, it was a fishing cabin at a place called Little Lost Lake, and it was because no one could stand talking to him. Phil suddenly started shivering.

"Cold?" April asked, giving him a slitty-eyed look. At first this red-haired lady seemed young and pretty cool, but now she seemed just plain nosy.

"Wet. You know, the rain?"

"Your brother kind of keeps to himself, doesn't he?"

"Sometimes he talks a lot," Phil said, giving Benjy a sneaky elbow jab. In fact, ever since Phil's lecture after Bea stormed off, Benjy hadn't said a thing, had sat slumped against the car door, staring out the window for the entire ride, as if he could see something more interesting out there than fog and streaks of rain. What landscape Phil could make out was all pretty depressing—rows of straggly pine trees, vandalized picnic areas, road shoulders choked with weeds. In other words, nothing. What had motivated their grandfather, or their mom for that matter, to hang out in this wasteland?

"So what's the cabin like?" Phil asked. April had told all about how her husband had done such a brilliant job fixing leaks and rotting beams , but not what it actually looked like.

"Not much to say. It's small, brown. At least it doesn't smell like raccoon poop anymore." April slowed the car to a crawl. "Well, we're here, so you can see for yourself." She turned the wheel sharply and the truck dipped, bumped over some invisible object, and dove down into the dripping woods.

We're here. He was about to see his mom, he thought, his heart leaping up, then crashing down with another thought. "You sure she's here?" he asked bleakly.

"Pretty sure. Where else could she be?" Soggy branches scraped along both windows like they were driving through a car wash.

Where else could she be besides this creepy place? Practically anything else made more sense—like in her studio back in Crowley, or at Crocker Software, even if she'd been demoted from head honcho to consultant. The new Crocker building with its constant hum of air conditioning, the brand-new smell of wall-to-wall carpet, the employee lounge where you could get cool stuff like Power Bars and Cup-A-Soup out of vending machines —who wouldn't want to spend every minute there?

The truck rocked and rattled along at about zero miles an hour until it coasted into a tiny clearing. Phil rubbed the fog off the windshield and pressed his nose against the glass for a closer look. There was the dented rear end of his mom's Taurus—awesome, she was there!—and past that loomed a rickety wooden stair, a slanted porch, a screen door with no screen, a single fogged window lit from the inside by a dim orange light.

April cut the engine, stopping the wipers in midsweep. "Okay, guys. You can climb out now."

Phil sank back in the seat, and let out a long sigh. "Why don't you go in first and tell her we're here. She doesn't know we ran . . . I mean, got out of camp early. You can break the news."

She made a fed-up clicking sound with her tongue. "Geez, you are a pair of odd ducks. She's your mom, she's going to be glad to see you. Trust me. So get going, I'll wait in the truck."

Benjy still wasn't budging, so Phil reached across his lap, opened the passenger door, kind of bodychecked him out, then flipped up his sweatshirt hood, slid across the seat, and clambered after him. He grabbed Benjy's by the sleeve and dragged him over to the stairs. "What are we going to tell Mom?" he whispered when they were out of range of April's truck.

"Just let me do the talking," said Benjy, not even sounding nervous.

Okay, let him. It wasn't like Phil had any brilliant ideas and besides, he'd had a stomach full of fibbing—or was it plain old lying?—for one day. He tagged behind Benjy, who marched up the stairs and rapped softly on what was left of the screened door. They waited for a few seconds, listening hard for any I'm-coming-to-answer-the-door sounds, but nothing except the splatter of rain on their heads. Benjy knocked again, three sharp whacks this time, but still nothing. He shrugged, then reached through the busted screen and turned the door handle. Locked—well, that was a friendly welcome! Now Benjy was really starting to get ripped. He twisted the handle back and forth so hard that Phil thought it might snap off, then hammered hard with the heel of his hand. "Open up!" he yelled.

A voice, two inches away on the other side of the door, growled back, "Who is that?" It took Phil a second or two to figure out it was actually his mom's, only weirder—his mom taken over by a pod person, his mom on angel dust, his mom being held hostage. "Mom? It's us. Benjy and Phil," he called over Benjy's shoulder.

"Oh!" A yelp of surprise. Then a squeaky sound as a key turned a rusty lock, a tug at the warped door until it popped open, and there stood his mom, but different. First of all, she'd done something totally bizarre to her hair—whacked it off and made it poke out all over in clumps. Secondly, she was holding up an Indian tomahawk with a big stone blade, like she was about to lunge out and brain them. "Benjy, Phil," she said, like she was about to start crying from pure happiness, then she reached for them with that tomahawk.

"Mom!" Benjy said, ducking.

"Oh, sorry," she said, staring down at the end of her hand as if she'd forgotten what she was holding. "I thought you were someone else."

"Like who? The last of the Mohicans?"

"Well, you never know, this is the north woods, right?" she said, letting out an embarrassed little chuckle. The tomahawk thunked to the floor and the next thing he knew he was being yanked inside and being subjected to major mom mauling. "Oh, Phil," she said, in a syrupy voice. "I can't believe it's you. You've gotten so tall, you're so tan. Oh, my gosh, you're soaking wet. Let's get you out of these wet clothes." And while she was saying this, he was being kissed first on the cheek and then on the forehead, and having his hair combed back and his shoulder squeezed, and having a hand shoved under his shirt up his backbone—all the typical mother poking and prodding that usually drove him crazy, only this time he didn't mind so much because no one had done it to him in quite a while.

Then it was Benjy's turn. "You look so thin. Look how long your hair has gotten. Your nose is sunburned. Is that poison ivy on your leg? I think there's some calamine lotion in the first aid box. Oh, you're soaked, too. Let's take off your shirt."

Even though Benjy hated the hugging stuff worse than Phil, he stood there and put up with it until finally he reached his breaking point. "Mom, cut it out," he said. "You're giving me an Indian rope burn."

"I am? Sorry," she said, jumping back and letting her arms

fall to her sides. Then she just stared at them in a goofy way, like she couldn't quite believe her eyes, and then without warning, she started to cry, big snuffling sobs, then wiped her nose on her sweatshirt sleeve.

Oh, man, not the crazy mom act again. First she flips out when she gets fired by dad even though she asked for it, then she flips out when she catches them on the Internet. Then when they go to camp like she wants them to, instead of acting glad, she turns into a crybaby at the blessing of the expedition. And now when they turn up at this Little Lost Lake place that she's so crazy about, she attacks them with a tomahawk and then does the boo-hoo business again. Why can't I just have a normal mother, thought Phil, even though he couldn't think who of all his friends had a mother who was exactly normal. Josh's mom was fat and always wore sweatpants, and Lila Shea's mom was divorced and went to aerobics class five times a week, and Nick's mom arranged flowers for the church altar and prayed before each meal. But still.

"Sorry, guys," she sniffled. "It's just that today I was feeling so lonely and was wishing so badly that I could see my boys, and poof, here you are. It's like a fairy tale where an enchanted frog grants you a wish. No, wait a second. You kiss the frog, and then he turns into a prince. Well, you know what I'm trying to say."

"You mean a fairy godmother who grants your wish, right? Like me," said April, clomping in out of the rain and giving herself a shake like a wet black Lab.

"You! You drove the boys here?" Uh oh, here comes the third degree, Phil thought.

"Well, sure. How else do you think they got here?" said April, sounding slightly put out that she hadn't gotten proper credit.

"I don't know. I was so busy hugging and kissing them that I forgot to ask. So how'd you guys get to Dunbar's? Why aren't you still at Kinahwee?"

"The senior canoe trip ended a couple of weeks early because one of the counselors got sick with appendicitis. They tried to call you from camp, but when they found out there was no telephone, the other counselor, the one that doesn't have appendicitis, dropped us off at Dunbar's. His name is Chris and he's a junior at Dartmouth. He's a really neat guy—you'd really like him," said Benjy, as innocently as a Boy Scout.

"I'm sure I would," said his mom in a distracted way, like she was barely listening. But April was listening plenty hard and she was scowling at Benjy like she didn't buy one single word. The major problem with Benjy's lies is he always put in too much information. April had probably seen them get dropped off by an old lady in a truck. And everyone knew that only people in books got burst appendixes, not real people.

But for whatever reason, their mom was in a gullible mood (as Benjy would say), and didn't feel like giving them the third degree. "Aren't my boys something?" she asked April dreamily.

"They sure are. They are very unique children," said April.

"Actually, it is improper English to say very unique," said Benjy, straightening his foggy glasses. "Because unique is a superlative, it can't be modified."

"Smart, too."

"So, Mom, who gave you that really disgusting haircut?" Benjy asked.

"I better hit the road," said April.

"Please stay. Let me make you a cup of tea," said his mom, suddenly remembering to have good manners.

"Nah, I'd feel like I was butting in on your little reunion. Besides, I need to get back to the store," April said, already halfway through the door, as if she couldn't wait to get out of there. "Bye, boys."

"Bye, April. I'm glad we had a chance to meet you. Thank you so much for giving us a ride. We really appreciate your thoughtfulness," Phil called after her as she thundered down the steps, back into the rain that had now accelerated into a deluge. Oh great, Benjy had done it again.

With April gone, the three of them stayed standing by the door, Benjy and him still dripping even though they'd had their shirts stripped off, the tomahawk still lying where it had been flung, as if no one knew what to do next. Phil finally gave his mom a good once-over and she looked both better and worse than she had a month ago. On second glance, her new haircut wasn't so ugly after all, it just needed a good combing, and besides, short hair made her look younger and cooler, like the other females who worked at Crocker. She was dressed like she was about to head off on a hike, in shorts and boots, which was a real switch from the swishy flowered dresses she usually wore all summer long. Her face was a healthy tan color, but her legs were covered with scabs and greenish-black bruises like she was suffering from some strange disease. "I like your new haircut," Phil said finally.

"Really," she said, running her fingers through it, which made it point straight up even more. "It's kind of a mess. I haven't brushed it in a couple of days." And here she used to rag on him and Benj when they didn't comb their hair every morning even if it was the weekend or they were wearing a baseball cap. "So, what do you think of your grandfather's cabin? Is it what you expected?" She stepped into the middle of the big living room, waving her arm around like a tour guide, and Phil checked it out for the first time.

Of course, he hadn't expected his granddad's cabin to be like anything, even though he could hardly tell his mom that, but nevertheless, it was still sort of a surprise. It was, as advertised, brown, but a nicer brown than all those brown shacks they'd driven by, made of clean-looking logs, not warped, mildewed plywood. It had a peaked log roof, and looked like the cowboy cabin in that dopey movie *Legends of the Fall,* which Lila Shea thought was so great because it starred Brad Pitt, whose eyes were too close together, like a collie dog's. There was old-fashioned stuff everywhere that must have belonged to his grandfather—two big shelves with leather books and dusty piles of papers, a 1958 calendar with a picture of a hunting dog, a crooked fishing rod and long rubber boots hanging on a hook by the door, and some Indian junk over the fireplace that must have been where she grabbed that tomahawk from.

The furniture was all pretty bare bones and ratty. The couch had stuffing springing out of the arms and big round dents on the cushions like a raccoon had spent the winter snoozing there. Phil took a couple of deep sniffs, but didn't notice any raccoon smells, thank goodness. It was hard to believe his grandmother Corky, who lived in a condo where all the chairs were covered with the same orange hummingbird cloth, had ever set one of her fancy Sak's Fifth Avenue shoes inside here, much less cooked anything in the closet-size kitchen with a one-burner stove and a sink with a pump instead of faucets. But as far as he could tell Corky never did, just sent her old stuttering husband off by himself, or with his daughter. She would call that getting him "out of her hair."

"So where are we supposed to sleep?" Benjy asked.

She pointed up a log ladder that led to a loft above the bookcases. "There's a bunk bed up there. That's where Uncle Larry and I used to sleep. It's pretty cozy up there, especially when there's a fire. I think you guys will like it." She said this doubtfully, as if she expected a bunch of complaints.

Benjy actually looked pleased, because for some unknown reason, bunk beds were one of the few normal kid things he liked. Whenever they spent the night at their friend Josh's house, Benj always went for the top bunk so he could swing down in the middle of the night and shine a flashlight in Phil's eyes. "Can we drive back to Crowley tomorrow?" he said.

"Crowley," she said, like it was a foreign word she'd forgotten the definition of. "That depends."

"Depends on what?" Benjy demanded.

"On what Dad's plans are. Did you call him from Dunbar's?"

"We tried him a lot of times but there was never any answer," said Benjy.

"There wasn't?" she said in a wobbly voice, sinking down on the raccoon couch and hanging her head over her knees like she'd just heard he'd gone down in a plane.

"He's probably just working late at Crocker," Phil offered.

"Yeah, right," she said in a way that was more furious than worried. "Well, that settles that. Why don't we stay here instead for another two weeks. That's when Dad's expecting us home."

"Two weeks? You must be kidding. Doing what?" said Benjy. He started pacing around the living room like a caged animal and Phil had to admit that the idea of being cooped up here all together made him feel pretty claustrophobic, especially if it kept on pouring, which it probably would.

"There are some jigsaw puzzles and checkers in the wooden chest. I could teach you guys pinochle. See those marks on the wall? Your grandfather spent one whole summer playing pinochle with his brother, Bart. And when the weather clears up we could go out in the canoe, maybe paddle over to Twin Pond. No, scratch that idea, but we can canoe somewhere else . . . " she rambled.

"More canoeing? Make me hurl."

For the first time in weeks, Phil actually agreed with Benjy. "Me, too."

Benjy had wound up in the corner by the picture window staring out at the pine trees thrashing back and forth, the greeny-brown soup that had swallowed up every trace of Little Lost Lake. Then he started pawing through the papers on a log worktable where his mom had spread out some of her painting supplies. "What are these?" he asked, moving the single kerosene lamp over from the couch so he could have a better look.

"Oh," she said, twisting around on the couch to see what

he was up to. "Well, you remember how I said I might try my hand at a children's book? I found some notes your grandfather made about old lumberjack tales. So I decided to illustrate a couple, like the one about Broadaxe Bill and the winter of the blue snow."

She'd read a book about Paul Bunyan to them when they were little kids, but Phil hadn't cared for it much. The idea of a giant lumberjack and a blue ox digging out the Great Lakes struck him as pretty farfetched.

"Then I kind of went off on my own tangent. Those are just a few rough sketches and false starts. Nothing is finished yet." She sounded like she was apologizing for something.

"Huh," Benjy grunted, and then nothing more for a few minutes as he hunched over the dim pool of lamplight, arranging and rearranging the drawings in little stacks. "Now, I see," he said finally.

"See what?" she asked, shuffling over timidly, like she was preparing herself for a typical Benjyism—a sneer, a put-down, a blowoff.

"The different levels."

"Like I said, Benj, it's not a computer game. They're unrelated story ideas for a book." Now her voice sounded exasperated as if to say, why does it always have to be about computers?

"No," he announced, shaking his head vigorously. "No, you're wrong, Mom. It's a computer game. It's the sequel to Maiden's Quest. Let me show you."

Even though he wanted no part of this squabble, Phil figured he better wander over and see what Benjy was up to this time. At the rate he'd been going with Chris and Bea and April, he'd get their mom so ticked off that they'd find themselves back at Camp Kinahwee. But for some reason, she seemed more amused than offended.

"You're too much," she said, shaking her head. "Okay, show me. I'm all ears."

"See, this castle with all the clocks is level one."

"The Clockwork Castle. Right."

"Now here's the heroine, Arabella."

"It's not Arabella, Benj. Arabella had blonde hair and this woman is a brunette," she said, starting to sound a little testy.

Phil managed to wedge in between Benjy's shoulder and her hip to get a closer look, patting his hair to make sure it wasn't dripping on anything. There were dozens of thick pages ripply with watercolor, stacked in six ragged piles. The pictures were peculiar, totally different than anything she'd drawn before—a lumberjack trapped in a frozen cave made out of words, a man who could peel off his face like a mask and inside his brain was made of clock gears, two dwarves carving strange letters on the side of a twisted-up tree, a wizard's cottage filled with rats. The whole effect was impressive but creepy, too, like they'd been created by a crazy person, making Phil wonder if his mom had gone off the deep end in the last month. "The lady looks like mom, sort of," Phil observed. He did not add, but younger and prettier.

Benjy jerked back so he could give her a doubtful once-over—mom, a heroine in a computer game, give me a break. "*Mmm*. Maybe you're right, only this one's a babe. All right, so she goes to this evil castle, see, looking for her boyfriend." He arranged the drawings in sequence across the table.

"That guy kind of looks like dad, only without the ponytail," Phil offered.

"Yeah, but not so dorky. Okay. So this lady, we'll call her Arabella just to make it simple, is searching for her heart-throb Ed, I mean . . . Edgar, and starts noticing everyone in this castle is acting pretty strangely." He held up a picture of Arabella watching a clockwork cat chase a clockwork mouse down a hallway lined with grandfather clocks. "She finally figures out the person behind all the funny business is the punk blonde lady clockmaker." He held up a watercolor of a spiky-haired woman dressed in a leather getup with a laced-up front that showed off half her boobs, working away in her tower clock shop filled with strange-shaped tools and spell books. "The sexpot clockmaker looks sort of like what's-her-name at Crocker . . ."

"The one with the big, you know. I think her name is Ingrid," said Phil helpfully.

His mom jumped back from the table like she'd seen a mouse scuttle by—a real possibility in this place—and started massaging her forehead hard enough to leave a big red welt. "Am I that transparent?" she half-whispered.

"No, you're not transparent. That's because skin has so many tiny blood vessels that you can't see through it," Benjy answered matter-of-factly. "Where was I? Oh, yeah. So Arabella twigs onto the evil clockmaker Ingrid."

"Let's call her something else, Benj," she said. It was not a request.

"The evil clockmaker I . . . I . . . Iris. So Arabella goes into Edgar's room to tell him about the evil Iris, and guess what? Old Edgar's been turned into a clock, too! His face is hanging on the bedpost like a pair of pj's. Now Arabella really flips out. She needs to escape or she's going to be turned into a big tick-tock herself. Then she escapes in the dead of night with the two dwarf guys, who must be her servants or something, right, Mom?"

"I guess so. You're making a whole lot more sense of this than I ever did."

As much as Phil hated to admit it even to himself, Benjy's presentation was pretty inspired, like he was telling a good story you didn't want to come to an end. Even though Benjy was a know-it-all pain in the butt, the sad truth was that he was a real brain, about a hundred times brainier than Phil, and now it seemed that he was the twin who had ended up with their mom's genius for designing computer games—talk about unfair. "Are those dwarves supposed to look like Benj a little bit?" Phil asked.

"No," corrected Benjy. "They look like you." Actually, they looked a little bit like both of them. "So next we come to level two. Arabella and the dwarves escape into a primeval forest where they meet up with this lumberjack."

Primeval? What the hell did primeval mean? Benjy never missed a chance to show off.

"This is the part I don't get, Mom. Is the lumberjack supposed to be good or evil? 'Cause in this scene, he's guiding her through the forest past the quicksand and wild boar, but in this next scene where his words freeze into blue snow, she looks scared of him."

His mom fell into what his grandmother would call a brown study. She hugged her elbows like she was suddenly feeling cold and rubbed one of those banged-up legs against the other, back and forth, back and forth. "Can't he be both?"

"Nope. This is a computer game. A character either has to be good or bad."

"Okay, in that case, I'd say he's bad. At first he seems like he's trying to help her. But see in this picture, when his words thaw out, they come out in a different order, and Arabella realizes he's been telling her lies. That the lumberjack is false, and Edgar is true."

"The lumberjack doesn't look like anyone I know," Phil offered.

"That's right." She seemed to be finding the whole who-was-who (or was it whom?) stuff pretty tiresome.

"So after Arabella figures out that the lumberjack's a psycho, we move onto the next level, which is this cottage in the woods where the rats live."

"They're not rats. They're minks."

Whatever they were, she'd made them look evil and nasty, their weasel-shaped bodies lounging across the furniture, holding cigarettes between yellowed teeth. "I thought minks were soft and friendly," said Phil.

She shuddered. "The only good mink is a coat."

"So what are they doing in this cottage?"

"It's not theirs, it's the wizard's," Benjy explained. "But

they've taken him prisoner. See, here's a picture of him in a wicker cage in the attic. They're trespassing—eating his food, smoking his tobacco, stealing his magic spells. So Arabella has to get rid of the minks, so she can get the spell book and rescue Edgar."

"How's she going to do that?" Phil asked.

"I don't know. Poison them, drown them?" she offered.

"Doesn't Crocker have a policy of no violence to animals in any of its games?" Benjy said.

"How about banish them to a remote island?" she suggested.

"Sweet," said Phil.

"Okay, Benjy. You've convinced me. I thought I was creating something original here, but maybe all I've done is come up with the sequel for Maiden's Quest I. When we get back, I'll give my drawings to Ingrid and Dad, and maybe they can fit it into the Robocop version they're working on. I'm sure Ingrid and Dad are really going to find my drawings . . . *inspirational.*" When she said the words *Ingrid and Dad,* droplets of spit splattered all over the lumberjack and his ice words. Phil guessed she would have gotten over being fired as head designer by this time. She was still a consultant after all, and it was hard to believe that any of those boring Crocker artists had come up with anything remotely as good as her evil clockmaker/ lying lumberjack/trespassing minks version.

"Do you have to give these drawings to Dad and the Crocker people?" Benjy asked, his voice pleading rather than wise-guy.

"Well, who else would I give it to?" she asked.

"No one. We could do it ourselves."

"Be realistic, Benj," she said gently, like she was comforting a little kid. "This would be much too big a project for BPCC. You know how many people it takes to design a computer game—programmers, artists, musicians, animators, actors for the live scenes. Dozens."

"I'm not saying we have to do the whole thing, just the

beginning part. Figure out the scenes in each level, the puzzles, scan in the images. The fun stuff," he insisted. Why was Benjy so fired up all of a sudden about designing a computer game? He'd never shown much interest before in what either of his parents did, had always thought that Crocker games were for simpletons.

His mom seemed to think Benjy was acting pretty strange, too, and she caught Phil's eye over Benjy's bent head and raised her eyebrows as if to say what gives, anyway. "Fine. If you want to do the storyboards and the puzzles, be my guest."

"Right, then we can hire the rest of the team later," he said.

"You mean start our own company?" Now she gave Phil a double eyebrow raise and he gave her one back.

"Why not? The Crocker designers are a bunch of bozos. Look at what they did with the MQII demo—it sucks eggs. Besides, it's not like you really work there anymore."

"Why not," she repeated, staring out the window, tapping her hiking boot in nervous spasms against the table leg. Then again, as if the two words together made some pretty melody: "Why not."

Over dinner, the three of them hammered out their plans to start their own company. She managed to whomp up a pretty incredible meal out of a few items in the rusty refrigerator that somehow ran on burning gas and a few boxes of dried stuff on the one and only shelf. She called it rotini primavera à la Mom, the primavera part being stunted vegetables, and the Mom part being cream and bacon—which always made something taste better, but which they usually never had at home because it was supposed to be bad for you. That was served up with some squishy Italian rolls and Chips Ahoys, which again was something they never had back at Crowley. But, you couldn't get brown bread with sprouts growing in it and organic cookies sweetened with apple juice at Dunbar's. Phil had forgotten what a great cook his mother was—better than grizzly gravy or diner burgers any day.

"Don't they sell full-grown vegetables at Dunbar's?" Phil asked, holding up a carrot that looked like a witch's finger.

"Those are handpicked from someone's garden," she said, sounding a little defensive.

Benjy went back to brainstorming for their as-yet-unnamed company while their mom kept minutes on a yellow legal pad. "Okay, tomorrow morning the three of us talk through the game level by level, scene by scene, and make a flow chart. Then you start making the additional watercolors, while me and Phil figure out the puzzles."

He's including me, Phil thought gratefully. Followed by, why the hell shouldn't he include me? I know almost as much about computers as he does. I saved his ass from drowning in Lake Hazard, not that he'd ever have the guts to admit it to Mom or Dad.

"I figure we could do a clock puzzle and a catacomb maze in level one, the lumberjack's frozen words which will need to be unscrambled, and then maybe the spells in the wizard's books can be written in a secret language which needs to be decoded. Those will all be pretty complicated so we'll probably need two terminals."

"We can save that part until we get back to Crowley," she suggested.

"No," Benjy corrected. "We'll do it here, starting tomorrow." Suddenly, he wasn't in any hurry to get back to Crowley, probably because he was worried that their dad would butt in somehow and hand the project over to Crocker programmers, banish him and Phil back to BPCC installing Windows 98 and designing Web pages.

"Notice anything missing around here?" she asked, pointing toward two wrought-iron candlesticks on the table covered with globs of melted wax.

"Like electricity, stupid," said Phil.

"Oh, that. Just bring it in from the road." Oh, right—for all his braininess, Benjy could be so dense sometimes.

"Okay. Hank said it wouldn't be a big deal to run in a temporary line," she said, jotting *install electricity* down on her list. "Where are we going to get a couple of high-powered computers in the boondocks?"

"I've figured that out," said Benjy. "Laszlo Zuk."

"Laszlo?" she asked. She looked like she was about to burst out laughing just hearing his name. "Benjy, we haven't talked to Laszlo in years. Not since he quit Crocker. I have no idea where he is."

Laszlo Zuk was the big, chain-smoking Hungarian who had been the most crazy programmer at Crocker ever. Dad had told them dozen of Laszlo stories over the years—how he'd spent one whole Christmas programming because he forgot it was a holiday, how once at a Crocker staff party he did a wild Cossack dance and put his foot through the monitor, how he left an open can of sardines on his desk for a week, and when Marla finally complained he quit in a huff.

"But I do," said Benjy, pulling his electronic organizer out of his pocket. "He runs a computer store in Wisconsin somewhere."

"How in the world do you know that?" their mother, said half-amused and half-amazed.

"Because he sent us a postcard, like, over a year ago announcing the grand opening of his store," Benjy said. Of course Benjy would be the only one in their family not only to notice the postcard, but record the address in his organizer. "Here it is. LZ Computers, Oshkosh, Wisconsin. Is that near here?"

"About three hours away. Close enough," she said, adding *buy computers from Laszlo* to her list.

Close enough, she says, just like that? Phil studied her face in the flickering light of the candles. Ever since Benjy had come up with this crazy scheme, she'd perked up, laughing like she really meant it, so you could see her small, pretty teeth, cooking like it was actually fun and not drudgery. Still it was hard to believe she seriously planned to run a power line down the road, find Laszlo Zuk, and set up a computer lab at Little Lost Lake, that she wasn't just humoring them.

It reminded him of the time when he was about eight and wanted to build a pirate ship, a real pirate ship, in the backyard. That's an excellent idea, Phil, she had said and they'd spent a whole afternoon making plans on graph paper—two masts, a crow's nest, an anchor, a galley, a head, a brig with hatches and portholes. She'd even had him call up the lumber yard to get a price for supplies. By the next day, he'd forgotten all about it, as she must have known he would.

"Oh, hey," she said, handing around the bag of Chips Ahoy. "I forgot to ask. How was Camp Kinahwee?"

The next morning, after they'd dropped by Dunbar's to leave a message for Hank to run a power line, they headed off to Oshkosh in search of Laszlo Zuk. Phil was in the front, flipping the channel to Howard Stern, a new taste he'd acquired from Bea, and Benjy was in the back with his nose buried in the crossword puzzle book they'd bought at the Battle Creek rest stop on the way to Kinahwee. (Phil had let Benjy do all the talking about camp, and he'd done a masterful job—the shimmering waves of northern lights, the taste of trout toasted on the end of a stick, the pleasant achy feel of your muscles after a hard day of paddling. He'd even managed to explain why they didn't have their packs or clothes with them—the camp was shipping them back to Crowley. Maybe you'd like to go back next summer, she'd beamed.) His mother was whistling to herself, as if she were trying to block out Howard Stern, who was interviewing a very deep-voiced cross-dresser.

At the outskirts of Oshkosh, they passed a Circuit City, then an Office Max. "Why don't we get our stuff there?" Phil said. Wouldn't it be much simpler just to go to a superstore and plunk down a charge card for a new, out-of-the-box Hewlett Packard?

"Sorry, Phil. Now I'm on a mission. We've got to find Laszlo," she said. Her sunshine mood had carried over from yesterday, but who knew why—him and Benjy being back from camp, starting her own computer game company, not having to rush back to Crowley, all of the above?

After considerable searching in downtown Oshkosh, they found the address on Central Street that had formerly been a Woolworth. A sign was taped to the inside window: LZ COMPUTERS, USED OR BUILD NEW, MAC OR PC, printed in purple marker on two sheets of yellow poster board, now faded a rippled cream color in the sun. "We're here," she announced, pulling up crookedly into the ten empty spaces along the front.

They followed her through the double glass doors into a twilight-echoing skeleton of a Woolworth, the empty shelves and checkout counter still in place, half the neon tubes burned out. There in the center, looking like a yard sale, was a clump of fold-up banquet tables covered with a motley assortment of beige boxes and monitors. "I'm having second thoughts," Benjy whispered.

"Too late," she whispered back. "Laszlo?" she yelled toward a swirling cloud of cigarette smoke.

A bushy head popped up from behind a bank of minitowers. "A . . . customer?" it said in a thick eastern European accent, and started lumbering toward them across the soiled checkerboard tiles like a drunken bear. The footsteps suddenly stopped. "Could it be . . . Lucy Crocker?"

The next thing Phil knew, his mom was being grabbed by a roly-poly, hairy man and twirled around so fast her feet lifted right off the ground, the cigarette butt dangling from his lips barely missing her hair. "Whew," she said when he plunked her back down. "I think you cracked a couple of ribs. Laszlo, you remember Benjy and Phil."

The man pulled the cigarette out of his mouth. "These cannot be little baby twin boys."

"Yup," she said, "all grown up."And the next thing Phil knew he was being hugged and spun off his feet and then getting his cheek pinched hard with yellow-stained fingers.

"What brings you to Oshkosh?" Laszlo asked, as if the amazing coincidence was suddenly striking him.

"You. We got your postcard. Ed still says you're the best programmer Crocker ever had."

"Ed, he said that?" said Laszlo, lifting his wooly head and concentrating hard on the ceiling for a minute, as if he were counting all the fluorescent light tubes that needed replacing.

"So Laszlo, what brings *you* to Oshkosh?" She made the question sound casual, but Phil knew what his mom was really asking was how come you ended up in a dump like this?

He waved his cigarette jauntily. "You know computer business. Start-up here, start-up there, help cousin repair computers in Madison, now this." He made it sound like he was discussing something deeply mysterious like the origin of black holes.

"Well, we need computers. We're starting a start-up, right boys?"

"You come to right place. And business she's slow, so maybe I help with this, too," Laszlo said, his fingers tapping out code in the smoky air.

CHAPTER 17

>>

For two days, two torturous endless days, Ed and Uncle Bo tracked the boys up mud creeks, across lead-colored lakes, around rocky islands, down unmarked sunless trails. Uncle Bo was like an L. L. Bean version of Sherlock Holmes, inspecting food wrappers, sifting through ash to figure out how long ago a campfire had been made, identifying tread marks from the bottom of both boys' sneakers. It was a lucky thing the boys were such slobs, leaving a swath of litter along their way.

On a barren bump in the middle of Lake Hazard, they found the charred remains of a Kinahwee manual, a crumpled Knorr gravy wrapper, and most alarmingly, a dirty sock with *Crocker* written in crooked black marker across the sole, stained with blood. "They spent the night here," Uncle Bo surmised, pointing to a spot where the blueberry bushes had been trampled flat. "And don't go getting worked up over that sock. That's just a few drops of blood, probably from a superficial cut." But Uncle Bo had no answers for Ed's more cosmic questions. Why would the boys have chosen this desolate hunk of rock and scrub to camp on, when in every direction there were lush islands with sheltering stands of spruce. Who cares where the boys were two days ago, where were they now?

He stood on a rocky spit and once again scanned the unbroken evergreen horizon for the tiniest hint of his boys—the flash of a neon yellow Yahoo! T-shirt, the glint of sunlight off Benjy's glasses, anything. "Ben, Phil," he yelled once again across the watery void, listening with every nerve ending for a muffled response, something besides the faint echo of his own croaky voice. "Ben, Phil!" He would not let himself even think the incomprehensible word *dead.* No, he only let himself say a word that was nearly as awful—*lost.* Lost and wandering out there in the three bands of dulled gray, green, and blue. When his unblinking eyes became too parched to focus any longer, he rubbed them hard. Then stared again, called again. "Ben, Phil!"

"They're all right," Uncle Bo pronounced every fifteen minutes or so, giving Ed's shoulder a reassuring squeeze. "Trust me. Ben and Phil are all right." On the one hand, Ed was relieved that at least Uncle Bo thought they were safe. But he still had to resist the urge to lunge at him, to wrap his hands around his leathery gizzard and throttle him. If Uncle Bo had the gift of clairvoyance, why couldn't he take it one step farther and figure out where they were right this second.

At the far shore of Lake Hazard they came across another campsite, this one with cigarette butts, a Campfire marshmallow, and a fragment of the Lake Hazard topo map. "They didn't have a fire here, that's an old site. Marshmallow wrapper and map are theirs, though," Uncle Bo said. "Now see how both boys' footprints go back and forth to the shore, but there's no scrape mark where they pulled the canoe up? My guess is they hitched the canoe, but it came untied and drifted off. That's when they decided to head off overland on the trail." He pointed at a faint trace of footsteps leading straight into the forest where, as far as Ed could make out, there was no blaze or path whatsoever. The so-called trail meandered back and forth through a buggy morass for a couple of miles, then landed them on a tar road that led, eventually, to something called Ogilvie's variety store. There, in a heap of burger wrappers, French fry boats, and old receipts from Benjy's wallet, the boys' trail vanished.

"Probably got picked up by a trucker," Uncle Bo concluded. "They'll turn up somewhere. Better start phoning around."

Ed called anyone he could think of to see if they'd heard from the boys—Camp Kinahwee, Crocker Software, Larry, Rosemary, but nothing. Then he checked the answering machine back in Crowley, but the only message was a strange one from Lucy, left five days ago, saying that she would always love him.

He saved the worst call for last—the one to Lucy. He had waited in the vain hope that his call would be one of rejoicing and relief—they gave us quite a scare, but we found them. Well, that was not to be. So here was Ed, standing at a pay phone outside of Ogilvie's with the phone receiver cradled in his hand, trying to figure out what words he would use to tell his dear, unsuspecting wife that their children were missing. Uncle Bo waited at a discreet distance, having tea and a honey bun on the front porch rocker, to give Ed some privacy as he faced his darkest hour. There are no words, he thought, tears streaming down his cheeks. With trembling fingers, he had dialed the number for Dunbar's general store and that unpleasant girl answered again.

"I need to leave a message for Lucy Crocker. It's an emergency," Ed managed to choke out.

"Is this her husband? What's the matter? You sound kind of upset."

He told her as best he could through the snuffles—the empty canoe, the food wrappers, and now this, gone without a trace.

She interrupted him with a big belly laugh—*yuk, yuk, yuk*. "So those little stinkers ran away, eh? I thought so. They're here, Ed," she said. "Safe and sound."

"Who is?"

"Benjy and Phil. A trucker dropped them off here a couple of days ago and I took them over to Lucy's at Little Lost Lake."

"Benjy and Phil Crocker? Are you sure it was them?"

Maybe she was mistaken; he couldn't let himself trust her words.

"Twins, right? Tall one with dark hair that falls in his eyes a lot. Small blond one with glasses, kind of a smart aleck, thinks he knows everything."

"That's them!" He was shouting. He pulled the receiver as far as it would reach on its chrome cable and waved his free arm at Uncle Bo, did a spastic Mexican hat dance. "They're at Lucy's. They're all right!" he hollered. Uncle Bo set the Styrofoam cup down on his knee and nodded sagely, as if this were pleasant but not unexpected news. How could he have known that, how could he have been so sure?

Ed retreated around the corner and pressed the receiver against his chest. They're alive, they're alive, they're alive. This is the most miraculous moment of my life, to have believed my precious children were gone and to have them restored to me in a single second. Thank you, God, he said even though he was a Unitarian and a lapsed one at that.

And then in the perverse and fickle way of human nature, this epiphany of fatherly love was bumped aside for one of pure rage. How could Benjy and Phil have pulled such a harebrained, immature stunt? First, to risk their lives by heading off by themselves when they couldn't swim for God's sake much less handle a tippy canoe across a ten-mile lake. And then when they finally did reach civilization not to have the common decency to call someone, anyone, to let everyone know they were safe. Didn't they know that he and Lucy would be frantic with worry?

Well, he was frantic with worry, but who could guess how old unfathomable Lucy felt. His fury made a 180-degree turn and headed straight for his wife's heart of stone. Why hadn't she bothered to tell anyone that the boys were at Little Lost Lake? Did she think that three days of wondering whether his children were dead or alive was somehow just punishment for his dalliance with Ingrid, that Ed deserved this? "Goddamn Lucy," he said.

"Hello? Hello? Ed, are you still there?" a muffled voice asked. Oh, right, the lady at Dunbar's.

"Sorry to keep you waiting. I had to tell the search party that we'd found our lost boys."

"No problem. You sure sound a lot better."

"Listen, it'll probably take me a couple of days to get from Canada to Little Lost Lake. Would you mind keeping this conversation under your hat? I want my arrival to be sort of a surprise."

"Want to give them hell personally, huh?" She let out a low, mean chuckle.

"Something like that."

After he hung up, Ed settled into an almost Zen-like calm—his breathing slowed, his heart rate dropped, his conversation shrank to cryptic monosyllables. When Uncle Bo suggested that Ed head to the nearest airport, he insisted that it was his sacred duty to help paddle their canoe back to Two Sister Lake. "We have come this far," Ed said in his new centered at-one-with-nature-and-himself mode. "We must finish our journey together."

By now, he and Uncle Bo were as synchronized as an Olympic scull, their canoe gliding forward without a ripple or splash, from Lake Hazard back to Two Sisters in half the time.

Uncle Bo seemed to find the new taciturn Ed disconcerting. "Now, don't be too hard on your boys," he chattered. "Chris and Dave admitted that the other boys had been teasing them. You've got to admire them for taking action and getting themselves back home without any mishaps. They probably had no idea we'd be so worried. Kids just don't understand the consequences of their actions."

"Youth is not an excuse for thoughtlessness."

"And don't be too hard on Lucy, either. I'm sure the boys didn't admit that they'd run away. Probably gave her some cockamamie story about getting out early and she believed them. I'm sure she had no idea we'd been on a manhunt for the last three days."

Ed pointed toward the sky, at a V-shaped formation of geese heading south. "Facing our responsibilities is inevitable, as one season leads to the next. I take responsibility for my actions. She must take responsibility for hers."

"Sure you haven't gotten too much sun, Ed?"

By the time Ed had bumped and weaved his Mr. Rent-A-Car through every pothole between Kinahwee Falls and Dunbar's general store, his inner peace had shaken loose. He whizzed past Dunbar's doing sixty, got a glimpse of the evergreen sign with the fawn in the rear view, did a U-turn, and squealed into the parking lot. When he slammed the screen door, a red-haired woman reading *TV Guide* behind the cash register looked up. "Hi, Ed. I wasn't expecting you so soon. How was your trip?"

"I'm not in much of a mood for conversation." For some reason, he was panting. "Just tell me how to get to Little Lost Lake, will you?"

"Sure."

He bought two six-packs of Old Milwaukee, either to be polite or because he wanted to get shit-faced, he wasn't sure which. By the time he was nosing into the scrubby turnoff to Little Lost Lake—identifiable only by the bright orange temporary power line running along the ground—he was opening his third bottle. He had rehearsed, or at least tried to rehearse, his script. Okay, I'm not going to be confrontational. I'm going to go in there, be everyone's favorite dad at first. Big hugs for the boys, a hug and a kiss for Lucy if she'll let me, which she probably will because she left that message that said she would always love me. A cheek kiss, not a wet mouth kiss—near the mouth, ardent, but dry. And then I sort of stand back and check out the lay of the land. If the boys seem repentant or scared, I act reasonable—this is a learning experience. But if they act like it's a great big joke, I go ballistic. But I must not act drunk, he thought, as the beer raced to his sun-soaked, stressed-out brain like hundred proof.

There were two cars pulled up crookedly in a little clearing in front of a cabin—Lucy's Taurus and an ancient gray Gremlin hatchback covered with a patchwork of tourist trap bumper stickers: THIS CAR CLIMBED MOUNT WASHINGTON, I SURVIVED HOWE'S CAVERN, GET CROCKED AT ZAM'S SWAMP TOUR. The Gremlin registered dully on some synapse from long, long ago, but I wouldn't know anyone who drives a car like that, Ed thought.

He stopped at a discreet distance out of sight of the cabin window, cut the engine, sat back nursing his third Old Milwaukee, and tried to get the lay of the land. So here he was at last, Little Lost Lake, this mythic place he'd heard invoked by Lucy for years. The spiritual home of poor beaten-down Cyrus. It seemed, at least at first glance, so very ordinary. Through the denuded lower trunks of red pine, the lake sparkled in the sunshine, lovely but no different from a dozen he'd seen in the last week. The brown log cabin was generic, like the ones at Kinahwee, only more dilapidated with the porch railings and stairs crudely patched. All that money extracted by Larry sure didn't buy much.

And then turning maudlin from the beer, Ed thought, my boys, my boys. It was a week ago since he'd opened Benjy's pathetic plea and he'd been searching desperately for them ever since—for hundreds of miles, over lakes, through forests. Calling their names until he had no voice left. So why was he waiting, why wasn't he dashing up the stairs to his sons? Maybe because he suspected that the idea of his family, safe and sound inside, was so much less complicated than the reality.

He set his now-empty bottle back into the carton on the passenger seat and tilted the mirror to inspect his face. It was certainly much changed from the last time Lucy and the boys had seen him—now a ruddy tan, darker than it had ever been before in his indoor-loving life, with creases fanning out from his eyes and mouth. How could he have aged so much in a single week? He climbed out and shut the car door softly and followed the orange power line snaking down the road, up the stairs, and across the porch. The weathered green door was cracked ajar to accommodate the cord, but he could see nothing, could only hear voices chattering from within. There was Lucy's sweet murmur, now Benjy's insistent grumble, probably pointing out someone's mistakes, followed by Phil's laugh, sounding deeper. They sure seemed to be having fun, all yakking and gabbing at once. And then another voice, a strange male one. Maybe Ed had waited too long.

He knocked twice on the splintery wood (hadn't they paid Larry $850 for a new door?) and waited, but there was no break in the hubbub (what were they doing, having a cocktail party?). He knocked again, good and loud this time. The mystery man said, "I get it."

The door ricocheted open and a bearded face with apple red cheeks like Saint Nick and an unfiltered Camel leered out. Ed's poor addled brain barely had time to register *Laszlo Zuk* before he was being grabbed around the middle and shaken up and down, like a sack of cornmeal being emptied. "Eet eez Ed, eet eez Ed," Laszlo repeated , hoisting Ed over the threshold and dumping him on the floor. He tried to stagger to his feet, only to be sent sprawling by a few more hearty thumps on the back. Lazlo had always loved him.

"Down, Laszlo," said Lucy's voice.

Ed steadied himself, pulled down his shirt, pushed his hair back, and looked around. He was standing in the middle of a large log living room with the usual fishing camp accoutrements—fieldstone fireplace, rickety furniture, moldy books. The only modern touch was a Crocker-size computer lab at one end of the room that completely obliterated the picture window with its scenic view of Little Lost Lake. Two Compaq towers, a Gordian knot of cables and surge protectors, and—as if they had been time traveled from their bedroom two months ago—his twin sons transfixed in front of twin monitors.

Phil glanced up. "Hi, Dad." Benjy's mouse didn't even slow down.

Then he spotted Lucy. She was leaning against a worktable covered with her painting supplies (was that the tin of pencils he had given her, finally being used?) her arms crossed skeptically across her chest, scrutinizing him in much the same way that he was scrutinizing her. She looked radically changed, but it took him a few moments to figure out how. First, there was a new shorter haircut. Not a supertrendy one like Ingrid's, but it did the job—enhanced her graceful neck and wide startled eyes, and let's face it, made her look about eight years younger. She seemed to be having a similar thought about him, and they simultaneously reached up and patted the backs of their own shorn heads. Her body was tanner and fitter than he'd ever seen her, especially since the last year of snoozing on her studio couch. But the real difference was the rubbery way her mouth was moving, the impish gleam in her eyes as if she were cooking up a big surprise. She was happy, he finally realized.

She spoke. "So Ed, I was wondering when you were going to turn up. What took you so long?"

Of course, it was the perfect entrée to announce exactly what had taken him so long—scouring the northwest territory for his runaway sons—but no one let him get a word in edgewise. First, Phil and Benjy had him by the elbow, steering him toward their monitors. "We're doing the puzzles for Mom's new game and they're awesome," said Phil—no doubt about it, that voice was getting deeper, but what new game of Mom's? They sat him down and scrolled through what frankly looked like chicken scratchings.

"Now, here are the lumberjack's words which have all gotten frozen and when they thaw, they come out scrambled in a different order. You see the word *lair.* It melts into the word *liar.* So that's when Arabella figures out the lumberjack is lying to her. Get it?" Benjy explained. When was the last time Benjy had looked so excited about anything, or wanted Ed's approval, for that matter?

"Wow, this is amazing," said Ed dutifully, catching a quick wink from Lucy.

Next, Laszlo threw a burly arm around his shoulder and ushered him down to the dock with the second six-pack and a package of Camels for a man-to-man chat. It had not gone so well for him, Laszlo admitted after he'd stormed out of Crocker over the sardine incident. There had been misunderstandings at other start-ups over silly little things, who knew why. And then this store in Oshkosh hadn't been the big hit he'd hoped for. "Happiest days in whole life at Crocker," Laszlo sighed, his bear paws pressing against his heart.

"Well, then," said Ed, fanning the smoke from his eyes. This was his first real gander at Little Lost Lake. Pretty in a generic north woods way, it even had an island—hadn't Lucy told him something about that island? "I guess you'll just have to come back. We haven't had a decent programmer since you left."

After he'd been scooped up for yet another bone-cracking hug, Ed wobbled back up to the cabin and this time Lucy waylaid him, her slender fingers lacing around his upper arm and squeezing. "I suppose I should show you this so-called computer game the boys are talking about. They're just a bunch of rough sketches. Benjy's the one who's convinced there's something more here." Benjy, with his matted hair and surly expression, trying to convince his mother that she had done something brilliant and creative? Maybe camp really had transformed him.

"I'd love to see what you've been working on," Ed lied. Just the thought of Lucy and her secretive little drawings made his temper rise—that's what had gotten their marriage into such a sorry mess to begin with. It wasn't just his prick's fault.

She arranged the drawings across the table, then held up a sheaf of faded legal pads. "I was looking through Dad's old research notes on lumberjack tales and decided to illustrate a couple of the more way-out ones." She pointed to a winter landscape with snow drifts the color of a robin's egg and another with a family of trees, mama, papa, and the baby, running along on legs made from their roots. "That was a starting point, but then along came these other images. I'm not sure from where, exactly." Her voice trailed off in an embarrassed way.

His first impression was scenes from her own life, viewed through a grotesquely deforming lens. The evil clockmaker was of course Ingrid. The hapless man who had been transformed into a clockwork human was himself. The woman fleeing into the wilderness was Lucy. The wizard's cottage was Cyrus's cabin. The lumberjack looked, unfortunately, a great deal like Sam McCarty with a beard, if memory served him correctly. And who could guess where those demented minks came from.

His second was that the images were too bizarre to be a computer game, but then he saw it, just like Benjy must have. It would be unlike any other kind of computer game—with a brooding mood, flirting along the dark edges of the unconscious. With a landscape that was not psuedo-medieval or psuedo-Greek mythology, but authentic, this—the great north woods. "These are very . . . Lucy," he said at last.

He reached out and ran a bashful index finger up her brown arm, along her shoulder and neck, through her dark clipped hair. There was a pause and then she stepped closer to him, reached out her hand to brush his cheek, comb her fingers through the back of his short hair. He tilted his head to one side and kissed her. Not a safe one as he had planned, but a hard, probing one right on the mouth. There were her firm, soft lips, the spicy scent of her neck, the curve of her long thin waist. And she kissed him back.

"Close eyes, boys," said Laszlo.

It wasn't until an hour later, when they were all out on the busted screen porch and Ed was flipping burgers on the rusty

Weber, that he said, "No one's asked me what I've been doing for the last week."

"So, what have you been doing, Dad?" Phil asked politely. He and Benjy were sitting cross-legged on the floor, examining the tiny dice cups of an old Parcheesi game as if they were mysterious artifacts found in a prehistoric tomb. Of course, his sons had never played anything as pedestrian as Parcheesi.

"Well, let's see. I hardly know where to start. Learning to paddle a canoe. Getting to know Uncle Bo and your counselors, Chris and Dave. Exploring all the islands of Lake Hazard. Shopping at Ogilvie's variety store. Lots of things." He was gratified to see both Benjy's and Phil's mouths sag open to form perfectly shaped Os.

"What?" said Lucy, shaking out a red-checked oilcloth and spreading it over a splintery picnic table. "What are you talking about, Ed?"

"Why don't you ask your sons."

Laszlo frowned at a dark line of clouds moving quickly across the lake. "Laszlo thinks big storm coming. Unplug now or big electricity surge." He smacked his knuckles together, as loud as Krakatoa.

CHAPTER 18

>>

Lucy and Ed spent the next morning at Dunbar's making phone calls.

"Just wanted to tell you the boys are all right," Lucy told her mother.

"Why wouldn't they be all right?" said Corky over the chatter of *Regis & Kathie Lee*.

"Because they were lost in the Canadian wilderness, remember? Ed called you."

"Of course I remember. You don't have to talk to me like I'm senile, Lucy. He told me they were lost but he didn't tell me I should be worried. I can't imagine what you're doing in that icky old cabin all summer. The boys should be learning how to play golf and there's not a golf course within thirty miles."

Next Lucy called Larry. "I told you not to send them to that Nazi youth camp," he crowed. "So, have you forgiven Ed for fooling around?"

"Who told you that?" said Lucy, glancing over at Ed, who was stretched across the front steps of Dunbar's, catching up with current events as best he could with the one and only daily paper available, the *Eagle River Gazette*.

"No one had to. Six weeks ago, you suddenly pick up and flee across the country. What other reason could there be?"

"Lots of other reasons," she said, not able to think of a single one.

"So, did you retaliate by hooking up again with your hunky forester?"

"You wish," she said, now able to read the headline of the *Gazette*: No New Clues in Mink Farm Raid.

"What have you been doing all summer at Little Lost Lake?" Larry always said the name as if it were the punch line of a joke.

"One thing I've been doing is going through Dad's notes on lumberjack tales."

A pause. "Forgot about those," he said, almost tenderly. He and Lucy used to listen to them, wrapped up in Hudson's Bay blankets in front of the fireplace. See, Larry, there are a few pleasant memories from our childhood. "Shot Gunderson and Hot Biscuit Slim."

"Blackie de Bois and Johnnie Inkslinger." Did Cyrus actually stutter less when he told them lumberjack tales or was her memory playing tricks.

"So, have you figured out how to immortalize Dad yet?"

"Kind of. I'm putting him in my next computer game."

A cynical laugh, the nostalgic moment blown away like a milkweed seed. "He'd be thrilled. So, what has Ed said about the, *um*, incomplete renovations."

Incomplete, that's one word for it. "Believe it or not, I don't think he's noticed yet."

"Do me a favor, Lu," Larry said in his sweetest baby-brother voice. "Don't point them out. Okay?"

Then there was Uncle Bo. "We've never actually had a boy succeed at running away before. Usually they give up after a couple of hours and come back with their tails between their legs." He actually sounded impressed. "How'd they figure out where they were going?"

"They had a GPS."

"A what?"

"It's a gadget that takes a reading off a satellite to figure out your exact latitude and longitude." At least, she thought that was what it did—she'd never heard of a GPS before last night, either.

"Oh, *phfff,*" he said dismissively. "That's cheating. I

thought they'd done it properly—with a compass, the stars, and their brains. Now, Lucy . . . " It was his blessing of the expedition tone—gravelly and grave.

"What?"

"I know Ed slipped his tether for a while, but I think he's ready to mend his ways. We spent six days together, and as I've always said, there's nothing like a canoe to take full measure of a man's character. I think you should give him a second chance."

Ed wasn't the only one who had slipped his tether. "Thanks for the advice, Uncle Bo. I'll think it over."

Next Ed checked in with his assistant Marla at Crocker for the first time in over a month and she gave him an earful. Things did not seem to be going very well in his absence. "Well, I'm sorry Ingrid said that to you. No, of course not, I didn't say she was in charge, you read my memo—the responsibilities were supposed to be shared by the creative team. Yes, I'll speak to her." Ed turned around to where Lucy was eavesdropping and gave a Black Panther salute as if to say, See, I'm finally standing up to the onslaught of Ingrid. "That bad, huh? The focus group really hated it? How many times did it crash? We can't be sending out games filled with bugs, Ralph should be catching those. We're just going to have to put out a press release saying that the release date for Maiden's Quest II has been postponed for another six months. I know we're going to catch a lot of shit, but what can we do? Now listen, tell the team that Lucy's come up with a new game that'll blow their socks off. Trust me. And I've rehired Laszlo Zuk. Yes, I'll talk with him about the sardines and it won't happen again. Yup, the boys are fine, but they put us through the wringer. Lucy's right here, yeah, I'll tell her. See you next week."

He hung up. "Marla says to tell you the place is falling apart and that almost everyone misses you."

"Thanks for the plug about my game." Why did it please her so much that Ed approved?

"It's the truth."

Next it was Lucy's turn to contend with Rosemary. "Look, I did call you before I left but you weren't home and I got the answering machine. I'm sorry if you were worried. And I'm sorry we finked out on the Wheeler bungalows at the last minute." I'm sorry, I'm sorry.

"Well, our vacation really sucked without you. Alfred moped around the whole time. You better not pull a stunt like this again."

"Next time I have a midlife crisis, I'll ask your permission first, okay?"

"*Hmph*. You actually expect me to believe you've been cooped up in a moldy cabin for a month making watercolors of ferrets?"

"Minks. Yes."

"And you expect me to believe that wimpy, white-bread Ed canoed across Canada doing a Sergeant Preston of the Yukon act?"

"Wait'll you see him. He's got Arnold Schwarzenegger arms."

"Oh, please. So, have you fallen into Arnold's arms yet?"

"We're still working on that part."

"You do that."

April was sitting at the lunch counter eating a Dunbar's special, an egg salad club with Miracle Whip, and catching up on the latest issue of the *Eagle River Gazette*. "Still no leads on the mink farm. They think it might be eco-nuts from out of state."

"Out-of-staters, huh?" said Ed. "Well, at least we know it wasn't Lucy. She hates minks."

"Foolish thing of it is that they herded up all the minks the next day. Every one of them, except two that got run over. Figured out how you're going to punish your boys?"

"They're writing letters of apology to the camp director, their counselors, and the Canadian troopers. Handwritten. Neatly. No spelling or grammatical errors," Lucy said, pulling out two Dunbar specials and the most gourmet wine available, a jug of Gallo, out of the cooler.

"That doesn't sound too bad."

"You don't know how bad their handwriting is. It'll take them about four days."

Later, leaving Laszlo to supervise the boys bent double over ink-blotted note paper, Lucy and Ed headed off in the canoe with their Dunbar's picnic so she could give him the Little Lost Lake grand tour, at last. With Ed in the bow and Lucy in stern, they pushed off from the dock with long sure sweeps in unison, as if they'd been doing this for years. Not surprising really, they'd had the same teacher. "Which way, boss," he twisted around to grin at her. She hadn't been lying to Rosemary. Her husband the computer geek had somehow in the last month been transformed into a hunk—the Oakley wraparound shades that had formerly looked so preposterous in the Crocker Software parking lot, his newly ponytail-less hair turned streaky blond in the sun, the arms with actual biceps, the shoulders now square instead of sloped, both flexing impressively with each stroke.

"Let's just paddle around the shore, just like I used to do with Dad when we were searching for a trout rise. No talking, that was the rule," she ordered.

"All right. In honor of Cyrus, I'll zip my lip."

In truth, she wanted a little peace and quiet to make sense of all the goings and comings of the last five days—first, Sam McCarty exploded out her life like a pipe bomb, then the boys turn up followed by Laszlo Zuk, and now her husband.

Last night after the dishes had been done and Laszlo had weaved off in his Gremlin and the boys had climbed up the ladder to the loft, she and Ed had had an awkward moment. Don't worry, I'll sleep on the couch, he'd said, casting a resigned glance toward the lumpy, sprung cushions. Don't be ridiculous, she'd said, but the tone had been more practical than welcoming. And in truth, once they found themselves enclosed in the tiny bedroom with the iron-frame bed, only barely a double, they lapsed into an awkward silence—undressing with backs turned, blowing out the lantern, and scrambling under the covers like a parody of a Mormon honeymoon.

"I know we need to talk," Ed whispered, and reached a hand over in the darkness to feel the shape of her shoulder, elbow, hip. It was not a sexual touch. It was almost as if he were checking to make sure her body was real flesh and bone, that nothing had changed. "But I just want you to know that I'm so glad to be here, next to you, again. I missed you so much."

"Me, too," she said. But how could she not remember the twenty-seven nights of Sam's body in this very spot. How was that fact going to be woven seamlessly back into the fabric of her marriage? She took Ed's hand in both of hers, felt the ridge of blisters along the palm, the new roughness of the fingers. Then closed her fingers around it and nestled his hand under her chin. But before she could say another word of concession or confession, Ed's breathing slipped into an even rhythm. Poor boy, what with all the canoeing, the stress, and the beer, he was worn out.

They skirted close to shore and every spot stirred a small memory—here was where she'd found a nest of box turtle eggs, here her father had caught his giant trout with Bart, here was where she'd bickered with Larry over a can of grape soda and smacked him on the head with a paddle (she always forgot how obnoxious he used to be, or maybe she had been the obnoxious one).

"Where's that go," Ed asked as they passed the outlet to Twin Pond. She hadn't been back since she'd dumped Sam at the airport. She imagined how the caboose must look—three-foot-long zucchinis in the garden, the corn stalks nibbled down to stubs by the deer, rain-soaked towels flapping on the line, a half-drunk mug of tea on the table, a hardened loaf of bread on the cutting board, the animal rights clippings yellowing in the accordion file, a family of mice already in residence in the fifty-pound sack of flour under the kitchen counter. All waiting for Sam's return—in a month, in a year, in ten—who knew or cared. Well, maybe the police cared, maybe they'd already been snooping around the place, but she suspected that Sam once again had slipped off the grid without a trace.

She could have lied. She could have said it doesn't go anywhere, or it used to go to Twin Pond but now it's all silted up. But if this marriage was going to survive, they had to be done with deceptions. "That leads over to Sam McCarty's cabin. Actually, it was an old Rock Island caboose." Something about the deliberate way she spoke made Ed turn around.

"So, have you been up there?" he asked, in an equally deliberate way.

"Yes."

"Caboose still standing?"

"Yup. It's in great shape. Roof fixed. Freshly painted." She rested her paddle across the gunwales.

"Any inhabitants?" He rested his paddle across his knees and flipped his sunglasses on top of his head so he could squint back at her. For a few moments, the only sound was the steady trickle of brown lake water off the paddle blades.

"Sam was living there for part of the summer. But he's gone now. I'm not sure if he'll ever be back," she said evenly. The canoe was drifting in aimless circles, then Ed pushed his sunglasses back down, turned forward, and picked up his paddle.

She pointed them away from shore. "There's a picnic spot on the island."

They hitched the canoe and scrambled up a scrubby embankment to a pine needle-covered promontory at the far end of the island, out of view of the cabin.

"Nice private spot,"said Ed, peeling off a sweaty T-shirt and splaying his pale chest and brown arms in the sun. No doubt about it—the flaccid, twenty-hours-a-day-under-fluorescent-lights look had vanished. Laszlo's raised voice echoed softly across the water, probably urging the boys forward with their chore.

Lucy unpacked the sandwiches, now squished, the white toast soggy, and unscrewed the Gallo. "That was always one of its attractions. When I was eight and was allowed to go out in the rowboat by myself, I used to come over here and build fairy houses made of twigs and moss, with acorns and pinecones for furniture."

"I don't think boys build fairy houses."

"And then when I was about fourteen, Larry and I would steal Dad's cigarettes and come over here and smoke. Later it was dope." She stripped off her tank top to her black satin bra, the same one she'd worn on her reunion dinner with Sam. An unavoidable coincidence—it was the only decent underwear she'd brought to Wisconsin.

"And did you come here with Sam McCarty, too?" Ed said, his eyes still closed, soaking up the rays.

"Do you really want me to answer that question."

"I guess not." Suddenly, Ed flipped over on his side and propped his head up on one elbow. "There's just one thing I don't understand, Lucy."

Uh oh, here it came. The third degree about everything she'd done with Sam in the last month. I will be completely honest, no matter how painful.

"One of the very first things you ever told me about yourself was about Little Lost Lake—how you spent all your summers here, fishing with your father, communing with nature, painting, whatever. If this place was so special, how come you never wanted to come back here. Or bring me?"

"You know the answer, I think. My last summer here, Dad was getting sick, but I was too busy with my new boyfriend to notice," she said, hugging her knees tightly. "Not something I'm very proud of."

"But it was more than that, I think," he said, turning his face to her, so she could see her own baffled face reflected back in the mirrored lenses of his glasses.

"You seem to know, so tell me," she said, not very pleasantly, but who was he to be accusing her.

"I think this place symbolized the person you were supposed to be—in tune with nature, self-sufficient, adventurous. And you thought if you brought old Ed here, and witnessed how the MIT geek couldn't fish, or swim, or paddle a canoe, you'd be reminded all over again what a big mistake you made. Right?"

"I never said anything like that." She stared down at her big toe with chipped red polish, nosing into the pine needles so he wouldn't read the truth in her eyes. That she'd been embarrassed by him, was afraid he wouldn't measure up under the shadow of Sam McCarty.

"You didn't have to." He shook his head, his expression unreadable behind blue glass.

"You know how you wrote and said that the boys and I were all the family you ever needed? That you felt no lacking? Well, you were right about me. For all the years together, I have wallowed in what I thought was missing from life. Another child, a different career, more adventures. I was so . . ." She searched for the right word. "Foolish," she said finally.

"I was a fool, too, just in a different way." His sunburned cheeks pulled tight and he laughed in a rueful way, the same expression he made when he described the latest goings-on at Crocker. A sense of humor about oneself—there was a quality she had new appreciation for. "I'm not in much of a position to criticize you, you know."

"Ed, I feel no lacking." She crawled over to him, kissed the top of his sun-warmed head.

"If I'd brought my violin, I'd serenade you with 'Go Tell Aunt Rhody.' That's Uncle Bo's favorite. I've been practicing, you know."

"I guess we'll have to think of another way to make up." Her hand slid up and down his spine like it was the neck of a violin, her fingers pressing deeply, searching for the spot to create the perfect note. Across the water came the faint echo of Laszlo's voice, no words, just the passionate rise and fall of it. As Ed turned to rub his bristly cheek against the tender skin of her belly, she searched under the trees for the lichen-covered remains of a fairy house. All gone, she would have to build another.

CHAPTER 19

>>

Gamer's Guide to

Maiden's Quest II: The Lumberjack's Lair

by Lucy Crocker

At long last, the adventures of brave Arabella continue in **Maiden's Quest II: The Lumberjack's Lair.** In MQII, Arabella embarks on her most perilous quest yet. Her beloved, Edgar, has been turned into a clockwork man by the wicked sorceress Iris. In order to free him from Iris's curse, Arabella and her faithful gnomes, Portus and Beno, must journey into the never-ending forest to retrieve the magic spell from the sorcerer Cyrus. They encounter many perils along the way—the deceitful lumberjack, the minks who have infested Cyrus's cottage—but eventually they vanquish their enemies.

The gamer's guide offers clues on how to get through each level of the game. Some questers prefer to stumble through the game with no hints at all, falling into every perilous trap along the way. Others like to know where they are going, and will take any helpful advice that is offered. As we all know, a clever computer game is like life itself, filled with wrong turns, tricky puzzles, messages written in code, and people who are not always what they seem. There are both difficult and easy ways to win the game. Who of us can say which path is better?

Happy questing!

CHAPTER 20

>>

Gossip Net

After sixteen months of delays, Crocker Software unveiled Maiden's Quest II: The Lumberjack's Lair at the P.C. Gamer's Convention at the Monterey Hyatt. Critics and players alike have raved about the dazzling graphics and intricate storyline, especially the Clockwork Castle in level one, the Lumberjack's Ice Cave of Words in level three, and the Mink Cottage in level four.

Rumors have been swirling for months about the unrest at Crocker Software. Serious disagreements among members of the MQII creative team resulted in the departure of several key Crocker players earlier this year. CFO Russell Mott, Publicity Director Ingrid Bascom, and Head Programmer Ralph Freed have now started their own game company, Hi-Jinx Software. Ms. Bascom is prohibited by the terms of her out-of-court settlement with Crocker Software from discussing the specific issues of conflict. "You could say that we had a more cutting-edge, innovative concept for computer games, which we hope to implement at Hi-Jinx. I have the greatest respect for the Crockers and wish them well," she said. The sequel was finally finished in a frantic six-month push with the yeoman efforts of Laszlo Zuk, one of the original Crocker programmers.

An inside source at Crocker reports that at the nadir of the crisis, Ed Crocker fired Lucy Crocker from the creative team and that the Crockers had separated after fifteen years of marriage. But at the Monterey gamer's conference, the Crockers appeared to be partners in every sense of the word.

The Crockers' twin fourteen-year-old sons, Ben and Phil, are also credited as designers for Maiden's Quest II. The Crocker boys have recently become teenage heartthrobs after a profile about the young software moguls appeared in *Teen People.* Their Web page has over ten thousand hits per week, but Phil Crocker appears unfazed by his newfound celebrity. He plans to spend the summer canoeing the Hudson's Bay region. "There's more to life than computer games, you know?" the dreadlocked teenager said when we caught up with him at the Monterey Hyatt.

When we asked Lucy Crocker where she found inspiration for her latest masterpiece, the famously cryptic designer replied, "I find inspiration in everyday life. Monsters disguised as heroes. Heroes disguised as monsters. Mazes, labyrinths, perilous journeys, treacherous women. These are the kinds of situations I encounter daily."

If you say so, Lucy!

ABOUT THE AUTHOR

CAROLINE PRESTON is married to the writer Christopher Tilghman and lives with him and their three sons in Massachusetts. A graduate of Dartmouth College, she earned her master's in American civilization at Brown University. Her first novel, *Jackie by Josie,* was a *New York Times* Notable Book of the Year.